Patrick Sean Kelley grew up in Rochester, New York, a frozen little borough somewhere between here and nowhere. After graduating from university, he moved to Miami (a tad warmer), where he met his wife, Marisa, and together, they moved on to Chicago in pursuit of his career, which has spanned over twenty years in the world of advertising, working as a writer, creative director, and executive. He currently resides in the great state of Indiana with his wife, two daughters and one obstinate Shiba Inu by the name of Remington (or Remy for short).

WHITE

Book One

Patrick Sean Kelley

WHITE

Book One
Inspired by true story

Vanguard Press

VANGUARD PAPERBACK

© Copyright 2024
Patrick Sean Kelley

The right of Patrick Sean Kelley to be identified as author of
this work has been asserted by him in accordance with the
Copyright, Designs and Patents Act 1988.

All Rights Reserved

No reproduction, copy or transmission of this publication
may be made without written permission.
No paragraph of this publication may be reproduced,
copied or transmitted save with the written permission of the
publisher, or in accordance with the provisions
of the Copyright Act 1956 (as amended).

Any person who commits any unauthorized act in relation to
this publication may be liable to criminal
prosecution and civil claims for damages.

A CIP catalogue record for this title is
available from the British Library.

ISBN 978 1 83794 037 0

This is a work of fiction. Names, characters, businesses, places, events, and
incidents, are either the product of the author's imagination or used in a
fictitious manner. Any resemblance to actual persons, living or dead, or actual
events is purely coincidental.

*Vanguard Press is an imprint of
Pegasus Elliot Mackenzie Publishers Ltd.*
www.pegasuspublishers.com

First Published in 2024

**Vanguard Press
Sheraton House Castle Park
Cambridge England**
Printed & Bound in Great Britain

To my family, Marisa, Daniella, and Christina. For your continued support across both the book writing process and all its inevitable ups and downs. And to my good friends—a certain group of boisterous thirteen-year-old boys, I once called pals.

Thanks to everyone on my publishing team. A special thanks of course to my family for their tireless support, and their innate ability to put up with me. And last, to the people and places that I've discovered and come to love on a path less traversed, I thank you.

Contents

Prologue	13
Awake	17
Middle-aged	29
Eddie	39
Best friends	44
Campin' out	48
The first encounter	54
Running in shadow	57
Beverly's white coat	66
William Henry O'Connor	73
Airport security can be a real bitch	98
Gone	108
The morning comes and goes	118
Finding the Spotted Green	129
Making the call	133
A hunt	142
Porch sitting	164
Change comes hard at the Springfield Inn	176
Badass	204
Memories don't come easy	217
Her and Billy	230
Terms to live (or die) by	276
Enter at your own peril	298
She	351

Prologue

1988
1:16 A.M.

The night's black covered my sleep with slithering dreams. I felt a warm unseen wind—I stirred. Ben was sitting upright, pushing blistered red embers with a crooked stick to flame. Tiny flares of light spit and spurted upward from our once glorious campfire. I rolled over in my sleeping bag, edging closer to its brightly flickering warmth.

"What time is it?" I asked of Ben's darkened profile. His shoulders shrugged silently as he continued to make work of the fire. Lost somewhere between thought and my own dream, I fisted my eye holes, working the sleep out, trying to bring life back out of the din of an uncomfortable sleep.

"Dude, what the fuck? Why you up?" Ben turned in a swirl of yellowed sparks to glare back at me. "Ma-ma-man, did you see it?" he asked, exasperated. Just a little out of breath, so unlike him, I thought. I looked up at his profile glowering in the fire's ebbing light. His skin glowed an unfavorable white; his eyes, a hooded mystery, flitted to-and-fro, seeming always to dart back upon the tangled mass of blackened forest just off in the distance.

I sat in silence for a moment following his blinking line of sight, looking upon the endless shadow of the most frightening forest I'd ever known in my full thirteen-years of life on this big blue marble. How many times had we'd sat under the edge of those ancient trees? Towering hundreds of feet above us, blanking out the sun, daring each other to enter… no one ever did.

"See what?" I asked sheepishly. Honestly not wanting to hear his answer. Something in his breathing, he appeared short of breath? Had he been crying? He never answered, hunching, lowering himself over the fire's apparent warmth. "See what, man?' I repeated, a little louder this time, causing Eddie to snort, then roll over in his sleeping bag angrily, disturbed from the space in the dreams where he now dwelt.

I caught the look in Ben's eyes as he turned his face to me. Sparkling orange light from the fire he'd romanced back to life, dancing in the reflection of his gold-framed glasses. Just enough to mask the red rims of his tear-soaked eyes, but not enough to mask the worry that burned there just beneath. A glint of fright simmering darkly behind the illuminated lens of his ever-trusted eyewear. Bent and dented, a tattered rhyme of sticky black tape holding one of the two arms unsteadily to its frame. I'd lost myself in his image for seconds uncounted before I noticed his fixed stare upon me. His face, ashen gray, startled me to sit up. "Ben, dude, you okay?"

His stare faltered when he finally chose to answer my question. "The wuh-wa-wolf, man," he said, again hesitating, breathing in deep. Uncomfortable with his own words, he kept on. "I-I-I saw it ma-ma-man." A tear rolled down his cheek, sparkling in the weak light.

"The fuh-fucking thing, ma-ma-man. It came r-r-r-ight out of there." He lifted a shaking hand to point to the place I knew he would and at the same time wished he wouldn't. *Ah, the forest*, I thought, *those damned woods…* and as my eyes followed the trail of his cadaverously pale hand, a flash appeared against the deep black wall of trees… Bouncing on a blur of darkly blued grass, it slashed violently across the yellow mooned night shocking me straight up and out of my sleeping bag.

"Ben, what the fuck?" I squealed, but as I turned again, panic a cold drain along my spine, Ben was no longer sitting alongside the fire. The moment cemented, I was barely able to make out his shadow, rolling down the hill, leaping away from our little camp.

All was still. I could hear his footsteps pounding, falling loosely, more distant. My heart thudding in time in my chest. "Ben," I cried weakly, but he was already gone. A cold chill ran the length of my neck while hot sweat trickled to warm its path. I was turning before I knew what I was doing, back to the thing that had caused my best friend to bolt blindly from camp in the middle of the night. Back to what awaited me, back to an inexplicable attraction, cold and contagious.

My mind created an image of what lie before me, a specter, a monster, a macabre beyond imagination… but what I saw, cloaked in white across the misted field, was well beyond all of that.

Chapter One

Awake

The wind stirred through the trees. Rustling low, its depth warming, smells of musty decay—so deliciously intoxicating. She stirred, ears twitching against the creatures that buzzed relentlessly against them. Her nose wrinkled, breathing in the scent of all she knew, all she had been for time beyond time. The sound of them filtered down from above like tinkling laughter. Her head rising from its place which had lain still deep within the nested burrow. Their yipping cries were joyous, pinching at her being, their beating hearts loud as thunder overhead. It was time, the earth had turned over. It was time to begin again. To alas lay claim to her true form once more.

She stretched forward, feeling the long dormant muscles clicking and popping into life. Vibrantly pulsing, the life she'd thought she once lost coursing through her limbs, neck, and body. Hunger a distant grumble, but nothing she had not experienced or been used to. There were times when she'd gone without warmth or substance for months on end. So many falling then. Their very essence, the only proof of life leaking out from within them as their bodies just stopped moving—stilled to lie where they fell. Their spirits swirling angrily, crying out in despair. Lost forever to the great rivers that tumble atop a demon's breath. Whipping and howling upward, ever upward until they were quieted, now one with earth, water, and sky.

She was up on her feet now. Shaking loose the fog that lay over her. Had laid with her, dragging her deep down for the great sleep. It was time. She scented deeply of the soil beneath her, scratching at it fervently. Feeling it loosening, warm, moist, and rich, once more. The others had stopped running now. She could still hear them though; they were all so close. Circling her place of rest, crying out to her, desperate in their need.

She remembered a time when they, those that circled above were all there was in these lands—her kin of white. A time and a place so unlike what were the present. These strange times she'd found herself living and now hiding within. No longer able to be her true self in the world. But she was alive, and life, after all, was the only thing that truly mattered, she thought. As the old one had once said when it shared its language with her. A language she'd not understood all that well at first. He, a male human child called Pieskaret, explained to her that all forms of life were to be revered, no matter what they were, or how short or long their time was to be. "Any life is a good one beneath the daylight's big yellow bird of fire and its twin of night, the pale eyed moon. And your life will take the shape of many," he'd said to her through a half grin. She couldn't help but grin herself in anticipation of the pale glow of the bloated moon that awaited above her. The eve of the earth's renewal, sodden with the warm scent of life that hovered lushly on the nights breeze.

He was of an ancient human race called the Huron and told her of so many worldly things, but that was a time long, long ago. She'd felt no apprehension or guilt in consuming his flesh, so alive with hot, steaming blood, meat, and bone. Every ounce of the timeworn human a prophet and seer, taken in, never shying away from it, the kill quick and as painless as she could make it. He was an elder of his people—wise and true. Bound to the old ways of the earth and guided by the moon's lonely, pale light. So very unlike the human brothers and sisters who would come to be. He was one of the last spirits of the Huron's tribe of light, formed upon words now long forgotten. He'd known that he would give himself to her, had spoken of the act almost, longingly. A sacrifice for a greater good, his true essence would live beyond the confines of his mortal vessel. She would take him and his human form far beyond the great river and out from under the world of the dead where he'd once found her. Along with the rest of her kind, the old gods of the forest, having all but passed over. Leaving the tall trees behind to become a dark, faceless whisper of what once was.

It had bothered her that she was the last of her kind and the elders had not saved them. That she'd no longer run under the yellow bird's night twin's pale eye with those that once ruled these fertile grounds. Out in the open for all other species to lay witness to. Trembling in their glorious presence. Their fierce tribe of giants, the only true earthly gods of that time. Before the hordes of man came with their shining sticks that ushered out death in a fired stream of silver. Their need to control, to conquer, ever growing. Destroying all in front of them, blind to the ways of the elders. Stupid and cruel beings that should have been torn apart, never allowed to force their will upon these grounds. But she would make them pay up in full. She would enter their world and walk amongst them. And have revenge. Cold and unforgiving.

But even her kind had underestimated them, all of them, as there were so many. They were cunning, bloodthirsty in their unquenchable hunger, dominating through destruction of the living things of this Earth. Polluting and tainting all under an ever-widening human footprint. Somehow, her kind had assumed they'd just go away, fade out from disease or famine—the weak and needy beings that they truly were. How wrong they'd been. The race of humans was a great sickness that would not be slowed or stopped. Even more of them came, consuming the land's once abundant offerings, and murdering those that lived upon them. It was vicious. A systemic extermination of all that surrounded them. Soon, they were all that was left of the natural lands. The gods of old and their tribes were no more.

We will rebuild, she thought brightly, seeing the new future so clearly now. The growing pack, her family, would reclaim it all and bring this modern human beast low. It was their time now, and the hot blood of the humans would flow. She'd become one of them. Use them, their pitiful ambitions exploited to get back what she—what they—had lost. As Pieskaret had once taught her. She'd find them along their own dark paths, their silly dreams, and enter their worlds upright. Promising them all that they longed for as only a lover, or a mother, their true mother, could ever do. Everything. Every sick and twisted desire the disease laden human could possibly want for, she'd grant to them. But only if they obeyed her. Gave themselves over to her. And one day, she would find the mate of old blood that she'd been sworn to. The old Indian had promised to her just before she'd taken his life. She remembered the conversation well, and how Pieskaret's words played back to her time and time again. "He will come to you in a time of great change. A human child to transcend all the spirits from above and below. Your destiny will be forever intertwined with the race of humans through the consummation of your coupling. The key to life's eternal mysteries lies within one mortal being. Only you will recognize this being as you would one of your own kind. You've seen him before—walking amongst the dream spirits... just a boy."

She rose quickly from the hollows beneath the earth, trotting freely now. Working her way ever upward, the tunnel to her lair, long and deep as they'd said it should be. Unknown to any of those who walked above, she'd kept it a secret place where she would lie—nurturing the strength that now sparked hot within her. The Earth would turn and move on while she slept, waiting as she was told to do when he'd first found her, laid low—so close to passing over.

***

Her life's light had all but been snuffed black as her pack and beloved family had already fallen prey to. She remembered hanging on to nothing yet everything when he gave back to her a last frayed thread of it. His bare limb laid open, hot liquid gushing between her teeth. *"Go. You must take this gift and go back. To the land of the living. To walk amongst them once more,"* he'd said to her as she rose upon trembling legs. The warm taste of his blood bringing her back, coursing with a bubbling vitality, providing the strength she'd needed to move forward.

Making her way blindly through the lands of those who had long since passed over. Across a place of so many dead—their bodies putrid and gaseous. Under a moonless, ashen gray sky that stared down blankly upon the cold, barren grounds, she ran. She'd laid amongst the dead for a long stretch of time, of nothingness, before he had come to her. He had made magic in the old ways, moving above her, singing and shaking in time with the sound of a crackling rattle. He'd brought her back from the brink of darkness. Why she'd wondered… he was no different than those other foul humans. No different from the abhorrent hairless beings who had wiped away her kin, destroying the lands and forests, forcing the very last of her kind into exile. Into a place of decay and darkness, this dead place for ever more.

"You, great white child of the moon, will return to the green grasses and the trees born beneath blue sky," he chanted, the reptilian rattle hissing now, faster and faster it went. She'd recognized the words he made. Dusty from a past she'd all but forgotten. "I am Pieskaret, the last remaining soldier of my tribe. I see you, Great Achak of White, here in the land of the dead, the ancestral grounds of our fathers." He moaned low. "I have been sent to bring you back. A promised oath made of blood, fire, and the sacrifice of the living. The elders have guided me to you, from dark to light, and made it so. You are to live on. To take to form as only a being of White can do," he'd told her, chanting in harmony with the rattling sound, commanding her to rise, to run like she'd never run before.

And she had. Weak, muscles flaring in agony, she could barely move at first. But she would find her stride, his energy pulsing, pumping through her as she ran on. Blinded by darkness, scenting her way through the endless miles of rot, decaying flesh and yellowed bones. She came upon a great open expanse, a clearing of sorts where she'd forced herself to stop, to be still. Her breathing came in ragged spurts. She worked her way slowly to the crest of the forested grounds to lay witness to a great rolling valley, blanketed in blue green grasses that bent gently to the night wind's will. Ancient instincts drew deep upon Achak, who lowered her massive head, nuzzling the damp, thick aromatics from the soils beneath her. Its fragrance overpowering her, pulling her to the ground, rolling upon it, trying to absorb its very essence, so rich in the life she'd all but forgotten. Her barking cries were of such grief and pain, they nearly broke the night's darkness in two.

"Time has moved on in a great sweeping motion, my child. It has washed away the lives of what once were and what once lived on the lands before you," he'd said to her, putting a warm hand gently to her back, rubbing deep beneath her furred hide. "Come, walk with me, Great Achak of White, you are home once more as am I, and there is much for you to know."

They sat high upon the deeply forested ridge, haloed beneath the silver eye of the moon. That would soon turn from a sliver of pale light to the day's full burst of the yellow bird's sun. He taught her many things across that time. The language of his people came naturally to her, so she listened intently as he told tales of both his and his tribal people's many lives past. They, like the towering trees above and the moss-covered earth below, existed in harmony with what lived and died around them. He spoke of old truths and what she must do to regain them. He fed her of himself in both knowledge and blood. The promise he'd made to his ancestors—the ancient ones—kept in full, strength of body and soul flowing back to her.

The wise man imparted all he had left to give and when it was time, gave his life willingly to her, ensuring that they would carry on as one being of light, from that time on. But the humankind's tenebrous foothold was more entrenched than ever before. Dug deep within the earth, growing, consuming all in its path. There would be no change until they, Pieskaret, the last Huron elder, and she, as he'd called her, the Great Achak of White, were united. Until she'd taken him into her, consuming his flesh, the essence of his long and powerful ancestral line. A sacrifice made so her kind, the children of White, would rise once more to reclaim what had been taken from them.

***

She hit the nights open air leaping, laying witness to those that had long awaited her return. Hundreds upon hundreds of them… There had not been anything even close to these numbers since her kind was removed from these very lands. Once again, they moved together, running over the rolling fields and across the shadowed forest grounds. Their souls forever committed as their blood intermingled with hers. "The Spotted Green." She made the human words so suddenly, remembering the one who had spoken to her and had called these lands so. A male child, once thought to be the one that Pieskaret had told her would come, but it was not to be.

After an endlessly frigid winter, the time had finally come, the time she'd longed for. The damp ground exhilarating beneath her, as she drew in the nights sharply scented air in large, gulping bites. She'd risen above, breaking free of the earth that had bound her. The male child who was named William, the very person who had given her those human words, the Spotted Green, fell to his knees, his fragile form atremble. She towered over him, at least two times his size—growling low, opening her jaws ever so slightly. Bending to bight down upon the furred collar of his garment. Nuzzling his head up with her snout, exposing the pink skin of his throat—her snarls menacing, daring him to move from under her. He offered himself without hesitation, stretching his neck fully before her, submitting to her will. "Take me, Achak of White. Take me, my foremother, and may my blood nurture your being and bring you great strength." She bared her immense fangs, growls deepening to a guttural hum that echoed through the tree limbs. But just as she came in for the kill that awaited her, that she craved so, she quickly turned away from the him, nodding her head, showing him mercy for his loyalty.

She'd found that most of the human children she came upon, were easily conquered. Shapeshifting was in her nature. She could become whomever or whatever they most desired her to be. And then, they would become hers, loyal allies in the protection against their own despicable kind. She would make those loyal to her stronger, stronger than their feeble brothers and sisters, through the exchange of blood. They would take from her, drinking of her, absorbing the power of her ancient lineage. They'd become immortal, with a singular purpose, to serve her, the foremother, Achaka. A small price for her really, considering what she would demand and ultimately receive in return. Her children would give themselves over to her for eternity and beyond, if there was even such a thing. The human children and her own would become one, loyal to her and none other.

Her new family surrounded her as she made her way through them, each bristling, nudging one another for her attention. She sat silently upon the forested ridge, the very same one she'd once sat upon with the old Indian chief so many moons before. Turning to them, her children, she rose up onto all fours, her full stature blocking out the moons pale glow. Her immense coat rustled on an unseen breeze, gleaming white in silhouette against the black of the night. She looked over them, her eyes the color of a pale blue sky sparked with such ferocious intensity, many turned away, avoiding her gaze. It had been a long time since she'd felt such contentedness, such joy, such anticipation of what was to come, she thought, lifting herself, opening her throat, releasing her voice to shake the ground they now crouched down upon. It felt so good—so alive. Almost better than the smell of... *bacon cooking on the stove in the comforts of a warm kitchen...* she suddenly thought. Not fully understanding the meaning behind the human words or why they'd been thrust into her head. But there was one that did understand their meaning. They were important to something or someone, she thought, reflecting, suddenly longing to hear it. The one voice she'd heard when she'd taken the weak human child that night not so long ago. There was another presence, there with her. One who had laid witness to all, to her.

For reasons she didn't understand, these thoughts of this 'other' human child, troubled her heart greatly.

Perhaps because he'd been there to witness it, seen through her disguise when she'd taken the boy's life. She'd often sought the advice of Pieskaret around this one kill in particular. But even he had stopped answering her endless questions about the strange human child that somehow had seen her that night. In time, the old Huron would speak more, but in confounding riddles rather than answers. Fiery anger boiling upward, his ridiculous riddling so frustratingly vague, served no purpose to her. *"You mustn't try to understand what is yet to be, Achak. The answer you seek will come when the truth is delivered. Soon great one, soon. There will be a deliverer."*

In the end, she chose to let his words simply flow through her, no longer questioning them. Remembering his great sacrifice to her, to all of them. She turned her head up to the bloated pale moon, its argent ghostly light dappled gently upon the trees of the forest. The song filled her lungs once more, the lonely voice of her kin released across the ebony skies. The baying howl grew to shake the earth and trees. Beckoning for them all to lay before her— to bow before the night's one true, Earthbound god.

Chapter Two

Middle-aged

"By the time you're up, you're down," some guy next to me says in my ear as I sit at another airport bar wondering what the fuck I was doing in another airport bar. What was I searching for exactly? I wondered quietly, as the guy to my right drained his third double Woodford Reserve, yet somehow was able to just keep on talking. "So, have yah ever been to Vero Beach, man?" he asked without waiting for my response (as if I was intending upon responding). "Man, Florida—yah got to go. The fishing there's off the charts. Off the freakin' hook for sure, man. And the women? Shii-iiiit—don't even get me started…" he says as I look the other way trying to do anything but get this guy started.

Just then four rough-and-tumble type tween-age boys come rumbling into the innocuous bar restaurant, I too somehow fell into. Irreverently named Chili's, or Champ's, or Chilean's, or Chitterling's, for all I knew, or cared. They were all depressingly the same. As was the clientele, I supposed. Just like the ass-clown sitting next to me, still talking…

The boys burst across the red-tiled floor in an awkward bunch of flailing appendages, piercing the air with unfiltered, high-pitched giggling that punches a big ole-hole right through the Chitterling-stale atmosphere. I find myself turning toward that sound, drawn to its purity. The boy in front shoves one of his buddies who falls into another, causing an even louder ruckus as they ram their way forward. Right through the rather dismayed patrons to find their glassy-eyed, and now somewhat mortified, parental units.

The red-faced male parental unit grabs the boy in front by the arm, pulling him roughly down onto the booth's wheezing seat cushion. Hissing words unheard into the boy's ear, who continues giggling just the same. "Good for you," I say, turning away from the little scene that now appears to be quieting. "Good for you, boyo," I cheer somewhat merrily to my increasingly more talkative bar-mate. Who is, unbelievably, still talking to me.

"…And then I was with this one chick, oh man, she had a fucking giant tattoo of Gandalf on the inside of her thigh…" He leans back smiling to himself, remembering his woven tale as if it did actually happen, and was not part of the bourbon-balls he'd been growing as he ordered yet another. "You know? Man, the really old wizard dude, with the long white beard and pointy hat? From that movie—man? Yah know? About those olden-time midget warriors or some shit…" He slurps at his fresh drink, rolling its ice around in his glass, still pondering. "Aw, man, what the fuck was the name of that flick?"

"*The Hobbit*," I say noncommittally as the man's bleary eyes come back to focus on me.

"The what? No man—what the fuck? Not that one, that wasn't it... There was this hot evil elf-chick in it..."

"*The Lord of the Rings*," I respond in conversational time but he is already off on another pointless tangent about elven 'chicks' and a porno film he'd recently rented... "The plot thickens," I add, but he ignores my quip which is just fine by me.

My mind wanders dutifully away from him, from this dreadful bar. I can hear the traces of giggling echoing, steering me, wandering backward across time. "We were just like that, weren't we?" I announce to the oversized Chitterling bar's mirrored wall. "How the hell did I become this? This desperate, red-faced guy sitting here—wishing I were somewhere—anywhere else? A middle-aged Caucasian male, working a middle-aged Caucasian guys job, traversing the ass-end of our country's way less-than-celebrated rural towns. Unheard of little burrows somewhere between here and there. Drinking mid-shelf bourbon with other middle-aged Caucasian men, eager to buy some made-to-plan market analysis I'd cobbled together in another innocuous airport just like this one. Identifying their oh-so-elusive target audience profiles and buying patterns for the hydrostatic tractor transmission oil, or industrial grade toilet bowl cleaner that they sold. Their little piece of human existence that no one truly gives a shit about but them, and me—when they're paying me to give a shit, that is.

"What happened to us? The rat-fucking-pack that we were?" I mumbled the question to no one, quivering as the words poured weakly from inside. Not wanting to remember, refusing to take the bait, to walk down that old path. But my mind raced back anyway, its roughened voice dismissing my cowardice plea, bitch-slapping me down, down to that time…

***

…where I was running, pacing quickly now behind him. Gaining ground steadily, my feet thundering beneath me as I watched myself close in on Ben. The night air cool on my face. "Wait up! Come on you guys, wait for mee-eee-eeee!" The girlish shouts rose and fell from somewhere behind, too far off in the distance, I had to focus. I would catch Ben, it was just a matter of time. Then we'd stop for a minute to talk this through and go back to the camp to get Franky and Eddie. *Just keep the pace, man, just keep the pace.* I could hear myself breathing, sucking in the dark cold air, chuffing it back out in puffs of gray. I looked back over my shoulder. I knew I shouldn't, but I couldn't help it. And there, a tiny blue-gray Franky was just cresting the top of the second hill. *He's so far back, shit he'll never catch up. I should stop—wait for him*, but my feet just kept going, gaining stride once more, his squeaky cries falling away.

Funny, I thought. The little fucker was always so self-conscious about his athletic abilities, or truth be told, lack of them. He wanted so bad to be the 'guy', the star on the athletic field. Any field for that matter, be it baseball, football, or even skiing. But sometimes yah just got to admit to whether you have 'it', you know, the stuff to be the big-swinging-dick-all-star-team-captain-guy. Or, sadly, you don't. And Franky just didn't. At all. And perhaps Ben and I were the only ones to ever acknowledge it I thought, slowing myself down to a jog, allowing Franky to begin to close the gap, his shouting growing louder from behind me. As I'd done before at football practice, or in baseball games, and or any other sport he just couldn't play like either Ben, Eddie, or I could. We felt for him. He was one of our own, he was a part of our little pack of misfits. *Our gang of four*, I thought, slowing to walk, then finally just standing still, watching anxiously as Ben shot out of my line of sight.

"What the fuck?" he queried loudly, falling upon the ground in front of me breathing in sharp bursting snorts, gasping through open mouth. "Dude, what… what the fuck…" he repeated.

"Catch your breath, man. Where's Eddie?" Franky didn't respond at first, taking my advice, breathing deeply. I knelt beside him grabbing hold of his shoulder, noticing his shirt was cold to the touch. "Is Eddie behind you, man?" I asked as he turned his face toward me, his eyes turning down, telling me all I needed to know. "You left his ass? Franky, you fucking left him?"

Franky shook me off and stood up quickly, avoiding my eyes, "If I left him, so did you." He spat back tersely, then turned to walk away.

But I was just a touch quicker, grabbing him by the arm, stopping him before he could turn completely away from me or say something else. Turning him back to face me. "Franky, we gotta go back…"

***

I snapped out from under the weight of memory, chilled goosebumps rising rigidly across my forearms. I was shivering, Franky's face in the early morning light some twenty-five years in the past as vivid as if he were right in front of me now. Being here, stuck in my old hometown I'm sure wasn't helping me much either. Shit, even if it was just a delay in my connecting flight to Chicago. I looked up to catch a glimpse of my reflection, floating pale in the glossy barroom mirror. Frozen there, a stranger staring back at me. "Eddie!" I shouted, standing up too fast, awkwardly stumbling back away from the queer man's image reflected in the hulking mirror. I was reaching out, clumsily knocking over my herculean beer mug. Too late—the untouched, yet highly recommended local pilsner toppling forward, splurging heady foam to slop through the air. I was turning away just the same, clutching the rolling travel bag nestled beside the barstool. Rearing back, the talkative, elf-loving idiot squealing, "Heyyy-eeyyy-ah!" Just as the amber contents from my glass splashed down onto his generous lap, his face squelched, silently shouting displeasure. I guessed he was perhaps more displeased at my untimely departure rather than the newly acquired wet, beer crotch. Well, more than likely yes, as I am sure he had another one of his highly titillating, ass-clown stories to tell.

I'd already been through airport security and now just needed to find the appropriate gate coded across my mobile ticket. I stopped in front of gate B3 and was just fishing my phone out of the inside of my suit coat when it erupted in a flurry of buzzing vibrations, which scared the living shit out of me. Looking down at the pissed off little device now whirring in hand, I noticed that the caller was "unidentified", deemed someone whom I or the device didn't recognize. I pushed the button to send the annoying unknown caller to voicemail hell, and noticed a familiar area code just a second too late. "Seven-one-six?" I said apparently way too loud, causing a stern looking woman holding a slumbering baby to look up at me and grimace.

I nodded to her in apology and she mouthed inappropriately back to me, "Move the fuck on, mister."

I smiled and began to walk once more. "B twenty-eight," I exhaled when finally finding the ticket on my phone, and began to head in the gate's general direction. The memory of that night crept back into my head—a cool night's air—a sparking campfire—my best friends… "That was a long time ago," I told myself. "Nothing you can do about it now," I said, completely forgetting about the unknown caller from an oddly recognized area code.

But back then, you could-ah done something, Seany-Boy, couldn't-chah? But maybe you were jus-tah too much of a faggot-pussy now—weren't cha? the roughened voice growled from the back of my head. *Faggot!* it suddenly shouted then began to fade out with rasping, laborious breaths.

I found myself standing in front of gate B28, still lost in my own tangled thoughts. There appeared to be some commotion happening at the little ticket counter. A group of obviously stressed-out fellow travelers were clustered in front of it, raising their hands (and voices) trying in vain to gain the attention of one harried airline agent. Who began barking testily into a handy pocket-sized microphone, her voice instantly booming through unseen cables and out onto the airport loud-speaker system. "*Good evening,*" she thundered. "Flight eight-seven-two-three, to Chicago O'Hare from Rochester International, has been delayed. Repeat, flight eight-seven-two-three, to Chicago O'Hare out of gate B-twenty-eight, is now delayed. We are looking at a new time for departure of ten-twenty-three p.m. We apologize for any inconvenience. If you have connecting flights to Milwaukee Mitchell International Airport, Minneapolis Saint Paul Airport, or… please come to the B-twenty-eight ticket counter for… we'll have more information shortly… Again, we apologize…"

The ticket agent's voice droned and rumbled on. The digital screen above the B28 ticket counter provided the current time of 6:18 p.m., Eastern Standard.

Unfortunately, there was just no way to drive to Chicago from Rochester, New York, it would be at least a ten-hour schlep, I thought angrily. In fact, nothing was actually very close to the Rochester airport besides a life I'd left behind many, many years ago. *Shit. Well, I guess I can just sit here and wait it out. No problem at all really.* The weather was certainly taking a turn for the worse too, I noticed gazing out at the airport tarmac. The blackening skies were closing in and pelting rain began to fall in swirling gusts of crackling ice. "Ah, upstate travel at its finest," a guy who was standing right behind me, said rather loudly. "Fuck it, I'm goin' to the bar." And with that, he turned and sauntered back the way we'd all just come from.

I thought about following him but was instantly reminded of my rather abrupt exit from Chitterling's, and decided instead to sit down in one of the many now vacant seats in front of gate B28. I pushed my rolling carryon up to rest alongside me, my head pounding just a little too loudly. *It must have been all the driving…* I told myself, leaning back and closing my eyes. It was as if my ever-loving inner voice had picked up exactly where it had just left off. Its grumblings echoing all around inside my head. *You don't get off that easy, faggot. You ran like the fucking dick-lovin-faggot that you is—and you know it.*

"We were just kids, man." I hissed quietly. "Just kids… and besides, I was running to catch Ben. To bring his ass back…"

Then why ain't you stayed in touch with 'em, Seany-Boy? They're your pals, ain't they? And pals don't just bail when shit gets sticky. Franky? Ben? They're still wandering around above terra firma, right? Ain't that hard to pick up a phone, now is it? The voice slowed, I could hear it breathing low. *Or you just afraid they gonna find out you became a pole-smokin-fag-boy?* Mechanical sounding laughter bristled then went silent.

"Just shut the fuck up already," I seethed angrily—too loudly. Watching as the woman sitting two seats down looked over at me, then averted her eyes quickly while grabbing up her things and moving away briskly. "Away from the crazy guy," I whispered, my tone softening. "We all just moved on, okay?" I mouthed quietly to the now dormant voice in my head. "Just like we were meant to. On to college and then landing jobs. Getting married and having kids, you know—life for Christ's sake. It gets in the way of just being pals—you know?" And when there was no response from it, my crude inner voice, I took a bit of time to fill in some blanks. "Besides," I continued. "We never really talked about it, all that shit, anyway. Any of what had really happened that night. Even when we were still freakin' talkin'. And none of us, as you fucking damn well know, ever went back there into those woods."

Chapter Three

Eddie

The dream kept Eddie down. Closed off from the voices he'd heard whispering just out of range. Ben and Sean, "Seany-Boy" as he'd liked to call him, were talking about somethin' serious, he'd thought. Sean was raising his voice for some reason, and fuckin' Ben sounded like he'd been crying? Nah, just some bullshit they was arguin' about. "Fuck it," he told the voices and flipped over in his sleeping bag, rolling closer to the fire, feeling the flames tickle hotly at the back of his neck.

***

In his dream Eddie's mother, Beverly Juniper Lahn, married to one Edward Jonathan Lahn, stood stock still before him. Her pale skin glowing in contrast against the backdrop of the night-black forest. She appeared to be draped in something. A light-colored coat or some shit that almost covered her completely. It rippled and stirred on the hot tremble of a breeze. At first, he tried to look away, repulsed by something he could not quite identify, but he just couldn't do that, he was drawn to the image of her. So soft… and white? She was smiling when she began speaking to him, yet he couldn't hear her voice at all. And he needed to hear her, right? He must listen very, very carefully to her, he told himself, having no idea to why. And as he leaned in, stepping closer, he could see her mouth moving but still, all was silent. Her lips moved ever so gracefully, smiling at him sweetly at first. But there was something wrong, wasn't there? Something odd. Her mouth looked kinda weird, crooked almost? And her lips were way too thick and caked in a red color. Like she was wearin' gobs of blotchy, red lipstick? Which wasn't at all right, he thought. 'Cause his mom never wore makeup let alone bright red, fucking lipstick. But she smiled again, a mom's smile he'd thought, full of warmth and things 'all good'. Like a sun-filled kitchen struck delicious by the smell of bacon frying in an iron skillet. Her aproned back turned to him as she placed the sizzling goodness on his plate. "Eat up, Eddie, you've got a big day today," she'd say, smiling fondly down upon him.

Eddie's mom was calling to him now—mouthing for him to come closer, smiling wide and red. Eddie took another step toward her, Beverly, who opened her rustling, fur-covered arms wide to embrace her only child. *Why is she wearing a coat?* he thought absently. *A fur coat? In the middle of freakin' summer?* he questioned lightly, but smiled back at his sweet mother just the same. His feet automatically in motion, stepping forward in anticipation of the glorious and loving "mom hug." The hot air picked up and Eddie suddenly caught a whiff of something dark and ripe. The musky scent of an animal dead and decaying, cloyingly thick. *And it must've been dead for a while to smell this bad*, he thought. *And close by too*. He pictured its flesh decomposing in the torrid night air—moist and now turning to rancid. His stomach rolled queasily.

The trees rustled on the wind above, his mom now stepping up closer as if to greet him. Placing her delicate hand on the front of his shirt, grabbing hold, twisting with an entirely unexpected ferocity. Eddie looking down to see his mother's long thin hand now covered in a coarse, white-gray hair that bristled on end upon the breeze. Before he could cry out to her—to Beverly, the woman who cleaned his room, did his laundry and sometimes, but not very often, raised her voice when she caught him smoking in the house—spat saliva on him as she opened her mouth wide, crookedly. Rows of unevenly aligned teeth sprang outward, jagged black and cruelly pointed. Covered over by loosely thick, rubbery red lips.

Beverly's face scrunched up to snarl, a growl released as she contentedly bit down. Her eyes rolling all the way back to reveal their shiny whites. Wet, ripping noises broke over the once silent night. *Funny*, Eddie thought, *now I can hear her?* The smell of animal decay turned suddenly over to the delectably yummy smell of bacon, frying on the stove. So heavenly was the aroma, he hardly felt it as his mom's teeth tore through his cotton tee-shirt to pierce deeply into his flesh just above his right nipple. And when he felt a hot liquid running along his rib cage, he looked down just in time to see his mom smiling sweetly... through all those teeth... a long flap of skin wrapped in dark red cotton hanging from her cheery, cherry red mouth.

***

Eddie came awake with a start, searing heat suddenly burning his wrist and forearm. "Ow! What the fuck?" he shouted, rolling back away from the fire. "Fuck!" he shouted again as he finally realized that he'd rolled out of his sleeping bag and into the smoldering, embers of their campfire. "No wonder I smelled something cooking," he said, grinning as he winced, gingerly touching his freshly singed arm. "But that sure as shit ain't the smell of bacon, cookin'. I ain't no freakin' hog," he said, giggling to himself. Eddie had completely forgotten about the camp, his friends, and or where he even was. His mind still wrapped in the disturbing dream of his ruby-red-lipped mom being some kinda white were-fucking-wolf, he thought, still chuckling, shaking his head to clear out the fucked up 'mom-wolf' image from his mind's eye.

"Damn. That was some crazy shit." Eddie spoke into his arm, still prodding it gently to make sure the skin wasn't broken which, thankfully, it wasn't. It came back to him quickly, his pals, their camp out, and the thought of Ben's sister naked—all flooding into him in one balled-up, blue second. "Ben? Dude, what the fuck?" Eddie jumped up and walked over to where his friends had parked their sleeping bags around the camps fire. He kicked at Ben's which was obviously empty, as were Franky's and Sean's too.

"Pole smokin' faggots," Eddie said and laughed a little, sitting down next to what was left of their fire. He grabbed a handful of the sticks that they'd all gathered earlier in the day and threw them onto the dying fire, which caught quickly aflame as they were well dried from the summer's already ball-breaking heat. He'd need to be careful, as it was likely the whole field could go up in smoke if he weren't. "And old grandpa O'Connor would have my peach fuzz covered balls on a plate," he said to the fire, chuckling lightly.

He watched as the flame caught, reaching into his worn Levi jacket he'd slept in to find his cigarettes. Shaking out a Marlboro Red into his hand, he popped it in his mouth and grabbed up a burning stick to light it. He sucked in deeply, feeling the cigarette smoke kiss his lungs, smelling the toasted tobacco; he sighed and reclined back upon his elbow. He tried not to think of his mom all fanged out and trying to chew on him, but it was hard to get the image out of his head. He laughed a little shakily. "A white fucking, fur coat? Fuckin' classic Stephen King, Silver Bullet, bullshit." Again, he snorted at the thought and took another drag off his cigarette.

Chapter Four

Best friends

His dad leaned against the old barn door contemplating Ben's question. He was a tall man, but back then, most all grown people were tall to me—to us. My mind drifted as it often did, the summer's sun tickling my skin as its hot breeze pushed my hair back, causing me to turn my face into its warming glory. I closed my eyes, scenting the freshly mowed grass and golden hay moldering just out of sight, deep within the shadow of the barn's cavernous double doors. A loud farting noise shook me from my daydream, that was followed by the chirping giggles that erupted all around us.

Ben's dad turned to walk away, shaking his head when Ben too fell into the ever-contagious fit of giggles, smacking Eddie on the arm as he was obviously the one who had delivered a most untimely, and richly aromatic, fart. "So?" I asked Ben. "What'd he say?"

Ben just smiled and threw up his hands and then punched Eddie once more, who turned to try and tackle him. But Ben was way faster than Eddie, probably than any of us really, and he easily bobbed and dodged Eddie's fumbled attempts to bring him low. And then we were all running, sleeping bags slung across our backs, random cooking pans jangling from outside our backpacks, while half of Ben's family food pantry lay hidden inside them.

"This is gonna be epic, man!" Franky shouted from behind. "The whole freakin' weekend on our own out under the stars? Man, I wish your sister could come with us, Ben! She'd love me and my fat-sausage 'longtime'!" he squealed, in a very awkwardly high-pitched, Asian inspired accent copped directly from Stanley Kubrick's masterpiece of a war movie, *Full Metal Jacket*. Which we'd all recently snuck into the East View Mall theater to watch. Fucking great film, but honestly, Franky sounded more like a little girl shrieking than anything even remotely 'Asian prostitute'—but we all cracked up just the same.

Our bikes were laying in the dirt just outside of the O'Connor farms fenced and sagging gate of entry. Several of the dozen or so brown spotted bovine looked up at us as we approached. Drowsily chewing their cud or whatever it was that they chewed-the-fuck-on. Their soft brown eyes not at all curious, stolid stares as they wisped their tails and nervously flexed their ample skins to move the bloat of summer black flies that buzzed relentlessly around them.

"You got the smokes?" I called out to Eddie, who just looked at me, smiling sideways.

And Franky chimed in, "And I got the matches—all your faces and my ass!" Which set us to giggling once more as we jumped on our bikes and Ben unlatched the gate to pull it open enough for us to snake through.

A lone and ominously heavy rain cloud blotted out the yellow of the sun. Throwing cool gray shade over the world as we'd known it just seconds before. "Man, we didn't even think about it—shit." Franky moaned. "What if it freakin' pours?" He looked up, pointing at the lone, puffy, gray-blue cloud. "We're gonna be way the hell out there and we'd be screwed if it rains, I mean really rains," Franky said with just a tad too much cry-baby added in for our ever-so-manly group of thirteen-year-old boys to tolerate. Who in turn, of course, set to chorus in mocking him, pretty much relentlessly.

"Oh, Franky baby! Wah-wah! Waa-aaahhh! Your hair might get wet! Oh no, not my hair! It won't stand up anymore!" And so it went on and on before Eddie shouted above us all.

"Shut up already, you guys! Ben's dad's gonna come back and tell us we ain't goin' at all, yah bunch ah fuckin' faggots," he threatened, which did snap us back to attention and we all took it down a few notches before breaking out laughing again when we looked at Franky's quaffed, poodle-do hair.

You see, Franky had an enormous gathering of tightly knit curls that stood tall atop his rather small head, that we happened to know he spent a great deal of time teasing up to an almost afro-like, crazy hair-do. We'd taken to teasing him (also relentlessly) about his 'real mother'. Which was not Mrs. Stella LaManno after all. Instead, his real and true mother must've been, according to Ben, Eddie and I, a skanky black street ho from the projects over on the lower east side. But then he got mad at us, so we'd stopped teasing him about his overly teased hair and what we all believed to be his true African American heritage. Well, at least not to his face.

"Hey, there's a shitload of tree coverage out there, man. We can always duck into the woods, Franky," I said, genuinely trying to solve the issue that obviously had him a bit too miffed. And with that said, the group went unusually quiet, suddenly finding a great interest in looking down at their dirt-caked Adidas. "F-f-f-fuh-uucck that," Ben stammered, representing the group's feelings ever so poignantly.

Chapter Five

Campin' out

There's that odd-ball age when a boy is not quite a man, yet not really a boy either. And that age, at least for me, was thirteen. To be more precise, the day school had ended and summer break had just begun. Still months before I was to turn fourteen, which when I think back on it, was when all hell broke loose and nothing else mattered except my new, profoundly desperate, obsession with girls.

But at thirteen, none of that female stuff really mattered. It was your pals that mattered and we did everything together. Sure, we boasted of our vast experiences with the fairer sex (mostly Ben's older and horribly bitchy sister), repeating word-for-word the dirty tales our older siblings shared with us, or stealing the lines we'd heard at the movies between handfuls of buttered popcorn. We each knew that the other was making up every bit of their storied, sexy encounters, be it in the back of the school bus, or behind the dumpster at our local 7-Eleven. But we listened intently to every word anyway. Gathering each juicy detail that we might indeed be able to string together when it came our own turn to, well, share.

Ben was a way's ahead of us trying to hold a "wheelie" as long as he could. His tongue jutting out of the left side of his mouth, engrossed in his own heroic competition with none other than himself. Riding on the back wheel, pulling, the bike's front end higher and higher until he almost flipped over onto his back. Franky and Eddie were riding slower, hanging back to compare notes on the New York Giants' players' roster and the year's rather daunting schedule. Both begrudgingly agreeing upon at least nine wins out of the regular sixteen game season. And I, I was lost in my own sparkling thoughts. Riding easily, closing my eyes while the new summer's sun beat down upon my head. Thinking only of just how incredible I felt in that moment of newly minted freedom. Freedom from school, angry parents, and aggressive siblings. Nope, none of that mattered now. Just the sound of bike tires crunching over dirt, my pals, and the expanse of green fields that lay unexplored ahead of us.

We'd probably rode a mile or so by then into the O'Connor's thousand-plus-acre plot. It was said to be some of the most beautiful acreage in all Upstate New York. And to me, it certainly was that and so much more. It was, I supposed, my own stretch of Heaven so to speak. Rolling hills of whispering green, tall grasses as far as the eye could see. Bending on the light breeze, framed by towered walls of green-blue forests, their depths to this day still not fully explored. Or at least that was what we were told, anyway. Old man O'Connor, Henry O'Connor, or just Hank as he was called by those familiar enough with him, never said much to us 'shit-for-brain' kids, as he so endearingly liked to refer to us as. Even if Ben was ole Hank's only male grandbaby and the one true and rightful heir to all his estate and properties. Which was, in total, a fuck of a lot. But when the old man talked about those woods, the Spotted Green as they'd been called back in the old days, man, the old dude would just talk your freakin' ear off.

"I ain't never been all the way through them damn woods neither," Hank claimed one day, sitting on his porch, sipping from a glistening can of beer and smoking a filter-less Pall Mall. We knew his brand pretty well, and had learned the hard way to shy away from them even when we were desperate for a smoke. We'd certainly stolen more than a few cigarettes from his crinkled, beat-up packs now and again, but man it was like smoking the ass-end of a rooster, as Eddie had once said. And he was more than right in his analogy.

"Never ever wanted to neither, boys. And I's own the lot of 'em for Christ-on-a-cross's-sake..." Old man O'Connor continued, jerking his thumb over in the general direction of his forest. "Damn cursed timber that they be, I should set a got-damn match to the 'ole lot of 'em and be done with it once and for all."

And then Ben's grandma, Mrs Elizabeth Audrey O'Connor, who was married to the old buzzard for time uncounted and always seemed to be just within earshot, would interrupt him in her most endearing, yet stern, old-lady voice. "Now, Henry, that's blasphemy yer talkin'. Now stop to that yackin' already—puttin' such ideas in these poor boys' heads. Lord, you're one crotchety ole-bugger-boo now ain't-cha just?" she'd say, smiling a little in our general direction. "Now, who wants some more of my butter crisp apple pie?" she'd ask in a slow drawl. Taking her sweet time, looking from one of us to the next, making each of us blush in time. 'Cause man, Grandma Elizabeth Audrey O'Connor made some of the finest freakin' apple pie in the entire Tri-State area. And that was just the simple truth of it. But we just never knew if her old man (and I do mean old, he was like eighty-six or seven years of age at the time and the last of his siblings still upright) was gonna haul off and slap one of us aside the head. And he always seemed to be about one can of Genesee Cream Ale away from doing just that. So, we'd just sit there, trying to look anywhere but into Grandma O'Connor's big blue, silky eyes. And finally, she'd just give up asking and bring the entire pie out to the little porch table and set it down with some new plates and forks. "Y'all help yourselves now." And she'd just smile as we set to demolishing that poor, helplessly delicious pie.

And old man O'Connor would grimace a bit, but then would set back into telling us stories about those 'infamous timbers'. Usually beginning with the snap, and whuusshing sound a fresh beer makes as it is being cracked open. We'd heard the sound often enough as he kept a large and heavily dented, once blue, Coleman cooler on the porch when he took to what he called sittin' and shit-talkin' for a spell. Course when he wasn't sitting there, that old battered cooler was nowhere to be found. Believe me, we searched for it high and low in those times.

"There's some powerful magic back in them spotted greens, boys, yes, sir, that'd be fact. Some bad shit if I be tellin' it truthful and all," he'd profess, his eyes taking to wandering back toward his fields, filled with wonder and devilish curiosity. "You little bastards need to stay the hell away from it, hear? I've wished often enough that we'd taken that advice ourselves back when…" And suddenly his voice would crack and he'd stare over at the four of us and we'd just nod, so again, he wouldn't take to slapping us each upside the head. "Y'all got shit between yer ears for brains and not a hair on your balls between the lot of yah. Shhii-iiit—those woods would eat you boys alive. Like a fat kid in an' all you can eat Neapolitan ice cream competition."

Eddie was prone to be the first to laugh at something that was not meant to be entirely funny. And that would normally set us all off. And as we giggled between mouthfuls of Grandma O'Connor's butter crisp apple pie, Mr. Henry O'Connor, Hank that is, would take to reminiscing. And truth be told, this was the part of the story we all hung around for. The scary shit, as Franky sometimes put it.

"When I was just a few years older than y'all, and one heck of a lot smarter and tougher for certain, my pappy took me and my kin back there to deer huntin'. Like fish in a barrel, it was. There was and still is so much game back in them trees, even dinguses like y'all could a brought somethin' down." His voice would raise up, suddenly angry, yet through a crooked smile. "But there were areas out there where even the natural game didn't take to travel," he'd then say, his voice growing quiet, hushed. "I guess 'cause it wasn't real natural to begin with in those areas. Dark places, that is…"

Chapter Six

The First Encounter

Eddie finished his cigarette and flicked the butt into the fire where it disappeared in a haze of red sparks. He stood up and stretched, walking to the edge of the camp to see if he could see *those faggots* that'd run off on him. "They didn't even pick up their shit," he said, looking around at the half-opened backpacks, rumpled sleeping bags and bicycles lying low in the grass. "For fuck-sake. Bunch ah pansy-ass pole smokers," he said and bent to pick up the first of the sleeping bags, rolling it back up and stringing its laces around the bundle. "I can only carry so much of your shit, you fuck-heads!" he shouted out into the night, then took to gathering another bag.

The bone shaking howl literally knocked him off his feet, stumbling backward, he landed hard on the dirt packed ground. "What the fuck?" he squealed, turning quickly toward the sound of the lone cry that still echoed over the rolling hills. He spotted something moving eerily fast against the black canopy of the forest's outer tree line. The image was blurred, but even so it was hard to mistake it as it loped up and over the wavering tall grasses. "It's a big fucker," was all Eddie could think to say under his breath as the animal stopped mid-stride. Its action so swift, so sudden, he had to rub the dust from his eyes to be sure that what he thought he was looking at, was actually there in front of him. Slowly, the animal's features came into focus, crystalized in stark contrast against the night black trees. It, which appeared to be a massive coyote or dog of some sort, bowed its overgrown head, turning to stare directly back at him. Eddie was struck silent by its enormous frame and stature, but it was the eyes that freaked him out the most. They threw off an otherworldly cast of pale blue light that oddly enough, glowed winter cold in the night's sultry darkness. The creature stood on all fours, a stiff, aggressive stance that clearly showed off its heavily muscled chest and shoulders. Baring bright white teeth, it almost looked to be grinning at Eddie.

Eddie's first reaction was to stomp the fire out, so whatever this thing was couldn't spot him that easily. But somewhere deep down he already knew that it was too late for that shit. So, he did what he thought would be the right thing—show no fear. He turned slowly toward it, staring right back at the gargantuan creature, hoping to show that he really wasn't afraid. "Come on, fucker, let's see what you can do." And as Eddie made to reach for his bike resting just a few feet from where he stood, the animal suddenly leapt forward. Coming to life in a flurry of tight-muscled movements, mirroring Eddie's actions, unleashing another snarling, bone-cracking howl. Eddie stopped and stood still, eyeballing it with new found wonder. "What the hell?" he breathed. "This bitch has already got me scented," he mumbled, deciding there and then that the thing before him was not someone's lost Fido, that much was for goddamn sure.

Eddie took a slow, deliberate step back, slapping the dust off the back of his pants almost casually, trying hard to be brave. He kept his eyes glued to the animal, smiling, while ever so slowly he pulled out the twelve-inch gravity knife he carried in the front pocket of his jeans. His 'happy-to-see-you-boner-knife' as the guys had coined the blade, he thought randomly. Allowing the boner-knife to silently unfold, its steely blade glowing yellow in the fires weakening light.

Eddie had grown up not so far from those damn woods and had seen, trapped and killed his fair share of wild game in his time, but never had he seen anything the likes of this monster, he thought. "So, you're the White?" he asked under his breath, holding the now fully extended blade close against his side. "The mystical white doggy-bitch Ben and Seany-Boy keep yammerin' on about, aren't cha?" he said aloud, taking a few tentative steps toward where it now had sat back on its wide haunches, panting. "It looks like the damn things waiting for me to come to it?" Eddie wheezed uneasily, watching as the white beast cocked its head as if to acknowledge Eddie's question, grinning back at him, wolfishly.

Chapter Seven

Running in shadow

Ben wasn't even really breathing hard as he sprinted over the next hilltop. He'd had a nagging suspicion that the rest of his friends were running up right behind him, but somehow that feeling had now gone bone cold. Finally touching down atop the massive hill, Ben allowed himself to stop running all together, taking a knee and breathing in deeply of the night's sticky-sweet air. He turned back toward where he'd just come from; off in the distance he could barely make out a pin prickling of yellow light, which he assumed was their dwindling campfire. "Come on, you guys. Get the fuck out of there," he said aloud, not stammering at all. Oddly, only when Ben was alone could he speak without a single stutter, or pesky embarrassing stammer on a word he knew to pronounce, but sometimes just couldn't. As if his voice somehow lost its way up some crazy, twisting path, adrift before it could ever be heard.

He stood up on the hilltop peering into the vast rolling lands, scouring the blackened hills for any sign of his pals, but his efforts were met quietly with only more shadowed darkness. He shivered a little even though the night's air was still wet and warm. Frosted fingers scratched just beneath the skin along the length of his spine. The image coming back to him again and again. A white undulating blaze rolling just above the tall blue grasses, muscled flanks shimmering sleekly in the moon's pallid light. Blue eyes floating pale against the night's black, teeth shining whitely as the beast turned to look upon him. As if in slow motion, Ben stepped ungracefully back into his own memory. He's trying to wake Sean, shaking him roughly by the shoulder while the thing turns once more to stare at him. Its glowing eyes connecting with him, piercing through the night's foggy veil, pushing through him. A sneering grin appears, ghostly white through impossibly long fangs. Every nerve in his body is jangling upward, on edge, on holy-shit-this-thing-is-real alert. He knows he shouldn't run, shouldn't leave them all behind, but they won't wake up, and every fiber of his being is screaming for him to flee. Ben doesn't know for certain what it is, but its presence even from a distance, is one of pure predator. He can feel it. It's growing restless, and soon it will come. As it had time and time again in his sweat-soaked nightmares.

"Come on, man, it's just some lost wolf that got loose out there," he says to himself, again without a single stammer. But he knows… He can hear his grandpa talking low. "Son, there ain't been no wolves in this part of the country for more than ah fifty goddamn years. I should know, boy, I hunted the last of 'em out." His granddad gives him a sly wink. "What's that you say?" His face crinkling like cellophane as a smile comes creeping forward. "You think Mister Barnum and ole Bailey come out here? Them two Ringling Brothers just up and let loose a five-hundred-pound snow white wolf? In these here woods?" Old man O'Connor's voice trailed off only to end with a few curt barks of laugher aimed at his grandson's absurdly stupid point of view.

"Then it's a fucking oversized freak show of a coyote!" Ben shouts back at the voice inside his head. "It's gotta be one or the other, man. Or it's all just my fucking imagination? Whatever the fuck it is, it's got to be the biggest whatever of its kind... and the dreams..." he says, now seeing the creature pacing back and forth in rapid succession. Restlessly circling, Ben swears he can hear it panting low. He's still trying to work out in his head what he's looking at when he recalls the first time he'd seen the... the thing. It was at least a few summers past on the night of the 4th of July fireworks. He and Sean had been sitting here, right on this exact hilltop, 'cause it had by far the best view of the lot, he thought. Sitting right here after the last of the fireworks had gone black under the night's sky. A sizzling blaze of bright pink and blue cacophonous booms still echoed in his head. Other than the ending, all in all it was a pretty lame showing of half-hearted fireworks, fizzling and popping around dully just atop the tree line, as he recalled. But the white thing, well, that was a showstopper that topped pretty much anything he'd ever seen before. *Hadn't Sean seen it too?* He couldn't quite remember either way, but this time, this time he'd make damn sure he saw it, that they all saw the fucker. He trembled, fidgeting with his tee-shirt, remembering how just a short time ago he'd taken to kicking at Sean's sleeping bag, just before he'd taken to running his ass off.

There was a single moment of clarity for him as he stood there alone looking down off the steep, black hill. The shakes slowing, finally subsiding. And that's when he knew that he would venture back to find his friends. "Because that's what friends do," he said clearly, emphatically. But even so, he just couldn't get his feet to moving back in the direction he'd just come from. He was frozen, suspended in that one moment in time. The image of the beast etched darkly in his head. "It was fuckin' smiling at me…" he said under his breath as he began to make his way back down the precipitous slope.

Ben began to pick up his pace as he entered the lower basin of the rolling landscape, jogging quietly, the long field grasses brushing softly up against him as he went. As if trying to slow him down—to perhaps even stop him mid-stride in his quest to find his pals. But he wasn't going to stop. "Not now, not ever," he said aloud as he pushed himself harder, darting forward with purpose. It wasn't long before he came upon them, standing there, just visible in the night's mist covered distance. Sean appeared to be pulling Franky to his feet, gesticulating with his hands while shouting something unintelligible into his darkened face. Ben could see them both clearly enough now, coming into his vision, their images twisting—they were scared. Angry words were being exchanged but their voices were somehow swallowed up by the night. Ben was instantly reminded of the old black and white movies he'd watched late at night when the rest of the house slept. The old-time actors with their faces painted greasy white, jittering about across long forgotten scenes. Their movements oddly mechanical, silently communicating from another time into an unknown future.

Sean's mouth opened and closed again silently. He looked pissed. He turned in a hurry, away from Ben's line of sight, to look back in the direction of where their camp was. It occurred to him that Eddie was not there—not with the two of them. His legs suddenly felt rubbery, the thought taking hold, Sean's anger; he sensed those chilled fingers again only this time touching down in the bottom of his stomach.

Franky was the first to see him coming on across the darkened fields. His hand up to wave him over but Sean, well, he never even turned to look. He was grabbing hold of Franky, pushing him backward roughly, and then he himself was off and running. Ben wanted to call out but the words wouldn't come, so he ran even faster toward them. Luckily, Franky caught hold of Sean's arm just as he was taking off, spinning him back around, pointing toward him wildly. "Hey!" Franky yelled. "Ben! Hey, over here!"

Ben raised his hand in response, still running. He shouted back in return, "I see you man!" His voice rang true and clear, a smile rose on his face as he realized he'd not stuttered at all in the most critical of moments.

***

We all stood together, shuffling on our feet, forming a loose circle. I was peppering Ben with questions about what exactly he'd seen over there. Flustered, Ben threw his arms into the air, hollering anxiously, something about the woods and the 4th of July? Then jumping over to some sort of dream he'd had about a 'white wolf' and Eddie. All in one completely illegible tirade. "Iii-iitt's ah mah-ma-monst-ster, mah-man. Where the f-fuh-fuck is Ed-ed-eddie?" was all I'd made out from his uncharacteristic rant, but that was more than enough to set my mind to working back. Yes, we'd left Eddie and I too had seen the creature in white skulking madly around those damn trees. And for the love of God, I couldn't think of one single, even half-assed explanation for it, or for leaving our pal behind.

Franky, apparently hadn't seen anything at all, he'd just took off when he'd spotted us running. But he was pretty damn shaken and full of nervy energy just the same. We were still miles away from anywhere and the night was black as pitch. Even the stars had seemed to run for cover under the sudden cloud coverage that washed the night's sky in sweeps of cottony gray. "I'm not goin' back, you guys. That's it, man," Franky stated, crossing his arms about his chest emphatically.

I looked at him closely, clocking the signs. He was more than scared. And really rattled by Ben's bizarrely animated reenactment of the white dog creature we'd thought we had seen back at camp. I reached over and put my hand on his shoulder, but he brushed me off, turning away. Not wanting to show any fear. I got it.

"I say we make our way the hell out of here," Franky spat out abruptly. "Just head over toward Ben's house, 'cause that's what Eddie probably already did anyway, right?" he said, looking to Ben. "And he's got his freakin' bike! He's probably way ahead of us by now! Maybe even there already? Just sittin' an chillin'. Smoking a cig at the gate, waitin' for us to hurry the fuck up and meet 'em!" Franky was getting wound up now. "Come on already, you guys! Let's get the fuck gone!" Franky shouted, pleading more to Ben than me. He already knew my position and was still pissed off at the way I'd shoved him just a few minutes earlier.

"We would've seen him," was all I said back to Franky, who again had decided not to meet my eyes. "We have to go back to the camp and get our shit anyway. Let's just go back and make sure he's not there and then we can head out, okay?" I declared evenly.

"No fucking way," he blustered. "Besides, we can get our bikes and shit when the sun comes up, man," Franky continued to counter. "No one's gonna steal three crappy bikes, a few backpacks and some dirty ole sleeping bags. Worse thing that happens is some squirrel chows down on the food we left there and takes a squirrel shit in your sleeping bag," he said through a clenched jaw. "Come on, man, let's just go!"

I smiled at the squirrel shit reference, but didn't give an inch. "Franky, I'm going back whether you come or not," I said, now looking directly at Ben. "And if you want to babysit his ass, you can stay here with him." I tossed my words out, aiming them directly at Ben, knowing he'd never back down from a direct challenge the likes of that one. And he didn't. He stared back at me and without a word, turned and started walking in the direction we needed to go in my book. I looked back at Franky and shrugged my shoulders in a nothin'-you-can-do-now type of shrug and turned on my heel to follow Ben.

"Fuck you," Franky hissed, still fuming from a position of losing the argument. "I'm heading back to the house. I'll see you assholes there later I guess," he said, turning away without looking over his shoulder, walking in the opposite direction. I stood for a few seconds there in between them both, feeling torn. If Franky had just looked back, I would have gone to him and tried harder to convince him to stay with us—to stay together. We were a fucking pack after all. But he never did turn, and quickly disappeared into the night's gloom.

I caught up with Ben and fell into step beside him. "He'll be okay," I said to him, punching him on the arm, knowing he too was worried about Franky, our weakest link, so to speak. And even though I was worried too, I knew Franky was heading away from any real or, well, perceived danger, or whatever the fuck it was we were all sweating about. Ben and I would just go on, collect Eddie who was probably still sound asleep by the fire, gather all our shit, including Franky's. And if all went according to our unspoken plan, we'd meet up back at O'Connor's farm just in time to hit up Grandma O'Connor for some apple and cinnamon hotcakes, smothered in syrup and home-churned butter. Yeah, but none of that shit ever happened.

Chapter Eight

Beverly's white coat

I could see Eddie grinning back in his own wolfish way, casually pulling out another cigarette and pressing it to his lips—rolling it back-n-forth playfully. "Fuck you, wolf-dick. I got no fear of yer country ass," he said, a bit more forcefully than meant, or perhaps felt? He peered down at the thing that sat still, shrouded in a weird, curtain like mist. It stared blankly back at him—invitingly? Eddie stepped forward again. "I ain't afraid…" he mumbled as if in a trance, stumbling ahead toward where it sat, staring. Its tongue lapping at its lips as if the largest porkchop it had ever seen just appeared before it.

Eddie's only clear thought was singular: *Mom's bacon*. A sunlit kitchen hovering in the backlot of his memory, she was humming something… "Mmm-hhmmm. Don't you… Mmm-hhmmm. Don't you worry 'bout a thing-ggg-ah…"

"Mmm-hhmmm. Don't you worry 'bout a thing-ggg-ahhh…" Over and over again, an intoxicating swing beat persevered in droning undercurrent. "Addicting," he said aloud, humming the verse to his mom's strangely bacon induced tune. He held the extended blade well in front of him as he made his way down the hill, ever closer to the forest wall and the white wolf that had somehow become the spitting image of his mother, cooking an aromatic breakfast for him in the comforts of a bright, morning lit kitchen.

The animal never moved a muscle as Eddie drew nearer to where it sat, smiling through a damn good imitation of Beverly's pasty white mask of a face. "Mom?" I heard him call as he stumbled across the tall grass, feeling himself falling forward, not caring. "Mommy," he mumbled as he fell to his knees, the strange song playing louder in his head. Feeling the cool ground press against his face, his body soundlessly slapping against it.

"Oh, Eddie, you little klutzy fuck," she or it said, still smiling. "You never were one for agility in a tight spot, were you, boy? Just like that clod-hopper father of yours." The voice droned on in his head accompanied by raspy spurts of laugher, his mother's features blurring between a wolf snout and motherly nose. Bright red lipstick stretching balloon like across canine teeth. All so familiar. "So good, really." The intoxicating smell of bacon buffering any sense of malevolence, no, all was good. "Really, really good," he said, rolling onto his belly, cuddled in his mother's loving embrace.

She was suddenly telling him that he'd need a good and substantial breakfast to enter the Spotted Green.

"Spotted what?" he asked the cool grass now tickling his forehead as he closed and stuffed the boner-blade back in the front pocket of this jeans without a care.

And then she said that he would really need his strength... "'Cause even though you're a super-duper, ever-growing healthy little boy, the Spotted Green can still be a real motherfucker and you know that, Edward, don't cha? It don't matter much how healthy you is right now, you pink-titted little oinker." And then she was laughing again.

Eddie smiled a bit but was honestly a little more embarrassed by her crude reference, missing entirely the low grumbling growl seated deeply underneath her voice. "Don't you worry 'bout a thing-ggg-ah..." came ringing out in beat with his mother's loving voice. The feeling was euphoric—orgasmic—all was right with every little thing in Eddie's mind, right as fucking spring dandy rain.

He pulled himself up, dragging his body away from the cool, soothing grasses. Staggering back on his feet, swaying just a tad too much as he made his way toward his mom's loving face, hovering just above the wolf's furry muzzle. A bleary red smile plastered against its exposed teeth.

Suddenly, my line of sight narrowed, focusing in like I was looking through the lens of a camera. I was suspended over Eddie's shoulder, the viewfinder shaking slightly as it zoomed in directly upon the grinning mombeast's lips. Which were now peeled all the way back to reveal its true nature, globs of pink saliva falling freely to the blue grass. The jazzy beat still playing on when the creature's eyes flickered, suddenly turning to a bright blue color, turning away from Eddie to look directly at me, into the lens. I held my breath, hoping it was looking elsewhere, anywhere else… But it never turned away, nodding as it drew closer toward me. Dropping its feral muzzle ever so slightly, its eyes sparking blue over the low, insistent baritone rumbling that rises from its being. I step back, pulling at my thoughts. "What the fuck?" I mumble, too scared to understand. "I'm not here. I can't be here—it's just a dream!" I was still backing away from it, the head of the beast cocked slightly to the right while Eddie's mom's image appeared again, hung, no stretched, abstractly to hover in front of the wolf's glaring muzzle. I could see tangles of white fur poking through Beverly's cheeks, and its scintillatingly carnivorous teeth that somehow fit perfectly within her own open mouth. And then she was grinning, a ghoulish chuckle belching out from her widespread lips, as both Eddie's mom and the wolf winked at me simultaneously…

"Ah-what-the-fuck!" I shouted, pushing myself back roughly. Away from the smiling monstrosity before me. "Oh, man stop it. Stop this shit! Eddie, get the fuck down!" I cried out, desperately swinging my arms forward, trying to pull us both back away from the thing. I hit the back of something hard, kicking out to send my carryon bag careening across the carpeted floor in smashing fashion. Someone or something screeched. The sound more like a devious prankster dragging their fingernails across a chalkboard than anything even remotely human. Again, I slammed myself backward and again I felt my body crash against a rigid object that sent shockwaves down my spine.

Their image way too close to me, it or they were laughing frantically now. Foamy saliva gathering at the corners of Mrs Lahn's mouth. Her ruby red lipstick smeared across the wolf's white furred muzzle.

I turned my head, my eyes open, the image of Eddie's mom's face dancing puppet like before me. But there was more to it now, someone else was there, standing up before me, pushing away, mouthing something. A woman? She's making the fingernails on the chalkboard sound. Her hand over her mouth and she's looking right at me.

Startled, I try to say something, anything, but I can't find any words but to ask, "Did you see it?" The image of Eddie's mom suddenly vanished. Poof, gone before my eyes. But it was there, I know it was there. "Did you fucking see it?" I shout again to the woman, now reeling backward, slamming once more into the back of my seat. Ah, that's what it was, I think to myself. And suddenly Eddie is there before me, it was Eddie—he was in danger. "Eddie! What the fuck was that?" I blurt out, apparently too loud for those that still sat around me, as people began grabbing their things, hustling to move away from the guy randomly shouting and belligerently bouncing around in his seat. The lady is still screaming; her fingernail voice continues to scrape loudly against an imaginary chalkboard.

I push myself down against the seat now, trying to breathe, to just calm the fuck down. I had to get control of my surroundings again, take stock of what I'd just somehow witnessed. I closed my mouth tight and shut my eyes against the commotion that seemed to have risen all around me. I wanted, no needed, to go back to the dream or whatever it was I'd just left. I had to find Eddie. I sat completely still. "Please..." I said quietly through my twitching jaw. "Please, let me find him." The smell of damp, blue grass crept up quietly, I continued to breathe in slowly. A cool breeze tickled my forehead, drying the trickling beads of jeweled sweat that formed there. I was standing just outside the forest wall, I could see the trees' darkened leaves, rustling...

Someone grabbed my shoulder, pulling me forward. I spun around in fear, smashing my fist into the unseen body. The wooded lands disappearing before me. Hot breath in my ear, someone was choking me, the night's cooling touch fading. I was sitting up; a voice accompanied the warm breath at my ear... "Sir! You need to calm down." A man's voice this time, a strangely determined and audibly much too loud—demanding that I pay attention. I tried to shake it off, shake him off, wanting only to go back, go back to Eddie and the dream that played before me just seconds ago. Or was it hours? Whatever, I had to know... I had to find out what happened to him...

"Sir! You need to sit down right now!" the voice demanded. "You're out of control, just calm down now!" Silence... "Sir!" The voice trailed off then, regaining strength, bellowed out before me, choking me, a new kind of fear entering my head. "*Security*! I need security over here. *Right now*!" Somewhere I heard the thunder of heavy boots, gaining ground, getting closer, then closer again. I thought of Ben, his crazy sudden bolting—running, his boot tread heavy as he headed away from the campfire. Sparking flames danced before me, then Eddie was calling quietly from inside of me, but I couldn't quite make out what he was saying. I was screaming again. How odd? I thought but just couldn't contain myself. I guess I knew that I was screaming but had no idea when it had started. "*Eddie! Stop!*" I yelled at the darkness behind my eyes, still slammed shut against those who now grabbed at me. "Aw, Eddie, don't do it. Don't go in there. Don't leave us... I gotta know..."

And that's just about the time they came. They came and shut it all down. The large men, that is. Hands moving to fists, thrashing me down, cold concrete smashing into my face. A knee connecting to the groin as my hands were wrenched upward—too far, the pain a bolt of white lightning against my skull. I lost my voice in the agony of it all, each man working feverishly to do their part in subduing me. *Why?* I thought. *Because I was screaming incessantly from my seat right in front of the ticket counter at gate B28? Smack dab in the middle of the Rochester International Airport? Well, my flight was delayed after all, wasn't it?* I giggled a little at my own joke, opening my eyes just as one of the airport security men lifted a small black baton. I heard a cracking sound and that was it. Lights out everybody. Lights out.

Chapter Nine

William Henry O'Connor Hank, as he was known

Back then, folks never did call anyone by their God given Christian name. No-sir. Whatever your daddy called you was good enough for the rest of 'em. Damn if it aint't for certain. And people just took to callin' him Hank right off instead a tryin' to stumble around with William, or even worse, Henry. Most folks said he even looked like a Hank. Like one o' them their movie stars like Hank Williams even. Yeah, ole Hank was a sort of lady killer if there ever was to be one. He grew up hard and lean, with the kinda face that looked to be chiseled directly out of a chunk of granite. And he stood just over six foot, which back then was something of an anomaly for sure. 'Cause there sure as shootin' weren't any of his kin, including his daddy, that reached anywhere near that height. Hank was also blessed with an impossibly thick shock of wavy black hair atop his head that sometime in the late 1920s he took to slicking straight back from his forehead with a thick, jelly like goop by the name of Murray's Pomade. Not to be no pretty boy, mind you, but it was the only pomade thick enough to hold the two-ton o' hair that sat atop his head out from his eyes.

And believe it or not, for Hank, it was all about function. And seein', and seein' clearly, was a most important function indeed for him back then. Especially when he took to the woods. Which back then, was pretty much any and every hour of a day.

He hailed from a large and bold family of Irish immigrants, who came straight over on the boat from the southwest part of Ireland, known to the locals as Cork. And as was with most Irish immigrants of the day, the only thing they came to America for was, quite simply, land. And in the years 1866, 1867 and 1868, when Hank's granddaddy and his brother, their wives, and their extended families, first set foot on the stony shores of Ellis Island, that's exactly what they set out to find. Loads of it, so to speak. The only real difference between the estimated 4.5 million poor and hungry Irish immigrants that made their way through the Ellis Island gateway to the Americas in those times, was that the O'Connor family, was no poverty-stricken lot. No, quite the opposite really. They came from generations of enterprising farmers who began in sheep, for both mutton meat and shearing. And would ultimately branch out into a wider association of animal husbandry that included chicken, goat, lamb, venison, cattle (for dairy farming and butchering) and even Connemara ponies, Ireland's last true work horse.

By most accounts, the O'Connor clan was quite well-to-do when they made their way by train to Albany County, New York's long-time capital. With the American Civil War just one year done, they found a bustling city loaded with new and burgeoning commerce from the import and export of all sorts of goods and commodities. And more importantly to the O'Connors, an exploding populous that needed, more than anything else, to be fed. The O'Connors quickly set up shop and were soon enough importing, raising and butchering their livestock cheaper, faster and of far better quality than even the local farmers could produce.

But it was only when Hank's granddad, William Richard O'Connor, known to most as Billy, at just twenty-five years of age, set out in search of what even then was said to be the most 'beautiful land on God's green Earth', that they truly found their home in the Americas. It was late summer, in the year of 1870, when on horseback he and his brother Ciaran fell upon the infamous lands that much later would be coined by Billy himself as, the Spotted Green. The property spread across a little-known village of sorts by the name of Victor, the namesake of its founder, way up at the tip of New York's Ontario County.

And Billy, well he was instantly smitten by the soft, ever rolling green hills ringed by majestic deep blue forest as far as the eye could see. And within the same year, Billy O'Connor had struck one hell of a bargain with the then mayor of Rochester, New York, a greasy little fella by the name of Mr Howard Pitkin, who said that he hoped that the O'Connor family would bring some 'well needed commerce' to the county and even more so, to his fair city. Billy felt from the start of their negotiations that the man was on the take. And a good chunk of what they'd negotiated as a price for the property, was going directly into Mr Pitkin's personal coffers.

Hank's granddad didn't much care either way to what that Mr Pitkin fella wanted or did. He was, in his eyes, a soft stomached, pimple of a man, who'd more than likely never once seen or done an honest day's work. And was driven far too easily by the lining of his own pockets. All of that mattered little to Billy, who purchased just over eighteen hundred acres of God's most beautiful land on Earth from the greedy little mayor just the same. And when Mr Pitkin's offered to personally escort both him and his brother on to the property in the comforts of his own carriage, Billy drew the line. He thanked the mayor first for the most generous offer, and then in the same breath, warned him too. "Mr Pitkin—" he began to say before Pitkin interrupted him.

"Please, William, call me Howard."

Billy stood for a moment staring down at the small man sitting smugly in his oversized leather chair. "Mr Pitkin," Billy continued, leaning his large frame over the desk to get his face nice and close to the mayor, who quickly leaned back, shying away from this rather large and foreign ruffian. "I'd think it best that we, you and I, ought not have no further dealings. And the land I just purchased from yah, laddie, well I need not remind you is now mine own and legally my private property. So, if I was to see you, or any of them nice fellas you've got hangin' around here…" Billy paused to point out the front window of Pitkin's office toward two, well-heeled, hard looking men leaning against the brick elevation of the town's general store just across its deeply rutted main roadway. "Well, let's just say we'd not be sittin' here in a fancy office havin' tea and discussin' the reasons for such a visit now, would we? You'd be best to know, Mr Pitkin, if we see any of yah, we'll take to shootin'. And my brother here's one hell-of-a-shot with that old Henry rifle he carries on his person at all times."

Mr Pitkin began to protest, but Ciaran pulled the rifle out from under his coat lightning quick, slamming the lever back with one hand, then casually pointed the business end of the weapon at the two men still standing there unknowingly across that old road.

"Mr O'Connor, you are not acting in a civil manner, please tell your brother—"

Billy cut him off. "That's right, boyo. And we'll be even less so if we see you anywhere nears our properties," he growled, staring directly into the mayor's eyes to make sure he took his meaning. And it wasn't until Pitkin tried to look anywhere else but Billy's baby-blues, that Billy himself stood up and turned away, smiling at the cowering man still sitting in his obscenely large chair. Billy bid the mayor a good day, which were the last words ever exchanged between the O'Connors and the mayor's 'office'.

He and his brother Ciaran spent the next several weeks of summer out there, roaming their new lands together, riding side-by-side on horseback. Camping by firelight under the endless stars wherever they found a plot that suited them. Exploring small bits of the wood where they could, pounding into the ground large rough-hewn wooden stakes as trail markers or areas of interest for hunting and trapping wild game. But there was only so much they could even begin to explore let alone catalog as the forests were deep and vast, thick with lush summer growth and teeming with game from the fattest wild turkeys to white tail deer the size of their horses. Yes, it was an incredible place, or so they thought at the time anyway.

***

It was early morning in the year of nineteen hundred and twenty-eight, well before first light when his daddy woke him. His two brothers were already in the barn layin' out the morning hay and saddling up their horses. Hank's Granddad Billy Senior, who normally would have come with them, had passed on a few years back at the age of eighty-four. Of what his granny said to be, 'some right suspicious circumstances'. But most of his kin knew that the man had gone crazy, foaming at the mouth, and hollering up a storm.

"Lot a nonsense," Hank muttered as he thought of the old man. A man he revered. A man who was in his eighties and still strong as an ox and sharp as a tack. "Rabid from a bite he got on himself off in them woods someplace by some type ah feral animal. Probably one o' them goddamn chucks or something," Hank thought aloud. "Miserable little bastards they be an' all," he said without smiling. He still missed his Granddaddy; even at eighteen years of age, it still hurt something fierce for him to think about him bein' gone and all. So, Hank tried not to think about it. But that rarely worked either, especially on mornings like these.

The O'Connor brothers and their kin had constructed over the years what most folks who had called Ontario County their home back then, 'a true agricultural wonder'. Literally cleaving off and tilling hundreds of the most pristine acres of flat lands on the northeastern sector of the property for planting feed sileage corn, alfalfa and hay. And to the west, they grew acres of the county's finest apple, tart cherry and maple producing trees in New York's entire northeastern quadrant. Along with fields of vined tomatoes, strawberries, grapes, onions, wheat, sweetcorn, and of course, golden brown potatoes seeded directly from their homelands of Cork, Ireland. In all, they built twelve total working barns and seventeen smaller outhouses to serve their ever-bustling operations. Mile upon mile of white, hand-split picket fence posts were dropped into hundreds of holes dug by teams of hired hands. All built with sturdy oak timber, cut and milled straight out of O'Connor's Spotted Green to hold and house their horses, cattle, sheep, pigs, chickens, pheasants, and at one time, even buffalo. All surrounding a singular, monolith of a structure, known as the O'Connor Head Quarters. Which for all intent, was their main barn, but back then, to anyone who'd laid eyes upon it, was considered to be something of an architectural marvel.

A twelve-thousand square foot barn by any account was a bit of a structural wonderment back then. But the O'Connor HQ as they took to callin' it, was glorious, a beauty painted in bright red with crystal white piping that stood over one hundred foot tall. The brains of the operation, ole Billy Senior used to say. And it sat within eye shot of their other architectural masterpiece, their sprawling, three-story family home. Or as many of the town folks referred it to as, the O'Connor mansion. Either way, the O'Connor home and main barn stood bright and tall, smack dab atop one of the prettiest hilled plots in all the vast and wild O'Connor acreage.

The house itself boasted monumental floor to ceiling sparkling glass windows, and two of its three stories had planked cedar porches that wrapped all the way across the home's elevation. Which from a distance appeared to meander on without an ending, disappearing miraculously around and into the deep green landscape. The home was constructed to face to the east for its extensively breathtaking views of nature's finest moments. A sublime vista that occurred each and every morning. An uninterrupted sun rising in a flood of yellow as far as the eye could see to finally break free above the forested lands, dappling all in its path with sparkling light. To the west, the second story porch was widened, extending far out and over the rolling hills. Built to hold a hundred guests comfortably if need be, all to enjoy those summer evening pink to purple sunsets that only the northeast part of the country was capable of creating. To put it plainly, the O'Connor home and all eighteen-hundred acres of nature's finest land that surrounded it, was paradise to say the least.

Hank shot through the front door with his mama hollerin' something from behind him about biscuits. The screen door slammed on its frame as he launched himself across the porch still hitching up his britches and at the same time trying desperately to pull his hat down over his head of unruly curls. "No thank yah, Mama!" he shouted over his shoulder, boots now slapping hard against the matted dirt of the front drive. He could just make out the shadowy silhouettes of his brothers Cullen and Thomas when his daddy, Billy Junior, appeared in his path.

"Whoa, there, big fella. Slow yer roll, boy," he said, grabbing hold of Hank's shoulder, literally stopping him in his tracks.

"Hey, Pa. Sorry, I thought I was runnin' behind is all," Hank said, digging the heels of his boots into the dirt while skidding to a standstill.

"Nah, you're all right, son. Your brothers got your rifle and bedroll out from under yah earlier this mornin' while yah was still sawin' wood there. Boy, you can sleep like the dead," he said, his teeth glowing white behind a smile in the early morning's fragile light. Hank grinned himself and then thanked his pa for getting his brothers to get his things together while he still slept. Lord knows they wouldn't have done it on their own.

"Now, Hank, I want to ask yah something here, and I need you to mind me true. All right?" Hank nodded, looking at his father's shadowed face that no longer held the glowing smile of just seconds before. "These woods is ours, as yah know. And there ain't no mistaken them for that, but you got to respect 'em," he said waving his arm out toward the now black tree line. "And all the creatures that call those woods home too," Billy Junior continued. "They ain't all doe-eyed, tail waggin' little targets for you and your brothers to just come up upon and start to shootin'. No, sir, you got to understand and respect that there are predators in the mix too." Hank's pa shoved his hands into his jacket pockets. "Ah shit, I know y'all think of your own selves as the biggest swingin' dicks in these parts, but I'm the one sayin' you ain't."

Hank started to object, but his daddy was not having any of it. He was in what Hank liked to refer to as his lecture mode. And when he got to it, there was just no point in trying to stop him. Best just to sit there and listen till he got it all out of him. *Like a storm passing*, he thought silently, still watching his father intently.

"What-cha need to wrap yer mind around is that not only is there animal type predators in them Spotted Green but there's other stuff too." Hank watched as his pa stopped for a second, scratching the bristle of white whiskers on his chin. He still couldn't see his face clearly, but knew he was to be frowning as he'd done before in approaching this same particular subject. "We all seen stuff out a there." Again, he raised an arm toward the rolling line of darkened timber that backed them. "Stuff, we ain't been able to explain all that easily. Stuff that mighta just brought my daddy, your granddaddy, low, if you hear what I'm sayin Hank?"

Hank nodded dutifully. Knowing all too well to do so in the right places or pay the price for not paying his pa mind when he was supposed to.

"There's stuff out there that's older than them damn woods and the black earth they spurt up from as saplings way back whenever that was. And within it, there is another kinda predator, an apex…"

Hank began to tune out as his daddy once again started talkin' about something that lived out there beyond both reason and explanation. A type of what he'd called a 'presence', or some made up shit that sounded more like a fairy tale than anything else. Well, to Hank anyway. He didn't believe in none of it, but respected his pa enough not to come up against him on the subject. He just continued to feign interest and nod in the right spots so his daddy wouldn't cuff him one for not doin' so.

"Now you just stick to the trail, Hank, and all will be just fine. And pay your brothers mind too in the process. Keep 'em on the straight and narrow, son. They'll listen to yah." Billy Junior was turning back toward the barn now and waving his hand for him to follow, which Hank did without another word.

Hank knew that even though he was the youngest of three, he was still the leader of the boys and proved it out time-and-time again. Hank was said to be absolutely fearless and could fight, shoot and drink any one of them under the table on any given Sunday. Well, if that's what the Sunday had instore for 'em that is. Most o' the time, Sunday morning was spent at the little white steepled church up the road, all being brung up under a stout Irish Catholic belief system, that again, Hank didn't have much belief in or use for. But the rest of the day was theirs, and they spent most of it out there in and between the trees. Yep, that's where the boys (all three of them) would be from the moment they returned home, stripping off their jackets, shirts and fussy neckties in a trail of crumpled piles on the floor. Running to grab their gear, heading to the spot where their entirely illegal potbellied copper still held the promise of the taste of bitter corn whiskey, promiscuous tales, and adventure well off the trail, so to speak.

But not this morning. No, they were heading out into the woods with a real and proper purpose. Something had been getting to their sheep and even cattle as of late and if it was some crazy presence as his old man mighta thought, it sure as shit was a hungry one. Either way, Hank's daddy had made his intention clear; kill whatever it was that was slaughtering their livestock. "Gut that son of a bitch and bring its bullet riddled hide home to hang above the mantle," he'd said and Hank couldn't wait to do just that. And to boot, show his pa just what he was made of when it came to hunting anything in them there woods. And certainly not just them 'doe eyed little woodland creatures' neither, as his daddy had put it.

"Nope I'll kill whatever crosses my path a sideways. If I can sight it, I can kill it," he said to himself, picking up his pace to catch up to his daddy. "'Cause I'm fearless…" He breathed out the words, tasting them, liking them perhaps just a little too much.

Thomas was talking quietly to Cullen when Hank and his daddy approached, but Hank heard 'em just the same. "By the looks of them mutilated carcasses this, ah, thing's leavin' behind, it ain't no black bear. Bite marks were clean, without no signs of them big-ass claw tears a bear leaves on an animal once turned to its prey."

Cullen was nodding in agreement, they'd all seen bear kills firsthand, many times. "Nope, this is different," Cullen set in. "It couldn't a been no coyote neither…"

Which made Hank remember his pa's words from just last night. "We got a lot of coyote in these parts. Scoundrel wild dogs is what they is. But they hunt in packs and packs don't leave nothing behind but the blood-soaked ground of the kill spot."

"There's two predators left in them woods that could kill an animal that way," Thomas said flatly. "A wolf or a mountain lion and we ain't seen no big cats in these parts ever. And no one else neither for at least a hundred years or more."

Cullen, the eldest of them all by three years and a bit, moved in toward where Thomas was leaning his back against the barns open door. "But this thing is one big fucking animal, that much is for damn sure." His voice rose. "You saw the size o' them fuckin' bite marks… them teeth got to be…"

But before he could continue Pa was a-top of them. "Language, Cullen Patrick. Watch your mouth, boy."

Cullen turned in surprise to see the two of them standing there just a few yards behind them. "Sorry, Pa," was all he could muster.

"You boys are gettin' soft in the head, that's the only thing for certain here," Billy Junior said. "Talkin' all this shite whilst we a creep up on yah without a turn o' the head. You take to actin' like that in them woods and I'll be hangin' your own hides over the mantle. And that's a fact sure as I'm standing here right now, boys."

Hank grinned, biting back the laugh that threatened to spill out of his mouth. He tipped his hat to his skulking brothers and made his way into the O'Connor HQ through its enormous, open double doors. Kerosene lanterns glowered from the overhead beams, shedding flickering amber light that seemed to threaten all who came under its fiery touch. He made his way deeper into the cavernous barn's main floor, toward the horses, who simmered calmly in the glow of the lanterns. Their long, forlorn faces lifting as he approached, hand outstretched to his mount, the blunt stem of a carrot protruding from his closed fist. The horse, his horse, nodded and extended his neck to gum at the breakfast treat he was being offered. Hank had named him Wind for reasons sorta obvious once you'd seen the animal in action. From the first day he'd laid eyes upon the colt trotting ahead of its dam, he knew that this one was meant for him. Or better yet, they were meant for each other. The colt was big for its age, with a jet-black mane and glistening russet hide, it was prone to wild outbursts of ferocity, bolting away from its mother, kicking and stomping until its coat glittered with shiny beaded sweat. And when in the open field, no horse in the O'Connor stable could even come close to catching him. He ran like the wind that blew across the high-grassed fields on a stormy day. There was just no stopping that wind, just like there was no stopping Hank's fire-eyed colt once it took to running.

Hank smiled back at his memories, and brushed Wind's long snout as he chewed the rest of his breakfast. Making his way to the saddle he checked his roll, re-cinching it because one of his brothers did a shit job in tying it up in the first place. Then pulled his rifle from the saddle scabbard and held it out for inspection. She too was a beauty, which was all he could think of every time he put his hands on her. The burled walnut stock coruscating as the light bounced off her, its smoky black barrel dulled in comparison. His kin pretty much stuck to a family tradition started by Billy Senior himself when he first stepped off that old steam ship from Ireland; they carried the Henry 16-shot, lever action rifles for the most part. And later, the Winchester 54, but Hank never took to either. Hank fell hard for the Savage 99 rifle at a gun show he'd been taken to as a boy.

It was late spring when he and his brothers, daddy and granddaddy, made their way east by way of carriage to a town by the name of Utica, way upstate in the New York wilds. Where Hank would come to find later to be the same place that the Savage 99 rifles were originally manufactured. Hank's granddad's brother and his great uncle, Ciaran Michael O'Connor, passed on the winter before, as did many back then. The winters in that part of the country were like none other ever seen before and it was true to the letter when they said, 'only the strong survived' them blasted winters. His wife Elizabeth, Hank's great aunt, found Ciaran stone cold in the bed on a dark and bitterly frigid December morning at the ass end of the year nineteen hundred and twenty. It was Granddad O'Connor who took care of Ciaran, wrapping him up tight in lengths of seed-bag burlap and carrying his stilled body silently outside to the woodshed. Where he then laid his brother down amongst the frozen chunks of charcoal and stacks of cut wood meant for burning. He'd known that no animals would get at him out there, and the flesh wouldn't spoil 'count of any warmth. 'Cause there sure as shit wasn't nothing warm about the woodshed out back, Hank had recalled.

Months later, on one of the first spring like mornings, they dropped Hank's great uncle into the sweet black soil just up the hill a-ways from the house. The ceremony was a simple affair led by Father Charles MacDonald, the pastor at St. Patrick's Catholic Church of Victor. Which all told with the mass, ended some forty-five minutes later. But the good Father and well over half of his congregation flocked to the house, obliged to pay their respects in person to the entirety of the O'Connor clan. And of course, Hank's mama and the rest of the O'Connor women being such gracious hosts, laid out a feast and spread beyond compare. Tables were lined up and draped with fine white linens. Steaming plates of smoked honey glazed ham and turkey with pickled corn jellies, homemade breads, and biscuits, were brought out for all to enjoy. And there was even a touch of the spirit (whiskey and ale shipped in directly from Cork, Ireland) put out for those who took a drink now and again. Truth be told, the request for a proper 'Irish spirit' to lift a glass with to the recently departed came straight from the good Father MacDonald himself.

As their guests began to really unwind, Billy Senior, not too tickled by any of it, spoke his mind in plain. "Damn freeloading lot of 'em, they didn't come to bury my brother, they came to raid out our pantry and drink us dry," he said under his breath. "Like a swarm o' damn flyin' locust, they is," he shouted in a whirl of frustration, storming down the back steps and away from Father MacDonald and the rest of his parishioner locusts. But there was more to it, Hank had thought, as he watched his grandpa go. There was a sadness too. And when you looked close enough, beyond the red-faced bluster, it was heartbreakingly profound. A gloom that never quite lifted even as each season came and went. Billy Senior was really never the same after his dear brother passed, just never the same at all.

The day was one of those bright blue ones, the smell of jasmine shyly kissing at the breezy air as it tugged and tussled at one's clothing. And with his brother just buried, Billy Senior loaded the boys up into their high wheeled wagon and without another word pointed the horses east, heading them all to the town of Utica, New York. Hank and his brothers found out along the way that the Utica Rifle Frolics Competition was the reason for the trip and according to their grandpa, they all could benefit from some shooting lessons. "Yah lads couldn't hit the broadside of a barn with a damn cannon," was all he had said on the matter.

When they'd finally arrived later that day, Hank, and the lot of his kin couldn't help but notice how industrious and alive the town of Utica was. Hank had no idea what to expect; he'd never been further outside the O'Connor estate than the town of Rochester in his entire ten years, and this place was just like something out of the picture books he read in school. "Magnificent," he'd whispered over his brothers' hootin'-and-hollerin'. The town was bustling with throngs of all kinds o' curious looking folks, from rough and ready ranch-hands to the more sophisticated, bowler wearing men in black suits with high shirt collars and bowties. They appeared to stroll rather than walk. Arm in arm with their lady folk who seemed to have not a care in the world, all dressed up in summer whites and twirling brightly colored parasols above their heads, making them appear more like a delicately stemmed wildflower than a person, Hank thought.

The festival itself offered activities that stretched all the way across downtown Fayette Street, right through its

State Street intersection, to finally spill out onto the Chenango Canal bridge. The streets were alive with people dressed in their Sunday finest, while the town itself was ablaze with street cars, vendors, magicians, cowboys, stilt walkers and circus creatures in giant barred cages. All lining the proper, red-bricked storefronts that were heavily decorated with red, white and blue banners, which rippled and waved on the steadily warming puffs of wind. The American flag rose high above and they could make it out easily over the top of the towns squat brick buildings as they entered her gates.

But the main attraction and the reason they'd all made the trek into Utica, was the Rifle Competition. Which was housed just off the Erie Canal in an old coal shed, which by and by, was the size of two city blocks for sure. And it was right there that a marksman wearing bruised leather chaps, a dusty black Stetson hat and star shaped spurs on his boots, used a Savage 99 rifle to fell thirty-two targets without missing a single shot. Besting all the other competitive shooters by more than two times. Hank couldn't take his eyes off the cowboy and more importantly, his rifle. And after all the shootin' was done, Hank's granddaddy introduced him to the competition's champion, a man by the name of Big Jesse Reinhardt, who hailed all the way from a place called Denver, Colorado.

Hank was struck dumb when the impossibly tall cowboy got down on his haunches to look Hank square in the eyes, winking once at him before saying, "Hank O'Connor, it's a pleasure to make your acquaintance."

And engulfed Hank's hand in his own and shook it twice, up then down. "And this here's my baby, and she goes by the name o' Heartbreak. 'Cause she'll break it every time she fires 'cause she's just that sweet to shoot..." The ole cowboy went on for a spell and Hank lost track of his words and took to just staring at his rifle, Heartbreak herself, that is.

By the time they'd crossed over the edge of the ridge toward the northern quadrant of the O'Connor estate, Hank had all but forgotten about that old-time cowboy, his focus turned to the Spotted Green just coming into view over the rolling horizon. Cullen and Thomas had fallen in behind him and he behind his pa, leading the way down the meandering game trail and out into the open fields of tall grass. Once they were off trail Hank couldn't resist letting ole Wind stretch his legs a bit, and with a quick, "Yah!" he just tapped at the horse's haunches and then held on for dear life as Wind took to what he did best—running. He broke away from the pack leaving Hank just enough time to grab his hat while turning in his saddle to wave back at the boys he was leaving in their dust. His pa was shaking his head, a grin breaking a mile wide across his face.

Then they were off and running, picking up speed as Wind found his stride through the flat lands. Gobbling up the space between them and the forest with such ferocity, Hank thought to slow him down, but in the end, he was just having too much fun. They came upon the tree line and were instantly engulfed in long, blue shadow under the first line of the trees' vast, umbrella like canopy. The air was already considerably cooler there, but Hank knew from experience that once they entered the wood, the temperature would drop another twenty degrees when the sun would disappeared behind the giant red oak, maple, sycamore, and mountain ash trees that were just some of the varietals that made up the forest. Hank dismounted, stringing Wind's rein to a low hanging branch as he walked toward the spot where the grasses ended and the forest began. He put his palm on what must have been a three-hundred-foot-tall elm tree, marveling at its sheer height and size. The tree looked to be very old, with many a gnarled twist and gash over its enormous base and rooted trunk. Oversized branches the width of a man's midsection shot straight up into the air, winding snake like toward the sky. He pulled out his buck knife from the sheath on his belt, figurin' this was as good of a place as any to mark their spot. And even provide a pretty simple reminder to his lazy-ass brothers as to who got here first. He grinned at the thought.

To Hank, this place, this one tree, and all the others that made up the Spotted Green, were the most beautiful gift mother nature coulda offered the world. And well, for him, it was like coming home every time he'd come up on them woods. He started to carving his initials, digging two long vertical slashes into the great tree's impossibly thick outer bark. But as he moved to cross the two lines with the blade, making the distinctive 'H', the first initial to his preferred name, when he suddenly felt something—something strangely out of place.

He stiffened, backing quickly away from the tree. A chilled gush of wind slapped at his back sending a dizzying spike of cold from the bottom of his spine all the way to the base of his neck. He spun around on heels as if there were… "Were what?" he asked aloud. Wind, his trusty mount, looked up with mild interest when hearing Hank's voice but quickly went back to chewing at the lush, green grasses. Hank froze in place, just as still as he could be. There was something that piqued him, something he couldn't quite put a finger on, but could sense just the same. It felt like… "Like I'm being watched," he said in a hushed voice, spinning around just as fast as he could to face the old trees, towering above him. Hoping to catch a glimpse of whatever his tingling senses had alerted him too. He stood completely still again, his blade held out toward the ominous tree line. Scanning the dense green, trying to see through the cloaked, leafy shadows. Nothing moved but the tree leaves themselves, bristling gently on an oddly cool summer's breeze. And then he heard it. A low rumbling sound coming out from behind the immense elm's barrel like trunk. The sound of something growling… low, barely audible at first, but then it changed. Hank fell back, stunned, not able to process what it was he was hearing. There were voices too… they were singing. "What the…" he mumbled, taking another unsteady step backward, something or someone was singing in there, he thought. Shocked by the fact that he even recognized the tune. It was from one of them nightly radio programs; one he'd taken to hummin' now and again while doin' his daily chores. *"The Spell of the Blues!"* He said aloud. "Yeah, by them Dorsey Brothers or somethin', that's right." He exclaimed just as a winding horn section took off once more as the famously sultry, baritone crooner sang out.

I turn my head to the sky
When you pass by.
But I want to cry because
My heart is under the spell of your blues.

Hank was lost in the songs haunting melody that came mysteriously from nowhere yet seemed to be everywhere around him when a foul odor, putrid and bloated just about bowled him over. Shaking him free from music's untimely spell, he stumbled, struggling to find his balance. The rancid stench of decay caused him to gag on hot bile that rose all too quickly into his mouth. Leaning over, trying with all he had not to throw up.

"Hank! What you think you're doin', runnin' the dang Kentucky Derby?" He suddenly heard his brother Thomas shout out. Well before he'd heard their horses' hooves pounding the ground as they finally caught up with him. The strange music still trembling about in his head when something rustled within the brush in front of him, right where he'd just been standing. An unseen presence of a potent nature took to drifting, slinking away, back into the wooded shadow. Hank just stood there frozen, trying to comprehend, then fumbled to sheath the blade still held tightly in hand. He turned around quickly, throwing a forced grin back toward his brother.

But it was his pa who took notice of Hank's expression. For an instant, he saw something else on the boy's face beside his silly grinning, something he'd really never seen on his face before, he thought: fear. "Hank, son, you all right?" he asked as he jumped from his mount, landing in stride, skip-stepping over to him. "Hank?" And when his youngest finally turned toward him there wasn't a trace of what he'd just seen left on his mug.

"Nah, everything's Jake, Pa. Just feelin' a bit o' Ma's biscuits is all. They got all jostled up when ole Wind here took to runnin'," Hank said with a queasy grimace.

"Aw, poor baby, got a bad tum-tum?" Cullen squealed, happy to finally have an opportunity to take a jab at his do-no-wrong little brother.

Hank was moving toward Wind before his pa could truly grab hold of him, but he got him by the back of the collar before Hank could make his getaway. His pa dragged him back to stand right there in front of him. Placing both hands on Hank's shoulders, he gripped down tightly. "Boy, you just cool your heels here and now," he hollered tersely into Hank's sweaty face. "You and I know goddamn well you ain't had no biscuits this morning—now don't we just?" he said pulling Hank closer. "Now, let's try this again and you best not even try to tell me another tale about breakfast, 'cause I saw the look on your face, boy. Now, what's got you so damn spooked?"

Hank stood silent for what felt like an eternity. At least enough time for his brothers to make their way to stand just behind their pa and stare blankly at him. "Speak up, boy," his pa urged him.

Hank turned his head to the woods, speaking slowly, almost methodically. "I heard, well no, I guess I felt? Felt and heard somethin'… somethin' watchin' over me. A queer feeling just come upon me and all, then whatever was watchin', started to well, uh, to growlin'. Deep and low, funny like, like in some kind a rhythm or some shit. But that ain't the half of it, Pa, I mean, that wasn't all a what got my skin to crawlin'." Hank was about to say something about the music that took to playing inside his head but wisely decided against it. Call it a hunch, but this was just too much already without addin' in ole Bing Crosby's singin' an all. Nah, he kept that part of the story quiet, 'cause they'd think he'd gone and popped a spring loose for sure. Instead, he looked directly into his pa's inquisitive face. "It was the smell pa. I, I-ah, I ain't never smelt nothin' so powerful hateful in all my days…"

Chapter Ten

Airport security can be a real bitch

My head rang like a bell when I lifted it up, trying desperately to open even just one eye. Which both felt to be sewn shut by needle and thread. The light was blinding when I finally was able to peer through a single, heavily encrusted eyelid. There were voices, but I couldn't make out a single word; everything was all slurred and rammed together in incoherent chattering. "Where am I?" I demanded of the voices. "My head..." And then everything went dark once more.

When I awoke the second time, things were quite a bit clearer although my head was still screaming with white hot pain. I found myself sitting at a desk, or table, or something, with my face pressed flat to its cold aluminum surface. "That's bizarre," I said and winced at the lightning bolt that shot across the back of my skull when I lifted my head slightly from where it lay. Instinctively, I moved my hand to soothe the pain, but couldn't lift it. I heard a chain rattle when pulling up my hands again, this time noticing that I was handcuffed and chained to a small metal loop that protruded from an otherwise empty aluminum table that I appeared to be sitting in front of.

"Yes, bazaar but apparently necessary Mr Kilpatrick. Uh, you are, that is at the moment, in the custody of the ACTS Aviation Security Department," a distinct baritone voice called out from somewhere beyond where I was seated. "My name is Agent Lenard Bishop and I am the person in charge, if you happened to be wondering. Do you know why you are being detained with us this evening, Mr Kilpatrick?"

His words bounced around in my head when I finally found the strength to open my eyes fully. The glare of the overhead light burned platinum bright as I took in the small, drab, gray, cinder-blocked room, I was now being held captive within. Adjusting my head to let my eyes roam a bit they landed upon what must have been one Agent Lenard Bishop, smack dab in the middle of it all. Which was only a matter of time, I supposed, because ole Agent Bishop was quite possibly the largest human being I'd ever laid eyes on.

He sat across from me making both the table and the chair he sat on appear to be somehow miniaturized to dollhouse status. His gargantuan head was clean shaven as was his face, which wasn't an unpleasant face really, it was just so enormous, it seemed to be misplaced, even on a man of his size.

"Mr Kilpatrick..." He said again, and I politely interrupted him putting on my best aw shucks, I fucked up smile.

"Please, Agent Bishop, call me Sean."

He stirred in his tiny chair before speaking again. "Okay then, Sean, that's real nice of you now, but before we get started let me ask you one more time, do you have any idea to why you're here? Why you're being detained?"

I looked at him, still grinning, as he crossed his giant arms over his chest and leaned back awkwardly. I lifted myself up from the aluminum table to sit upright as best I could, before answering the question. "'Cause my flight was delayed?" I answered sheepishly, hoping a little levity might soften the tension hanging there between us. The agent just continued to clock me, solemnly unmoved. "Okay, okay, I get it," I said placing my palms flat on the cool surface of the table. "It's just that I've been under some stress lately, job shit—you know the drill, right? And I, I just sort of lost my composure I guess," I said, exhaling deeply as if the weight of the world was suddenly lifting off me. "I'm sorry. Really. I didn't mean—"

Agent Bishop raised his hand up, interrupting my supposed confession that was now only just beginning to flow. "Mr, uh, Sean. I fully understand that in this day-and-age people can be, as you've said, suffering under a great deal of stress. But Mr Kilpatrick, your particular outburst appeared to be well beyond just a run of the mill release of job-related stress. We deployed three of our security personnel just to subdue you." He breathed deeply. "Frankly, er, Sean, passenger related melt-downs born of the garden variety stress of life are not all that uncommon here in our airport, but you, Sean, you've entered an entirely new realm of so-called stress release." He turned his upper body toward a small monitor hung on the wall just above my line of sight. Lifting his arm to point the tiny remote control that was buried within a catcher's mitt sized hand, toward the dark screen.

The monitor blipped on, crackling static shredding the heavy silence that had moved uncomfortably into the small room. I turned my head slowly, watching closely as a fuzzy image appeared centered on screen. Clearing as if by one pixel at a time to finally reveal itself as an aerial view of a large airport terminal. The camera spun automatically to the right, showing what looked like a gateway between multiple terminal bays. Hundreds of gray-faced travelers moved about in black and white, sporadically hustling to unknown destinations only they held the key to discover. A hum of activity poured through the monitor's little speakers as Agent Bishop increased the volume from the tiny remote control. Ghostly voices whispered unintelligibly from the screen, intermixing with loud robotic sounding airline representatives making their uninspired announcements. "United flight one-three-five-eight is now boarding at Gate thirty-two C. Please have your boarding passes…" The voices blurred together dully in my head, pounding painfully from temple to temple. I was fading out a bit when a single high-pitched scream sliced through the slur of mundane voices, cutting deep into my memory. "Fingernails on a chalkboard…" I said softly, not knowing exactly why.

Just then, the camera stopped cold, leaving the echo of the scream to play again in my head. Then it was pulling away, retreating from the piercing sound that picked up once more, even more urgently this time than before. The lens readjusted, zooming quickly down, right into the crowded terminal gateway. I'm not sure when it happened, but both my hands were locked down on the table's edge, gripping it as if my life depended on it. There was something so unsettling about the camera's unabashed singular focus, pushing relentlessly inward, closing in upon…

And then it just stopped. The screaming silenced so suddenly, it left a faint ringing in both my ears. A tangled mob of distressed looking people pushed into frame in a wave. Grunting, crying out then pushing at each other, cursing as they took to flight. Human chaos erupts in front of my eyes. The camera is unforgiving, pressing ever closer into the mass, capturing the detail as a man in a gray pinstripe suit shoves a woman brusquely as she tries to cut in front of him. The boarding gate comes into view in the background. I can just make it out, B… B28… Gate B28 floods the screen. "That's my gate…" I say breathlessly, my eyes wide, glued to the screen. A male voice suddenly shouts out above the rest of the buzzing human panic and turmoil. A woman falls into frame, rolling across the carpeted floor to grab hold of a small shrieking child. She jerks the kid by the back of his coat and starts dragging him like a discarded stuffed toy across the floor.

There's a commonness to the movement now; these people are trying to get away from something that is somewhere right around Gate B28. Something is there, but I still can't make it out. Then ever so slowly, I see it. A man is sitting just to the left of the gate. He's convulsing. His shoulders are shaking violently and his head, it's twisting back and forth too rapidly, frighteningly odd as if possessed by an unseen demon. He's shouting... No, more like shrieking. "Hey," I say, rising from my chair, trying to point at the screen, my cuff stopping me dead in my tracks. "What the hell is that? Look, it's that guy. He's causing all this crazy shit. The guy's completely out of it," I say, looking back at the agent. "The crazy fucker's just sitting there going ballistic."

Agent Bishop is staring at me calmly, and without saying a word, raises his balloon sized hand in front of me, waving me back to sit down once again. I feel myself hesitate, staring at Bishop's face. His expression, it's oddly curious. There's something hanging on his giant mug that catches me off guard. I turn my head back to face the screen. The fucking camera is moving again, zooming in, drilling down—cutting through the clutter of people now falling away. I feel my insides clench as the man in question comes into focus. "Oh, come on. Nah, man, no fucking way..." I breathe, watching the crazy fucker's face, recognition pinning me back. Then I'm dropping to my seat, watching this guy on screen twisting and turning, in his chair, foaming at the mouth, deep guttural screams come forth without a break, one incoherent rant after another.

Agent Bishop is suddenly on his feet, pointing the remote toward the image, freezing the video to allow the tormented face to float bloatedly into the full light of the frame. The air stills across the room, I can't look away; staring back at me is a face with features straight out of a nineteenth century psych ward. Eyes crookedly ablaze, a broken snarl frozen there, mouth open to throw thick gobs of white spittle out into the space between me and my freak-show twin.

Bishop sets the remote down gently on the table and quietly turns to look directly into my eyes. "I think we can agree, Sean, that this person is not a person that is, how'd you say, 'stressed out' from a rough week on the job, no?" He moves in agile steps for a man his size, maneuvering expertly around the table, which becomes that much smaller as his enormous form stands before me. He looks saddened when stepping back, turning once more to the screen, lifting a sausage sized finger to point directly at the face there, which is in fact my face. "So, let me ask yah again, Sean, 'cause as we've established, this isn't anything even close to well, normal behavior. Do you, Mr Kilpatrick, have any history of mental illness? And if so, we're not here to judge you, we simply want to get you back to where, uh, wherever it is you belong. So, is there someone we can call to perhaps bring you back to..." He paused, dropping his massive hands to his sides.

"You mean is there anyone I can call to take me back to the nuthatch I recently escaped from, Agent Bishop?"

He never responded to my sarcastic inquiry, but instead, turned to speak to several men who must have just entered the room. I could hear him talking, but really, I wasn't paying much attention to their words, or even the fact that additional security personnel entered our already cramped little space. I was lost in the image floating before me on the screen. Startled by its sheer ferocity as it stared wildly back at me, still not entirely believing that it was even me at all. When was this? It couldn't have been just a few hours earlier in the evening, could it? I tore my gaze away from the screen, scouring the wall for a clock, and of course there it was, an oversized two-handed model in the far corner, just like the ones we'd had in grade school. Its hands read 12:23 a.m. My flight was supposed to have boarded at 7:06 p.m. before the weather delay was announced. Was that right? Due to weather? "The weather?" I mumbled.

Looking around the room again I noticed the additional staff—three bulky men in dark blue uniforms, each carrying a standard issue Glock-nine sidearm holstered to their oversized black belts. Could six hours really have gone by without me knowing it? I felt my head throb and remembered the men, the men that now stood here in this room—they were beating me... I looked from grim face to face. Frantically trying to work out the why in my head.

"Mr Kilpatrick, are you, all right?" Agent Bishop was on his feet and leaning toward where I sat.

"Get these bastards away from me." I stammered. "Can you fucking spell e-x-c-e-s-s-i-v-e force?" I breathed in deeply. "I wonder if you have any footage of these fine gentleman their Agent Bishop…" I said, pointing at the large, Hitler's SS looking dude scowling at me from where he stood, hands clasped together tightly in front of him— too tightly. "So big boy, been to any Nazi Youth rally's lately?" I probed gently, watching his jaw clench then twitch before I pressed on. "I bet if we stripped that shirt off, we might find a few rather interesting tattoos, no? A little old-fashioned 'Fatherland' representation? A little Deutschland loyalty, no?"

The guard seemed to have had enough and stepped up to me, but Agent Bishop blocked his path. "Stand down, Richter, that's enough."

"Richter?" I challenged. "Richter? You're German, yes…" I smiled knowingly.

"Mr Kilpatrick, enough." Bishop shot me a look that said it all.

I put my hands up in mock surrender. "What do you know about 'excessive force', Agent Bishop. If I asked, I'm sure I, or perhaps my attorney, could get this footage." I pointed at the screen where my insane asylum friendly twin silently raged, seething outward. "Yeah, from the airport authorities, or maybe even your supervisors—I'd also venture to bet that there were plenty of witnesses to support—"

Agent Bishop held up his hand before me. "Mr Kilpatrick, please. You were and may even still be, clearly out of control and a danger to both yourself and the multitude of innocent patrons of this airport." His voice stretched tightly over the last few words. "But let me try to understand your point—it's—it is what, exactly? That Richter here is some sort of Nazi reincarnate and he beat you in an anti-Semite, anti-lunatic, type of rage?" He stopped mid-sentence, holding his hands up in apology. "Mr Kilpatrick, these accusations aren't even remotely necessary. We simply would like to ensure that you are looked after and get the care you so deserve. Now once more, is there anyone that we can call for you?"

I looked up into his moon sized face. "Well, yes, Lenard," I answered rather enthusiastically. "Yes, indeedy, boys, there in fact is. There's a fella that I think just might vouch for me as being somewhat sane. Haven't spoken with him in a dog's age, but what the hell, I'm game if you are. Sure as shit, beats sitting here with you and your sauerkraut eating friends…"

Chapter Eleven

Gone

Ben and I stood on the edge of the hill looking down at the black veil of forest. We'd not spoken a word to each other since we arrived back at our campsite. I could barely see the last smoldering embers of our campfire, which was more smoke than embers. The camp area was completely still, and to our surprise, completely empty. Granted, all our shit was still there, lying about pretty much how we'd left it just a few hours earlier, only a couple of our things appearing to have been tidied away. As if being readied for a quick departure. But Eddie was nowhere to be found. We'd taken turns scouring the hillside below the camp and ultimately shouting out to Eddie in what rapidly was becoming desperation.

"Dude." I turned back and looked at Ben. "Maybe Eddie just bolted home too. Cut through the fields and we just missed him when we were coming back here. Maybe Franky was right and shit?"

Ben looked up at the sound of my voice, responding with a half-hearted shrug of his shoulders. True, this place was an area of massive proportion and honestly Eddie could have been anywhere. But somewhere deep down, we both knew better. Eddie wouldn't have just taken off. He knew these back woods better than any of us and would have headed back in the exact same way we'd come. Exact. He would have known that he'd eventually either catch up to us or meet us at the home base later.

Ben stood very still, staring at the forest's inky edges. He was looking for something, I thought, as I watched him scan the vast horizon.

"He's not in there, man," I said, following his line of sight. "There's no way Eddie would run into those woods alone at night."

Ben turned and stared at me for a long uncomfortable beat. "Ye-ye-yes he wah-would," he said quietly turning back to peer out at the woods some more. "I-i-if he ha-had a ga-ga-good enough rah-ra-reason, he wah-would, ma-man—du-d-dude ain't afraid of nah-nothin'."

I wanted to ask, but decided against it. Eddie may not have been afraid, but were we? Would we go into those woods after him right now? I suddenly felt cold all over. We had a choice to make. We could either keep looking for him across the endless rolling hills, which might just include a trip into that foreboding forest, or we could head back hoping that Eddie had already made his way out of here.

In the end, Ben and I simply stalled. We wandered around the camp, played with our fire, rolled up all the remaining sleeping bags, collected the rest of the packs and gear, then arranged it all in an orderly pile. When there was nothing left for us to do, we both sat down by the fire.

I looked at my watch which read 3:48 a.m. Dawn would be coming soon and there was absolutely no sign of our friend. Ben stared intently into the flames as I searched for the words to say. When they finally came, I hesitated briefly, then just spat them out. "Look, man, I think he headed back. There's literally no trace of him..." As I was talking, I happened to catch a glimpse of a cigarette butt, ground out in the dirt just beyond where Ben was now perched. I froze, not really understanding what I was even looking at. Then got up to take a closer look. I could feel Ben's eyes on me as I walked to the edge of our camp sight, looking down, scouring the grounds.

"Dude, throw me your flashlight," I said as I knelt in the dirt. Ben was up and moving, rustling through his pack to grab a light and before I could ask again, he too was kneeling beside me with the light shining before us over the darkened patch of packed dirt and pebbly rocks. I couldn't help but smile when I saw the lone cigarette butt half covered in the dirt and dusty debris. Obviously crushed down under the weight of a heavy booted foot. I shone the light over the area and instantly recognized a series of multiple boot prints. "Eddie was standing right here, man," I said, as I remembered the first time I'd seen the tracks that lay before us.

We'd been hiking the back trails behind the O'Connors house right after a heavy rain and the trail was slick with gooey mud. Eddie was walking in front of me and I happened to be looking down at the trail when I first noticed his boot tread. I'd laughed out loud in spotting his little joke, responding in kind with a, "Fuck you too, Eddie." Which caused him to turn around in mid-step and grin at me, then flip me off before he turned back to the trail. You see, Eddie had a great sense of humor if you knew him, he just didn't show it all that often. Well, probably more like never, but I saw it often enough and knew this little trick was meant for me. You see, somewhere before we went on that rainy-day hike, Eddie had taken the time to carve two large letters, one each in the middle of the rubber sole of his right and left boot. F and U. Carved deep in big capital letters, which were really hard to miss if you were walking right behind him on a muddy trail.

"Funny shit," I said as I shone the light closer to the sparse grounds, spotting a multitude of tread marks with the infamous F and U's carved out of the middle. I stood up, skirting the edge of the dusty patch and followed the tread marks. To my dismay, they headed directly toward the forest, and where the scrape of dirt patch ended, so too did Eddie's boot prints. But as I turned the light directly into the dark, grassy field, I was startled to see the obvious path he must have taken. The long sweeping grasses were bent and broken, as if a large person had been running through them. "He was running... and heading straight for woods?" I said over my shoulder to Ben.

"Who-who wah-w-was r-running, mah-man? Wha-wa-what are y-you tah-talking about?" he'd barked back tersely.

I stopped and shone the light up the hill at him. "Dude, come down here and look. It was Eddie. They're Eddie's tracks, and you can see where he started to run…"

Ben worked his way around the dirt so as not to disturb the tracks and ran down the hill to meet up with me.

I shone the light into the black and blue grasses to show him what I'd already seen. I watched as Ben looked out across the fields and ultimately asked for the flashlight back, which I handed to him without question. We both fell silently into step walking alongside what we'd guessed to be Eddie's tracks, where he had run through the field toward the woods.

We came upon the rim of the deep timbered forest all too suddenly. Eddie's boot prints disappearing abruptly at the edge of a large, matted down bed in the otherwise waist high weeds and grass. It was as if he'd just stopped walking, then laid down to take a little nap right at the forest's edge. We stood there as Ben swept the flashlight back and forth over the flattened grasses. And then turned the light to the woods where it was quickly deadened under the deep blackness of its interior. Meaning, well, we couldn't see shit from where we stood. I was pacing, edging my way closer to the trees as Ben pinned the light ahead of me, directly into the forest. There was something peculiar about all of this, but I just couldn't place it.

I stepped up, running a hand over the first tree in my path, an imposingly large oak that soared ever upward, disappearing into the night sky. Its base was at least eight feet across, my fingers closing in upon the deep ridges that ran over the tree's entire outer bark. It was cool to the touch and somehow, I felt comforted by that. Ben shone the flashlight over my shoulder then back into the weald. I could almost make out the second line of thick, leafy trees, just inside the perimeter. Nothing moved or stirred. All was unnervingly still as I stepped over the thicket's threshold and into the forest's chilled embrace.

"Ben, bring the light down here, I need to see…" And right then a sulfurous odor hit me like a punch to the face. I fell back a step, choking. Raising my tee-shirt to cover my nose, the rank stench simply overwhelmed me so suddenly… a bone deep exhaustion taking over my body…

"Dude, you all right?" Ben was shouting from somewhere behind, his voice seemed so far away. I was fading, the blood rushing at my temples in meaty thuds as my knees gave way beneath me. Something was pulling me, dragging me out from the cottony sleep I so wanted to give into. A distant rattle, coughing sounds, my arms being lifted, dragging me out from the tainted grounds.

"Wha-wa-what the fuh-f-fuck, mah-m-man?" Ben was stammering wildly in my ear, I was just coming out of the daze when I heard what sounded like thunder rumbling from the thick bramble bushes that covered the forest grounds outer parameter. The growling broke out unexpectedly, charging into a cracking barrage of shocked howling. Deeply ripping, tearing at my sanity as it grew even louder, more insistent. Ben was pulling me, his arm around my neck taking hold, prying me up to my feet. My head spun woozily when we took to flight, head lolling, a razor-sharp wave of fear planted itself deep, pushing me forward. We were moving fast, the freakish howls still snapping in my ears. We were trying to put as much distance between ourselves and it, whatever the fuck it was. Cresting the hill, we scrambled into our camp sight, our fire cast a dull glow at its center. I looked to Ben, his eyes two red dots that stared back at me—terror stamped white across his face.

I turned away from him slowly, cold sweat oozing down my back, I had to see it, I had to know… The forest was pitch black from where they now stood, nothing to be seen at all, relief suddenly washing over me when I spotted something? A tiny stream of white light shining at an odd angle through the grass. "The flashlight." I mumbled, turning toward him. "We dropped the flashlight."

Ben was grabbing his pack. "Ll-la-leave it!" he shouted, clenching my shoulder and spinning me back around to face him. I wanted to say something, but my mouth was cinched closed, every muscle locked down in fear. "Oh, m-m-man…" Was all I heard from him before he bolted away from me. I turned for an instance, just seeing the back of his head as he fled down the other side of the hill away from me. I wanted to call to him; I lifted my hand but couldn't move my lips to speak let alone shout after him. And then he was gone and I was alone, the gravity of the moment's realization falling over me in thick black waves.

I stood there like that for God knew how long, trembling, then shaking uncontrollably. I couldn't move. But I had to, I had to see it for myself... I was turning my head toward it, tamping down the cold fear that rose too quickly, the fallen flashlight's lone beam of light shown small against the vast black woods and whatever lie within. My stomach lurched so suddenly that I heard a popping sound inside my head as my eyes fell upon it. "Oh God..." I heard myself whisper, my body frozen, my eyes locked onto the, the... it was just sitting there, plain as day, only a few feet away from the flashlight I'd held in my hand just moments before. Its fur swaying gently even though there was no breeze. It's glossy white pelt aglow in the sallow moonlight. It was so still, I thought. And when our eyes finally met, it tilted its massive head ever so slowly, almost quizzically. The blue of the animal's eyes shone brightly, beaming out to me, enchanting me, beckoning to come closer. Perhaps a fun little sit down with the nice, shaggy white doggy... it was no longer growling and in fact, the night was eerily silent, even the cicada had mysteriously gone to quiet; all around me was a thick, almost numbing silence. Until it wasn't.

It began in a whisper, faint at first, some sort of rhythmic beat, I couldn't quite make it out. I turned around thinking maybe Franky had left his transistor radio on in his backpack, but no, that couldn't be it, could it? But there was a distinct sound moving the air around me, and then a voice sprang from the darkness, crooning all quiet like, building, edging its way into existence. "Mmm-hhmmm.

Don't you... Mmm-hhmmm. Don't you worry 'bout a thing-ggg-ah..."

Then, the crooner's mysterious voice slammed itself inside my head, forcing me to my knees. I cupped both hands over my ears to try and stop it. *"Don't you worry 'bout a thing, mammaaa-aaaah..."* Screamed within me, playing on relentlessly. The songs verse suddenly shifting, pitch dropping. "But just don't you feel too badddd-aahhhh..." A surreal swing beat in ghostly chorus takes over. *I know this song*, I think, at the roller-skating parties... they played this... Stevie Wonder. *"When you get fooled by smiling faces!"* screams inside me again, I turn to the animal, there's a connection somehow between the two. I notice it's moved closer; I can see every muscle as its broad chest rises and falls in breadth. I can smell it; dark earthy taint penetrating my nostrils. I try to look away, but it's drawing me in, its faded blue eyes dancing a lively jig through me. Its head moving in time with the song's beat... It's smiling at me...

"Don't you worry 'bout a thing, mammaaa-aaaah," Is all I hear when I turn tail and begin to run. I'm moving in pure instinct mode. I have no idea what I'm doing, self-preservation taking over; I'm on auto pilot and picking up speed.

I don't stop until I reach the flats which had to be a mile or more from our camp. I can't breathe, my heart racing as I fall to the ground, trying to catch hold of each fleeting breath. Panic pushing every nerve to high alert, my entire body jangling with prickling energy. I crawl into the brush; I need to stay hidden or so I think I do. Falling onto my back I suck in the moist air until my breathing finally levels out. My eyes wide, checking the path I'd just run, waiting for it to show up behind me, but it never does. The darkness creeps back in when I realize that the music has ceased playing entirely. I can't hear anything except my tortured breathing. And then I hear the cicada, once again dominating the night's early morning airwaves.

My watch reads 5:32 a.m. Just about two hours had gone by since Ben and I approached those woods. "Fuck, Ben?" I question the early morning gloom, then come to the somewhat obvious conclusion that he's long gone by now and probably, hopefully, close to home. I look at the sky and see that morning is finally upon us, purple bruises of lightening sky rising from the east. I can't seem to stop shaking. My mind is trying to rationalize what I just witnessed, but it's bending well beyond reality and or any form of acceptance. Without thinking or looking back, I'm running once more, again picking up speed; the more distance I can put between me and whatever that was, the better.

Chapter Twelve

The morning comes and goes

Ben, Franky and I were sitting quietly in the kitchen at Ben's house. Thankfully both parental units had already headed out to work and beyond a brief good morning and a rustling of the hair, we hardly said a handful of words to them. Wildly, they didn't even notice Eddie wasn't with us. Disheveled doesn't begin to describe what my two best friends looked like. Haunted, or better yet, filthy and scared shitless was more appropriate. And I hadn't even begun to tell them what I'd seen out there in those early morning hours. And if the truth be told, they didn't ask to hear any of it either. I finally broke the icy silence that was just kinda hanging there between us.

"We should call over to Eddie's to see if he went home last night or this morning, or whatever—you know what I mean."

Ben looked up for a second and then nodded. Just a few hours earlier I'd run into the two of them sitting outside the same sagging gate we'd all snaked our way through some eighteen hours earlier. The sun being fully up did nothing to lighten the look that hung on their tired faces. Franky had obviously been crying, I could still see where his tears ran runners through the dirt and dust covering his cheeks. Ben had eyed me sheepishly and later would say he was sorry for leaving my ass back there again, and that he was glad I was okay. I'd just nodded back to him silently, not wanting to talk about any of it just yet.

I did, however, take the time to inform them of what they already knew, that Eddie was nowhere to be found and that whatever was in the woods had disappeared when I'd begun my trek back here. Franky had confronted me, saying, "If you would have just listened in the first place none of this shit would have ever happened." I reminded him that regardless, it doesn't change the fact that Eddie is still missing. He stared at his untouched Captain Crunch, which was starting to sink into a sea of ever warming, yellow colored milk.

Ben picked up the phone's receiver on his dad's desk in the study and began to dial the seven-digit number we all knew by heart to be Eddie's home phone. Mrs Lahn, Beverly, as we secretly liked to call her, answered the phone on the first ring. Franky and I were standing right next to him with our heads all pressed together so we could each hear the conversation for ourselves. After beating around the bush a little with some awkward small talk — Ben was terrible at this, I'd thought — he finally asked if Eddie had shown up there at the house this morning.

"Not to my recollection, Ben, but let me call him," Beverly responded, then was shouting his name which we all heard loud and clear. After several attempts she came back on the line and asked Ben to hold while she 'checked in' on her son. She set the phone down roughly causing a loud clacking on our end and marched off and up the hollow sounding wooden stairs to where we all knew Eddie's bedroom was. The Lahns really never bought into the idea of purchasing a portable telephone. Why would they, when they had a perfectly good, pea green rotary model hanging right there on the kitchen wall.

We could hear her calling him in her mom voice, "Eddie. Eddd-iii-eeee?" Stomping feet echoing as she crossed the hall. "Edward, are you up?" Pounding on the old wood paneled door to his bedroom. "Eddie?" Softer this time as she pries open the door. All is quiet on the other end of the phone for a brief, tense moment.

All three of us are holding our breath—hoping. "Come on, Eddie, be there," Franky moans low.

"I'm sorry, Ben, he's not here. Say, wasn't he with you last night sleeping over out back?" The silence on our end is beyond deafening. We hadn't thought this through and had no response for the most obvious of questions. "U-uh, yah-yep he wah-was with us, Bev... I mah-mean uh-uh-uhm, Mrs La-Lahn. Ye-ye-e-ah, wah-wa-we split up th-this mah-morn-n-ing and wah-we ha-hadn't heard fra-fra-from him," Ben finally responds, which surprisingly does the trick.

"I'll let him know you boys are looking for him when I see him. Okay, love, bye for now." The line clicks off and Beverly is gone. Gone without suspecting that her son has somehow disappeared in the dead of night pretty much right before all our eyes.

Ben places the phone back on its cradle quietly. We're just standing there in a little circle when Franky speaks up. "We, we should really call the cops." He looks around to gage Ben's and my reaction, which is mild agreement, before he plows on. "I mean, he's really missing and shit. And they need to search for him. He might be hurt out there or some shit…" His voice trailing off then coming back around. "Or they might even think we did something to him."

Ben and I both look up at the same time.

"We? We did something to Eddie? Who the fuck would think that?" I ask Franky directly.

"Anybody," he hisses. "Anybody lookin' in on this has got tah wonder, right? Wonder if we all decided to off our buddy for some stupid reason. No one gives a shit about the reason, but they'd think we did it. We need to get our shit together and come up with a story, you guys, or we're all totally fucked."

I find myself staring at Franky's dirt-streaked face. He's scared, really scared and ironically, he doesn't even know half of what we'd actually seen and heard out there. I can suddenly hear a nostalgic chorus ringing quietly in my head. *Don't cha worry 'bout a thiin-gah…* I close my eyes, trying to shut out the image of the smiling dog or wolf that was grooving to the beat. What the fuck was that thing?

When Ben breaks through the moment. "Yah-you wah-watch ta-too mah-much f-fuh-fuh-fuckin' TV, Fra-Franky. Wah-we got to ca-call my ma-ma-mother. We ga-got to ta-tell an adult."

"Yep, an adult," Franky spits out, staring back at Ben.

"And we're going to tell them what, exactly?"

Ben looks defiantly to me and says, "The tru-tru-truth? Exactly wha-what we sa-saw out th-the-there!" he says, while pointing across the small formal living room toward the back of the house. Toward the fields and the woods.

"*Wait! Stop for* a fuckin' minute! That's not gonna work at all, dude," Franky whines in exasperation. "Let me play this out for a second. So, we tell some adult, or Ben's mom even, that we saw a giant white dog thing in the woods—then we all just ran away 'cause we got scared an' shit? But then we just somehow decided to go back? Only to find our buddy, the one that hadn't run away with us in the first place, had somehow up and disappeared in the night?" Franky's voice edging up to a lively shout, crackling too brightly around the edges of his words. "Some of us ran. And then some of us went back too, Franky," I point out to him while he turns his rapidly reddening face away from the group.

"Th tha-that's ra-right, Franky. L-li-like I sah-sa-said, we ta-te-tell 'em the tra-tra-tru-uth," Ben repeats, ignoring my jab.

"Well, I hope you like big black dick up your ass, cause their gonna dump us all on Riker's Island and throw away the fucking key," Franky whispers back hotly, his voice trembling, rich with a blatant contempt.

"Whoa," I say, putting my hands palm side up to them. "Slow this down man. No one's dumping us anywhere let alone in a prison. We didn't do anything but lose our friend out back while camping. And for all we know he might even still be out there somewhere. Like you said, Franky," I say to him, slapping him on the shoulder, hoping to reengage him in a more meaningful discussion and rational decision. "We've got to go back out there now that it's daylight again. And Ben, you're right too, we've got to talk to an adult, like the old man," I say, smiling at him now.

"I'd r-ra-rather tah-ta-talk to my ma-ma-mom, she'll be-beh-be ee-easier to de-deal with the-then mah-my—"

I cut him off before he could finish. "Not *your* old man, Ben, *the* old man. Grandpa O'Connor."

Both Franky and Ben throw their collective hands up in dramatic display of obvious dismay. "What the fuck, Sean? Are you freakin' nuts? There's no way we can talk to that, that old dude, Ben's grandad and shit," Franky stumbles in saying, while Ben aggressively nods his head in agreement, both hands still up in the air above his head.

"Besides, he'll skin us alive for bein' back there in the first place Sean, and you fuckin' know it."

It's my turn to put my hands up in effort to calm the two of them down, nodding my head in violent agreement with them. And when they finally do begin to quiet their tirade on how stupid my idea was, I start talking. "Guys, I know this is goin' to be a bitch, but it's our only shot at getting someone to believe us and even go back out there with us right freakin' now." They both take to laughing at me, but I press on anyway. "Like it or not man, he's the only person on the planet right here and now that might just believe our crazy, fuckin' story. And it's the truth of it, ain't it, Ben?" I stare at him as he shrugs his shoulders, still, disapproving of my idea, but perhaps just a little less so? "He's told us more stories about those woods and the land they stand on than anyone ever has, or ever will. And he sure as shit believes that there's something out there in the… what did he call it again? Oh yeah, the Spotted Green." I looked over my little audience as they both seemed to be coming around to the point of view I was trying so hard to get across. "And if Eddie is hurt and is still out there, we need to get our asses into those woods and find him, like right fuckin' now. And I for one, well, would much rather do it in the light of day accompanied by somebody who actually knows what the fuck they're doing out there."

"And what are you going to say about what we saw *out there*?" Franky asks, his voice registering just enough capitulation for me to hope.

"Well, Franky, we're going to tell him everything. Every fuckin' detail of what, whatever it was that we saw out there last night." I looked up quickly at Ben before finishing my thought. "What we all saw, heard and did out there in those fields last night." I looked to them both in earnest, trying to read through their fear, trying to find a way to move this forward with or without them.

We headed out the back way, cutting through the rolling fields that backed up to the O'Connors' estate and farm. The morning was brightly sunny and already simmering hot at 8:46 a.m., I thought, looking at my watch, the sweat trickling down my back in small streams. Must have been ninety-plus degrees and heading toward a midday scorcher for sure. I lost myself in my own spirited thoughts, noticing that the fields looked so beautiful in the crisp, cinematic morning light. The soft, undulating hills of green capturing my imagination, I wanted to just lay down and forget all about last night. But I knew I couldn't. And there, over the second hill we could just see the O'Connor homestead. Stunningly bright, its red and white siding a dazzling contradiction, draped in the early sun's intense yellows and mellow golds. I could make out the home's winding porches, where we'd soon be sitting down to tell our tale. They wrapped around the entire length of the great, elegant home, seemingly meandering on forever. Franky had fallen well behind us, and appeared to be sulking. But Ben and I continued to walk on, shoulder to shoulder, each of our hands reaching out now and again to brush the tops of the tall grasses.

"So, are you going to tell me what you heard last night?"

I looked over at him, still taken off guard when he didn't stammer. He sounded so much different, older—maybe even wiser, I guessed. "I suppose I should tell you before we get in front of the old man. Try it on for size so you can tell me how crazy you think it all sounds," I said, looking ahead as we walked on.

"Well, lah-l-look. I-I-I kna-kn-know I le-le-lefft—"

I put my hand on his shoulder before he could finish the thought. "It's okay, man. I can't blame you for running," I say.

"Bla-blame me?" Ben countered. "Wha-what the fuh-fuck, du-dude, I th-th-thought you were ri-ri-right be-be-behind me. We bah-both ran from the wah-wa-woods when th-tha-that smah-sma-smell, fuh-fuckin' hit mah-man…" He stopped for a second to catch his breath. "And wah-wa-when I saw th-the thi-th-thing, I just tha-th-thought you wah-we-were rah-run-na-ning tah-t-too." He looked at me for a beat then looked ahead again.

"Did you ever think to come back?" I asked quietly. "To see if I was okay?"

This time Ben put his hand up and grabbed my arm to stop me from walking on. "Dude. I di-did wah-wa-want to come bah-back for ya-you. Fuh-fah-fuck!" He breathed out harshly. "But I ra-ra-ran into h-him." He jerked his thumb back in Franky's general direction, who was still lagging behind us, well out of listening range. "He wah-was cra-cryin an' sh-shi-shit. Sca-sca-scared out of h-hi-his fuh-fah-fuckin' wits. He wah-would-n-n't let me go, ma-man. And then y-ya-you came flah-fl-flyin' over the h-hi-hill…" He stopped walking again to look over at me. "Y-y-you wah-were safe, de-du-dude. Th-tha-that's all that mah-ma-mattered to me."

I nodded in understanding, turning away to look ahead, I started to walk. I did get it. What he was trying to say that is, which was primarily due to my own experience with Franky earlier that very morning when I was trying to get him to come back to camp to find Eddie. Regardless, I knew Ben was telling the truth; he just wasn't the type to lie about anything. And he sure as shit was no coward.

"You saw it too? The white... well, wolf?" I asked him as we both picked up our pace. "You saw it, right? I'm not fucking imagining that part, a huge fuckin' wolf, right?"

He looked at me, then nodded slowly. Adding, "I've se-se-seen it be-before too. Ah-a-and ss-so-so ha-have yah-you." I looked back at him, trying to see if he was joking, but his expression was blank, entirely unreadable. I decided not to press him, something was definitely weird about his expression. So, I proceeded to tell my best friend the rest of the story. The part of it I'd witnessed on my own, exactly as I remembered it.

By the time we crossed the road onto the O'Connors' pea gravel driveway, I'd told Ben everything I could recall. Not skipping a single moment, no matter how strange my words sounded, even to me. He never stopped or interrupted me once, he just looked ahead grimly as I continued to take him through the frighteningly bazaar events I'd experienced after he'd taken off. Franky was finally closing in on us when Ben suddenly stopped walking, asking me, "Do-do y-yah th-think th-that tha-thin-thing... tha-tha-that wah-wa-wolf, took E-ed-eddie?"

At that moment, I hadn't a true or definitive answer to his question, but it was sure as shit hard to skirt around what I'd or even we'd, both seen. We'd both seen the boot marks in the dirt and the broken path through the tall grass that led right up to the edge of those fuckin' woods. And the boot tracks, were undeniably Eddie's. Unless someone, or something, somehow came along unseen, stole his boots, then ran toward the forest wearing em, that is. I shrugged my shoulders. I really didn't want to think about the 'maybes' any more. I'd had a night full of them. What I really wanted was to get to ole Hank O'Connor, the old man, and sit eye-to-eye with the old bastard and tell him every inch of our totally unbelievable tale. To watch his face crinkle when he got hot, to hear him tell us that we were all so-full-of-little-girly-shit, and what we saw was just some low hanging fog and nothin' more.

But there was just one thing he or we couldn't deny, one truth to fact that no one could actually deny. And that is our pal, Eddie, was just fucking gone. Poof. Nowhere to be seen since the early morning hours. And the only logical answer was to get our narrow asses moving, and get into those spotted, fuckin' green woods and find him.

Chapter Thirteen

Finding the Spotted Green

'I've walked right up to the face of the abyss, starin' square into her pale blue eyes. In all my eighty some years on God's lovin' Earth, I ain't never seen a sight more dangerously beautiful. It was like coming home to suckle at my mah's tit, it was. Me an' her was all there was in them black woods when night come on. Just the two of us when she opened her mouth wide and tried to tear out my throat…'
— *1922: from the pages of William (Billy Senior) O'Connor's memoirs*

***

Hank stared back at his brothers' disbelieving faces. Cullen was smirking as his pa continued to quiz him in quick, perfunctory fashion. "What sort a smell you talkin' about, boy?" Then, "What exactly did you see in them wood?" And even asking, "You been drinkin', son?" To each question Hank just kept his eyes ahead, trained on his two-smirking brothers. What he was really trying to do, was to think. What had he actually seen, or more so, smelled? He'd never scented anything the likes of that. And in truth, he'd seen nothing, but he had heard something, right? So, the only real answer he could muster was about the drinking. "No, Pa, I ain't been drinkin' none. Geeze... I been with y'all the entire time. I just, just smelled somethin' powerfully off, and heard somethin' too."

"Boy, there ain't no smell here except your own bad breath," his pa exclaimed to the delight of his brothers. "Now let's just take this down a peg or two, shall we? You heard somethin' in there." He turned and pointed his gloved hands to the wood line. "Which probably just kilt its breakfast and that's what yah smelled." Then he turned to his two other sons, who were trying unsuccessfully to contain their amusement at Hank's expense. "Cullen, git your ass in them woods and see if you find any animal scat. Could be our 'monster' here, might a just been taken to doin' its morning constitution." Cullen nodded once and walked up to the wooded line and quickly disappeared into the deep brush.

Hank wasn't at all comfortable with his brother going in there alone. Even if he was makin' fun of him. Something was wrong, he could feel it in his stomach. And over his years, Hank's stomach was rarely wrong about stuff that made it tense up and turn to queasy.

Cullen broke back through the brush with his hands stretched out in front of him. "No scat, Pa, but there's somethin' there," he said, pushing his leather, flat brimmed hat back off his forehead. "There're some tracks,

Pa, but they can't be... They can't be what I'm thinkin' they is," he said, scratching at his morning chin stubble. "Spit it out boy, we ain't got all day to sit here a lollygaggin' about what you think or don't," his father called out tersely.

"Well, they look like a coyote tracked there. Or maybe even a wolf? But Pa, they're way too big to be either, really. I mean way bigger than anything I ever seen, even in them picture books we look at sometimes at school. The ones with them prehistoric carnivores in 'em. One time, I saw this giant old-time wolf called a, uh, 'Canis dirus' or somethin', no wait, it was a... a 'Dire wolf' was what it was called." Cullen smiled to himself for being able to remember. "Which was roamin' these woods some ten thousand years ago, or some shit like that. Uh, sorry, Pa, for the curse word, but whoa, these were some big dogs and—"

"Stop yer yammer and get down here out o' them woods," their pa yelled waving Cullen over. Once they all came together, they each tied their horses off to graze while their pa made his way into the woods with Cullen in tow. He wanted to see the tracks for himself, so they could perhaps even determine if this was the same 'carnivore' as Cullen had put it, that was tearin' up their livestock. When the two of them finally made their way back to where Hank and Thomas sat, Hank could see the excitement in his pa's eyes. "God damn biggest dog I've ever seen, boys," he said with a flash of a smile. "Paw prints are the size ah my hand if not bigger," he exclaimed excitedly. "And that big bastard is gonna hang over our hearth as of tonight, 'cause the thing's so big, it ain't gonna be hard to follow none, neither. Like following a truck through them woods by the signs it's leavin' back, that much is for sure." Hank's pa ended his point wearing a big Cheshire cat grin. "We got this, boys, it's ours to lose." And with all said, he stood up and went over to his saddle and pulled out his .50-110 WCF Winchester rifle and sighted it toward the woods. That thing could take down a buffalo at a hundred yards with one well-placed shot. And that wasn't just talk neither, Hank had seen his daddy do it back on the farm when they used to raise buffalo. Put the animal down, that is.

The four of them moved slowly at first, leading their horses on foot, their pa taking the lead position as they walked straight into the Spotted Green. They'd all been in the woods plenty of times before, but to Hank, something still felt, well, different.

Chapter Fourteen

Making the call

I hit my cell phone's address book quickly, scrolling over the alphabetized names and numbers I recognized immediately and others I'd forgotten I even had. I was searching for a name and number I'd not forgotten, no I'd never forgotten it, just hadn't used it in over a decade now. Sure, there had been a few quick calls over the holiday season to check in, more or less. Talk about the wife and kids, the job, and maybe even stumble over a select few current events. But that was it. There was never any reminiscing, or questions asked about a certain pal of ours. Nope, we both just stuck to the script we'd made all those years ago.

'Mr Benjamin Moyer • 716…' appeared across the screen and I stopped my thumb scroll abruptly. Agent Bishop had uncuffed me from the metal table, walking us out into a long, rectangular office space that was full of shadow and empty cubicles. I assumed silently that this was the actual working area for Rochester, New York's Aviation Security Department. I also assumed that at this hour, the actual occupants of all these little cubicles were home tucked away safely in their beds.

"So, this is where all the security magic happens, eh, Agent Bishop?" I'd asked lightly of the hulking agent, who just continued to frown, staring straight ahead as he escorted me into the center of the hundred or so empty office cubes.

"You should have plenty of privacy here, Mr Kilpatrick. As you can see, our staff has retired for the evening," he said, turning to face me again.

"Well, most of your staff that is," I answered, nodding my head toward the three surly looking goons standing at attention in front of the main office's double glass doors. "Man, only the very best put in the extra hours when you really need them to, don't they, Agent Bishop?"

The agent refused to take the bait again and simply moved on. "Please take your time, uh, Sean," he said quietly. "I'll be right out front here if you should, well, require my services for uh, whatever." He smiled flatly and turned his herculean sized body away and began walking toward the front of the office where his security awaited him.

I only realized the late hour after I'd already hit the 'call' number. "Shit. I haven't talked to Ben in how many years? And now I'm calling him well after midnight smack dab in the middle of a work week? And I'm going to say what to him, exactly?" I mumbled to myself, unable to answer my own question, but also unable to click off the line either. 'Ringing…' I see the word float across the phone's black screen. Letting me know that I'm one step closer to this very awkward encounter. I also know, if someone doesn't alas come here to the airport and pick me up, I'll be spending the night in a cell with Lenard's three amigos. The thought of it spurred me on.

'Ringing...' A third ring and then a mumbling, flustered male voice grunts over the little phone's tiny speaker. "Hel-lo." The voice resounds, so agonizingly familiar, the memories rush in—his face turned ashen gray as we sat on that porch so many years ago. His grandfather standing up, his hands shaking as he reaches out and slaps Ben hard across the cheek... the sound it makes echoing dully in my head. "*Hel-lo!*" Ben shouts this time. I can hear him breathing across the cellular line. He's pissed, I can feel it. But there was no turning back now. So, I just jump into the moment.

"Uhm, hey, man. Ben?" I hear myself saying, my voice scratching, weirdly high pitched. "Hey, man, I'm sorry for the late call. You're not gonna believe who this is..." I say then stall out, words just evading me. "Uhm, anyway, man, I just needed to..."

"Sean? Sean?" he asks through the line without hesitation. "Dude, you okay? What time is it? Where are you?"

I breathe in, falling back into the cushioned office chair, pushing myself away on its rolling castors. Suddenly forced to stare at the random framed pictures of the unknown cubicle owner whose personal space I've unknowingly invaded. Running a shaking hand through my hair, I repeat my first words. "Ben. Man, sorry for the late call. I just wanted..." Again, my words stop, I feel the tears welling up inside me. *Don't cry dude, not that*, I say to myself, just barely pulling myself together enough to continue. "I just wanted to let you know that I'm in town. Uh, at the airport actually." I let out an obviously forced laugh. "And yeah, man, I know it's really freakin' late, but thought maybe we could grab a beer?"

There's a long silence on the other end, I can hear him shifting the phone, pulling it closer to his cheek. Finally, he speaks up. "Uh, yeah. Sure, man," he says half-heartedly. "You wanna meet somewhere? I just need to get dressed—"

I cut him off before he can continue. "Well, honestly, I was hoping you could pick me up. Uh, here at the airport? See, my flight got all jacked up and I just found out that there's no more flights to Chicago till morning, so I wanted to call you. I thought maybe we could catch up a little?"

Ben was now quick to respond and I could already hear him whispering to someone whom I only assumed to be his wife, Holly? Yeah, I think that's right. I'd never met her, but remembered the name from the family Christmas cards they used to send out. When was the last time we received one? Had to have been five years ago, I thought sadly. "Yeah, man, of course, of course," he answered, his voice sounding more and more as if he were waking up. "I can be out there in about forty-five minutes or so. Do you have a place to stay?"

Shit, I hadn't even thought about that, but answered that I did, and it was not a problem at all. We worked out a few details of where to meet and then hung up the line without further conversation.

I sat there staring at the family photos lined up before me. A grinningly handsome husband and wife team kneeling before a tall, sparkling Christmas tree. Their two kids, a boy and girl, both glisteningly pretty, looking earnestly into the lens of the camera. Orthodontist approved toothy smiles plastered upon their faces. "When was the last time I'd even heard from Ben?" I asked the row of perfectly, pretty little family photos. "Shit, when was the last time he heard from me? A way better fucking question indeed," I told them quietly.

I stood up and gathered myself and my rolling carryon luggage and headed toward the front of the office. Where my 'keepers' awaited me and by the look they gave me upon my approach, couldn't wait to be rid of me. I shook Agent Bishop's hand after letting him know that one of my oldest and 'dearest friends' would be picking me up out front at the airport's ticketing area in an hour or so. I thanked him for his handling of this most unfortunate incident, and moved to take my leave. But at the last second, in an act of admitted boyish immaturity, I turned back to the three long graduated Hitler youth and provided them with my best attempt at the infamous Nazi salute, clicking my heels together as I did so. The expression Richter provided said it all: 'If I catch you outside these walls jack-ass, I don't care how crazy you fucking are, I'm going to seriously fuck you up.' Well, that's what it looked and perhaps felt like he'd wanted to say to me anyway. So,

I just smiled my own toothy grin, and headed down the long hallway back into the main terminal of the airport.

Ben's what looked to be a brand new, white BMW M6 series, was pretty hard to miss in front of the Rochester International ticketing terminal. First of all, it was the only car out there, but more so, it was an automobile with a sticker price well north of $100,000.00. You just didn't see cars like that way up here in upstate, I thought, admiring its sleek, glowering body lines. With winter being a spectacular bitch at least six-months out of every year, and the amount of salt the city dumped on its streets, there just weren't many Rochester residents willing to let a vehicle of the M6's stature, and cost, become a rusted-out piece of worthless shit at the end of its first lovely, upstate winter.

As if confirming my point, the wind picked up and literally howled as I pushed through the automatic doors and out into the night's frigid air. The gleaming car's exhaust puffed up white clouds that streaked out on the wind as Ben revved the running, hungry motor. He jumped out of the driver's side when he saw me coming. We shook hands tersely before he grabbed hold of my rolling bag and turned to toss it into the now open trunk of the beautiful, rumbling automobile. I dove through the passenger side door to get out of whipping cold that I was certainly not dressed for. As I slammed the door closed the music on the radio gripped hold of me hard, throwing me back in time as ACDC stamped out their youthful anthem, *Back in Black*. The lead guitarist we all knew by the name of just Angus, shredded his infamous, red Gibson SG in the head-slamming, strangled guitar solo, across the multitude of high-end speakers within the plush interior of the German made car.

Ben had just banged the trunk closed and was making his way back toward the driver's side when the wind picked up and nearly knocked him off his feet. I moved to get out and help him, but he'd already regained his footing and was grabbing hold of the driver's side door handle for support. And then he was in the car, his door closing with a solid *whump*. Man, these cars were solid, was all I could think of as he reached to turn the volume down on ACDC's screeching crescendo and then turned to look at me. We looked each other over for an uncomfortable few silent seconds, before I broke in.

"You look good, man. Married life suits you."

Ben just nodded and then threw the car into drive. "Where to?" he asked abruptly and pulled away from the sidewalk, punching the accelerator hard before I could even get my seatbelt fastened.

"Nice car," was all I could say before we were screaming off into the night.

"You up for the Cottage?" I said, staring ahead, resisting the urge to put my hand on the dashboard to brace myself as Ben downshifted the automatic transmission hard, stomping the gas as he made the turn out of the airport and onto Brooks Avenue. Where he gunned the motor upshifting back into drive. The car barely swerved as it found its groove. *He's testing me*, I thought. As teenagers, we often did this type of testosterone fueled testing of each other's manhood. Whose balls were bigger type of shit. I smiled as I looked over at him and he back at me. Taking his eyes completely from the road as he raised our speed in steady ten mile per hour increments, the speedometer already reading out at seventy-five… eighty-five… ninety-five miles per hour. The car was quite literally flying down the empty avenue before Ben spoke again.

"The Cottage, huh. Haven't been there in a while. Hey, how about the Springfield Inn instead? Remember that place? You me and Eddie…" Before I could answer he swerved deftly around the only other vehicle out on the road beyond us. Downshifting smoothly, the motor's blazing six-cylinder revving contentedly, as we blew past the unsuspecting vehicle. He could still drive, that was for sure. Just like a bat out of hell as we used to say, he always was a bit on the crazy side. Particularly after we lost Eddie.

The next song came belting out on the stereo's unseen speakers. The dashboard's amber faceplate's digital readout confirming what I already knew to be Queen's opus, *Bohemian Rhapsody*. As the harmonics swelled, I smiled saying, "Ninety-seven-point-nine, right? Rochester's infamous K-ROCK. The only *ass-kicking* classic rock station in the tri-county area." I smiled contentedly as Ben revved the engine higher, and watched as the street signs melted together in a gray blur. "Yeah, the Springfield Inn will be just fine. Didn't know it still existed, but yeah, perfect, dude."

Ben turned his face toward me again, his obviously new, sleek glasses reflecting the lights that whizzed past us in a blinking carnival like styling. "There's a lot you don't know, Sean," he said, then turned his attention back to the road and I, well, I hung on for dear life.

Chapter Fifteen

A Hunt

They quickly found their pace and worked the horses into a single file with Hank's pa in front, then Cullen, then Thomas, and Hank bringing up the rear. Hank's one job was to protect their backs. There were no real trails in this part of the woods, just the game paths that oftentimes ran in crazy circles and could get one lost right quick out there, that was for damn sure. So, they each took turns checking their pocket compasses to at the very least, establish cardinal direction and all. Which in the end, just lead to more arguin' over each other's reported coordinates than anything else. Anyway, anything could sneak up from behind them and Hank's pa knew it—that's why he put Hank in the rear.

Hank kept his head on a swivel and his eyes on the tracks they'd been following for close to an hour now. Which seemed to be moving them in a large arcing formation, heading deeper and deeper into the forest's "wilder" areas. At least that's what Hank thought. It was for certain that he'd never been anywhere near this part of the woods, and in truth, he'd been further in than any of them, even his pa. Only his granddaddy knew that about him, as he too held that same deeply burning curiosity gene. Some might even have said it was a need to go deeper, to go to the place's others dared never to go. Hank wondered if ole Billy had been out this far in his own travels. The thought somehow comforted him, as he was sure as shootin' that if anyone had come this far in, it would have been his granddaddy. He couldn't help but wish he was here now, bringing up the rear with him.

His pa suddenly let out a low whistle, and held a fist up into the air, which was the sign for them all to stop where they were right quick. No one questioned the signal and when his pa dismounted and moved to tie his horse off, the boys all did the same. Hank took Wind by the reins to try and find a grassy spot for him, but there was nothing but ground moss, rotting tree debris, roots, and a whole lot of black rock. This part of the forest saw absolutely no sunlight, and in fact, felt a bit too uncomfortably like nighttime when Hank knew full well by the hands on his pocket watch that it was not yet even midday.

His brothers and Pa spread out as they'd already done several times, looking for any more signs of the animal that left those big tracks behind. Hank stayed back with the horses; the less confusion you had looking for tracks the better. Before you know it yah got everyone stompin' around and erasin' any sure sign of the beast. Hank crouched down on his haunches and scoured his surroundings. Taking his time, eyeballing all he could see just above ground level. Nothing moved in this shadow land which wasn't all that strange really; it wasn't like the smaller woodland creatures hadn't heard them all coming on from a mile away and took to hiding. Shit, they may as well have drove a wagon through here by the noise they'd been making, he thought. No, if the truth be told, Hank liked to hunt on his own. Quiet like. He'd yet to be bested in the woods when it came to bringing home a prize like the enormous eighteen-point buck he brought down just a few weeks back. But that wasn't way the hell out here to the north, though. In fact, none of them had really hunted in any of these parts of the forest. No reason to come all the way up here when there was just so much game less than an hour's ride to the south of the farm. Just as Hank started to feel a little disenchanted with it all, something moved up on the low ridge about a hundred yards northwest from where they'd all just dismounted. Hank froze, focusing all his concentration on the spot, daring it, whatever it was, to move again.

When the first shot rang out, Hank was so startled he fell backward onto the uneven terrain, sliding down the slick, moss covered ravine on his backside until he landed between one of the many exposed and gnarled root systems of the forests trees. He was on his feet before another blue-second ticked off his pocket watch, running to grab his rifle from Wind's saddle. He stayed low, trying to make out who fired the shot, but could see nothing more than the darkened ridge and a bit of stray gun smoke sifting down the path. His brothers and Pa were nowhere to be seen. He knew better than to call out, so instead he dropped the hammer back on his weapon and bent down on one knee, rifle at the ready. There was a sudden burst of movement again, coming straight down the rocky ridgeline. His brother was running recklessly, leaping over fallen tree limbs and large rocks, heading right for him. "Thomas!" Hank hissed, then waved a gloved hand. "Over here," he spat, expecting him to spill at any second. But when Thomas finally sighted him, he slowed enough to regain control, sliding down right beside him.

"Okay…" he wheezed, trying to catch his breath.

Hank grabbed hold of Thomas's arm trying to steady him. "Calm down, damnit. Where they at?" Hank asked tersely.

Thomas looked up at him and pointed toward the very summit of the ridge he'd just come blasting down. "They be over the hill just above them rocks. And they got the critter in their sights for damn sure. I think I might o' even seen it too…"

Before Hank could respond another shot rang out, accompanied by a low whistle. Pa was calling them to him. "Thomas, you wait here with the horses, stay low and I'll go see what's up."

He turned, frowning at Hank, who was already moving out and away. "Wait, Hank!" he whispered harshly. "For fucks-sake, little brother, Pa wants us all to be together on this one. The horses and all our shit will be just fine here on their own."

Hank was deadlocked, turning back to see Thomas jump to his feet, running toward his horse to grab his rifle, the same one he'd stupidly left behind. "Ah, so that's the real reason he'd come back this way," Hank said under his breath, grinning just a bit. "What kinda dumb-ass goes out in the wood to hunt without a rifle to shoot with?" he asked of his brother, who chose to ignore his remark. Shaking his head in disgust, Hank turned to grab hold of Wind's reins, making certain the horse was securely tied off to the tree. "Uh, you might want to make sure your mount is tied down there brother, you's probably gonna need that horse to get back home on," he said, smiling over at Thomas, who stared back flatly at him, not finding humor in his little brother's japes. But eventually, second guessing himself, headed back to retie his mount's reins more securely just the same. Which truth be told, weren't secure in the first damn place, and Hank had known it all along.

He was off and racing through the dense trees before his brother could even ask for him to wait up. Hank was surefooted when it came to running in the woods and he made his way quickly up the steep embankment and over the other side of the brush line. As he climbed up and over the rocky ledge, he couldn't help but notice that the forest seemed to close in all around him. The trees were much older and bigger here. Tightly knit together making visibility and movement much more difficult. Hank could barely make out the rifle that set there in his own hands, it was so dense with shadow in these parts. He pushed on, working his way methodically over the water slick stones, and through the thick mud, and endless tangles of underbrush that twisted and turned dangerously beneath the goliath trees. The air grew thick, damp with a clinging mist, any sign of a trail or even an animal path, all but impossible to find. If they were going to try to bring their horses through this muck, they might have to find another route, Hank thought to himself.

He spotted his father, his head bobbing up and down just north of where he now crouched. Neither Cullen nor his pa heard him come up on them and jumped up, all jittery, when he suddenly knelt beside them.

"Damn it, Hank. You scared the livin' bejesus outta me, boy. Can't you signal us when you're to come a creepin'?"

Hank answered his pa's question with a question. "So, if I was to let you know I was comin', then it wouldn't be creepin', now would it?"

His pa's face reddened just a touch then he got down to business. "Okay, smart guy, we got an eye on this thing and it's just over yonder hunkered down in them brambles. Looks like it might be nested up there with a mate. But we ain't fer certain… can't see fer shit in this here place."

Cullen turned to Hank with a grizzled grin stretched taught over his face. "Brother, you've got to see this thing. It's o' got-damn monster."

Hank had to admit that he felt a certain excitement in the moment of the hunt, and that they'd come on to the animal so quickly and all, but something just didn't quite feel right. Almost like this was all just a tad too easy? The animal suddenly moved, the low brush around it shaking as it struggled to make its way out of what might indeed be a nest or winter's den. But what Hank didn't expect to see was a second animal, which sprang up right beside the first. Hank had a decent line of sight on both, and even through the smoggy murk he could tell that neither of these four-legged predators were the ones that made the paw tracks they'd been following. In Hank's estimation, they would need to be at least twice the size of what they were to make the tracks he'd seen—they'd all seen. There was no doubt that these were some pretty damn big dogs, by the likes of any he'd seen before, but not the one they'd been after. And they was coyote too, and coyote didn't carry the weight to make an indent that size and more particularly, the depth of the ones they'd been set to trackin' all damn mornin' now.

Hank knew better than to say anything, but in the end couldn't stop his tongue from waggin'. "Pa, neither of these dogs are the critter that made them tracks back yonder and you damn well know it just as I do. Sides, there's two of 'em. We didn't see no second set of tracks that brung us all the way out here," Hank whispered forcefully, regretting the words after they'd already come out.

His father turned his head, and put a finger to his mouth, telling Hank to just shush already. Hank pushed his hat down tighter on his head while trying to bite back his rising frustration before it boiled over. Not only had they lost sight of the mysterious creature they'd actually been trackin', but now they were chasing a couple of oversized but run o' the mill coyotes instead.

"We're wastin' our damn time," Hank said quietly, not caring whether Cullen or his pa had heard him. Breathing low, he crawled out of the brushy area they'd chosen to hole up in and tried to get a better vantage point to view what they was really huntin'. It was just so damn gloomy in these parts, he could hardly make out the two black spots movin' about just above where he now lay. *Maybe if we take them down, we can get back to the business of trackin' the real monster*, as his brother had said it, Hank thought. "I can make the shot for sure from here, Pa," he whispered, as he sprawled low over a downed tree and sighted his rifle. He noticed that one of the pair was limping on its hind leg pretty good. Cullen or his pa must a got a piece of it with a lucky shot.

The animals were scampering about now, making their way upward, trotting the steep incline toward the top of the ridge. Heading even further north by the looks of it, well away from where his party was sittin'. Cullen was moving, jogging low behind their quarry, agile as ever, leaping across the blackened landscape with ease. He watched as his pa lay still, looking through the scope mounted to that cannon of a rifle he carried. And that's when he knew what they was up to. Pa would take out the larger of the two from a distance and Cullen would get in close to hit the gimp one as it would be slower to react and he'd be closer to the kill spot than their pa. It was a good plan, he thought as the first shot rang out, echoing dully off the silent, ancient trees that stood at attention over them, appearing to be judging them for what they were about to do. Hank watched as the larger animal went down flat and then two more distant shots rang true as Cullen closed in, taking the second on the run. Hank's pa stood up to see his eldest son raise his rifle above his head in silent cheer of the kill.

Thomas had come up from behind; they all turned in unison as they heard him coming from at least fifty yards back, like a tank blasting his way through the layers of ground cover and bramble. Hank caught his father's eye, who just shook his head as if understanding exactly what Hank was thinking and willing him not to say a damn word about it.

The four of them decided to set up camp just atop the crest of the forested ridge which was ideal, providing unimpeded views of the forest in most all directions. Not to mention the best available light, which wasn't much to start with, but continued to fall rapidly, leaking away as early evening set in. They'd skin, hide and tan the animals, then smoke the meat to make it all a whole hell of a lot easier to carry back with them at first light. There was no sense in trying to make their way out of the woods now that nightfall would be on them in just a few short hours. For the most part, Hank kept to himself, stayin' quiet as his brothers worked expertly in preparing the hides. Their pa watched over 'em, making a comment or two here and there, but for the most part, they were all pretty well versed when it come to huntin', trappin' and skinnin', whatever called the woods their home.

Billy Junior was his father's son for sure, and knew instinctively when one of his boys had taken to acting peculiar. And his youngest was sure as shit doin' just that. It wasn't like Hank to be all silent like, not bustin' his older brothers' chops about all the shite they was constantly doin' wrong or at the very least, half assed. No, Hank took to just sitting there hugging that damn rifle to his chest and staring off into the ever-blackening wood.

He sidled up next to his youngest and poured him another cup of coffee in the tin cup he'd left there by his foot on the dirt. "Drink this, boy, looks like you need somethin' to wake your ass up," he said, smiling as he sat down next to Hank on the old, knurled log they'd dragged over to their cook fire just for sittin'. Hank barely acknowledged his pa, keeping his eyes ahead, looking off into the distance. His pa turned to follow his boy's line of sight and noticed Hank was staring out, past the tree line, his head pointed due north. But there was nothin' to see, he realized, and elbowed Hank in question. "What's got you so spooked, boy?" he said without looking away from where they both took to staring.

Hank spoke slowly at first, then began to dig in. "Pa, these dogs we kilt, they ain't our quarry. And you damn well know it. So why are we stoppin' here? Actin' like we're the king-o'-the-forest or some dumb shit, when in fact all we done is bring down a couple o' big, mangey coyotes."

His pa turned to his son. "They all is predators, son. And even though they might not be the lone son of a bitch we took to trackin' originally, don't mean these critters aren't responsible for chewin' up our livestock."

"Neither of these dogs did any of it and you damn well know it, Pa," Hank belted out, letting his frustration get the better of him, as he stood up and tossed the coffee his pa just poured for him out into the woods. His father never moved, he just looked at his son with sad, but hardened eyes. "Yeah, you're right, Hank. But they don't know that," he said, jerking his head over toward Cullen and Thomas who were busy finishing up the field hiding. "And they need this, boy. So, let's just end this evening in victory and get a bit of shuteye, okay?" Hank got what his pa was trying to tell him readily enough and agreed to the unspoken deal he'd been presented with. But it didn't mean that he'd liked it any better either ways.

***

Hank opened his eyes to see the orange embers of the fire smoldering warmly before him. The temperature outside had dropped considerably, setting him to shivering as he reached out to pile a few more twigs onto the fire. Night had come on quick, eclipsing all in its pitch-dark path, swallowing up entire chunks of the universe just beyond the campfires protective circle. He heard light snoring coming from somewhere beyond the fire's glow, comforted by the thought that someone was able to find sleep in this cold, dank place. He rose to stretch his chilled limbs, turning toward the fire, warming the side of his body he'd been layin' on over the unforgivingly frigid, forest grounds. No amount of tree brush underneath your sleeping gear was going to stave off this type o' cold. This frost was old in nature, it had worked its way well into the earth over the years, embedding itself deep, never to worry about the suns warming rays here. Quiet like, he moved away from the camp's fire so not to disturb his pa and brothers as he took to jumping up and down to get some feeling back into his outer extremities. "Mid-June my ass. It's still as cold as winter up here for Christ-sake," he mumbled, flexing his fingers and toes in a livelier fashion.

A sudden noise, high pitched whinnies followed by snorting, a horse shaking its head causing its bridle to jangle loudly across the bleak and barren night. Hank turned toward the sounds, walking quickly to where their horses were tied off to check on them. It sure as shit wouldn't have been the first time a horse's strap hold had gotten tangled up in a low hanging branch, leaving the animal to struggle, even panic, Hank thought, as he moved into the utter darkness. He stretched his hands out before him, stumbling forward all but blind, the nights black embracing him fully. He thought about grabbing a chunk of burning wood from the fire to light his way, but decided against it, knowing that it might spook the animals even more. But at the last second, he reached down to grab his rifle just in case. "In case of what?" he asked himself quietly. Still feeling that whatever had been clutching at his inners all day, had yet to ease its talons out from him.

He approached the horses, their eyes widened in recognition, glistening wetly against the dulled to black surroundings. He reached out, brushing down upon the first horse's nose, when it retreated, rearing up, delivering a loud fluttering sound from its steaming nostrils. "Whoa there. It's okay, just me—there, now. Just let me see how you're fixed up here, boy—"

"Damn, boyo. You still carryin' that Savage rifle around with yah where's ever it is you get to? Humph. That's a smart lad, now ain't you just."

Hank gasped, stumbled backward, feeling all the hair on the back of his neck standing up in sudden alarm. "What the hell?" he squealed, turning the barrel of his rifle in the general direction he'd thought the noise, or voice, had just come from. He stumbled again, his motor functions shocked stupid, unable to grasp what was happening. A hand suddenly shot out from the ebony, wrenching the barrel of Hank's rifle out of his stunned hands—lightning fast. Then Hank heard the gun being disengaged, but still could not move or begin to comprehend what was going on. His first thoughts were that a bandit had got the drop on him. But why would there be bandit's way the hell out here in the middle of nowhere? Before he could really consider the question, the voice called out again. So familiar, he thought…

"And you was loaded up for firin' too, boy, wasn't cha?"

Hank heard a slight chuffing of laughter, asserting to himself that its owner was male, but still couldn't see anything of the interloper that was talking at him. He needed to remain calm. Gather his strength. "What do you want?" he queried, the invisible man standing somewhere before him, trying hard not to stammer or allow his voice to betray the fear he felt low in his guts.

"What cha got?" the voice answered, followed by more chuffing and snickering. "I just wanted to see yah, was all laddie," the man continued in a more intimate fashion, stepping into Hank's view. It was still so dark, Hank couldn't be totally sure of what he was really looking at, but… "And don't be tellin' me you got a couple o' grade-A hides you'd look to be trading to save your own scrawny behind. I know's them dogs your daddy brung low. Shit, they's not worth a half o' one o' you, boyo."

Hank felt his bladder kick in squeamishly as he stared in wonder at the giant of a man who now stood before him holding his rifle in one hand and in his other, the two coyote pelts. "Grandpa?" Hank managed to just squeak out as no other words would come to him.

"Ah, that's right, boyo. It does my eyes good to see you again, Hank. You was always my favorite, but I knows yah already knew that to be true. You and me, well, we just alike," he said and then winked at Hank. "Fearless. Right, boyo?"

Hank was struck to dumb as he stared at his grandfather. A man they'd buried almost two years back now in the spring of 1926. A man that well into his eighties could still best any of them with his brains, or his brawn. All until that night. That night he'd… Hank suddenly noticed the peculiar look of the old man before him. His dress was odd, out of place for the times. He appeared to be wearing some kind of homespun clothing. The kind of stuff he'd seen the early settlers, or mountain men in the history books at school had always seemed to be wearin'. His hat and jersey alike were made up of thick bristled animal fur. The jacket cinched around the waist with rough-edged straps of well-beaten leather, and sheathed there in the front was a long, bone-handled bowie knife. Hank looked up to see his grandfather's face, but it was hidden under the fur-line of the oversized hat he wore. But when his eyes finally fell over him, their intensity was so bright, they sparked ice blue, beaming with what felt to be a sort of, well, hunger.

His grandfather spoke again before he could recover from his ferocious gaze. "You look strong, boyo. But you know you shouldn't be this far out in these here timbers, now don't cha? How many times I took to telling you that laddie—how many damn times?" Billy Senior's voice dropped low to a rolling dark grumble when he stepped closer, right up to Hank. The odor was like being gut punched, literally doubling him over to stop from retching. "Ah, but you're more like me in other ways too, aren't cha just? More than any the others, that's for damn sure."

The smell was so pungent, Hank couldn't bring himself to stand straight again. Each breath he drew in gagging him further.

"Ah, boy, you git used to the smell eventually," his grandpa, said then snickered some more. Which sounded more like growling than any sort of laughter, Hank thought. "You knew it too didn't yah, boy? Yep, you knew that there's maybe a much bigger prize out here than just these two mangey scavengers." He held up the coyote carcasses his brothers had spent the entire afternoon skinning and hiding in one large leathery fist. "No matter though, son. And I'm sorry to say to yah, that I can't let you leave with 'em." He shook his head back-n-forth. "They's a part of these here timbers and they stay where they lay." Billy Senior breathed out loudly. "But you, you and the rest o' my kin, you'll need to get gone from here now. And I mean right fucking now, boyo."

With that, the old man turned away, walking toward the horses, who in turn began to panic once more as he approached, their eyes wide when he slapped Thomas's horse hard across its hind quarters. The horse bolted upright, rearing wildly in fear, smashing into the others, who also took to bucking and snorting in the way spooked horses did. Hank never moved a muscle. Watching as the old man suddenly turned back toward him, standing just down the hill, staring up at him, barely visible. Then, without a word, he put a hand into the air to wave to Hank before disappearing into the cloak of darkness that sprawled forever between them.

Hank's pa and brothers were suddenly surrounding him, his pa shouting commands in between the ruckus the horses were making. His father's voice booming up, over the chaos, even still, Hank never moved. "Thomas, get hold of them horses now! Quick-like, boy. Move 'em out of the way from one another before one of 'em kills the other! And Cullen! Point that damn rifle any where's but at my head, boy—pronto!"

Hank could just make each of them out, they were right next to him, yet he just couldn't seem to move, his grandpa's ghostly image still clinging too tightly to him.

"Hank? Hank!" He heard his pa holler. "Boy, what are you doin' up here? What in God's creation is goin' on? Boy! Move your ass outta the way now!" his father yelled right into his face, taking Hank by the arm, roughly spinning him around, pushing him away from the panic-stricken horses.

But Hank still didn't move much, watching as his daddy ran over to grab onto Wind, who of all the horses acted the unruliest, spooked out of control. Hank's hand remained held out, as if expecting the long dead apparition of his granddaddy to come back and hand his rifle over to him. The rifle he'd taken from his person just minutes before. Several gun shots rang out, echoing off in his head as his brothers, for whatever reason, took to firing their weapons. Three of the four horses, now fully untethered and free from tie, ran wild off into the gloom. "Shit-fire, boys! Put those goddamn rifles o' yours on the ground right now before I use one of 'em to beat you on the head with!" Hank looked up to see them do as their pa had told them, just as the last horse, Wind, bolted away, bucking and jostling to run blindly off into the forest.

***

Gray light trickled in as morning came to rise weakly in the dark wood. Hank was sitting on the same log in front of a now roaring campfire. His mind racing back and forth as his pa carpeted him with questions that he just could not think fast enough to answer. "Who the hell would come all the way out here to steal a couple a coyote pelts?" he'd ask first of Hank, and then of his brothers. Who shrugged in both disbelief and agreement with their daddy's ask. They were both pretty tuckered out after chasing down their horses and bringing them back to the camp, both of 'em heads down, lyin' next to the fire. "And Hank, damn it, why in the hell were you up and wanderin' about in the early mornin' like you was? Coulda got yourself kilt just as sure as we is sittin' here for Christ sake! What's gone and got into that head o' yours boy?"

Hank's head was actually still in a fog, his ability to reason coming back to him slower than he would have liked. The shock of what he'd witnessed, or maybe thought he'd seen, was weighing him down like a sack of rocks. All the questioning his pa was throwin' his way just got jumbled up inside his noggin. And try as he might, even he couldn't get his mind around what had just happened to him. Hank wasn't one who scared all that easy or believed in none o' that hocus-pocus type stuff neither. But this was different, and tryin' to be rational, to apply logic to what he'd witnessed, just wasn't workin'. So, the best he'd come up with, well, was that this was all some kinda bad dream he'd been havin' and he'd taken to walkin' in his sleep over to where the horses had been tied up. "But that dog just don't hunt." He mumbled, remembering pretty-plainly when he'd woke up in a shiver, stoking the fire, then hearing them horses rustling about…

"And what about them pelts gone to missin' just like my rifle done too?" He hissed, reinforcing the truth of his early morning story and the events that he just didn't want to be so. He remembered the image of his granddaddy raising his hand up off in the shadow. He'd thought, more like hoped, that he'd been just wavin' goodbye to him, but in fact, he'd been holdin' Hank's old Savage rifle right above his head. "Wavin' it around like some kinda trophy, or some shit," Hank groused.

Since the moment they'd entered the Spotted Green just shy of twenty-four hours ago, there was a tangle of shit rollin' around in Hank's head that he just couldn't quite get hold of. The only thing he did know for certain, was that whatever the hell was goin' on out here in these woods, he sure as shit was gonna get to the bottom of it. And if there were bandits, bandits pretending to be his grandpa—well, stealing from the O'Connors wasn't somethin' he was goin' to tolerate, no sir. Especially the thievin' of his very own goddamn rifle. "That shit ain't gonna stand no how no way," Hank threatened angrily.

But at the same time, he knew that telling his pa the rightful truth of his story, one that included his dead for more than two years pappy, comin' here in the middle of the night for god knows what, wasn't a conversation he wanted to have—not now anyway. Even if he tried to tell his pa that the bandit, or bandits, was all just dressed up kinda like grandpa might to spook us into thinkin' he'd rose from the grave or some shit, the story was still paper thin. Besides, he wasn't dressed like his granddaddy at all, was he? No sir, he'd been dressed like some mountain man, 'trapper john' type o'guy. "So why in the blue hell did he, whoever he was, take those damn pelts anyhow? I mean I get takin' the weapon, but them pelts weren't worth a damn," Hank whispered hotly under his breath. He was still stewin', his daddy's voice now far-far away, when something just clicked in his addled brain. Like some welcome bit of light bein' switched on, Hank remembered, blurting the words out, "These here pelts belong to the woods and that they needed to, uh, *stay where they lay.*" Hank felt lighter somehow, finally being able to remember something about his encounter more clearly was like a fog being lifted from him.

"What's that yer yammerin' on about, boy? Speak up. If you got somethin' to say, just say it for Christ-sake." Hank's father had been standing right behind him when he had his strange epiphany. "What's that you say about them pelts now boy?"

Hank wasn't very good at coming up with stories on the fly, but tried his best to get his daddy off the trail he was now taken to runnin' down. "Uh, I was just playin' it back in my head, Pa. Tryin' to piece together how some kinda sneak-thief could just wander right into our camp, steal our pelts, and wander back out again without none o' you all wakin' up neither."

His father turned his head for a moment, contemplating his youngest son's words, then came over and sat down on the log next to him. "Son, not a one of us thinks less of anyone 'cause these boys got into our camp. But it was you standing out there next to the horses in the middle o' the night. We was thinkin' you gave those boys a chase, no?" He breathed in hard, the air whistling in his nose. "You tried to catch 'em, boy, didn't cha? And what I want to know is what it is you seen. But for some god forsaken reason you gone all deaf, dumb and blind on us here, and I for one don't like it. Now, last time, son." Billy Junior reached over and put his hand on Hank's sloping shoulder. "Tell me what you seen and then we can all get to catchin' the thievin' little bastards, right quick."

But Hank only shook his head, wanting to tell his pa the truth of it, but in the end couldn't. "It was awful dark Pa, I didn't get a good look at him…"

His pa jumped on those words. "But yah said 'him', boy. Meaning there was only one of 'em that got in, right?" Hank stared into the fire while his pa continued to poke at his words. "One lone marauder stole our pelts hangin' right over there, then managed to take that Savage rifle you's carry right off your person too?" Hank turned to look at his father in surprise. "Ah, you didn't think I noticed that one, did you now?" A stern grin came to life across his face. "Son, I know damn well you sleep with that firearm and it ain't on your person now, nor is it in your bedroll."

He shook his head in disbelief. "And what's got me puzzled is that there's just no way on God's green earth that some one person as you say, is just gonna waltz up on you, on us, and take that rifle out from under yah. Or the pelts hangin' just ten feet from camp. Something ain't adding up, boy. And the only thing I know right now for certain, is you is holding back. Yes sir, you is. And you better come around soon, son, 'cause we're not gonna let this just lay there, that much you know to be the truth."

Hank's dad got up in a hurry and started barking orders in the general direction of his brothers who still were laying down by the campfire. "Get this camp cleared out and douse that fire before you burn down the lot of these damn timbers. Get your asses up an' movin'!" he shouted as all of them jumped into action, including Hank.

Hank caught up to his father and tried to speak. "Pa?" he stammered, then looked down.

"Save it, boy. You'll tell me here when you is ready, I know that. And we got a long ride back to the house in front of us." With that he turned back toward the horses and didn't say another word until they were well outside of those damned timbers.

Chapter Sixteen

Porch sitting

Franky came jogging up alongside Ben and I, a little more winded than he should have been in my humble opinion. "Well, you guys ready to get the shit beat out of you?" he said, half a smile breaking on his dirt-streaked face. Ben and I just looked at him, his joke lost on us entirely.

"We're just going to tell him the truth, guys. Exactly what happened out there last night," I said, turning to face Ben mostly. "Let's not pull any punches, okay? No matter how crazy shit gets, or how crazy he thinks we are, remember we have one mission and that's to find Eddie."

Ben looked up and smiled tiredly. "G-g-good spa-spe-speech," was all he said and then we all started walking up the dirt and pea gravel driveway that led to the O'Connor family house.

Grandpa O'Connor was nowhere to be seen in the front yard or on the porch where he usually sat in the shade on hot summer mornings the likes of this one. But the door to the house was open and through the screen we all could smell something beyond delicious happening right there in the O'Connor kitchen. Ben was the first to speak as he banged his fist lightly on the old screen door. "Gr-grandma? Hey… ii-it's us. Y-y-you home?" His voice rang out empty across the massive kitchen until we heard footsteps coming from the way back of the house.

"Ben honey? Is that you?" His grandmother came around the corner wearing the infamous powder blue apron with little pies embroidered in lemon yellow thread across the front of it.

"That's a good sign," Franky said, leaning over and whispering in my ear. I smiled because I knew exactly what he meant. Whenever grandma O'Connor was wearing that apron, good things were usually about to come out of one of the several ovens they had lined up in that kitchen. And by the intoxicating smells this morning brought on, it had to be her holy-shit-unbelievable peach cobbler.

"Well, Ben! Oh, and boys! What a pleasure to see you all so bright and early in the mornin'. And well, I'll be, just in time for some peach cobbler too. Did you boys smell it o' cookin' from wherever it is you just crawled out from under?" She smiled whimsically, wiping her delicate hands purposefully on her apron before coming to the door. "You boys look a fright. Now get into that bathroom and wash up before you touch anything." She reached out and cradled Franky's face in her long fingers, shaking her head. "Mr LaManno, you especially. Don't forget to wash that cute little face of yours too!" Franky blushed a little, and looked down. "Scoot, boys. You know where the washroom is," she said, opening the screen door all the way to let each of us pass into the aromatic kitchen.

"Thank you, Mrs O'Connor," we each called out sheepishly in unison as we piled into the O'Connor home.

Ben looked at me and I nodded my head, whispering, "Just ask her."

Ben turned to his grandma. "Gr-grandma, wha-where's Gra-grand-pa-pah?"

Grandma O'Connor was putting on her oven mitts and paused to answer Ben. "Dear, he's out back on that horrible ATV thingy his Richie bought him last Christmas. Can't get the ole bugger-boo off that crazy four-wheeler once he's taken to riding it."

We all looked at each other at the same time. "Uncle Richie," I said under my breath. You see, we all knew that Uncle Richie, Richard Henry O'Connor that is, was going to be a problem if he was off with Ben's grandpa riding. He was Grandpa O'Connor's first-born son, and a real hard-on as we liked to call him. Behind his back, of course. He was also in direct competition with Ben to inherit all the O'Connor wealth and property, once Grandpa O'Connor passed on. And ole Richie knew that Ben would get his fair shake of the inheritance if there weren't another male O'Connor in the picture. Ben wasn't like a full-on O'Connor, but his mom was, and he was the only *other* male born to the family at that time. When the *hard-on* Richie looked at Ben, you could just feel the hatred burning in his eyes. All because, as Grandpa O'Connor himself had said on more than one very public occasion,

"All you got to do is knock up that pretty wife o' yours with a bouncing baby boy, and the rest is history."

'Cause as Richie knew all too well, without a son, he'd be divvying up anything and everything he (in his own mind) was due with his nephew, Ben. And thankfully for Ben, Uncle Richie had been married for ten-plus years and was still shooting blanks as Grandpa O'Connor also liked to say. Again, very publicly.

We all three piled into the bathroom at once just out of sight of Ben's grandma. Franky was the first to speak. But before he could get a word out, I turned the water on, thinking to drown out our conversation from prying ears. Both Franky and Ben looked at me, smirking. "What? You never know who could be listening," was all I said before Franky busted in.

"We can't tell your uncle any of this shit, Ben. Man, he's just going to shit all over our story, and then probably even call the cops on us." Franky was the first to put his dirt black hands in the running water and start to scrubbing.

"Franky's right," I said agreeing with him and looking at Ben in the little bathroom mirror's reflection. "There's no way we can let your uncle in on any of this."

Ben nodded in return.

"He's got too big of an axe to grind with you and what better way to get you out of the way then to get you placed in juvey way far away upstate."

Franky was now patting water on his face, but nodding his head in solid affirmation.

"A-al-all we ca-can do is wah-wa-wait." Ben said, pushing Franky out of the way to get his own hands in the now steaming water.

That was when we heard the distinct, winding sound of the ATVs' dueling motors as they approached the house. And it was definitely plural. Meaning more than one of them. We all froze for a beat, listening. "Okay, let's play it cool. We just stopped over to say hello. The best we can hope for is that Richie has shit to do at the Polaris shop and will be leaving here shortly," I said, placing my hands back in the water and resuming the cleaning ritual Grandma O'Connor set us to.

***

Ben pushed his way back out through the screen door, Franky grabbing it just before it slammed on its squeaky hinges. We all knew Grandpa O'Connor hated it when we let the door slam. I nodded to Franky, thanking him silently for his quick thinking and action. The two men were sitting sideways on their matching red Polaris ATV four-wheelers, chatting breezily in what appeared to be an amicable father and son moment. But that was when Uncle Richie's hands flew up into the air and the moment turned to shit in a flutter of expletives. From what we could hear, it seemed Richie was tired of manning the little Polaris shop they'd opened a few years back, particularly in the summer months when there were no goddamn customers, according to Richie. We watched as Ben's uncle continued to rant and rave while Grandpa O'Connor never once stirred or moved to calm his only, albeit red-faced, son. He just seemed to stare over at him as he carried on. And when the old man finally moved, standing up and placing his finger firmly in son Richie's chest, he cowered backward, stumbling onto his shiny machine, revving its two-stroke motor, and taking off in a hail of flying dirt, dust and choice expletives.

Ben turned back to us and grinned, then we all took off down the porch steps to greet ole Hank in person. He had a curt smile for Ben, and a rather elongated grimace for Franky and I. "You freeloading little bastards come by to eat up all my food again?" he said as he crushed the cigarette he'd been smoking out under his big, heavy boot.

"Gra-grand-mah-ma kn-know you're sti-still sm-smokin', Grandpa?" Ben asked lightly.

His head turned quickly to clock his grandson. "No, boy. And you ain't gonna tell her neither, is you?"

Ben looked down, shaking his head. "Nah-no. No si-sir," was all he said, but I could see he was still grinning just the same.

We followed the old man up on to the porch where he found his favorite wicker chair and sat down heavily, the seat cushions wheezing ungraciously under his weight. Ole Hank wasn't fat at all, mind you, on the contrary really. He was lean and still solid as a rock for a very old dude. But there was just a lot of him was all. He was a big and pretty intimidating old dude, as we all told Ben time and time again.

He never really invited us to come sit with him, but instead we heard the creaking of the old Coleman cooler being opened, and then him sloshing around in the ice-choked water as he fished out one of the many chilled, Genesee Cream Ale beer cans it always somehow contained. Ben walked up to his grandpa just as the first beer can was cracked in a *whuuu-ssshiiing* sound none of us could mistake as anything else. "Gr-grand-pah-pa, I-I-I ya-yah nah-need to ta-ta-talk to you."

Hank looked up, his blue eyes locking down on Ben, anger simmering deep beneath them as it always seemed to be. But then something changed and his eyes softened just a little before he spread his hand out to the other chairs on the porch. "Sit, boy. What's got you troubled?" he said, sensing there was something wrong by Ben's tone.

Grandma O'Connor came swooshing through the screen door carrying a great big platter holding a glistening pitcher of sweet tea, plenty of plates, glasses, cutlery and one steaming peach cobbler smack-dab in the middle of it all. "Henry, don't yah know it's still barely mornin'? And you be already into the ale?" A look of disgust rose on her normally pleasant face.

"Just cuttin' the dust out o' my throat, woman. Leave it be," Hank answered tersely, but then smiled at her just the same. Ole Hank was a true hard ass, but when it come to the missus, well, he was just as soft as a little kitten. At least that's what we thought anyway.

"Don't you boys just look so nice and fresh and clean now. Just look at that darling face. So handsome when you scrub the ten pounds of dirt from it, now isn't it such?" she said, looking directly at Franky, who blushed on cue and looked down at the porch floor. She set the festive platter on the little glass coffee table that sat in between all of us. "Now you boys dig right in. Just go on and help yourselves cause there's plenty more cobbler here in the kitchen." She smiled while looking at all of us. "And get yourselves some fresh, sun brewed sweet tea that I just made this morning. Mercy me, it's going to be a hot one today," she said, turning back toward the kitchen. "Oh, and Henry, maybe you ought to put down that old beer can and take some of the tea too," she said, staring over at her husband of years beyond our capacity to consider. Hank smirked at his lovely wife, raising the can in salute to her leaving, we supposed. Which she did after taking a deep, exaggerated breath and sighing loudly for all to hear.

"Helluva woman," was all the old man said as he cracked another beer and we dug into the feast that lay before us. "Where's that other one a yahs? That shit-for-brains wise crackin', smart-ass boy. I come to be a little fond of the peckerwood. So, where's he at?"

The old man asked all of us, but it was Ben who responded, blurting out, "Eddie's gah-gone ma-missing, Gr-grand-pa-pah."

Hank didn't respond right away. He just took another sip of his beer. "That so? Is that why you all is here?" he asked quietly, watching on as each of us nodded in agreement to him. "Okay, boys," he said, putting his beer can down on the glass table. "I'm sure there's one helluva story here that you needs to tell me. But if that boy is in trouble, you better get to spillin' it right quick, now. So, start to talkin', I'm all ears."

I turned to Franky and then Ben, who nodded for me to go ahead and tell the story. We'd all decided back at Ben's house that I was the best at talking to grownups and therefore should do the regaling of all the shit that had happened. So, I started from the very beginning, talking the old man through from the very start of our little adventure, which he impatiently interrupted, asking me to, "Get on with it already, for Christ's-sake." When I got to the part of what we'd seen over the past night's events, well some of us had seen anyway, he got real quiet like. And when I talked about Eddie, and how he'd just up and disappeared, he sat back in his chair with a huff. For some reason, I decided to leave out the part where I confronted the creature on my own. The strange music, and the feeling I'd had, it really wasn't something I could easily articulate anyway. It just all seemed so unreal, and it was only me that was there... so I left it out.

When, for the most part, our story was finally told, we all sat in silence waiting for the old man to respond. But he didn't. He just seemed to stare off into the distance. Gazing silently across the northern fields and toward the woods that lay beyond them. The same woods we'd left Eddie in last night, I thought. He was rubbing his chin when he finally came around to saying something. "How many times I tell you, Benjamin, not to go in them blasted woods? How many times?"

Ben began to stammer a response, but the old man jumped up so fast and slapped him hard across the head before he could duck out of the way.

"You little idiots! What the hell were you thinkin' goin' off in them woods all by your lonesome! On some stupid, piss-ant adventure, nonetheless! Them timbers is dangerous and you all damn well know that!" he shouted, tipping his beer over to fall to the floor in a soupy mess of foam and amber liquid.

Grandma O'Connor came through the door on the run at the sound of her husband's raised voice. "What in tarnation is going on out here, Henry?" she asked exasperated, looking around at all our stunned faces, while Ben covered his head, hoping not to get smacked again.

"Goddamn boys been out in them goddamned woods again and got their friend here lost," he shouted out, still standing over the three of us threateningly.

"What? Wait, who got lost? Where was it yah just said exactly? Benjamin—where's your mother? Is it Edward? Where's Edward?"

The questions bounced around us relentlessly, each of us answering in time, trying to be as clear as we possibly could in our responses. It was all out in the open now, and we needed their help and knew if we were going to find Eddie, this was the only way. Grandma O'Connor was on the phone to her daughter like lightning set free from a bottle. That's when we realized that the shit had only just begun to hit the proverbial fan.

"We need to get back out into those dang woods and find him," I said, standing to look directly up at the old man. "It's been way too freakin' long now already. We got to go back and get him, he might be hurt out there. Mr O'Connor, you're the only one that knows that part of the woods, certainly way better than any of us, better than Eddie too. That's why we're here. We need you to take us back in there, like right freakin' now!" I said, raising my voice an octave then shutting my eyes as I braced myself for the wrath of old man O'Connor. And when nothing came, I opened them again slowly, only to see the old man ambling off the porch, heading toward his truck.

Mrs O'Connor was still on the phone. We heard her saying something in a loud shrill voice about calling Mrs Lahn, "Right pronto." Then she was asking Ben's mom if they should file a missing person's report…

We all froze on those last words as the gravity of the situation began to finally sink in. Franky slid lower in his chair and closed his eyes. My mind kept going back to Eddie and a new possibility entered my brain uninterrupted without any softening or preamble. What if Eddie was already dead?

"Well, you little bastards, comin' or ain't-cha?" the old man hollered from across the driveway as he opened the cab door to his two-tone, rust-laden, Ford pickup. He pulled a long-barrel shotgun out from the truck's cab, cracking it open then snapping it shut quickly with just one hand. "Get yourselves in a different gear and do it right now. 'Cause we got us a lot of ground to cover."

We all looked up together, and instantly beelined for the truck. Grandma O'Connor was hollering something from the kitchen, but none of that mattered to us anymore. We were finally on the move and not o' one of us hesitated when asked to go back to them damn woods. I felt pretty darn proud of us all at that moment as we climbed into the passenger side of the old truck. That was until the old man said abruptly, "First thing we got to do is stop by the house and pick up Richie. We'll need him out in them blasted timbers." He then jammed the key in the ignition and turned her over without hesitation.

Chapter Seventeen

Change comes hard at the Springfield Inn

Ben pumped the brakes, fishtailing into the dirt and gravel parking lot, spraying stones and a torrent wave of gray water across it. Jamming the accelerator one more time to straighten the vehicle out, we skidded to a tire ripping stop just a few feet shy of the main entryway into the illustrious Springfield Inn. There were just three other cars on the frozen yet still muddy lot that early morning, two pickup trucks, and an ancient, dilapidated Buick Regal, sitting crookedly on four frighteningly bald tires. The Regal was anything but regal and seemed to have more rust than metal. I was just starting to second guess our choice of drinking establishments when Ben bounced out from the driver's seat and headed toward the Springfield Inn's sagging front door without looking back, or waiting for his old pal either.

I released my seatbelt and followed suit with Ben, making my way into the little one story, cinder block building. The Springfield Inn had seen little in the way of improvements over the past twenty-plus years as far as I could tell. In fact, it looked pretty much the same. The exterior's gray paint might have been a bit more faded, but it was hard to tell with the amount of dirt, cobwebs and other debris clinging to it. The old lighted sign hanging over the front door was missing more than a couple of light bulbs, and was riddled with small caliber bullet holes to boot. "Ah, the townies just love their firearms," I said aloud as I walked past the two somewhat typical looking (for these parts) pickup trucks. Both had seen better days too, paint faded, deeply scratched and dented beyond repair. Looking through each clouded windshield I noticed the trucks both had matching guns racks. I smiled for a second, imagining the two rednecks going together to shop for their holiday gun toting apparel. The smile faded right quick when I noticed both racks were empty.

Stepping into a place like the Springfield Inn was like stepping through a time warp back into the late 1970s. Lynyrd Skynyrd was blasting *Give me three steps* from the old Wurlitzer juke box, still sitting in the same corner I remembered it to be. The brown, banquet style tables surrounded by too many mismatched steel back chairs were also the same as I'd remembered. I stomped my feet at the front door, as one always did, careful not to track in any ground filth into a fine establishment the likes of the Springfield. I spotted the corner where Franky, Eddie, Ben and I had sat when all the parents took us on a cross-county snowmobile race all those years back. As I recalled, it wasn't much of a race in any true sense of the term, but more of a stop-at-every-do-drop-in-kinda-bar across the northern Great Lakes territory and get totally and recklessly, shit-faced, type a race. "The Springfield was the last stop in a long line of do-drop-ins that night too," I said a little too loudly, walking into the bar's memory laden embrace.

There were two tragically large male Springfield Inn patrons slouched over the somewhat sad and certainly leaning, bar. Each sat on one of the half-dozen battered, backless barstools. A cloudy, plastic pitcher filled halfway with flat, amber beer, sat between the two, who in turn slumped dangerously forward with beer mugs still in hand. Each wore baseball caps that, over time, had turned the distinct color of brackish grime and a past its prime blackened engine oil. One gentleman wore the John Deere insignia on his and the other held the esteemed CAT logo. Which I instantly recognized, having grown up in these parts, knowing that it stood for Caterpillar Equipment. Local boys who worked one of the many farms or industrial crews that roamed these areas, I deduced.

"What'd you say, faggot?" the John Deere hat wearing one mumbled in my general direction just as I passed by him going into the inn's-tired barroom. Before I even had a chance to acknowledge the rather unpleasant welcome thrown rather belligerently my way, I heard the loud scraping of metal, the barstool's feet sliding against the broken and uneven concrete floor.

"Ah, shit. Things really haven't changed at all, now have they," I said, turning to meet my more than likely assailant, head on.

The large, bearded man stood there swaying slightly, clutching his beer mug by the handle. Then repeated his earlier question, but this time while pointing at yours truly with his beer mug holding hand. "What'd yah say there, faggot?"

Original, I thought, while scanning the place quickly to see who else might be here if this were to turn into a true, bar emptying brawl. But the dim little barroom was completely empty of any type of crowd, or even a bartender. And even more disconcertingly, Ben was nowhere to be seen either. "Probably took a leak," I said, turning my attention back to the slurring, bearded asshole who now took another wobbly step closer to me. Probably to ask me another question about my sexual preferences, I thought, smiling back at him.

I moved quickly. And in one fluid motion I closed the bit of distance that was still left between us. Addressing the obviously inebriated patron right into his beady, red eyes. "Shut the fuck up, farm boy, and sit your fat, drunk ass back on that stool before you get yourself hurt." I leaned in close enough to smell the layers of old motor oil and copious amounts of Genesee Cream Ale, wafting off his person.

That's when John Deere leaned back slightly and gave up a, 'well I'll be damned' hard ass grin, filled to the gums with heavily tobacco stained, crooked teeth. He turned and slapped his buddy on the shoulder — still smiling at me — who didn't budge an inch. "Sammy, did you hear what this cock-sucking faggot, just ah... Just uhm, said to me? To us? To you too, fuck-o?" His grin never faltered when he reached over again, this time to smack ole Sammy harder, as if to wake him up from the beer induced coma that he appeared to be now drowning in.

I took advantage of the moment when ole John Deere turned his eyes away from clocking me, to further investigate Sammy's apparent complete lack of enthusiasm on my commentary toward the two of them. "Sammy? Dude, you fuckin'… you fuckin' listenin' to me…" were the last words he uttered for the night, thankfully.

Being a lefty, I surprised him with a quick, thrusting left jab to the side of his nose. Feeling my fist connecting, driving into the soft tissue at the base of it. I knew from some pretty substantive, and perhaps even qualifiable experience, it was a blow few 'dudes' could recover from. His weight shifted to the right from the force of the punch, which I deftly followed up with a loping right hook, landing smack on the right side of his jaw, using his considerable body weight against him. My right fist landed perfectly, standing John Deere almost upright again, his beer mug tumbling from his hand to smash on the concrete in a hail of crystal splinters and foamy, cheap smelling ale. I moved in for the final shot on goal. Raising my knee up and into his groin with all I had to once and for all shut Mr John Deere down for good.

His breath whooshed out of him as I drove my knee deep into the fleshy part of his body. His chin dropped, his face reddening while his eyes slapped closed. I stepped aside just in time to watch his big body crumple, then topple forward, falling to the floor loosely where he landed flat and stopped moving all together. Ironically, his partner, Sammy, never moved either, never even looked up from the bar. "Some friend you are," I said to Sammy, stepping over the out cold John Deere guy and walking past them both, heading to where I knew the men's room to be.

I rounded the corner to see Ben, leaning against the wall, his ear pressed to his cell. "Yeah, baby, he's here," he said, putting his free hand over his other ear to better hear as the music changed over to Bob Seager's stirring and quite obvious love for women of the night, smash hit of those rocking seventies, *Down on Main Street*. I was holding my left hand out which was covered in John Deere's blood.

"Nose bleeds are the worst," I said to Ben, passing in front of him to go wash up in the bathroom.

He looked up at me a tad puzzled, then put a finger up. "Yeah, he's staying with us. Make up the guest room. We'll be back to the house in a bit. Yeah, love you too," he said, then pulled the phone from his ear and disconnected the call.

I'd just gotten the long-frozen tap handle to turn to on above the battered, dirt encrusted bathroom sink, when I heard Ben click off his call. The hot water handle was so badly rusted out, it wouldn't move at all. So, I settled for the rust colored, just above freezing water to wash my blood-stained hand under. The door squealed offensively on long ago shot hinges, as Ben pushed his way into the cramped and 'hasn't been cleaned in twenty-plus years' smelling men's room.

"Making new friends?" he asked, as he plowed past me to the once lemon-yellow colored urinal to take a leak.

I looked up at his reflection in the cracked and foggy little mirror that hung crookedly over the sink, and just grinned. "I see nothing ever changes really here in Mendon, does it?"

Ben looked up, smiling a no shit type of smile.

We made our way back to the bar where the mysteriously *just missing* bartender was sweeping up the broken glass and last dregs of the beer John Deere had dropped in our little 'welcome back to the Springfield' conversation. He stopped what he was doing and then looked up at us, a cigarette glowing between broken and darkly cracked lips. "Uhm, you boy's all right?" the ancient proprietor of this fine establishment asked sheepishly while placing the broom to lean against the stool John Deere had most recently occupied. "I threw them out," he said, pointing a large, red finger toward the entryway. "Just Vick and Sam." He shook his blotchy, hairless head back and forth slowly. "Uhm well, you boys know the drill. Them two have a bad week on the job, take to drinkin'..." He jerked his head up, looking at us through heavily hooded, red-shot eyes. "And well, yah know how the story goes, right?" He tried on a smile that just didn't seem to fit his severely wrinkled, pug-like face.

Ben answered before I was able to respond, or at the very least, thank the old fucker for all the help he'd been just moments before. "All good, Dusty. Now go and bring out the bottle of Dalmore Fifteen you've got stashed back there for my friend and I, would yah? And be quick, we ain't got all night." Ben winked at me and slapped a crisp, new, one-hundred-dollar bill on the old bar top's marred counter, and then pulled a barstool under himself to sit down.

I stood for a second, unsure of what to do as old Dusty literally dropped what he'd been doing, and made his way quickly around behind the bar. "Sure thing, Mr Moyer, sir. I've been just holding it back there for you, uhm, sir. That much yah can be bloody damn sure of. Nobody else would be drinkin' that high-end hooch in here anyhow. Not in these times, anyway."

Ben turned away from Dusty, dismissing him summarily with a hand wave before giving him one last, rather brusque order. "Make sure you bring us some clean glasses to drink from. Not the filthy shit you serve the likes of Victor and Samuel. You know what I'm talking about and what I mean." Dusty was nodding in vigorous agreement as Ben turned back around to usher me up to the bar with an exaggeratedly grand and sweeping gesture. "Welcome home, Sean. It's been way too fucking long now, hasn't it?" he said in a mock, old-timey kingly voice, grinning at me then turning into the bar to await our drinks.

Dusty left the bottle with us and again, seemed to gush all over Ben even more than I or anyone might think to be even close to somewhat normal, particularly with a guy who hadn't even been in the Springfield Inn in years. Or so Ben had mentioned anyway. Ben handed Dusty the hundred-dollar bill telling him quietly to, "Keep it," and to, for lack of a better way to say it, "Get lost." Which he did, thanking Ben profusely and in turn, making sure I was all set and comfortable while at the same time now truly apologizing for 'those local boys'' most unfortunate behavior earlier. "They don't mean nothin' by it there, er, uh…" he turned toward Ben for help as he obviously didn't know my name.

"Ah yes, Dustin, my apologies for not introducing my pal here sooner. Dusty, meet my oldest and dearest friend, Mr Sean Kilpatrick."

Dustin's smile was a most unfortunate melody of entirely missing teeth mixed in with a hand full of burnt match colored errant stumps. But he offered it just the same before continuing *the boy's* sad tale of woah in way of some sort of fucked up apology. "It's a pleasure to meet yah's Mr Kilpatrick. Any friend of Mr Moyer here's a friend o' mine, that's for darn certain." He intoned humbly, to which I just smiled and nodded my head in kind. "Any who, them poor boy's, they're just, well, just intimidated by the likes o' strangers in these parts," he said, genuinely trying to smooth over Vick's, or Victor's version of welcoming patrons into his warm and loving little establishment. I wanted to ask ole Dustin where he'd been when the little episode went down, because if I'd not been able to handle myself, I might have been more than just a little banged up. But I just continued to stare back at him blankly, the strange, surreal events that had been unfolding all around me starting to close in. Well, those that happened since I was dropped into this forgotten little town in the burrows of Upstate New York, anyway.

Ben poured our drinks neat in what appeared to be two sparklingly clean, heavy cut, crystal whisky tumblers. After hoisting our glasses a few times to each other's health, and other ancillary bullshit, we settled into a more formative conversation somewhere between reminiscing and those always daunting yet sometimes a bit fictionalized, 'future plans'. He'd been genuinely saddened to hear of my divorce and how my now ex-wife, had taken our children and skedaddled for greener pastures, so to speak. A well-built sensitive type, who taught marine biology over at the University of Chicago, was more the reason than anything else, I'd thought distractedly. But what the hell, right? And as I described my travels across the rustier parts of the country, for a job I was a tad less than enamored with, he just shook his head.

"Dude, you were always way too talented of an artist to get bogged down in all that... that bull shit. Marketing? What does that even mean?" he admonished lightly, pouring yet another round of the fifteen-year-old Scotch whiskey from a quickly evaporating bottle.

On the other hand, Ben had seemed to truly prosper here in our little hometown. Taking control of the O'Connor family business, raising a family of his own, and becoming a somewhat influential member of the greater community of Victor New York. So, he said, at least. He belonged here, I thought. Just as our little gang had always hoped he one day would. He'd been blessed with four children, three girls, Sara twelve, Isabelle fourteen, and Elizabeth (Beth for short) just turned sixteen, and one boy, Henry (named after his granddad), his eldest, who'd be celebrating his eighteenth birthday in just a few short months. I smiled at the thought of either of us having soon to be adult children. How far we'd come from our rough and tumble roots, I thought a bit sadly.

The old Wurlitzer continued its preplanned flight across rock-n-roll's biggest hits of the 1970s. Never halting or hesitating as the needle dropped again and again. Nostalgic tune upon tune filled the little bar with those balmy sundown summer evenings and memories long past to time's relentless embrace. Michael Martin Murphey's one epic hit, *Wildfire* sprang out of the little speakers, causing both Ben and me to drift off in contented silence. Humming along to a song we'd all but grown up to, but neither one of us had ever bothered to learn the lyrics to.

I took another long, slow pull from my glass, savoring its smooth, smoky contents. It was Ben's voice that pulled me begrudgingly away from those dusky nights long past, under the blushing twinkle of carnival lights, her hand softly nestled in mine. He spoke in warmed whispers of his parents and their lives, but when he shared the news of their all too sudden departure, his voice scratched hoarsely low, his eyes cast down upon the bar in front of him.

"Departure?" I mumbled, somehow expecting the worst. Actually, I had no idea what to expect as I'd kept up on pretty much nothing that pertained to our hometown or the history we'd shared over the years. Which included friends and family too. *Your best fucking friends, Seany-Boy*, a voice rattled out between my ears dully.

"Yep, they departed." Ben breathed huskily, working to clear the bourbon from his throat. "Meaning, they up and bailed out, man." His tone drained, as he turned to look at me. "Just up and decided to fuckin' split one fine freakin' day. Guess they'd had enough, of all this, I suppose." He leaned back from the bar, a quick grin popping across his tired face. "Yeah man, they left to move back to 'the homeland', or so they'd called it. Whatever man. The place my mom droned on about more and more, especially after a few glasses of, well, you know." He smiled sadly and raised his glass toward me. "Cork, fuckin' Ireland of all places." He set his glass back on the bar pondering his statement stiffly. "She'd been nagging my dad for years about wantin' to go there. To go back to claim her part in the O'Conner family's history, or some shit. A family history she'd never even fuckin' known was more like it," he said, before lifting his glass again to sip.

The troubling subject sat mutely between us. I really had nothing to add, but just as I thought to, Ben abruptly changed gears before I got the chance. "I have to admit, dude…" he said, all smiles now. "I was really wondering if you'd gone all soft an' shit on me after all these years."

He was staring closely at me now. "But you ain't. And that's damn good to see, Sean—damn good indeed."

Ben suddenly bounced up from his stool, wobbling a little, just enough for me to notice, he held his glass up high, a true and proper shit eating grin (as we used to call it) plastered across his happy, ruddy mug. Frozen in the moment, I looked upon him thoroughly amused, having no fucking idea what he was up to. "Course, I would-ah stepped in had yah needed me too. I know you know that, don't-cha?" He winked back in my general direction.

I wasn't following, my exhausted, and now pretty damn inebriated brain stuck on pause. "Wait?" I slurred, "What's that your…" but Ben plowed on with his little ruse of a speech, and what sounded to be some sort of toast.

"Ah, fuck, Seany-Sean, Sean-Sean and the ole bad-to-the boner-Vick-ster. The fuckin' man of our youth himself. And of course, his ever-sleepy bud-bud Sam-Sam. I suppose ole Vick's lost a few steps over the years." He was doubled over with laughter now. "One fuck of a lot tougher of an hombre when we was kids running these streets mind you, but still…"

The proverbial lightbulb suddenly bursting right above my head. "Vick Thayer? Wait, that was fucking Vick Thayer?" I asked incredulously.

Ben nodded, still smirking widely. "Yes, Siree Bobby. Live and in-fuckin'-person, my Seany-Boy." He waved his fist in the air. "Oh, and ole Sammy Miller too," he added choking back bouts of barking laughter. "Well, what's left of them anyhow. Their booze drenched, alcoholic selves that is." He burst out with fresh peels of uncontrolled chuckling, slapping me hard on the shoulder, unable to contain the overarching joke any longer. "Sean my man, you just kicked the living shit out of one of the scariest, toughest, hoods in all the tri-state boroughs!" he hollered in his best imitation of a sports announcer, mingled in with loose fits of chirping giggles, as he again raised his glass high in what felt to me, a ridiculous salutation.

Our glasses met, clacking together so hard, I thought they might shatter in hand. We downed the rest of our drink, while the situation I'd found myself in upon arriving at this dump, finally hit home. I felt it more than anything else, swelling upward, swirling around inside of me, a burning anger chewing its way through to the surface.

"So that's it?" I asked, standing up slowly. "That's how you're gonna do me? 'Your oldest and dearest friend?'" I seethed, my voice bristling, rage trickling out in tightly coiled spurts. "You fuckin' left me to just hang out there like that?" I set my glass down on the bar, hands trembling as they balled to clenched fists, the moment being rewound then replayed before my eyes, the belligerent bad-to-the boner-Vick-ster's sinister grinning face floating before me just before I put my fist into it.

"Ah come on Sean. Vicky-boy ain't the virile and youthful stud of a tough-guy he used to be, now is he?" Ben responded quietly, setting his empty glass next to mine. Pushing himself back from the bar, squaring off in front of me.

I felt the hot blood flush in my temples, the old anger snapping dangerously bright, all this tough guy shit from the past now getting the best of me. *But this is how it is fuck-stick. How it's always been and will always be, Seany-Boy*, the voice crept in, adding a touch more fuel to the fire. I too stepped quickly onto the floor, gaging Ben, trying to feel out what his first move might be. *He was always faster than the rest of us*. I thought feeling way too old for all of this, this boys-in-the-hood, banger shit. But it was hard to suppress those old instincts when your blood was up.

"So," I asked the guy I was a hair's breadth away from dropping with my left jab. "So, that's the best you got?" I asked louder this time, feeling the tension between us slide down a notch. "That's your welcome back to our hood after a decade or so, test?" I probed, egging him on. "Ah, I suppose ole fuck-face Dusty back there was in on it too? How much did you pay that old fuck to uh, turn his back?" I breathed in deeply, the smell of molded decay and spoiling beer rich, potent. "Well, Benjamin, why don't we go and ask the old fuck what his part was in your little ruse of a 'welcome home' for me was?" I turned around quickly, moving away from him, making my way around the shitty little bar in short order. But Ben was fast, still fast that is.

"Whoa—whoa, there, man. Slow down, cowboy," he said, laughing a little, placing his hand upon my shoulder stopping me before I could get behind the bar. Something he really shouldn't have done. I spun on him, smacking his hand away, pushing him hard in the chest. And as he stumbled back, I moved in, hands readied, my left cocked and aimed, now poised to strike. "Okay, take it easy, Sean," he eased, putting both hands up in front of him. "Dude, just chill for a second. I, or we, was just havin' a bit of fun is all," he soothed, backing up another step. "Man, I guess you're still the hot-head I remember you were. Hair-fucking-fuse as always," he said, trying on a grim smile. "Just take it easy, calm down, okay?"

"You calm the fuck down!" I shouted back at him. "What the fuck's wrong with you?" I shouted even louder, watching as Dusty finally stumbled his way back into the barroom, a heavily marred and gouged Louisville Slugger baseball bat slung over his shoulder. "Ah, so now you show up Fuck-face?" I yelled, directing my heated attention squarely on the old, pug-faced bartender.

"We don't want no trouble in here, mister," Dusty said meekly, looking over to Ben for support.

"No! Keep your fucking eyes on me—asshole! Before I come over there and shove that bat up your wrinkly old ass!" I roared, the day's events and the copious amounts of expensive Scotch whiskey taking their collective toll on me and my severely frazzled nerves.

Dusty never averted his eyes from Ben as I proceeded to consider hopping over the bar to deliver on the threats I'd thrown out, but Ben spoke first in a loud, firm voice. "Dustin O'Leary, get your ass in the back where it belongs right fucking now! And drop that bat for fuck's sake. This is between us, two very old friends and nothing more. And

I, well we, owe our guest here an apology, and right fucking quick too."

Dusty backed up immediately, placing the oversized bat on the back counter, exiting the bar through the back-office door. Never looking back, or uttering another word. I was still watching the old bartender exit when Ben sat down at the bar, and once again took to filling our glasses. I began to protest, the last thing I needed was another drink, but as was always, Ben was just a touch faster than I.

"I haven't seen you, in what? Ten years, for Christ-sake? And then you just show up out a nowhere, drag my ass out of bed to come carry your carcass for a, a 'drink.' As if nothin's changed and we were still just as tight as we was when we we're kids?" He held my glass up to me, waiting for me to take it. "Okay, okay. Sean I'm truly sorry, man." He let his breath go with a huff, "Fuck man, you happy now?"

I took the glass from his hand slowly, still trying to read him. Trying to understand something, anything about this stupid place, my muscles twitching, confused by what's to come next. After an uncomfortable minute or so, I nodded, just letting the moments tautness deflate, soften. I swung my leg over the stool and sat down heavily next to him. My anger still tingling, all nervous energy and shit, still on high alert, danger pulsing brightly before my eyes. But in the end, I did nothing.

"I know I told yah this, but I would have jumped in, man. You know that, right? I mean, if you'd needed it and all…" Ben tossed out lightly. "But you did all right for yourself, my friend. Come on, let's just start again. Okay? Cool?"

I nodded once more and sipped at my drink, trying to just calm down already. To chill the fuck out.

"And honestly, if anything, you should be actually thanking my ass." Ben looked up over his glass earnestly, pushing his glasses back onto his face. When had he removed them? I asked myself absently. "Just think of the stories Sean. The glorious tales you can now regale to all that might listen." His voice rose briskly. "You just kicked the shit out o' living, upstate, tri-fucking-county legend…" He cracked an infectiously crooked smile and soon enough he had me smiling too. Somehow no longer wanting to choke the grin off his stupid, smug face.

Eventually, I just let it all go and accepted his apology. After all, he was right. I was the one who just sort of dropped in from literally nowhere and at the ass-end of a brutal winter's night to boot. The conversation eventually came back around to my arrival or 'dropping in from out of nowheres' here in our little town of Mendon, New York. Ben took his time, poking at the subject lightly, not wanting to flare up the strain between us again. But I'd all but forgotten about old fuck-face Dusty, and Vick-ster, the bad-to-the-boner, now fat, but still legendary, tough guy, I'd dropped earlier. I'd lost myself in more booze and one sorry-ass tale about being held in the Rochester International Airport Correctional Center earlier this very same fucked up evening. From the nostalgic, yet bizarre encounter with the kids in the Chitterling Tavern, straight through to the moment I'd apparently lost every inch of my shit, which admittedly, was still pretty damn fuzzy to recall. I even detailed out my detainees, describing Agent Bishop as the largest black man I'd ever laid eyes upon, and his goose-stepping goons, who had all taken a liking to manhandling my ass. But still, in all, I hadn't mentioned a word about what had pushed me over the edge, what I'd seen while sitting in the airport at my gate. Or the voice I'd been hearing in my head ever since… ever since when? I really couldn't remember any more.

But Ben was still probing at me. Something in his head, as he put it, didn't quite add up. And much like the line of questioning I'd recently endured from the big boy, Agent Bishop, Ben dug in. I wanted to tell him to be careful, not to dig too deep, as he might not like what he found and all. But after a time, I just spilled my guts. It was weirdly cathartic and at the same time, scary as shit. As I'd expected, the conversation turned a bit dark when I started to talk about Eddie. How that night, when we were kids… how I kept going back to that time. And how I'd watched as something took him away. How I'd somehow been transported back to that time, and so on and so forth. And then I told him about the voice. Eddie's voice. And how it was inside my head, like all the time and shit. I suppose that's about when Ben had had enough, or just couldn't follow my wildly flawed storyline any longer. Raising a hand, telling me to just stop talking without having to say it. "Dude, you had a rough night. Let's just leave it at that, okay?" And then he turned away to stare into his glass without another word.

The silence hung between us. Mick Jagger's Rolling Stones sang passionately about a girl he'd probably boned by the name of *Angie*. And Ben and me just took to listening and sipping at our drinks. But after a while, I started up again. The need to tell somebody, anybody, about the crazy shit I'd been experiencing, was overwhelmingly powerful. And honestly, who better than Ben to lay it out there with.

I grabbed him by the shoulder, pulling him back onto the barstool so he could sit up and face me before I began to tell what I'd thought to be the most fucked up part of my story. "So, dude, Ben, I know all this shit sounds batshit crazy, I get that," I said, staring at him, his face totally unreadable—a blank slate. "But this, well, this just might sound even fuckin' crazier," I blurted out, his attention turning, his eyes screwing down upon me coldly. I held his gaze and continued, slowly at first. "You see, I've been, uh—I've been not just hearing Eddie's voice in my head like some fucked up dream or some shit. No, it's not like that. He's, well, he's fuckin' talking to me man. Conversing with me and shit," I said quietly, watching Ben's eyes widen in dismay. "No, that's not even really quite right either," I recanted, a nervous laugh quivering out as I spoke. "It's more like he's, Eddie's, not just talking to me, he's showing me stuff. Like events from the past, man. Our past, dude." I gulped at the air, tasting its sourness. "That night, Ben. I think he's trying to show me what really happened to him. How he was taken the night we lost him, man…"

Ben stiffened, suddenly looking away from me, his head on a quick swivel. Then with a concerted effort to keep his hand steady, he set his glass down onto the bar.

I put my hand up into the air. "Wait, let me explain this, I know it sounds like I'm one step shy of the loony bin upstate, believe me I do, but it's the God's honest truth."

Ben lifted the bottle and began to pour generously into our glasses again. "One more for the ditch, my odd little friend?" he said, without looking up.

"Ben, believe me, I've got no idea why this shit is happenin'—it just is. I've been sort of lost over these past few years, since my family left me," I said, looking straight ahead, not wanting to look at anyone, particularly not Ben. "I think about us, you know. About our pack an' all. You know, how it was with us. How we were back then." I caught a sideways glance, he was back to staring into his glass. "We were so tight, yah know? I mean we've not talked in forever, totally on me, I've been goin' through a lot of my own shit like I said, but fuckin' Eddie has been reaching out to me, dude. And on a pretty regular basis too."

I did my best to describe the batshit crazy vision I'd had back at Rochester International. Sitting at my gate, gate B28. While Eddie took to sharing all kinds of shit with me. At least that's the way I saw it. I even went as far as surmising how my flight delay might not have been a mere coincidence and I was somehow meant to be here, right now.

Ben suddenly interrupted my flow, my walk backward in time. "Sean, man, slow it down a bit, okay? You're all over the place, man." He sounded exasperated. "Look, Eddie's been gone for more than twenty years and we all have fuckin' missed him. It was a very fucked up time back then," he said, shaking his head. "But dude, there's just no way he's up an' walkin' around out there tryin' to make some kinda contact." He let out his breath in an exaggerated whistle. "Besides, even if this shit were somehow happening, why now? And why with just you?"

I was listening to Ben intently when it occurred to me. Clicking over in my head, I couldn't help but suddenly blurt out. "Your stammer? Dude, you're not stuttering. At all. I mean it's totally gone? How—"

Before I could finish, he answered tersely. "You and me haven't had any meaningful contact in like a lot of years, Sean. As I said before, things do change," he answered tersely, picking up his glass and sipping lightly from it.

"Yeah, yeah, sure, man, I know… but it's really, really fantastic to hear—"

Again, he cut me off, pulling the conversation back to where we'd started. "You always did have a way-out-there imagination, man. That's what made you, well, really you." He smiled little. "And such an amazing artist too. Do you remember what that was like?" he questioned, his voice wobbling warmly as he placed a cold hand on my shoulder, squeezing down.

"Uh, yeah sure, I guess so. Maybe still do from time to time," I answered reluctantly. Remembering all too well what it felt like to hold a paint brush in my hand. Gesso white canvas, a new and refreshingly blank world just waiting there for just me. The smell of linseed oil, so hauntingly tantalizing, so far removed from my life today. "Wait," I asked suddenly. "You don't believe me? You don't believe any of this, do you?" I'd somehow made the connection with his last words.

Ben sighed heavily. "Well, look, you've had a fuck of a day. Besides, you've, or we've, been drinking quite a bit. So maybe some o' that shit you're preaching is true, or maybe you just want it to be true. Either way, come on— let's lighten it up a little—cool?" he said through a wavering grin, but then was suddenly serious again. "Jesus, man, you're all about hearing and seeing some sorta ghosts and shit? Freakin' out in the airport… What the fuck do you expect me to say? What nut-hatch did you fuckin' break out of? Man—seriously."

I broke out with a barking laugh at that comment. Thinking back again to Bishop, the black agent goliath, and how he'd asked me the exact question just a few hours prior. Well, he was a bit subtler of course, but maybe they both had a point. I was losing control. I'd been losing my shit for some time now, hadn't I? I could almost feel myself unraveling as I drained the last of my Scotch, shaking my head to free some of the more stubborn cobwebs that'd recently taken to roost there.

I couldn't hold back the giggles. They'd set to dwell deep down inside for quite a while now. Quietly waiting their turn. All of it, all the shit I'd been going through, so sudden and overwhelming. My best friend, with whom I hadn't had a real conversation with in over a decade. Sitting here of all places. In this shithole of a bar where it all had begun so many years back. A place I hadn't stepped foot into in what, twenty-something years? Yeah, the cracks in my once smooth elevation were really starting to tear apart at the seams. My eyes were leaking warm salty tears, while I choked back another uncontrollable fit of hot giggling. I noticed Ben looking over at me, his expression bordering somewhere between amusement and outright distain.

Ole Dusty, the fuck-faced bartender, peeked out from around the bathroom in the corner of the bar. Looking concerned too.

"Hey, fuck-face!" I shouted at him. "I thought your master here..." I jerked my thumb in Ben's general direction, "told you to fuck off outta here?"

Dusty ducked back out of sight, but it was already too late. I was laughing now, raucous, roaring laughter. Ben had become very still, watching me as my laughter finally doubled me over and my head hit the bar top hard enough for me to see stars.

"You okay?" I heard a voice ask from somewhere far, far away. My ability to comprehend anything at this point becoming more than difficult. Because truth be told, I wasn't even close to being fucking 'okay'. None of this shit was fucking okay. I tried to get my head up from the bar, but I was so comfortable there. Alone in my misery. My contemplation of death, Eddie, and of course, my own self-loathing. I placed both hands down on the bar, pushing—willing myself to lift upward. To stand and put both feet down upon terra firma, to turn and look them all in the eyeballs and answer the one bitch of an all-consuming question: am I really fucking all right?

And when I finally did stagger to a somewhat upright position, I looked up to see a much more concerned best friend still sitting there, right next to me. "Well, I'm going to answer your question…" I slurred. Ben still staring at me, appeared bewildered. "To answer you, or anyone that might ask me if I'm fuckin' 'okay,' well, the answer is a resounding fuck no." I chuckled. "In fact, I'm in no way, shape or form, even close to being *fucking all right*!" I shouted, feeling my knees buckle beneath me, but Ben was true to form, quickly grabbing ahold of the front of my jacket before I collapsed loosely to the floor.

"Okay, you're cut off," he said sternly, prodding and pushing me back up onto my stool where he kept his hand tightly on my shoulder to ensure I'd stay put. I couldn't help myself, it was all too comical, and once again I was laughing, tears streaming hotly down my cheeks.

"Dustin!" he shouted without looking around to see where the old fuck-face was. "Dusty. We're outta here. My friend is uh, ready to go."

I heard Dusty shuffling around and then watched uneasily as he made his way back behind the bar. "Hey, none o' my business, Mr Moyer, but ah, you ain't gonna let this guy drive is yah? He's a fuckin' mess, and that's not something I can have falling back on me. Yah know what I'm sayin, Mr Moyer?"

I turned toward him, feeling a tad beyond sick of ole fuck-face. Red colored rage danced before my eyes as I again relived my entry into his fine, shithole of an establishment. I leaned across the bar so quickly that Ben's hand fell away from my shoulder. I was waving ole Dusty to come closer, smiling all the while. Ben was trying to say something, but I hushed him up, pushing him away from me.

"It's all right, man. I just want to thank our most wonderful host here, Dustin!" I smiled enthusiastically, turning on the charm. Dusty couldn't help but grin himself at my drunken self, taking pity on me as he shook his head.

"Aw, okay, my boy, you can thank me all yah like, but…" he said grinning darkly at his one paying customer while leaning into meet me across the battered bar.

My hand shot out before he had time to react, grabbing ole Dusty by the neck hard, twisting it to the side, then slamming his face down onto the bar top. A loud slapping thud echoed across the barroom as Dusty squealed, "What the fuck? Let go of me!" He gasped indignantly. And then I pressed my full weight down on him, my elbow square in the back of his neck.

"The next time I come in here, fuck-face," I seethed, trying hard to suppress the chortling that wafted up into my throat, "you better fuckin throw me some respect. Or I'll do you like your little playmate, Vick—only not so nice like."

I breathed heavy as Ben pulled me back and my laughter kicked in, full of deep throaty force.

"Get him the fuck outta here, now! That's it! I'm not takin' no shit from the likes of some drunk fuck, like him!" Dusty screeched, jumping up, his cheek a bright crimson red from being smacked hard against the bar. He was backing away, pointing at me while he continued to holler at Ben.

"Dusty, shut the fuck up!" Ben shouted back across the bar and all was suddenly quiet again. Well, except for a wee bit of snickering I still couldn't seem to control. Ben had his arm around me while Dusty and I continued to stare at each other from a now much safer distance. I was just thinking about what I might do to ole Dusty—the fuck-face—Dustin—if I were to get my hands on him, when Ben slapped something loudly down onto the bar. "This is for you, Dustin. For your troubles." I looked down to see two more crisp, one hundred-dollar bills sitting there all pretty, like.

Dusty eyeballed the bills, his expression softening instantly as he scooped them up in a flash. "Hey, no problem there, Mr Moyer. But you know, this kinda shit?" He turned a frightened gaze my way. "Well, I can't have it in here—yah, yah, know what I'm sayin, right?"

Ben was staring at Dusty hard when he responded. "What kinda shit are you talking about, Dusty?" he asked calmly, to which Dusty just looked down to the floor. "You mean bar fights? Like there's never been a fuckin' bar fight in this fuckin' place? Is that what you're trying to say, Dusty?" he asked.

"Uh, no, not just fights. Just, you know what I'm sayin' here is, well, this fucker…" he said, looking up tempestuously, pointing a stubby finger in my general direction. "He can't be puttin' his fuckin' hands on me no matter who he is, or what he's a part of. That's all I'm sayin'."

I leapt forward, watching Dusty flinch. Wide-eyed, he stumbled backward, falling into several empty beer kegs on the floor behind him. Ben had hold of the back of my jacket now, but there was no need. I just wanted to confirm what I'd already known. I stood up, stepping back again, still grinning.

"The next time, Dusty, I might not be here to hold him back. It will do you good to remember that," Ben said quietly, then turned us both toward the door and out into the blustering, frozen darkness of early morning

Chapter Eighteen

Badass

The old truck had certainly seen better days, but still ran like it was meant to, all power and growls as the old man punched the accelerator, tires catching blacktop, chirping in protest. The cabin of the vehicle was just as beat up as its exterior and the smell of tobacco and stale beer was anything but subtle. The four of us all crammed into its two-man cab sure didn't help it much. But thankfully Ben got in first and was closest to the old man, 'cause he'd be the first to catch a slap should his granddad feel the urge to release one.

We turned the corner onto Route 64, and made the quick jaunt over to Richie O'Connor's sagging estate. Everything from the driveway full of ruts and potholes, to the broken-down front porch, was in desperate need of repair. "Boy can't fix a damn thing around here. Good for nothin' sorry excuse for a man that he be," Grandpa O'Connor exclaimed as he squinted through the truck's dirt-streaked windshield. His son's apparent lack of care when it came to anything about or around his home was pretty freakin' obvious. We bounced our way up the uneven driveway's steep elevation, passing one rusted out, weed choked, what once was some kind of machine, after another. There were old snowmobile skeletons, ancient cars on blocks, and even a washing machine that just seemed to have been tossed in for good measure. It was a creepy place, and Richie, well Richie, was a creepy dude. At least to the three of us anyway.

The old man came to a skidding stop just inches in front of what used to be a detached, one car garage. But the years of neglect had gotten the better of her and the tall grasses, weeds and trees alike, were slowly reclaiming the spot it once occupied. He was shaking his head as he pushed open the driver's side door and hopped out of the cab, like a much younger man might do. I pushed open the passenger door, with more effort than I thought would be needed, listening to the screeching of the door's rusted metal hinges, just waiting for the old man to curse at me. But he just eyeballed us, impatiently waiting for us to get our lazy, good for nothin' carcasses, out of his truck. He didn't have to say a word, we could just see it on his face, as we piled out and lined up in front of him on what once served as a driveway.

Just then there appeared to be a shadowy figure of someone standing in the front doorway, hidden behind a badly rusted and torn aluminum screen door. "Pa, whatcha forget?" a deep voice purred from within the grim porches dilapidated overhang.

"I ain't forgot nothin', boy," The old man barked, scaring us all into standing a bit straighter. "Uhm, I, or we…" He threw a glance our way, his voice softening a bit around the edges. "Well, we need to talk to you is all, son," he said in an uncharacteristically civil tone. "Now come on outta there 'cause I sure as shit don't want to come into this house o' yours." His voice cracked in a much more 'old man' like way. "If it be this bad on the outside, can't imagine what its inners might ah taken to lookin' like."

The old man stepped back off what was left of the front sidewalk to find a spot of shade to stave off the already soaring summer heat. The sun was stifling hot indeed, and the air around the once proud O'Connor estate that'd been left most unfortunately to ole Richie, just seemed to have stopped moving. Giving up altogether as if it were just too damn hot to even try to blow.

The screen door screamed as Richie pushed his way out from behind it, hopping down the busted out front steps two at a time, all cat like and shit. Richie had removed the shirt he'd been wearing earlier when the two of them were out riding, revealing his lean, heavily tattooed upper body. He wasn't all built up like some tough guy, body builder. No, he was just razor cut, or ripped, as some of the women folk had commented before when he took to hanging around bareback at the family gatherings and such. Most of the women couldn't peel their eyes off him, truth be told. Ogling him like a bunch a silly schoolgirl's an shit.

Richie never paid much attention to it outwardly, but oh, he knew that they were looking at him, and every once in a while, he'd throw one of them his killer, shark like smile. His teeth tombstone straight and bright white against his sun darkened features. I swear one of the housewives from the neighborhood outright swooned and had collapsed into her lawn chair, all on account of Richie's toothy grin. Well, and everything else that came with that smile, I supposed.

Richie was somewhere in his late twenties and had seen plenty of his share of women around town, and his wife of the past decade Debbie, Debbie Clemons was her maiden name before she got hitched, was once Miss Victor, New York, or some crazy shit. But the years were certainly not as kind to her as they'd been to ole Richie. No, she was a beat down hag of her original self, that was for damn sure. And when she'd show up with a new shiner of a black eye, hardly disguised under the pound of concealer make up she wore, we all knew that her looks were deteriorating mostly due to the amount of beatings she took from Ben's asshole of an uncle.

Regardless, to us, Richie looked more like some kind of feral animal. And just as dangerous too. Not an ounce of fat on him, every muscle tight, corded vein rippling under the copious amounts of ink he'd had tattooed into his arms, chest, shoulders, and back alike. And he had a complete hard-on for Ben, as we all knew. He was a real badass, as Eddie had liked to refer to him as. Eddie's grinning face appeared before my eyes, and I tried to shut it out; I needed to focus here and now.

Richie made his way toward the old man's truck, gliding over various chunks of busted concrete and indiscernible metal objects that looked to be more a part of the overgrown lawn than anything of use or value. He moved with a predatorial ease, sauntering across to where we all stood, staring back at him. Straightening up to his full six foot plus frame, he was more than intimidating; he embodied every inch of a badass if there were a definition of one. As per usual, really, as always, he was wearing the same deeply stained, blackened by motor grease and grime, pair of seriously filthy Levi jeans. A thick waisted, studded black belt with a big silver buckle, was barely enough to keep those jeans from falling off his hardened hide. The belt's buckle was always super shiny and glinted brightly in the hot sun, which in turn blurred out whatever was written on it. I likened the buckle to the kind the cowboys of old used to wear. And just as I'd thought of cowboys, I noticed the old toe worn, pointy black, cowboy style boots he wore. Jutting out dangerously from his pant legs like two black stiletto blades in search of something to pierce.

"What's the matter, Pa? You okay? Why'd you bring them peckerwoods with yah there? What they done got up to now?" he asked, hooking his thumbs in the wide belt, his arm muscles tensing, teetering on popping, as he leaned his back against the house's weather beaten, browned out siding.

The old man turned and reached into the truck to pull out his rifle off the gun rack that hung over the benched front seat. Sighting the barrel at his son who never even flinched, he spun to shoulder the weapon in one fluid motion. He really knew his firearms, was all I could think, as I eyed the gleaming blue-black barrel of the weapon now slung across his back. Richie eyed his father up and down, then pulled out a crumpled Cellophane pack of Marlboro Reds and shook out two, one for himself, and one for the old man. He moved silky smooth, handing the unlit cigarette to his pappy and then balancing on one foot, struck a wooden match across his glowing belt buckle to light both their smokes.

Richie leaned back again against the house, taking a long pull from his cigarette as his daddy nodded then turned his eyes to us, exhaling a thick cloud of blue gray smoke into the air.

"Ben, step up here, boy." He waved him over, his hand glistening from the heat. "Now tell your uncle what the lot ah y'all just told me and the missus. And don't spare nothin' boy, I don't want to be goin' over this twice now. We got a shitload o' work to do and we need to get on with it right pronto like."

Richie never took his eyes off his father, and when Ben started out by trying to greet his badass uncle, Richie simply nodded his head once in his nephew's general direction. So, Ben just began talking, telling our story from the beginning. Starting with the original plan that we'd all hatched, which consisted of the four of us getting away from the parental units for the weekend. The plan to camp out in the fields behind his house was really just the byproduct; we wanted to getaway for the first weekend of summer, you know? "Ju-just the fa-fa-four of us gu-guys." Ben stammered a little on that one, but no one really noticed but me and Franky, who looked my way, fear painted across his face. *If Ben fucks this up, we'll never get out there in those woods, and Richie will be the first to shoot the entire story full of holes*, I thought.

Ben kept going just the same, telling them how we'd asked permission and all, and then the four of us were going to set up camp about two miles out…

"Four?" Richie suddenly blurted out. His voice dripping with malicious question. Interrupting so fast, not missing a single beat, and more importantly, not letting Ben continue.

The old man came out of his quietly pondering gaze, jumping in quick to answer his son, because Richie was addressing him, not Ben, or any of us for that matter. But we all knew, including Richie, that the interruption was designed to throw Ben off balance and for Richie to take over. As Richie was normally prone to do. "That's the entirety of the reason we're here, son. One o' them." The old man threw up his hand toward the three of us, all still standing in a row as if we were now on trial. "Uh, Eddie is the boy's name, he's the missing fourth," he spat out, still looking directly at us. "Eddie Lahn that is. Lives just up the road there with his mom and dad." Again, he waved, only this time toward Route 64, pointing north as he did so. "Well, it appears the lad has gone to missin'." The old man turned to look back at where we were all still just standing there, silent as the mice we'd become. "How long has he been out there in them timbers, boys?"

Richie took the opportunity to steal the old man's attention, again, never once looking to any of us. "Too long. I'm sure as shit it's been too long, Daddy. And soon this place will be crawlin' with the whole lot from that sheriff's office of ours. All those fuckers stomping around in the trees and shit. Tourists that no nothing about them woods." He took another drag off his cigarette, watching his daddy's face as he nodded in agreement. He had the attention now and knew it as his killer smile peeked out from around the smoke he was busy exhaling. "Daddy, we need to get in them timbers before those fuck-heads come and muck up any real sign to where them boy mighta gotten to. "And these three?" he said slowly, turning his oily gaze upon us. "These three should be down to the station house fillin' out a missing person's report. Matter o' fact, I can throw the lot of 'em in my car and drive them over and meet you back at the gate behind Sis's house, there."

The old man nodded, then stomped out his smoke. "That's sounds about right, son, but hear the boys out, there's some shit in this here story that we need to be mindful of and you need to open your ears to."

It was Ben's turn to smile over at Richie, not quite the killer display of his badass uncle, but we all felt pretty good about it just the same. But Ben's nerves were just too splayed out and eventually they got the better of him. He again began to stammer and soon enough fell into a full-on stutter, that was so badly incoherent, I thought the old man was going to smack him across the head just to shut him up. Richie listened awhile with feigned interest, until

Ben really started to fall apart and Richie couldn't resist taking a shot at him.

"Pa, I can't understand a word that boy o' hers is sayin'. How the hell we gonna get anythin' done listenin' to this garbled load of horse shit? Jesus-H-Christ, nephew, could you just shut the fuck up and let someone else do the talkin' around here?"

Richie obviously meant that he was the one to do the talking, and never anticipated my jumping in right where Ben had, literally, just left off. I stepped up and just started to speak before he could say anything more.

I started out fast, getting to the meat of the adventure quickly, leaving out certain details around who ran and who stayed back, which to me, mattered little. I stayed to the story line's main theme, the missing boy by the name of Eddie Lahn. When I came to the part where Ben and I approached the forest's edge after locating Eddie's boot tracks, I again left out things like Stevie Wonder's jazzy little tune that played on between my ears. And that this larger-than-life white wolf appeared to be grooving too. *No, stick to the main facts of the story*, I thought. And when I finally came around to us seeing an actual wolf, a white wolf, I found myself talking directly to the old man. There was something in the way he was looking back at me that told me he'd believed me, or us. In fact, believed every word of our fucking way unbelievable story, really. But ole Richie on the other hand, he'd taken to making exaggeratedly deep sighing noises, and at some point, even laughing out loud, particularly when I took to describing the oversized white predator we'd claimed to have seen.

Upon closing, I felt winded, unsure of really anything I'd just said. And when I looked over to the old man for perhaps a little support, he appeared to be no longer interested in any of it. He'd taken to stroking the long barrel of his rifle and staring off across the weedy, dirt patches Richie tried to pass off as a front lawn. I heard the rustle of a deep throated giggling first. Which quickly turned over to a cackling laugh that ripped out of Richie's mouth and all but doubled him over, even while still leaning against possibly the only straight beam left on that derelict, old carriage house. When he finally recovered, he was smiling like the fat cat that just consumed the yellow-feathered canary, its entire birdy family, and all its little birdy friends.

"What the fuck were you boys drinkin' out there, for Christ-fuckin' sake? That's got to be one of the dumbest yarns anyone's ever had the balls to let out." He wheezed back another dirty bout of laughter. "What a pile of horse shit, Pa, ah, come on? Goddamn, these three is a bunch a dumb-ass, little crybabies, too fuckin' fearful to say what truly happened out there." He breathed in deep this time, his face suddenly under blue shadow, deadly serious in a blink of an eye. "Pa, these boys obviously got out in them woods, maybe was tokin' on something?" He threw a sly, mean eye in Ben's direction. "Smokin' a little weed and drinkin' some ah that Strawberry Boones Farm wine they stole from their mama's pantry." Again, he looked over to

Ben, who turned around to gaze nervously back at us, as we each simultaneously flushed dull red with acknowledgment. "I fuckin' knew it!" he shouted. Reading into the glowering embarrassment plastered across all our sweat slicked faces. "You little shits just got fuckin' wasted. And then got your stupid selves lost out there in them woods is all."

Richie stood up from the sagging garage he'd taken to leaning against, sauntering over to us, leaning dangerously close into Ben's frightened face. Then whipping around in a flurry to talk to the old man again. "Pa, we need to get our asses in gear and get out there before that little pecker, Eddie-boy, wakes up from his stoned and drunkin' stupor." His malicious grin lit up his darkened features, which didn't go unnoticed by yours truly. "Stupid little bastard, might even take to tryin' to make his way out of them damn timbers, for fuck's sake, Pa."

"We weren't drinking or smoking anything beyond a few Marlboros Eddie had brought with him," I said impatiently, mustering up all my courage to stare directly into Richie's gruesomely handsome face. "The reason we were, well, I guess embarrassed about your Boones Farm wine comment, is that we actually did that last summer. So, you were right. We had stolen a bottle from Ben's dad's liquor cabinet, and we all got pretty fucking sick, for sure. But you're wrong about one thing, Richie," I said, letting my words hang out here for good measure. "It wasn't this summer, it was last. An entire year ago to be exact." I didn't bother to get the rest of that story out; the old man had already turned back to his truck and was opening its driver's side door without saying or listening to anything more. He placed his rifle back onto the interior rack and jumped up into the cab, slamming the door closed behind. The Ford's 350 big-block motor grumbled to life when he flipped the ignition and stomped on the accelerator to gas it up.

The old man then leaned his arm out the window, Richie moving in toward the truck. But the old man turned his head ever-so-slowly toward the three of us instead of his son. "Well, you fuck-nuts comin', or we gonna stand here jawin' all day?"

Richie stopped dead in his tracks. His mouth open, his obvious protest hanging silently in air. Franky, Ben and I put our feet into motion, running off for the other side of the truck. Richie shouting, "Pa, are you fuckin' out of your ever lovin'—" But he never got to finish, his pa cutting him off.

"Hold your water boy. You ain't gonna tell me anythin' I ain't already thought-ah. And you sure as shit ain't gonna be helpful. So, 'cause you is as useless as tits on a bull, we ain't gonna be needin' yah after all on this one."

Richie's eyes widened in deadly protest as the three of us piled into the truck's passenger side. The truck's interior cabin was already a hundred-plus degrees from the ever-rising summer heat. Richie straightened slowly, his heavily inked arms taught and glistening as he stared down each one of us sitting there jammed inside that truck.

Maybe he hadn't fully comprehended what had just transpired, but he sure as shit knew who to blame for it. The old man waved him off with a curt salute, jamming the shifter on the old truck's steering column into reverse, spraying dusty gravel into the hot air as we jerked backward into motion. And I, I took the liberty of giving ole badass Richie my middle finger and my own version of his shit-eating, shark-like grin. While both Ben and Franky burst out into peals of uncontrollable laughter. And when I turned to look over to the old man, I noticed he too wore a rare grin upon his sunbeaten, deeply lined face.

Chapter Nineteen

Memories don't come easy

"Hey, man, you can drop me off at the nearest motel. No worries at all, seriously." I said, struggling to keep my eyes open while thousands of giant white blotches exploded across the BMW's windshield. I could hear the soft swishing sound of its wiper blades trying desperately to keep up with the onslaught of snow that was now swirling down in torrential waves.

"Yeah, you do remember where we are, right?" he said, grinning, his eyes never leaving what was left of the little roadway all but obliterated under a blanket of white stuff.

"Ah, yes. I do," I mumbled, not really understanding what he meant.

"Nearest motel is in Pittsford, and I'm not driving twenty miles in this shit. No, you can stay with me. We got lots of room."

I was thinking to myself, hadn't he already told his wife I was coming to stay with them in the bar? But I answered just the same. "Cool. Thanks, man. Hey, you said earlier that you'd moved though. Where to?" I asked, my words crashing all together in messy slurs. "You still fuckin' in town? I assume you is, right, man?" I opened my eyes just enough to see Ben's face awash in the red glow of the Beemer's dashboard lights. His head tilted slightly as he focused on his driving along a now non-existent road. The snow blinding, pelting down in hurling white gusts as he pressed the car forward out over the great white expanse.

How's he doing it? How can he even be driving? I'm flat out drunk off my ass, yet he's... I wondered foggily, watching him navigate through a complete whiteout snowstorm without even a single nervous swerve of the wheel, or jerking of the brakes.

"Yep. We've moved. And you'll see for yourself soon enough, Sean," he answered calmly, clearly. "Hey. I almost forgot. Holly, my wife, is really looking forward to finally meeting your ass, too."

As he said her name, only then had it occurred to me that I'd not met his Holly before. I'd actually never met any of his family. *How could that be?* I asked myself but then lost the thought as Ben started to talk again.

"I can't wait for you to see the old place, man. Lot's o' memories still hangin' around it for sure. Well, maybe not right this second, anyway. You are a little worse for wear so to speak," he said with a clipped laugh, then reached out to punch me teasingly on the shoulder. My head bounced back against the soft leather seat, my eyes slamming shut once more.

"What place?" I asked dreamily, head swimming and spinning in great buckets of fiery booze. "Fuck, man, I can't wait to see it—them…" I slobbered, my words instantly stolen as Eddie's voice cut through me.

You fucked it all up, pussy. You were right there, and you fucked it all up, again. Man, you really are a pole smoker ain't cha? Cry-fucking-baby, can't handle your liquor or nothin'. I'm tryin' to teach you somethin' here, dick breath. But you ain't listening*! We're pals, remember Seany-Boy? Remember what it was like to have pals, cocksucker? To have a friend even?*

Howling rasps of gritty laughter follow his terse, all but damning words. I suddenly can't breathe. "Oh, man, stop it already, my head—it's splitting." I begged him to stop. To just go away. But he's always so relentless. "Some things never change," I whispered to myself.

Nah. That ain't gonna happen. Been too long. We're gonna all be pals again whether you want to or not dickweed. And ole Ben here is gonna make sure of it. You'll see, you ain't never leavin' now…

"*Shut the fuck up, Eddie*!" I screamed, pushing myself to sit up. I felt like I was drowning under the weight of his words. Ben must have swerved or something, startled by my sudden outburst. But that didn't even begin to deter me, nothing or no one would stop me from trying to shut that voice down, Eddies voice. Which remarkably, continued to rattle on undeterred in its own right inside my head. *"What do you want from me, man? Just leave me the fuck alone already—please!"* I heard myself shouting, pleading.

I can't feel much of anything, but somehow, I know that I'm no longer a passenger in Ben's luxury automobile. There's a spotty memory of Ben pulling me out from the car's passenger side, putting his shoulder under me and dragging my limp self out and then up a series of steps… *it's so fuckin' cold.* Then there's a female, her voice filled with concern. She too is now helping me up even more steps. Ben's voice is distant, a blur. "Just give me a hand getting him into the bed, baby… I'll take it from there," he says, his voice strained, anger bristling there, subtle but there.

***

I somehow sit myself up, throwing back an innocuous, but delightfully warm comforter that covered my upper body. A blue-colored haze coats my eyes, my head spins in queasy, loping circles. Nausea sets into motion in hard sloppy turns within my lower bowels. I feel the vomit reach my throat before I fall back upon the bed's thick, feather light pillows. I'm willing myself to stop the room from spinning all topsy-turvy like when I drift back into a troubled, turbulent doze.

***

My eyes slap open heavily, furious streaks of blinding light pierce through the edges of a closed set of window curtains. White hot pain booming blatantly around inside my skull. I try again to sit up, shielding my eyes from the scathing light. I notice that I'm fully clothed, all the way down to both socks and shoes. Eddie's voice suddenly interrupting, edging its way into my already clouded thoughts. *Ole Ben here is gonna make sure of it. You'll see, you'll...* I block out his voice as best I can, trying to get a hold of myself. "Fuck," is about all I can muster. "Fuck. I'm going to be sick..."

I swing both legs over the side of the massive bed, pressing my feet firmly down upon the floor. As if to test it to make sure it's level before I can even try stand. "My head..." I whisper groggily, taking a moment to have a look around, but more importantly to find a freakin' bathroom. It took all I had to get on to my feet, wobbling, I lurch forward across the hardwood floors, staggering, my shoes clopping too loudly beneath me. I wrench open the first of several closed door in the spacious bedroom, only to confront a shadow filled closet. Moving on to door number two, praying for it as I turn the oversized brass door knob—Yahtzee—a fucking toilet. I let go, hitting the extensive and brightly-colored tile flooring that lay in complex patterns before me, reckless in my approach as nothing can stop me from getting to the illustrious toilet before it's too late. Throwing myself over the wide rimmed bowl just as an eruption of burning liquid is ejected from my mouth.

The intensity of the "hangover" sickness brought on by a night of professional-style drinking, thankfully begins to fade. I stand before an oval, ornately Victorian in style, mirror with my hands pressed tightly around the sink's basin. Desperately trying to wash away the vile, boozy taste from my desert dry mouth. *If there were only some aspirin in here. Shit, what I wouldn't do for just one freakin' tablet*, I tell myself, as a rapping of knuckles hammers loudly (too loudly) on a door somewhere outside the bathroom's vicinity. My head pounding once more as if on cue.

"Yo-yo, Sean. Oh Seany?" I hear Ben's voice muffled, filtering in across the spacious and graciously appointed, suite of a bedroom. I wipe my mouth and face upon one of several thick hand towels hanging to either side of me, staring back at my reflection in the mirror with a grimace.

"Shit, I look almost as good as I feel," I croak, grinning bravely at my tattered reflection. "Well, old boy, you're never fuckin' drinking again, that's for damn sure," I tell my mirror image, trying unsuccessfully to put on my best face, a face ready for the company of others.

"Hello—hello? Wakey, wakey, time to drop the snaky." A jocular voice advises. Knuckles rapping again, harder this time. "Dude, you alive?"

I make my way out from the bathroom, plodding methodically across the abounding floors to open the door for whom I knew would be none other than Ben. And there he stood fresh as a daisy, dressed and ready for another productive day. "Uh, hey. What, what time is it?" I manage in a raspy whisper, dragging a shaking hand through my bed-headed hair.

"Well good morning, or should I say good afternoon, to you too. It's just past one buddy." He smiled wanly. "You uh, you really went out hard last night, my friend," he teased just a little. "I'm sure it was all that shit you had to put up with at the airport earlier. Just wore your ass out," he said grinning wider in an 'I know the truth of it' sort of way. "Or perhaps, and this might be a stretch, but maybe the bottle of fifteen-year-old Scotch we consumed last night? I don't know, but that might just have somethin' to do with it too?" he added, a tad too merrily.

To which I responded hoarsely, "Oh, yeah, that. Remind me to thank you for that, that little bit of socially acceptable drinking, by the way. I'm not hungover in the slightest."

Ben laughed, then pushed past me with my carry-on bag in tow, throwing it unceremoniously upon the bed. Turning back, he tossed something my way, which I almost caught, bobbled, then dropped to the floor. I bent down to pick up the small plastic container, groaning thankfully as I read the bright red label aloud. "Excedrin. Extra strength headache relief. Shit, there actually is a god…" I said, looking back at Ben, nodding in gratitude at his smiling face.

Ben was all laughs and bursts of child-like giggling as he strolled over to the bedrooms ample sitting area. "Okay…" He said between bouts of laughter, "get in the damn shower, get yourself back together, and come downstairs when you is ready. I want to chat you up about some work I might have for yah. Shit's right up your alley too," he said, reaching over to pull back the first of several heavily embroidered curtains. The full light of the day pouring over the room as he pulls back yet another curtain, tying each off to their wall mounts to ensure that they stay nice and wide-open.

My head buzzes, the daylight seemingly having the same adverse effect on me that a vampire might describe... I smile at the thought, forcing myself to be brave and embrace the light. And once I do, I suddenly can't help but stare through the stately windows, mesmerized by the foreboding gray skies peppered by slanted flurries of white whipped snowflakes. Ben turns over his shoulder to say, "Ah, upstate winter weather at its finest, my friend." I finally turn away, covering my eyes as the swirling snow becomes almost blinding, my head a ticking timebomb just waiting to explode. "Our weather here is always so warm and welcoming, like a great big hug, yeah?" he stated lightly, turning to make his exit from the room, the place I'd somehow managed to wind up in. "I'll wait for yah downstairs Sean. Oh yeah, I almost forgot, Holly's already tried to get you back to Chicago on the next available flight. I took the liberty of looking at your ticketed flight information last night while you were, uhm, in a snoring coma. Hope you don't mind?" he questioned openly, never waiting for my response. "I'm sorry to say it partner, but you ain't gettin' out of this burg anytime soon, that's for damn sure. Not with this shit comin' down the way it is." He smiled earnestly. winking at me in a "don't you worry about nothin'" kind of way. And with that he was out the door, closing it swiftly behind him. "Coffee's still on, dude, sure you could use a cup..." he hollered, his voice fading as he moved further away. Boots clomping along on what sounded like hollow, yet well-padded, carpeted stairs.

I stood there for a few extra seconds, just trying to get my bearings and take in my new surroundings by the light of the day. The bed itself was king in size, an old-fashioned wrought iron type of unit, like one might imagine furniture out of the Queen Victoria era to be. Sitting atop ornately wrought, clawed iron feet, that almost looked like they might tear into thick, oriental carpet that lay just beneath them. But the bedroom itself was so unusually large, grand in all aspects of size. With two intricately carved mahogany tallboy dressers, and a matching table for sitting at, well positioned just in front of the rooms floor to ceiling, now light filled, windows. Two high-back, bruised leather chairs sat regally alongside the sitting table, enticing one to come on over and sit for a spell and gaze out the oversized paned glass windows. Which I noticed were heavily incased in a deeply engraved crown molding that stretched over the rooms twelve foot-plus plaster ceiling. And on the wall adjacent to the bed, was a beautifully carved, gleaming, oak mantle with a real wood burning fireplace. And above it hung one of the largest, 4k, LG thin-line flat screen televisions I'd ever seen.

"Man, it's got to be over one hundred some inches? Shit..." I whispered, stepping up to it, admiring its sleek, paper-thin frame. "This is a pretty damn nice place," I said to myself quietly, swaying on my feet as I turned to gaze back out the window, staring directly into the mouth of a spectacular winter storm. I still hadn't figured out exactly where I was, because I didn't even know Ben's address any more. *Had I ever known where he'd moved to over the years?* I asked myself again and at the same time, wishing I'd taken the damn Excedrin already.

After a long, luxuriously hot shower and four Excedrin tablets, I almost felt human again. Almost. I sat wrapped in several cottony white towels upon one of the two oversized chairs. It was almost impossible to see outside now as the continuous snowfall had quite literally blotted out any last remnants of the out-of-doors. A complete and utter whiteout if I'd ever seen one, I thought tragically, remembering just what it was like growing up here in this perpetually frosted part of the world. On average about six horrific months of dead cold, gray winter. And at any given time, from late September straight through to early May, one might see up to twenty inches of the white stuff in a single night if the snow really took to flying. The most serious accumulation generously driven off the massive Great Lakes that stretched their way well into Canada. But Lake Ontario was our main culprit for the copious amounts of dumping snow Rochester and even more so, Buffalo, received. And really, any of the countless other frozen little boroughs across the vast upstate region of New York. I cupped my hands over the cold window glass, squinting through the boil of countlessly whirling, white flakes. Trying to make out anything outside on this day, was simply not possible. Through the blurred, frigid winds I was however able to pick out a large, darkened structure some hundred yards or so to the south. The wildly blowing winds obscured just about everything atop the great white landscape of softly rolling hills and distant valleys. But just below, I could all but make it out, a massive, slat wood structure that may have been a balcony, or patio of some sort? "A patio?" I asked the window, fogging it with my hot and nauseatingly stale breath.

I then noticed a darkened rim of gray that appeared to surround the grounds from almost every direction. Coming intermittently into focus between the gusts of billowing snow. I could see that the grayish black wall like object was actually a vast stretch of tree line. Which looked to be struck bare of any color at all. My stomach gurgled when I pulled my face away from the heavily fogged window glass. "Nah, that's not right," I said, still staring out. "This can't be… the same place?" I stumbled on my words, leaning forward again, cupping my hands around my face to peer out the windows. "Wait, is it?"

I remembered hearing years ago, when I was still somewhat in touch with things, that Ben's uncle—fuckin' badass Richie—had taken over the O'Connor estate when the old man passed. "But that was years ago though, right?" I asked the glass, feeling a skittish surge in the pit of my stomach. "Richie had a kid, a son, Zack or Zackary, right? He'd finally put one in ole Debbie after all." I whispered, chuckling nervously. "Who would have held full claim to the entire kit-and-caboodle as the one true male heir to the O'Connor estate, and all the shit that came with it, whatever that meant." I told the glass. "Which should have iced Ben out... 'cause he's only half O'Connor on his mom's side..."

A strange bout of giddiness crept over me, lifting the corners of my mouth into a hard grin. "Somethin' must've changed then... most seriously fuckin' changed," I said aloud, standing up, wanting now only to get my ass dressed and downstairs to ask Ben the one singularly burning question. The one that left me staring breathlessly across what I now knew to be a rather familiar, wrap around patio. More precisely, the old man's wrap around patio.

I felt a bitter draft waft over my bare shoulders as I made my way back toward the bathroom. My head throbbed dully, reminding me that I wasn't quite out of the ole hangover woods just yet. I thought about the bottle of Excedrin, maybe taking another capsule (or twelve) to help stave off any unwelcome reoccurrences. But in the end, I chose to grab my shaving kit and proceed to make myself somewhat presentable before I sucked back any more pills. My palms were greased in sweat when I placed my hand on the door handle. Feeling anxious, but better now. I tucked the little aspirin bottle in the pocket of my jeans for safe keeping, and proceeded to open the door to the hallway.

As kids, I remembered that we were never allowed anywhere near the upstairs of the O'Connor house. So, I really had little in the way of expectations when I finally stepped out onto a generously carpeted, second floor landing. Which opened onto a gloriously winding staircase. The ceilings soared high above me, full of sweeping angles that were framed together by thick, hand-cut, oak beams that glowed in warm contrast with the multitude of modern, track lighting. I stepped forward, whistling low, in awe of just how spectacular this place truly was. Touching down on the first padded step, the rounded stairwell looked as if it might just meander on forever. "Just spectacular," I stated emphatically. "Somebody, or a lot of somebody's, have done some serious work on this place over the years," I assured myself, humming a little bit of a tune that had been playing quietly in my head since—when? A classic really, brought to me directly from the infamous Springfield Inn's own private collection of moldy-oldies. All slapped inside my head and plopped on repeat. "What was the name of it again? Something about a horse..." I asked myself, hearing the melody more clearly now. "*Wildfire*. That's totally it," I answered, singing in a hushed whisper from the tune's main chorus, which was all I, or I'd venture to guess, anyone, really knew of the song. Breathy bursts of the lyrics came forth more than slightly off key. *"In a blizz-zzard he was lost. Mmmm. She ran call-lliinng Wii-iiildfire. She ran call-lliinng Wah-wii-iildfiii-iiirrre..."*

Chapter Twenty

Her and Billy

The winter's wind howled and blustered outside the home's insulated walls. Twirling sheets of frozen blue snowflakes pelted at the home's window glass lightly, as if knocking timidly to be allowed inside. The chimney pushed swirling puffs of smoke up into the winter's endless night. While inside the home's fireplace crackled and popped with quartered oak logs, known for their hardiness and a long-standing quality burn.

She was listening to one of her favorite tracks by a band called Pearl Jam. One she'd recently stumbled upon. The song's narration about a human boy called *Jeremy* captivated her implicitly, as she paced evenly across the blond carpet's thick pile. Feeling herself smile when the deep throated singer spouted the line: *'Lemon yellow sun. Arms raised in a V. And the dead lay in pools of maroon below.'* But looking out from inside the home's glistening window glass served only to quickly snap her back to the somber loneliness she couldn't seem to shake. The outdoors's icy whispers calling to her, soothing her blistering soul. She'd dressed that afternoon in what was, she felt, appropriate for these long cycles of inclement weather. Even donning a long, ocher colored scarf of cashmere (her favorite) to complete the ensemble. But it was of little matter. A trivial thing, really. Just something she had to do to blend in, so to speak. And at her heart, she longed to strip down to the flesh, discard the beautifully tailored, stylish (everyone always commented on how 'put together' she appeared to be) garments she'd wrapped her warm skin within. Always feeling just a bit too trapped in them somehow. Confined by the clothing she so carefully selected to wear, and by all of this, she thought, looking tentatively around the opulently furnished, expansive room. The place she now called her home.

"More like the place they've stuck me in for safe keeping. Well, better than the caves I suppose," she groused, plopping down on the swollen, high-backed, leather sofa. She liked the feel of it. The sofa's stretched and tanned animal skin being so close to her own always just felt right. She picked up the phone and thumbed her way to the 'recent calls' section and pressed the number she already knew by memory alone. Listening as the device chirped somewhere out into the darkened world. "But you're not too far from me, now are you? Never too far…" she whispered softly, pushing herself back into the warm folds of the sofa.

The voices in her head had been strong of late. For many a night now. Alive and well upon the beginning of the winter's night solstice. Her spirit, the old guide from many days passed, seemed to be trying to tell her something of great importance. His muddled voice sounded desperate to her ears. But for reasons beyond even her comprehension, she could not quite grasp his repeated, yet nonsensical messages. His face so clear under the moon's glow, but the human words he wished to make would not come forth to be understood. Not to her anyway. But the look on his face, his expression, was one she'd not seen on the old Huron chief before. There was more to it somehow. Something troubled him but he could not make his words travel, which again, was new to her.

She clicked off the phone deciding against the call at the last minute. Tossing the bothersome device to the floor where it thumped and slid toward the fireplace unharmed. It began buzzing the moment it stopped skidding, the person she'd wanted to reach already calling her back.

"Ah, there's really nothing I want to say to any of them now." She spoke aloud and as soon as she did, the man was there. Standing before her, his head bowed slightly forward.

"What can I do for you, Foremother?" His voice rumbled deeply across the cavernous living area. Unintentionally opening a floodgate into her otherwise walled off subconscious. She could smell him now, much as she had then. Suddenly, the day exploded before her… a clear midnight's blue sky, sparkling and wet with the coming moon. The scent of it miraculously swelling up within her, feeding her, providing welcome moisture to her dry, scorched being. As if she were there once more, in that very moment. *So much life*, she thought, felt. Breathing in deeply of his dusky words, scenting their rich, succulent flavor, akin only to the deep black soil she had once risen from. The earth was moist, full of newly burgeoning life too. The memory brought tingling arousal to her, a heated desire pulsing desperately within her. The feeling of despair, a longing so great, she shuddered to breathe again.

"Go away!" she barked. "You are not needed here. Your foolish presence displeases me. I wish to be alone," were the thoughts that gushed forth from her. She could not control the feeling this child brought forward in her. And the human words she unleashed were filled with deceit and ill-intent. Her true feelings masked, its spirit bruised and wanton. A need she no longer held sway over, coursing hot through her veins.

He bowed deeply, backing away with his head down, his wide shoulders narrowed in what she took to be great sadness.

"Before you go. Be a lamb and put more wood on the fire, my young one. The chilled air is rife with dark spirits," she called from behind him. Her voice softening just enough. His head suddenly raised, blue eyes flashing with renewed energy, a hard line of a smile spreading over the gray whiskers he wore—had always worn upon his deeply lined jaw. He hurried out from the room to do her bidding, returning in mere seconds, both arms filled to their limit with stacks of heavy, split firewood. A dusting of bright white snow clung to both his clothing and hair. Her keen eyes watched each individual snowflake dissolve, disappearing into tiny runnels of water as he leaned ever closer to the heat of the fire. She could hear them trickle down to the floor, being absorbed to vanish from this world as if never to exist. *But they did exist*, she thought. *As I exist. And I will not disappear like they.* It was time. The days had grown far too long sitting in this gilded cage, she thought.

She could hear her cell phone trembling and buzzing from across the room as she rose from the couch and strode across the carpet to the mantled fireplace. She wanted to be near him. The smell, deliciously intoxicating, made her legs tremble as she approached from behind. Running a well-appointed fingernail down the center of his back caused him to jerk forward, tensing in surprise and almost dropping the gathered wood from his arms. She pushed her hands beneath the loose clothing, drawing the same line down his back with her nails. Scenting the salty flesh as she raked her nails harder across the rippling, worm-shaped scars that covered his upper torso. The first of many 'love marks' she'd made upon his body—upon his soul. He was hers, in both.

"Take me out, William. I need to roam a bit, my darling." She panted wetly in his ear, nipping at the fatty lobe, hanging there for just that purpose, or so it seemed to her. The human body was a frail and pampered thing, she thought mildly. Nothing to cover or protect it from the elements, its parts and limbs soft, easily exposed. Better for consuming than living within, she thought, growling lightly. But no matter how inferior they, all of them, were, they still had climbed to a place of dominance in nature's kingdom. The kingdom of all living creatures, really. Those old thoughts never quite leaving her. Still so troublesome even after however many millennia. Pushing a time and place so long past only she alone could recall. When they, the white, roamed freely, the true kings and queens of earth, water, and sky. Why had she not been able to produce the child? The children he had promised to her? The old Huron seer's words drifting back to her, taunting her.

"He will come to you in a time of great change. A human child of pure blood to transcend all the spirits from above and below. Your destiny will be forever intertwined with the race of man..."

The wind picked up outside, producing a piercing howl.

"Daughter of the Moon will live forever amongst the race of humans through the coupling with the one human child. And your children will walk amongst their rulers as kings and as queens..."

"Get the vehicle started. I will be out in a moment, my love," she whispered huskily, resisting the temptation to tear into the earlobe dangling before her. Just tasting it with the tip of her tongue released the rush she'd soon enough feel. Fiery hot liquid bursting from pierced flesh. Again, she shivered with anticipation as the old Huron chief's face thankfully faded away from sight.

He stood stock still. Not a muscle to move, knowing full well what could come to pass. And he certainly had the scars to prove it. But he would do what she asked of him, without hesitation, no matter what. It wasn't that he was afraid, he no longer feared anything really, since he'd become the abomination he'd become, way back when. *A walking corpse in the eyes of the Lord*, he thought, grimacing. He often wondered what his long dead Mary Elizabeth might've thought of him now. How he'd watched her pass over to the Lord's hands without her ever knowing he had. And how when she arrived at Heaven's Gate, he himself was not there to greet her. Or his son William Junior, or even his sons, Cullen Patrick, Thomas or Hank, for that matter.

Ah, Hank. That boy was a special one that much was for certain. He'd been offered her favor, and mind you, not many were offered it at all. She had to approve of them first, which she rarely if ever, did. But Hank she had seen for herself and eagerly approved of his turning. But in the end, the boy had turned him down flat. Hank hadn't judged his own decision to take on her 'favor' and become what he had become. No, that was not something his grandson would have done. Instead, he just drew down with that Savage 99 rifle of his, the one he'd just returned to his dumbstruck hands, and with a tear in his eye, had told him he was leaving. "Get out of my way, Grandpa," he'd said, with the rifle barrel pressed cold against his forehead.

Billy Senior respected the boy and had allowed him to pass, but had also warned him not to come back into the Spotted Green woods. Ever. Which he'd done for a time… and when Hank finally passed on, Billy was there. He had told himself he just needed to see him one more time before the ground took him as one of its own. But even then, he knew it was more than just that. He needed to see, yes, but the real question that had plagued him all these years simply remained. Even after the body passed on, could she still, well, turn them? He spent his time in shadow peering at the grave site, hidden from the many prying eyes. But that was all but impossible in these times, he thought. All them new phones and camera gadgets everyone carried on their person now, made it pretty tough for someone who looked like him to stay hidden. But Billy did what he could and was cautious when traveling amongst them. All those strange people who had somehow found their way to their little corner of the world that he and his brother Ciaran thought to be heaven on Earth all those years ago. And many were in some way his kin, too. Faces he did not know, but recognized certain traits within them plain as day. Inflections, smiles and even the shape of their nose, all pointed to one thing: these people were of his blood. Which got him to thinking, why go after the dead one when all these young vibrant relations of his were just as good as ole Hank had been even in his prime?

So, he did. And by the end of it, he'd raised an entire clan of O'Connors under the foremother's favor. Which was not a small feat, but did his heart good to see all these young ones embrace a life and lifestyle Hank had summarily dismissed, years and years ago. And for him, well, time just sort of blended together and the years passed into relative obscurity. "Heck," he mumbled, it didn't seem all that long ago when he and his brother

Ciaran rode up on these woods and founded all this, truth be told. "More game than we'd ever laid eyes upon…" he whispered to himself. "And somethin' else be there too. She was there—she'd always been there," he said quietly, lost in thoughts that seemed to ramble and tumble across large unidentified chunks of time. Time he no longer actually counted…

"Did you hear me?" Her voice came screeching into his head, abruptly stifling the little stroll down memory lane. "Hello? Are you there?" The voice demanded his attention. "I asked you to go and get the vehicle prepared, didn't I? And yet, here you still stand. William?"

Any thoughts beyond her demands disappeared. And fearing the worst, Billy apologized quickly before setting down the rest of the wood he still held in his arms. "Yes, yes, of course, Foremother. I'm so sorry for my mind's wanderin' nature. I was just thinkin' 'bout the weather an' all. Might be a trifle on the dangerous side to be travelin' in it, the way I see it. Specially in the dead of night as we'd be doin'." He ventured a glance at her face, which basically told him all he needed to know. She wasn't having any of his bullshit this evening—which was more than readily apparent. "Yes, ma'am. Right away," he answered without question. Turning to make his exit just as she stepped gracefully in front of him. Her large almond shaped eyes boring into him. Their austere sky-blue color turned to a cool, slated gray.

"Tonight, William. We will go tonight," she flashed coldly, her jaw clenching in time. "And you will not use that name, 'Foremother', when addressing me. You do know better than that, don't you?"

He nodded obediently, averting his eyes, finding renewed interest in the plush carpet beneath them.

"*Look at me!*" she shouted suddenly. Commanding him to do so, which he did without hesitation. "Look at me when I'm speaking to you, William," she insisted, her voice calming, slowing. "Not looking directly at someone when communicating reveals, well, a cowardly nature, my love." She sighed lightly, the trace of a smile lighting upon her face. "And you, my William, are anything but a coward." The smile she now wore graciously dazzling. "That's why I chose you, my pet. And that's why we chose all of 'them' isn't it, William?"

He held her luminous gaze, bowing his head toward her in affirmation.

"Ah, that's wonderful, my love. I'm glad we do see eye to eye," she said almost tenderly, whimsically brushing at his face with her open palm. Her mouth opening slightly, revealing an instant flash of sonic white teeth behind claret red lips. "Come, come, William. Tonight, we hunt, yes?" Her laughter suddenly cracking, splintering the quiet home like sheets of glass being smashed into millions of brittlely glistening, razor-sharp shards. She brushed by him, calling over shoulder as she drifted out from the shattered living room. "Do remember my 'name' this evening, young one. My hunger is great, so we, well you, will need to stay within character. So, try not to disappoint me, my love." Her tittering laughter broke free once more, echoing uncomfortably throughout the old mansion's billowy, shadowed halls.

Billy held up the key fob to the brand-new white-on-white Range Rover after flipping on the modified, five car garage, interior track lighting system. With the weather conditions being nothing less than a whiteout blizzard, he knew damn well that they'd need the option of the Rover's four-wheel drive. That is if they were to have a shot at staying on those country roads at all tonight. The chunky SUV barked brightly, blinking lights in acknowledgement of his request, seemingly excited to 'go for a little drive in the snow if we dare'. Once upon a time, her anger hadn't really frightened or even bothered him in the least. But over time, playing witness to all of what she, their foremother, was truly capable of doing, had certainly changed him. She was a predator in the truest sense of the word. One the likes he'd never seen or known, perhaps nobody had ever seen or known. And now, well, he knew to fold his damn cards and back up in a hurry when her tempestuous moods took to flight. Granted, she'd never been overly cruel to him anyway, but to others… he'd witnessed firsthand the meting out of her displeasure. And it was safe to say, very safe indeed, that if she wanted to send you a warning, a message, you can be damn certain that it would stick. As it was normally written in blood—your blood.

She was their mother and the alpha leader rolled into one extraordinary being. Ruling over an ever-growing pack of new human recruits was no simple thing, he thought. And she would never let any of her pack, including Billy himself, forget that she was in fact ruling. But it wasn't just brute strength, or the viciousness that she often displayed that kept the lot of them in line. Truth be told, it was more likely just her presence, an unrivaled beauty that so disarmed all that chose to surround her. Because it was a choice after all.

Which was the same way it had been for Billy when he'd stumbled upon her nesting in the furthest reaches of that forest. Which were still his trees sitting upon his land at the time, he thought blandly. "Just lyin' there helpless upon those great black stones... so beautiful and so out o' place in them wilds," he whispered. Remembering her long tangles of raven black hair that tumbled over skin white as the winter's first snows. Calling softly, sweetly, to him. Falling to his knees before her, watching on helplessly while she began to shift, changing before his eyes. Her body shaking in great waves, skins set to quiver, sliding in fast motion as her body took on a new form. Changing, stretching and pulling both bone and muscle until his long dead mother, Alicia, lay still before him. Her motherly eyes flashing open wide, watery, pleading for him to come to her. He'd reached out, watching her as she began to smile, his hand touching down upon her bare shoulder. An oversized row of pointed teeth protruding from her mouth as her smile took to a cruel grinning. So out of place, he'd thought frantically.

"Trickery," he whispered. "Enchantment and trickery. That's the way of it. The ways she gets to 'em, for sure."

He breathed out, opening the vehicle door, listening to the faint sound of a bell chirping, before pressing the ignition, igniting the sleek and sturdy automobile into roaring action. He pushed the heat sensor to its highest function of 90 degrees, knowing that she would ask for it, no, demand it. He would ensure that the luxurious interior was not just warm, but borderline sweltering before she stepped through the door. Pleasing her now was all he could think to do.

He remembered the first and last time he ever lay with her; it was just days after she'd turned him. A highly physical act that was never to happen again, she'd made that brutally clear. Her voice dark, trembling beneath him. "You are not the one!" she'd screamed into his face, throwing him off her with a single hand, sending him cartwheeling from the bed. Her strength only beginning to be uncorked as her mindless rage unfurled around and upon his person. *"You are not the one!"* she bellowed hurtfully into the darkened room. *"Why!"* she cried in agony. *"Damn you!* Damn your cursed blood!" she'd wailed repeatedly, her open hands flailing down upon him, clawing thin chunks of pink flesh from his hide. Her brightly polished fingernails arcing through the air continuously as he tried at first to defend himself, but too soon ended in curling into a tight ball, taking the blows as they came. The evening's pain even now, so many years past, still sharp in both memory and flesh.

Billy stepped out from the driver's side and moved to stand at the rear door, awaiting her impending arrival. She would come soon enough, he thought stoically. "Her damn blood be up and she be hotter than the July sun," he groused. But looking for a positive to all this, it may indeed mean that the 'hunt' might just be a quick one this bitterly cold evening. "One can only hope and perhaps maybe pray…" he said in a low grumble, the winter night's frigid air creeping boldly into the heated garage, working its way through him, prickling tingles buzzing lively upon his flesh. And then she was standing there. Pale and lovely upon the threshold of the entryway into the garage from the home's living area.

He'd turned just in time to see her staring at him, never hearing her; she was simply breathtaking in ways only a woman could be. Her age could not be determined so easily just by looking at her, but she appeared youthful, innocently vibrant, in a more than pleasing way. A creature the likes of she was not something he'd ever witnessed before and each time he caught sight of her still was like the very first time. A thick mane of luxurious hair fell in long shimmering waves of obsidian, framing her Renaissance face in a perfection of purely female artistry. It was as if you were seeing an old master's finished painting before anyone had the chance to lay claim to it. One's breath instantly punched out from the gut by her indescribably rare and devastatingly alluring beauty.

Billy had certainly witnessed his share of grown, hard-backed men break down to teary submission before her. Her physical person was long and dangerously lean, statuesque to lend a distinct air of nobility that she carried ever so naturally. But it was her eyes of deep cerulean blue above all else that really stole one's breath away, and for some, their soul. The moment she laid them so wantonly upon you, catching you with her broad sight, you were hers. Destined to drown in the unfathomable sea of endless blue storms, just as Billy had when they first fell upon him in those woods so long ago.

She wore a tightly fitted white turtleneck sweater that clung to her, allowing for a startlingly clear view of her well-rounded breasts, their darkened areola and nipples easily identifiable, as she rarely wore a bra. Tight black jeans and heeled leather boots made her legs seem to roll on forever. Completing her ensemble was a floor length, midnight blue, suede overcoat, which she wore tantalizingly open, as if inviting one to step right inside it with her and feel her warmth. She was simply devastating, Billy thought sadly. And some poor, struck-to-dumb man-boy, she did like them young, was going to fall head first into her deadly grasp this very evening. "A mistake they'll never get the chance to reconcile," he grumbled, an inflexible grimace spreading over his knowing features.

Billy moved swiftly, taking her arm in his own and escorting her gallantly to the rear of the vehicle, where he opened the door and helped her into its now uncomfortably warm cabin. Not a word was exchanged between them. He made his way into the driver's seat, strapping his safety belt into place then adjusting the review mirror to make sure he had clear visibility to back out… but his sight was instantly stolen away. She stared back into the compact mirror, filling it with her image. She was smiling…

He backed the rumbling Range Rover out into the blustering night's snowy covering, its low stance gripping down firmly onto the intrepid slice of ice slicked gravel. Sure footed, they made their way to the route that lay before them blanketed in white. Which the county's vast team of clearing trucks had not even begun to perform the most tertiary of snow plowing or salt dumping on. In short, the roads were eviscerated under the weight of the winter's storm. But Billy had grown more than accustomed to these mechanical miracles of the present, easing the vehicle expertly to where the road stretched out invisibly before them. Dropping the shifter into its low mode to engage the four-wheel drive system, they drove on without trepidation into the sprawling and spitting night.

"Shall we make a stop at the Cottage Hotel for a quick drink, William?" she asked lightly, her face heavily shadowed under the night's murk.

He could smell her now, her scent wildly captivating, absorbing his very sense of being. Her chosen perfume had been of late Strangelove's Dead of Night. She'd made him smell it once from the bottle and its musky amber and rose bouquet had made him almost recoil, but when she removed her robes and stood naked before him, spraying the perfume liberally upon her body, he was transfixed. The fragrance transformed into an essence that made him shiver with excitement just to recall. He remembered the evening she'd found it online, giggling like a schoolgirl at the name of both purveyor and brand. Purchasing it on sheer whim at just over $200.00 an ounce. Which she promptly bought seven one hundred milliliters bottles of. "Enough for each day of the week," she'd purred, then fell back into her unbridled laughter. The Dead of Night odor became a most intoxicating pheromone for her, one her suitors of the night could hardly resist.

"Of course, my dear," he replied amicably enough, trying to hold back the sudden strain in his voice. Playing her game as she wanted him to—demanded him to. All the while thinking that the place, the Cottage Inn and Hotel's restaurant and bar, was just far too close to home for, well, what was damn well bound to come. "Why there?" he whispered, the thought poking at him uncomfortably. This would indeed be an act well beyond reckless, and she was anything but reckless. His mind racing, the eminent danger far too obvious to ignore, knowing damn well what lie ahead. His eyes fell back to the blustering white swept road, not wanting to show her the growing fear that was crawling over him, needling and throbbing dangerously hot upon his flesh.

"Oh, and do remember, my love… to call me by my, uhm, my chosen name this evening, okay?"

He looked into the rearview mirror again, catching the blue light of her eyes, the storm simmering within. "Of course, Alaina," he answered in time, averting those eyes for the moment.

"Alaina O'Connor." She spoke out, whimsically playful. "Such a regular girl type of name, right? Even after all these years I still can't associate myself with it."

He smiled dutifully at her. "Yes, my dear, a name regular enough to fit in with the regulars certainly will never suit you entirely." He smiled brightly, his witty turn of phrase causing her to grin. The smile uncomfortably wide, showing too many sparkling white teeth, he thought. He remembered when he'd made the name Alaina O'Connor legal, placing it on the books, so to speak, all those years ago. They'd known for quite a time that they couldn't just go on calling her the foremother, or perhaps even more conspicuous, Achak, which by right, was her birth name given to her by the ancient Huron elders. A name that in translation, meant 'white spirit queen'. But back then, clerical things, like registering a new citizen with a new name, were far easier than it would in fact be in today's computerized world. A few dollars spread out here and there, to a few of the 'right' people and voila, you had a brand new, perfectly legal, birth name and identity. Alaina Ophelia O'Connor. Which the family has come to refer to her as, but only when in mixed, human company.

She turned abruptly away from the reflection in mirror, satisfied with his answer for now. In truth, she cared quite little of what any of them, the humankind, thought about her or about anything, really. *None of their kind matter*, she thought pleasantly. *They're all a means to an end.* A practicality she had been forced to endure. And the less they knew about her, name, place of origin, or even her appearance, the better. She caught her own reflection in the clouded door window. Her image intermixed with flecks of white, she leaned closer, staring just there, trying in vain to see what perhaps others saw in her, her beauty. But it was not something she found easily, even after the countless times she gazed upon herself in wonder. Her likeness in human form was still foreign to her, like looking upon another. A surprise waiting for her each time she saw the reflection. Such a lovely and delicate creature that stared back upon her. So different from the ferocity that lived within the vessel. Which brought a wicked grin to explode across her face.

And as of late, it seemed that she'd been spending more and more time in this human vessel than her true form. This point was not alarming nor frightening to her really. "Just a means to an end," she quipped to herself. "That's all it is and ever will be," she said to her reflection, watching as the signs came into glowing view beneath the vehicle's stark white headlamps. And on this night, she wanted to be seen. Seen by all of them as she now saw her reflected self. An innocent to be noticed, to perhaps be taken advantage of even... forced against her timid will.

Her smile darkened as she thought of all of them. Their musk, the heat that traveled dark beneath the flesh, awaiting her taste. "And the more local the place and its hungering and lecherous patrons, the better," she said, a burst of dark chuckling erupting from her, causing her man-child to investigate, gazing into the little mirror at her. His eyes troubled, sad. But she cared little as it was almost time. Time their local population started hiding from her rather than the other way around. Her smile beamed, brightly firing back at Billy's reflection as she licked at her reddened lips hungrily.

Billy pulled the snow-covered vehicle right up to the steps of the front entryway of the establishment. The lights from within the Cottage Hotel loomed warmly through frosted over, four-paned windows. He leapt unsteadily from the driver's side, struggling in the gusting, icy gale to open Alaina's door for her. The wind screamed and whipped up to a howl around him as he took hold of her arm, helping her out from the warm interior.

"Park this thing somewhere close by for a moment, my love, and then do come join me when it's all sorted out." She grinned prettily. "I'll be sitting at the bar all by my lonesome," she proposed teasingly, her laughter hotly breaking across the cold blasts of frigid air. Stepping lightly from his firm grasp, she moved swiftly away, agile as a gazelle.

"A gazelle with fangs," he said to her back without humor. He stood still in the blowing snow, watching her as she made her way up the slick, snow covered steps without hesitation. Entering through the delipidated doors that led into the belly of the time worn hotel and public house. Disappearing into its interior without the slightest look back.

Staring after her in the dark for time uncounted, deliberating meekly. Knowing this 'mistake' would bear significant consequences if she… "If she what?" he asked the flurrying snows that pelted down upon his exposed face and head. "If she's come to do what's in her nature to do, we're fucked," he answered himself obliquely. Knowing that the 'family boundaries' set for all within their kin to abide by would be in fact breached. And deep down, he knew the true why behind what she was doing, the point she was making by coming here, to this place on this night. A place that was in direct violation of their laws… "She's makin a damn point is what she's doin for fuck's sake, man," he breathed out puffs of white. "She never gave a damn about the laws as they be hers to make and break. And tonight, she's goin to break 'em in a big way," he proposed to the chilled air.

"And who for fucks sake is goin to stop her, boyo?" he said aloud, the reality of the situation now setting in nice and firm like. "But maybe it's just a quick drink. Maybe that's all it shall be?" he queried, unconvincingly. "Nah. She's come to make her point known."

A point she'd been wanting, needing to make for some time now. He'd been there watching her growing more and more restless, lashing out, killing without cause. Her anger and fury just boiling over.

"God help us, I can't stop her no more," he said, turning back to the automobile behind him. He could just take off and leave her. Leave her to 'the one drink' she'd promised. It was tempting—it was always tempting. But in the end, he knew just one thing clearly—no matter where he ran to, no matter how far he ran, she'd find him. And she'd make him pay dearly for his disloyalty. "Oh, so very dearly, laddiebuck," he said, jumping behind the wheel and searching for an out of the way place to park the vehicle as she'd asked him to do. Away from any prying eyes, which in this weather, wasn't all that difficult to do.

She entered the quaint little establishment in long, lithe strides, her muscles taut and trembling with giddy anticipation. The crowd was depressingly thin, but on a night the likes of this one, it was, she supposed, understandable of the weakling race. But she was pleased to see more of the local rough and ready types hadn't let a little inclement weather stop them from venturing out. Of whatever hole they lived within, she thought, gazing over the scruffy, all male patrons. All young men, both bold and brash, ready for whatever came their way. The type that craved to drink away the doldrums that plagued their pathetically inconsequential little worlds. The type that above all else sought to fulfill the fantasies that drove them out from their miserable hidey holes.

Fantasies of finding a mate. Finding that one elusive female to take for their own. By force if need be. Nothing more than fulfilling the need, the fantasy of hot, sweaty copulation. There was no desire for love; on the contrary, it was deeper, older. A carnal lust as old as the hills and she could smell it on them. Pungent and dank, filling the air, squashing the ribbons of tobacco smoke beneath its powerful musk. And she couldn't get enough of it. Breathing in deep as she scoured the small, dark barroom.

It was all so wonderfully predictable, she thought, feeling their burning eyes upon her. The jackals coming ever closer together, leaning forward, leering thirsty stares filled with a dark, lecherous hope. She meets several of their eyes before edging up to the battered and marred bar, selecting her stool carefully, wanting only to make sure the boys, or more like pack of jackals, felt she could be easily cornered. Allowing them to feel they had a chance, even before the actual hunt had begun. She sat down gingerly on the worn and rickety stool, wobbling just a little too much for show. Laughing just a little too loudly at her own clumsiness.

"Oh, shit. I guess I've had a few too many after all." She giggles. The exact mousey laugh the bratty little girl had made on the television program. The gruesome girl's patterned and soft femininity she'd been practicing repeatedly. She lifted her softly bewildered eyes to the room, making sure all had noticed. They had.

A funny thought came to her most unexpectedly as she finally sat down. After all these years, she'd never once stepped foot into this place. This Cottage Hotel. Not once. "Never shit where you eat," she said, a touch too loudly. A deep, throaty chuckle bursting from her before she could stop it. So different from the girly snickering she'd just expelled. But they hadn't noticed. Not one bit. All too preoccupied by the 'what if?' "Just a bunch of blunt instruments looking for a nice nail to pound. Am I right?" she spouted out to the room and again the grinding chuckling rose from her lips.

The boys from all around the room smiled back at her, elbowing their buddies playfully as they did so. All thinking the same thing, that perhaps this little wayward lamb has had a wee bit too much to drink? Or smoke, or who gives a shit what else? Perhaps now is longing for a stud to quell her hot, wet desires. Their smiling young faces turning quickly into the depraved hollow grins of the cat upon a well cornered mouse.

She was getting the lay of the land now, noticing that the barroom was a somewhat odd configuration. With the bar itself running the entire length of a front area just inside the doorway, and to the left was a small nesting of seating with several empty and defeated booths. Which looked to have been unoccupied since the turn of the century. She smiled at her own little joke. Then, over to the right, must have been where the action happened. The bar area opened onto a sprawling wood planked dancefloor, with an elevated platform standing behind it to host a modest sized, live singing band, which she loved the idea of. Then to the back of the dance area, there were a few pool tables intermixed with several mismatched tables and chairs for seating. And along the far wall were even more of those time worn booths to seat even more suspiciously absent bar patrons. The hotel could hold quite a crowd, she thought lightly. "If there were ever a need for such a thing. And poor little me, just one drunken little helpless lamb to satisfy all these jackals' growing hunger," she mused lightly, her own little pun quite unexpected.

She suddenly burst out with a bout of uncontrollable laughter, a real gut buster as some might think to call it. Placing several highly manicured fingers bashfully over her mouth, she feigned a rumbling, yet highly controlled, coughing spell. When she looked up again, several of the boys in the back had made their way closer to the bar. As did the handful that were already perhaps too close by. They were moving in. In for the kill. She tilted her head slightly, smiling as she breathed deeply of their scent.

By the time Billy trudged through the bar's snow blocked entranceway, two of the bolder young lads had ventured right up to where she was playfully seated. Alaina had shed her long coat and thrown it over the stool next to her. The tantalizingly curved shape of her body boldly exposed even in the bar area's diminished light. The boys were right there, all standing just a tad too close to her, hovering like large birds of prey. Making certain blatant and overt overtures, like resting a dust cracked hand upon the top of her shoulder, prodding ever so lightly, pulling her closer to them, whispers of lecherous propositions falling from saliva filled mouths.

How easy this all must be for her, he thought suddenly, desperately. "Like shootin' fish in a fuckin' barrel it be," he whispered gruffly, letting the bar doors slam to shut loudly from behind him. Their heads suddenly set to swivel, turning rapaciously to eye him up and down. The red flashing warning signs not missed by Billy, this was their lamb to feed upon and no fuckin' interlopers were welcome to the feast.

Her well-practiced theatrics were doin' the job, that much was for damn sure, he thought, just as she sprung free a flirtatiously devastating little smile to the young buck closest to her being. But what the smitten lad didn't see, chose not to see, was that smile was chock-full of large, menacingly sharp, teeth.

Billy took in the room, scanning the premises, noting another half-dozen or so more forlorn young men filling out the establishment's evening roster of enthused, 'lust stupid' patrons. Of course, this didn't include the hulking, handlebar mustache wearing bartender. He was one to watch, Billy thought.

The boys took to circling the area slowly, methodically making their way just a little closer to the 'catch', a seemingly oblivious little girl in need of some, well, some male company. Now, whether she knew that or not, wasn't really their concern; they'd take to getting what they wanted soon enough. "Or die tryin'…" he said confidently, his eyes falling over the small crowd bounding inward to form before him.

He placed his attention on the two closest to her, each in turn putting a protective hand upon her person. Billy grinned broadly; stomping the snow from his boots, he made his way up to the bar. He grabbed a stool by its leg, hoisted it up and carried it over to plop it down right there between the three of them. Then, taking a few liberties with the script they'd rehearsed, he leaned into the boy closest to him and shoved him hard against the chest. The unexpecting lad literally flew from his stool, toppling backward to land on the fatigued bar which creaked and shuddered against the boy's weight. Billy never stopped, moving abruptly between them, squeezing his large form to stop smack in front of the other, dumbstruck boy.

"All a part of the act is all," he mumbled, Alaina's eyes suddenly coming alight, her stagecraft in full melodramatic mode. She really got into this whole innocent little girl bit, he thought. "Nah, she just likes to rile her pray, get their blood nice an' high, scentin' that hot meal before it's to come," he whispered, avoiding those imploring eyes of hers.

The boy's, full of what could only be classified as indignant embarrassment, anger steaming hot in great white puffs of machismo, took the bait, the inevitable confrontation was now ripe for the picking. Billy knew that he'd set it all to motion by shoving the kid, but there was no harm in it at this point; it wasn't like they were going to just go on and let the lamb, their lamb, walk away scot-free. And she knew it just as well, all too well in fact. The boy he'd knocked from his perch on the bar stool couldn't have been more than twenty or maybe twenty-two years of age by the look of him. Billy's personal affront bringing the lad straight up, swinging his large, reddened fists.

Unfortunately, he was just a tad too slow, and just a tad too far into his cups with his buddies, to do any real damage. He swung a wildly loping right hook, which Billy dodged with ease, never even moving from the barstool he'd taken to sitting upon. So again, he placed his own large mitts on the would be, and slightly wobbly, assailant's chest and shoved into it. The scruffy faced kid literally flew off his feet backwards, careening his arms in pinwheeling fashion as he came crashing down on a cluster of unoccupied stools. A cacophony of clattering and shattering rang out, echoing loudly as the brittle stools erupted in a hailstorm of splintered shards and busted wood pieces. Bringing all the esteemed patrons of The Cottage Hotel and eatery on this fine and socially civilized evening, to attention—right quick. Billy was keen to notice that the space around him, well them really, was also closing in—right quick.

"Hey, old man!" the last boy sittin' next to Alaina shouted, his voice cracking, stretched too thin. "What the fuck you think you're doin? You better git to backin' the fuck up before you get yourself hurt!" the straight jawed boy-man warned, less than amicably. Standing up from his stool suddenly, much more adroit than his buddy, clutching an empty beer bottle in his fist. Cocking his hand back, well above his head, his lean form quivering, a rattle snake ready to strike. "What's your glitch, dad?" he asked in a hazy rasp of a whisper. "You think you's Chuck Norris or some shit?" A few dark chuckles breaking out from the now closing in crowd of Cottage Hotel devotees. "Here we are just mindin' our business, talkin' to the pretty little lady here…" his gaze falling back onto her, his other hand tightening down upon her shoulder. "And here you come all tough-guy Norris an' shit. Bustin' up the place and hurtin' Joey here to boot." the boy's voice rising, poison dripping from his venomously open mouth. His eyes moving past Billy while the rest of him remained still, his weapon of choice cocked and loaded above his head, explicitly marking him as the rest of his 'pack' closed in. The crooked grin that rolled across his face said it all; he was liking the odds unfolding around them.

He turned, still smiling to Billy, as he set the beer bottle down on the bar ever so gentle like. "Charlie, boys, get Joey up from that mess o' chairs, would yah?" he asked quietly, nodding to the young men who moved stealthily forward to do his bidding. Pulling a rather red-faced Joey out from the debris covered floor and propping him up on a stool, his head lolling forward, chin upon his chest from too much drink. Billy watched as the apparent leader of the pack ran a dark, motor oil-stained hand through his long, matted hair, then casually turned his attention back to him, awaiting his answer to what his 'glitch' actually was."

"Well, so what now, boys?" Billy asked of the group, a fatherly smile warming upon his furred mug. Turning to the boy that was giving the orders. "You must be the leader, of this here, er, what might you call yourselves? Ah, wait now, let me guess, a charitable church youth group out for an evenin' of prayer?"

A few of them snickered, but were quickly shut up by the look from their greasy haired captain whose anger was starting to get the better of him again. "What's it to you, old man?" he challenged, "who the fuck we is or ain't?" his anger seizing, as he clenched and unclenched his fists, finally dropping them to his thighs.

She turned toward Billy and with an impish smirk, nodding for him to continue. She was reveling in the moment, squeezing the tension for all it was worth.

"Hey, Grandpa? Yoo-hoo, old man!" the kid snapped at Billy, who turned his attention back to him. "Look at me when I'm speakin' to yah… yah crazy old fucker." his words trailed off, something about the look on the old guy's face didn't sit right, but he couldn't put his finger on it quite yet. "What are you, doin' here?" he asked Billy pointedly, lifting his hand, poking Billy on the shoulder. "Ain't it just a little past old-geezers' bed time at where ever the fuck place you's come from?" The question causing loud barking cackling from the boys who wound ever closer around Billy and Alaina.

Billy ignored the question all together and turned back to her, his voice never wavering. "So, this is the way you want the evening to go, my dear? This… is what we came for?" he asked her, his sincerity bordering on warning.

She stared back at him silently, her eyes filled with frosted contempt. Which he knew was in fact her own warning: 'just shut the fuck up already and get on with this or there will be true hell to pay, boyo' type o' warning. Billy nodded silently back to her, lifting his hands up palms first. "So be it, Alaina," was all he said in return.

The mustachioed bartender suddenly appeared from deep behind the bar where he'd produced a large, heavily scarred, home-made club of sorts from somewhere unseen beneath the bar's sagging counter. Slinging the make shift weapon briskly over his head, he bellowed, "Can I get you something, Dad?" grinning mysteriously beneath his heavily waxed facial hair, he unslung the 'oversized piece of kindling he was passin' off as a weapon' from his broad shoulder and pointed the thicker, business end of it toward Billy. "How 'bout a nice cup of warm milk for yah, now? That way you can piss off outta here and go back to the old folks' home and nighty-night land where you's fuckin' belong…"

A raucous laughter broke out across the room as the boy-men patrons howled in unison at the bartender's most hysterical remark. A few of the braver boys raised up their pool cues, swinging them back and forth to further egg on their colleagues, pushing the temperature of the room up just a skootch more.

Billy never took his eyes off the foremother as she was not going to back down, ever. So, he bowed his head to his queen in obedience and unquestioned capitulation. And with that, he turned his attention back to the gaggle of boys who had tightened their ranks, closing in for the kill, so to speak. He feigned his surrender, raising his hands well above his head for all to see.

"Now, boys, I'm simply here to take my granddaughter home to her worried sick mother as maybe some ah yah might ah already taken to guessin'? Yah see she's had a bit too much in the way o' the drink, we were, uhm, celebratin' and all. Yes, celebratin' her high school graduation that is…"

One of the boys, at the back of the room, wearing a grim, once red colored baseball cap backwards over his long, unruly head of hair shouted out, "How 'bout she celebrates on my cock, Grandpa?" Which in total, was really all it took to get the rest of the boys' blood up to a rolling boil, which in fact, she admittedly preferred.

And soon enough, they'd all taken to hollerin' obscene and rather egregious statements about their own inflated private parts. The night's fervor ratcheting steadily upward, slinging ever cruder sexual overtones toward Alaina and what they were promising to do with, or more accurately, to, her. Feeling strong, the force and unmatched power that a pack can so dangerously wield, they closed in, the grand finale finally within their sweat-soaked reach.

"We don't want no trouble here, lads." Billy spoke out calmly, slowly standing up from his stool. "Alaina, my dear, let's get to goin' here, your ma will be more than pleased to see yah now." He reached his hand out to her, which she simply stared at, her eyes wide, a burgeoning madness dancing there just behind the scene. "Look, fellas, let's be civil and all. Tells yah what, I'll buy yah all another round and we can just forget any of this shite ever were to happen." his voice rose and fell over the barroom. "Whatcha say boys, we got ourselves a deal?"

The leader of the little group had sat down quietly next to Alaina, when he suddenly stood up, his bar stool screeching loud across the uneven, wood-planked floors. He threw a taut forearm around her neck, yanking Alaina right up from her seat, dragging her forcefully into him. His sneering smirk quickly switched over to brutish smiles as he wrapped both of his heavily tattooed arms across her chest, thrusting himself obscenely against her backside as he did so. His open mouth flared wide as he rubbed his face into the back of her hair, scenting her roughly. A crooked line of undersized teeth the color of orange blossom, came into view as his mouth sprung blissfully all the way to open. He set his hands to caress and pull at Alaina's all too visible breasts. His laughter guttural, contagiously hot. "You ain't from around these parts, is you, pops?" he hissed, pulling Alaina tight, pressing himself lewdly into her, kneading at her breasts, turning toward the crowd so all could lay witness. "Tell yah what I'm gonna do, pops. Instead o' you buyin' us a drink," he shouted above the clamor, his voice husky, filled with dark lust, "we'll just let yah walk your wrinkly ole ass outta here right quick. That is while I'm still in the mood to letcha." He stroked one hand across her stiffened nipples as the other made its way down over her stomach to rest at the top of her jeans. "Best deal you's gettin' tonight, dad. So, I'd advise you take it whiles you can and let us men..." he paused for affect, as the boys took to hootin' and hollarin' even louder. "Us men, take care of this fine little piece o' fluff. 'Cause she's just beggin' for some o' my big-ass pole now, ain't she just?"

As he spoke he jiggled both her breasts in unison to the explosive crowd of revved up boys. And of course, Alaina, being the consummate actor, played her part to the letter. Her face filled with newfound fear, tears pouring down her pouty cheeks as she struggled against her captor who, alas, was just too powerful for her to break free from.

"That's right, kitty-cat. Me and you is gonna get along just fine this evening. I do like some fight in my women, but don't be alarmed if I fights back some too," he growled, biting down on her ear, raking his hands up and down her, slapping her breasts one after the other.

"So, you called this little slit Alaina, pops. Hmmm, I like that name. Suits the bitch just fine. But one thing's for sure, old man, and that's that little Alaina here, ain't goin nowhere. Well, nowhere until we all got a chance to break off a piece of her ass—right, boys?"

Their response was pure chaos. The proverbial shit hitting the fan as three of the boys sprung forward, shouting their battle cry as they rushed in, smashing into Billy head on, punching, kicking and tearing him down to the barroom floor where they fell upon him, holding him subdued. Billy didn't resist, never moving a muscle as they continued to punch and kick him even after he'd been pinned to the deeply splintered, wooden floor.

"Enough!" the leader suddenly shouted. In turn each boy stopping dead in their tracks instantly, releasing Billy, the room rolling to a deafening quiet. "Enough, boys. Let's not kill the old bugger now. I'm not takin' a murder rap for this ancient asshole neither." Several chirping giggles erupted but were quickly snuffed out. "Turn him the fuck over, I want him to see me." They did as they were told and flipped Billy over onto his back, darkened streaks of dirt and debris smeared generously across the entire left side of his face.

Billy stared up at the kid, unable to blink or conceal the grim feeling that fell over him.

"Aw, ain't you sweet all sad an' shit. You gonna cry?" the kid mocked, grinning capriciously as Alaina continued to wriggle around, still so much in character, *Now that's dedication*, he thought to himself. "Told yah to leave when yah could-ah, now didn't I? But you's a stubborn old fuck, ain't yah. Well, I guess you get to watch your little bitch granddaughter here, ole Alaina, in action after all," he told Billy brightly. "And if you go to make a move, even once, ole Joey here will gladly cut yah groin to throat, get me?"

The young man Billy had shoved was still holding his chest, his face a sickly yellow in color. Joey was struggling to just hold his head up let alone cut someone from stem to stern. Billy smiled sadly up at him. He turned to see his queen, Alaina, staring back at him. Showing absolutely no emotion yet goading him on, silently encouraging him to just stay the course and it would all be over soon enough. Billy breathed out, knowing he had no choice but to stay the course she'd now set, no matter how bad this were to get.

"This one isn't goin to end well," he whispered to no avail. *There's goin to be long-term cleanup of this*, he thought, stumbling to find his voice. "My Achak." he suddenly spoke, breaking the silence, a pleading tone in his cracking voice. "I know this, this episode, is, er, only just begun and all, but it doesn't have to be this way. We can just walk away. No harm no foul, it's still not too late," he implored to her softly, gently.

The room going entirely too still. The gaggle of boys confused, looking around to one another for answers.

"We can go elsewhere, my lady. Anywhere you like. And we can do this together, more private like. Please trust me when I say…"

The leader of the pack broke in before Billy could finish his heartfelt plea. "Who, or what the fuck is Achak? Are yah whacked out on old people medication or somethin'?" he cackled loudly, but no one else followed him, still lost in their own confused state. He then looked around too, his pack of jackals turning attention back to him, lasciviously grinning and drooling again on cue. "This old fuck's gone soft in the—"

The sudden nails-on-the-chalkboard squealing noise shocked everyone in the bar, heads instantly turning in unison to where the horrifying sound came from. It was like things were suddenly moving in stop motion, images staggering forward in staccato rhythm, the abhorred sounds echoing flatly across the old barroom's acoustically bereft interior. Panic falling neatly into place as those sounds became more recognizable, became more human—a human screaming in agony.

Time slowed in the moment, the rough-shot leader of the little pack holding his arm up, a fount of shooting liquid crimson replacing where his hand had just been. His eyes glassy, bulging outward like some cartoon character after a cartoon anvil was dropped upon their unexpecting cartoon head. Copious amounts of juicy red fluid jettisoned thickly into the still air, splattering unceremoniously in dotted black pools across the barroom floor.

No one moved; his screams continued and continued.

The hand that had just been seen roughly petting Alaina's breasts landed with a meaty thud at the feet of the stunned pack. The tattered flesh just below the wrist was a muddy brown color that spurted semi solid pink tissue out over the floor upon impact.

"What the fuck…" Joey managed to slur just before collapsing to the floor in an untidy heap of total unconsciousness.

Billy turned, his eyes seeking her out, still believing that he could stop this. She was standing now, right in front of the boy leader, who oddly was still trying to hold onto her with his one good hand. Her lips curved, stretching, the Cheshire grin forming across otherwise stoic features. In the moment, she appeared for all intent, picture perfect when she tore his arm off at the shoulder. Smiling wide, high school graduation photo written all over her. *Just as proud as punch*, Billy thought. The screeching began to taper off, replaced by loud gurgles and bubbling sounds as blood began to fill the boy's throat. His knees buckled under him and she cast him down, pushing him face first to the floor.

"You dare to use my name in front of these jackals?" she hissed just loud enough for Billy to hear. "You dare challenge me?" She seethed, letting her words be over pronounced, drawn out.

Billy made his way from the ground, not a soul in the place tried to hold him down. They'd each begun their own retreat, silently backing away, expressions shocked to pale. He bowed his head to her before speaking. "Please… I only want what's best for us, for you… we can stop this now," he never finished the sentence. His words hung there in the air, her expression ferocious when without warning her mouth opened to reveal a cavernous black hole lined with sparkling white, barbed teeth. Her jaw dropping downward abruptly, delicate skin ripping away, left to dangle in rubbery sheets of tangled flesh. Whited clumps of unidentifiable matter spewed outward as if shot from a cannon. Her upper body convulsing, deafening grunts and snarls cracked and snapped over the stunned quiet of the room. The little bar spinning, its patrons frenzied, stampeding over one another, blinded by fear, as the unseated shrieking erupted once more.

Her teeth glittered white as they exploded outward like gunfire, her head jerking violently back as rows of jagged, canine shaped fangs spat forth. Her once pretty mouth opening and closing in a viciously rapid motion as oversized serrated teeth clacked and clashed together in menacing rhythm. Billy stepped back too, understanding all too well that the transformation, her shifting, had only just begun. "And when she's done, god help these poor bastards…" he said, moving steadily away, knowing there was no one, or no god, that could help any of those 'poor bastards' now.

But the change never really came—not exactly anyway. It was as if she chose not to complete her full transformation, not to reveal her true identity. Billy kept his eyes glued to her, anxiously awaiting the final moment, the shape-shifting that never came to be. But what he witnessed, if it were possible, was somehow even worse. The abomination that stood, hunched before him, fleshy pink tissue dripping from its open mouth, appeared to be trapped between the beast and the human that made her whole.

He'd never seen or been exposed to anything like this before. She was indeed showing him what could be—teaching him. Her eyes stared flatly into his, glaring red as she ripped and tore the flesh of the boy that once stood before her. The sheer insanity of the moment cresting, her power just beginning to unleash itself. "Please…" was the only word he could find, his body and soul complicit, locked into all she wrought on the unwitting patrons of the evening. Smashing him down, helplessness his only comfort as he looked away, cowardly. Allowing the voracious carnage to commence and consume the once unassuming Cottage Hotel and each of its most unfortunate occupants.

She reached out, her hands sprayed sporadically with strands of coarse, glistening white hair, grabbing hold of what was left of the boy he'd thought to be their leader. Long, razor tipped fingers bent obscenely upon bulbous knuckles, latched down onto the crown of the boy's head. Billy couldn't help but notice the remnants of rose-colored nail polish, flaked and chipped over what appeared to be more claws than fingernails. She bore down hard, tugging savagely at the top of the bleeding head, as if trying to separate its scalp from the head and body it occupied. The boy's mouth suddenly shot open, his lips forming an 'O' shape as if to protest what was being done to him, but not a word was heard. Gruesomely reminding Billy of the stories he'd been told about the local Native Americans and how they scalped their enemies in battle. Preferring the dull end of a knife blade to cut the top layer of the head's scalp just beneath the hairline first, before tugging the flesh away from the unlucky scalping recipient. The sound it made sent chills down his spine while she proceeded to rip the skin back, spurting wide torrents of reddish spray and pink colored gore into the still air.

The entirety of the boy's scalp and thickly matted hair discharged almost comically. As if he'd been wearing a cheap wig all along that was surprisingly easy to remove. *"Ta da! And for my next trick, I'll remove his spleen with my bare hands!"* an oddly giddy female voice chimed into his head, followed by a series of course, barking laughter. Billy's throat closed and his stomach lurched upon hearing her voice inside his head. Great peals of laughter echoed inside of him until he caught the boy's eyes blankly staring ahead; they were screaming too. Dark red liquid drenched the boy's forehead then ran in long swerving rivulets down and over his cheeks and chin. His mouth remained open, large blots of gray colored spittle launching from it on unseen breath.

A sulfurous smell rose unimpeded over the room. Billy watched on, her laughter still ringing in his ears. She tossed the dripping mass of hair and scalp aside, eagerly driving her claws deep into the fleshy part of his exposed throat. Snapping his neck like a dried twig. He lay witness to the life-light that escaped mercifully from the boy's eyes. In her other hand, she took hold of the head just beneath its jaw, deliberately pulling upon it, a steady, swift motion that literally removed the head from its neck. A fount of blood sprayed upward as the carotid artery was severed. Laughter replaced with guttural rumbling's, as she greedily placed her thick red lips over the ragged hole where the boy's head had just sat. Grisly tearing noises coupled by aggressively loud slurps, drove Billy to a shivering panic.

The room stood eerily still in that second, nothing moved. Those who lay witness to this, this inexplicable atrocity, were simply frozen in disbelief. Shocked by the rawness of the horror unfolding right there in front of them. *"Had the music always been playing?"* Billy asked in hushed whispers as the old juke-joint Wurlitzer whirred to play its song. *An oldy but a goody*, Billy thought, when Tammy Wynette's late sixties country classic, *Stand by Your Man* spilled forth from the tinny speakers. Its swirling lyrics and harmonies well out of sync with the moment's chaos.

Billy snapped out from trance, her commands low, drenched in syrupy wet tones. "Make sure they're all still here, Wiiilll-yaahhmmm-uummm-aaahhhh… let's not let any of the little piggies loose from the barn now…" her gluttonous laughter ensuing, throwing his feet back into motion.

He quickly scanned the room, counting the pale, unhinged faces, their fate becoming an all too real reality at this point of the evening. They were all accounted for, even the bartender, Billy made sure of it. Tammy's lullaby inspired voice crooned on uninterrupted when the bartender's esteemed club fell from his hands, hitting the hard wood floor with a hollow clunking sound.

The foremother was lapping up the last bit of the meal she'd made of the boy's headless corpse. The two wrapped together, intertwined in what appeared to be almost that of a lover's, burning embrace. Only one of the lover's was headless, while the other bore a nightmarish resemblance to some hell born grotesquerie caught somewhere between a human and a wolf.

Her tongue lapped liberally at it, gulping the thick fluids that poured from the body's torn neck hole. Not unlike a rather hungry child might slurp around an ice cream cone melting in the hot sun. Her eyes dulled in deep satisfaction sprung to open upon the fallen club. Almost as if for a fleeting moment, she'd forgotten all that was around her, devoting herself selflessly upon her headless lover.

It didn't take long for her to remember, no time at all really. And it was only a matter of moments before she'd gotten at the others. Each scattering themselves about the little tavern, desperately seeking a place, any place, to hide. Ah, but they never had a chance, once she'd scented them that is. She drank deeply of their fear, and the more they panicked, moving about recklessly like their hair was set to flame, the better. The carnage unmatched by any Billy had been forced to lay testimony to, spinning up at such a feverish pitch of unfettered blood-letting, the shrill screams of those being torn to pieces while very much alive, echoing over the taverns paneled walls.

She moved with the ferocity and agility of a big cat, roaring from one shocked soul to the next. Slashing and gouging, hacking at them until each were nothing more than indiscernible chunks of twisted pink gristle, and bits of exposed white bone. She removed one boy's head clean off at the shoulders with a single swipe of her gruesomely disfigured, claw-like hand. Sending the wide-eyed head twirling in midair, leaving a trail of ominous maroon colored splashing's to mark its sudden trajectory. It landed with a wet thud, bouncing then rolling to stop just beneath one of the three pool tables. Its recently separated body stood alone, teetering in front of her, arms raised in defense, perhaps still in hopes of thwarting off the attack. She or it paused, head cocked to one side, staring curiously upon the headless figure before punching her open hand right through its chest, shattering the ribs, tearing loose a gelatinous chunk of dripping wet boy meat.

Their blood ran in thick, sluicing runnels from her body, her image beyond horrific, a blood-soaked ghoul straight out of the fourteenth century Italian writer Dante Alighieri's epic poem, *Inferno*. Pandemonium ratcheting ever upward as the last few straggling boys that still remained upright searched in vain for an exit that unfortunately, did not exist. Billy had made certain of it, blocking the establishments main entryway and the only exit with his person, which in part, also served to keep him well out of her path too. "You've made your bed boyo, now you got to lie in it amongst the slaughterin' and undead," he whispered to himself, watching as she suddenly got hold of another, tearing away his booted shin at the knee.

Time warped, wrapping itself in looping circles around the meaty havoc she'd, or they'd, set to pass. But her intensity was abating, the flagrant acts of violence subsiding, as if she were taking the time now to savor the last few kills, her blood lusting thirst slaked alas. And her prey, what was left of it, so torn and damaged, was no longer of real interest. The tavern's music as if oblivious, played on as Patsy Cline sung her moody and perhaps too appropriate hit song, *Crazy*. Billy made his way over to the last remaining survivor, stepping over the endless line of broken bodies, taking care not to slip on the offal slickened floorboards. The boy had rolled himself into an impenetrable fetal like position, his entire form shaking without reprise. Ms Cline's sultry voice rang out longingly over the execrable atrocities that now caked and coated every square inch of the bar and restaurant. *'Crazy. I'm crazy for feeling so lonely. I'm crazy. Crazy for feeling so blue...'* All but drowning out the sounds of her contented feeding, but not quite. One could still hear it, the biting, snapping and sucking at the limbs of the fallen, if one actually cared to listen. Tearing sinewy human muscle at the joint, rupturing bones loudly between her teeth while sucking upon them stingily. Mining with her tongue for the dark and meaty marrow that was nestled within. Feeding, draining them of every precious ounce of the life they had once held dear.

Billy's nerves took to jangling brightly; sweat collected across his furrowed brow as he knowingly watched the night of horror beyond horrors come to a sticky close. There was so much to do, but first, he had to reach out to the family. There was just no other way around it. They'd crossed the line. They'd broken the rules and even he wasn't sure how to clean this one up unscathed. "There's always a price for breakin' the rules and it ain't never been cheap..." he mouthed, looking across the bar at the horrifying amounts of damnable carnage he'd need to rid the little establishment of. And he would have to deal with the still quivering, lone survivor. Nudging the bartender with the toe of his boot set the boy into a screeching fit, his body flinching reflexively, trying to dig itself into the floorboards. Billy watched on, nodding with a practiced understanding.

In the past, they'd been able to save and sometimes, even convert those who may have seen or witnessed, well, shit they really shouldn't have. Shit they really should never have witnessed and lived to tell about that is. But by either dumb luck, or just an innate ability to hide better than their colleagues, some witnesses did actually survive. But the overarching question really never changed; *might they just talk?* You know, tell their horrific little tale as unbelievable as it might sound, to anyone who might take to listening? In the end, that was the way of it and both he and the rest of 'em knew it to be true. So, one way or another, alive or dead, they'd come around to seein' their way o' things. The alternative was just too damn gruesome to fathom, so they kept their mouths tightly shut. And in time, became a part, in some way, of their growing family.

Billy kicked him harder this time, the illustrious, club toting bartender of the esteemed Cottage Hotel and bar. "Ah shit. Get up, boyo if yah want to keep all yer parts intact, now," he hollered down at him. "Get the fuck up if you want to live," he insisted, knowing that she'd leave this one alone; she always left one in the end. Even she knew that they needed a person of the 'establishment', who knew their way around the joint, to help them pull off a cleansing of this size, and most unfortunate locality.

"Stop yer weepin', you little girl and git your ass up. We got a lot o' shit to do before the sun come up, now move!" he shouted, the man grew perfectly still, willing himself not to be seen. Billy took advantage of what he considered to be the quiet after the storm, pulling out his cell phone and swiping it open to ring his great, great, grandson, Ben.

Chapter Twenty-One

Terms to live (or die) by

Just before the clock struck the midnight hour, Hank had already made his way out the side door—slipping unseen into the soon to be coming morning. He'd a solid plan all laid out, finishing all the preparations earlier that same evening. He only had to wait till his Daddy concluded in listening to his evening radio program, which he finally had. Then tamp out his pipe and sip off the last of the Irish whiskey he'd poured himself earlier. "Waste not want not," he mumbled, hearing his mother's words spoken in his head.

He unlatched the door and pushed it quick like, as he'd learned to do over the years to keep the hinge squeaks to an absolute minimum. Which normally worked like a charm except of course, for this night. The damn door hinges squealed and screeched like a stuck pig. Loud enough for the whole house to hear 'em. "Shit fire," he hissed, standing stock still with the door wide open in hand. Waiting to hear the dreaded clomping of his daddy jumping up to see what, or who the hell was messin' around tryin' to get in or out of his home. He held his breath and counted slowly to ten. By the time he was done counting, not another sound was heard. He moved out onto the brick steps silently and swung the door closed, clicking the latch back into place without another sound.

He cinched the bedroll tighter around his shoulders, feeling the weight of the supplies he'd packed. "Might ah over done it a bit," he whispered. "Never can be too safe, though," he answered quickly, keeping himself moving before he had time to reconsider what it was he was even doing, heading out at this hour of the night. But he no longer wanted to think about it. Any of it. He knew exactly what he was doing and he also knew if he didn't go through with this, his plan, that is, he might never sleep again— ever. "I got to close this door once and for all and that's all there is to it," he said, looking up to the bloated moon that hung pale yellow on the night sky. It was warm even for the first part of July, rivulets of watery perspiration sliding down his back under the heavy load he now toiled to carry.

His shadow appeared behind him in long spider-like patches, exaggerating his every move. He looked over his shoulder now and again to ensure the house remained dark and still. The moon was a sliver from full, and cast a buttercream-colored light over all it touched. He slid the barn's main door partially open, just enough to let the light of the night spread across its floors. Wind looked up in his direction, immediately sensing his rider's presence. His ebony eyes glistened and sparked in the moon's waning light. Ah, he knew that adventure was damn near a foot. He always knew, Hank thought, a little unsettled.

Hank pulled the horse's blanket from Wind's gleaming flanks. Brushing him lightly, he fed the carrot nub he'd saved to his old friend while walking him out from his stall and into the dimly lit stables. Laying the saddle into place, Hank took a moment to open the bedroll he'd so thoughtfully packed just hours before. First pulling out the 16-shot Henry rifle and placing it in the proper saddle holder. He'd taken it off the mantle it had sat on ever since his granddad's funeral. He knew no one would notice it had gone to missing if he replaced it with one of the half dozen or so Winchester 54's they had lying about the house. He left the food—some deer jerky, a loaf of bread, and a satchel of ground coffee—in the bedroll sack, but pulled out the bottle of Irish whiskey that was stuffed in there a bit awkwardly. "Ah, you're a rare beauty, now ain't yah just," Hank whispered holding the bottle of Bushmills Irish whiskey up into the dim light.

Rare indeed for these parts, he thought. But his granddad always had a few cases stowed away in the containers they still imported from the homeland of Cork, Ireland. Funny, his grandpa knew full well that he and his brothers had constructed a corn liquor still out in the back woods. He'd even supplied most of the copper sheets and tubing they'd needed for its construction. Yet he never did take a drop. He'd always said, with a bit of Irish flourish, "The only liquor that passes these gums is me own mother's milk, Bushmills. The one thing the Irish ever got right." Then often adding a fatherly warning, which everyone knew he just did for show. "That shite you boys is cookin' up in them their woods will make your pecker soft and your eyes turn to dull. And there goes any chance o' my havin' any grand-babies, or better yet, any grand-babies that ain't struck blind, from the lot o' you. That is for damn sure."

Deep down, everyone also knew he was darn proud of us boys for going up against Johnny Law (as he referred to any government or official office) and their long list of insipid laws and even sillier rules. Showed we had 'a right proper pair of bull's balls.' Hank couldn't help but smile at the thought of him. And then broke into a laugh thinking about the 'soft pecker' comment. 'Cause he certainly didn't have any problems in that department, and he damn sure drank more corn liquor from that still than both his brothers combined.

He led Wind outside into the night's warm summer scented air. Wind lifted his head, turning into the breeze just as Hank did. Both appearing to be looking forward to a long run together. Hank checked his pocket watch and noted the time to be 12:46 a.m. He looked one last time back up to the main house; all was quiet and dark as he'd hoped. But he walked alongside Wind just the same for a hundred meters or so, just to be safe, before jumping up into the saddle. He had no idea when he might return, that was for sure. So, he left a note on his pillow in hopes that his ma would find it and not need to worry over him gone missing and such.

Ma,

By the time you find this note I'll hopefully be heading back home. Don't you worry about me, I'm just back in the woods is all. Tell Pa that my rifle and them coyote hides that was taken from us just ain't sittin' exactly right with me. And I'm going to make it right and bring 'em home where they belong.

See you soon.
Hank

Wind couldn't help but move the way he did. He was just all fire and brimstone when it came to running free, and the best thing Hank could do was let him get it out of his system, so to speak. So, once they hit the open fields under the light of the all but full moon, Wind took off like a shot from a rifle. And all Hank could really do was lean into the saddle, and hang on for the ride. He watched the long shadows they made flicker and stretch out behind them and listened to the thunder of Wind's hooves upon the grassy grounds. His grin was just about as wide as it could go, and he knew if his horse could grin too, he'd be doing the same about now.

They rode on that way for a time, until Wind finally eased up a bit and they took to a more reasonable pace. Hank loved this time of the morning, especially being out in the brush on his own with just his horse for company. "He's much better company than either my good for nothin' brothers, that's for damn sure. Never stop talkin' shit… chattering on about nonsense," he said, leaning over and patting Wind's generously muscled neck.

The tree line appeared just over the first set of hills, just as black as the inside of a cow's ass, he thought quietly. That anxious feeling swelling up in the pit of his stomach as it always seemed to do when he got sight of them blasted timbers. Something about it just made Hank uneasy. And it wasn't any forest that got him to feeling this way. "Shit, I practically live in the woods out back of the house," he said to Wind, who turned his head slightly, as if to listen. "No, it was these woods that done it. The Spotted Green and all the hocus-pocus shit that came with 'em…" he groused, watching as Wind's ears flickered at the change in his tone. "Yeah, boy, I know, I know. Give me the willies too," he said, patting his horse once more for reassurance.

When they came up to the edge of the forest, it was just after four in the morning. Hank tried to remember what day it was, finally landing on Tuesday after doing some clouded calculations in his head. He dismounted and tied Wind off to a barrel sized log to graze some hundred feet out from the Spotted Green's towering tree line. He approached the forest cautiously, respecting it for what he knew it to be—dangerous. Using his daddy's old Zippo lighter, he scoured the tree base before him. Looking for the sign under its flickering yellow light. The sign he'd left there just a few weeks back. And there before him it was, just as plain as day. The swirling 'H' he'd carved into the tree's wide trunk while waiting on his daddy and brothers to arrive that day. He couldn't put his finger to why, but he suddenly had the urge to finish the work he'd begun. Something just didn't feel right to him, leaving his first initial all by its lonesome like it was. He unsheathed the buck knife at his belt, just as he'd done before, and set to finishing the task he'd started some weeks prior.

When it was done, he stepped back to admire his handy work, holding the lighter up high to gain a better view. The initials, 'H.O.', stood out in stark comparison to the deeply grooved bark of the ancient tree. "Even my idiot brother Cullen could spot her from a mile off," he said with a grin, then took a moment to study the rustling branches above. Their dark leaves bristling on the low wind, the forest itself eerily alive, as if daring him to enter.

Tucking the lighter back into his trousers, he stepped up, right under the forest canopy's murky shadow. His stomach tense, he hesitated there at the edge, breathing the air deeply, trying to sense anything unusual. But there was nothing amiss here, and no foul odor assaulted him like the last time he'd stood in this exact spot. He stood there frozen, listening to the sounds of night, the lonely stir of the tall grasses being pulled along by a passing breeze.

Satisfied, Hank stepped back from the forest and made his way back to his horse, who looked up intuitively as he approached. "Yep, the coast is clear, my friend, and we're goin' on in," he said to Wind, patting his long nose before getting up in the saddle. The trailhead was all but covered over, but once inside the belly of the woods, it would be child's play to follow the trampling of tracks they'd left back then, he thought. "Back to camp. Where all this shit began," Hank mumbled, ducking his head under a low branch while steering Wind straight into the forest brush.

They arrived at the abandoned camp just before dawn. The deep tracks they'd left behind proved out perfectly, leading them right to the makeshift campground even in the pitch. Hank kicked at the stones around the long cold fire pit, watching as the tiny specks of spent ash twirled up into the thick, motionless air. The initial excitement of their journey now floundering. The humid, stifling air of the forest's interior pulling them both low. Lack of food and sleep tingling deep within his limbs. He tied Wind off to the same tree as he had before, unburdening the animal of saddle and the more human necessities he carried.

Hank got to lighting a small cook fire with the leftover twigs and branches they'd left behind. "Coffee might certainly hit the spot. And a drop ah Bushmills to take the edge off." He smiled, placing his canteen water into the charred black pan to heat over the fire's now sparking embers. He then set out two tin cups and stood the bottle of Bushmills between them on the sitting log his brothers had dragged into camp. *All in plain sight*, he thought. *Sitting there just as pretty as a picture*. Unrolling his bedding, he stretched his tired arms up and lay down. *Just for a minute*, he told himself, placing the Henry rifle across his chest, forefinger resting comfortably on its trigger.

He awoke with a start, jerking the rifle straight up to a shoulder, aiming out at an unseen target. There was something, a rustling sound that had pulled him away from his supposed light nap. He swung the business end of the weapon toward the noise, instantly startled by the large, male figure sitting there bathed in warm firelight. Holding one of the two tin cups out toward him.

"You mind pointin' that rifle o' mine anywhere else but on me? I'm just a wee bit uncomfortable lookin' down that dark hole of that damn barrel."

Hank fell back, stumbling. Trying desperately to gain his balance—pushing himself away from a now roaring fire. "Coffee's good and hot, boy, and it looks like you could use a cup, no? I'm assumin' and do correct me if I'm wrong, but yer layin' out the two tins and uh, a bottle of me favorite whiskey here, was sort o' your way of, well, of invitin' yours truly to join yah, now wasn't it?" He let out a deep chuckle and set the cup down on the ground for Hank to either take or leave. "I helped myself to the grounds there in your satchel, I just love the smell of coffee steaming over a good hot campfire. And the bottle, well she's comin' with me. But I added a touch to your cup there, boyo. So, don't be shy. Drink up."

Hank scrambled his way up unsteadily to his feet. His brain still not kicking in, acting on instinct alone, the rifle still pointed in the visitor's general direction.

"Son, I'm not gonna ask you again about pointin' that thing another way than on me. You gone deaf since the last time I seen you?"

Hank's brain finally caught up with his motor skills, and he lowered his grandfather's rifle quickly enough.

"I thank you, son. And I'm also assumin' you brought my old Henry firearm there to make a trade? With a certain Savage rifle, I took off you last time we met?" He grinned through a thick mesh of wiry, gray beard. "Ah, I knew you'd come for her. Not wantin' to trick yah and all, as you know boyo, but I had to be sure. You can understand that, can't cha?"

Hank didn't respond, his mind working its way back to their last encounter, clicking into the memory of it. A strange relief washing over him. Because it did happen. He was there. And he wasn't just 'seein' things' as his brothers had teased him about relentlessly ever since their return home.

"Lemme guess—your pa was more pissed about them coyote pelts gone to missing than this here Savage rifle being stolen off yah?" He held out Hank's rifle, its blue-black barrel glowing duskily in the fire's light. "Damn thick headed, is all. Boy always cared more about what people thought o' him than what was, in fact, important. Like this here rifle o' yours." He brought the weapon closer in, as if to inspect it. "Don't get me wrong, boy, he is my first-born son Billy Junior, and I love him more than anythin'. And miss him every wakin' minute now." Hank could hear a tinge of sorrow in his voice. "But let's face one truth between us. It couldn't ah never been him sittin' here with his dead father, now could it?" He stretched his long legs out from under himself, pushing his boots closer to the flame. "'Cause he wouldn't ah never believed it, boyo." He sighed. "No, Junior would ah made up some shit to cover for himself, not able to comprehend any o' this, 'cause it just wasn't natural to him. He just ain't able to look at what's really got to happenin', to find the truth of it and all. And he damn sure didn't understand the importance of this here rifle to you, son. Damn shame too."

The two were quiet for a while as the morning moved on to day. Although it was honestly hard to tell the difference this deep into the wood, Hank thought. He set the Henry rifle down next to him, squatting just above the ground. The tension he'd felt earlier slowly rolling out from him. But the questions now percolating inside his skull needed to be asked—and answered.

"Okay, Grandpa. I got it. Your being here and all. In the person, and you ain't some figment of my imagination neither." He broke the brooding silence, causing Billy Senior to look up from the fire. "But you is dead. I know, 'cause I buried yah. We all buried yah. Next to your brother up on that hill, two springs past." Hank shifted his feet, watching the man before him. His dead grandfather. Watching as he sat up straighter, tilting his head just a little to the right when Hank spoke to him. Doing people things. Normal things. Normal things dead people can't do. "So, you is dead and all, right? But here you are, sittin' with me just as if you really ain't. But I'm comin' around to acceptin' that this, whatever it is, just ain't natural. No, sir. But it's a fact, plain as day." Hank paused, his grandfather nodding lightly in agreement. "You also mentioned a 'truth' in all o' this. You said my Daddy wouldn't look for it, but you think that I would?"

"You is here ain't yah, boyo?" he said with a grin. "Just as I knew you'd be. And you do know why, don't cha now?" His features turning hard, staring at Hank from across the dancing fire light.

"Yeah, I'm here. I guess you was expectin' me and all…" Hank was about to continue, but was overrun with a flood of raw emotion, forcing him to turn away, his grandfather filling the gap in conversation.

"You are here, son. And the reason is plain," he said, letting his words die out against the crackling fire before continuing. "I was just kiddin' yah about the rifle, you know that don't cha? But it was a good and proper backup nonetheless. But yes, boyo, I knew you'd a comeback no matter what, and you knew it too." Billy Senior stopped talking, allowing Hank some time to recover. "The reason, well, is damn simple really—you had no choice in it is all. You, boyo, had to know." He grabbed his stick and took to stirring up the fire some more. "You had to know that you ain't gone bat-shit, mad first off. And that you did indeed see and talk with your long-passed granddaddy on that early morning just a few weeks ago now. So, you had to come back to learn the truth behind why and perhaps how all this crazy shite come to pass." He set down his untouched cup of coffee and went back to stirring the campfire's now diminishing embers.

"So, the truth, Grandpa?" Hank blurted out unexpectedly. "Tell it to me before I bust, would yah? How, or why, or whatever—I don't give two shits neither ways. Just tell me what in blue blazes is set to happenin' here? You can't just be here, sittin' all upright. Can you?" Hank was shaking when he picked up his coffee cup and drank from it deeply. Tasting the smoky whisky burning at the back of his throat. Hoping only to clear his head even just a little.

"Okay, okay now. Put your horses back in the barn so I can talk to yah here." Billy Senior breathed in. "The truth. She's all that matters, Hank. Nothin' else. But I got to warn yah, boyo, the truth ain't for the faint o' heart. That's why I chose you, son." He stared back at Hank somberly, letting his words settle in.

And for some reason, Hank had to fight back the trembling urge to walk right over to his grandpa, and well, touch him. Poke him really. So, he could see for himself if the old man might just evaporate on the wind and blow away. Just a fleeting chunk of Hank's overactive imagination. But the main problem with that was that Hank didn't have an overactive imagination. No, he had little imagination at all. Hank was a realist. A pragmatist by nature and quite frankly, had little use for silly daydreams, nor other imaginative such nonsense. But in the end, Hank took to sitting, waiting patiently for his grandpa to just get on with it already, the truth and all.

"When she turned me, son, it was like nothin' I can describe to yah that you might be able to relate to. It was a ritual of sorts, but it was somethin' a person of a more spiritual nature, more so than the two of us that's for sure, might call a profound feeling of, uh, bliss."

***

Hank had been listening to his granddaddy for close to an hour now. Spoutin' on about what he'd called the truth in all of this, but Hank just couldn't get his mind around any of it. And began to question most everything he said. "So, wait. Grandpa, you is tellin' me that you was, uhm, turned into some kinda creature right here in these very woods? The Spotted Green? And now whatever it is you are, you ain't dead no more? And in the meantime, before you became this creature, you came home to us first? And you didn't tell not a one of us?" Hank's voice rose dangerously high. "Then you just up and died come spring with the secret still tucked between them gums o' yours?" Hank pushed himself to his feet, dusting off his backside, shaking his head angrily. "That just fuckin' don't add up," he grumbled. "No, sir. And I ain't sorry to say that none of this truth shit adds up neither, Grandpa. None of it."

"Boy, take the wax outta yer ears and listen to me now." Billy Senior's voice crackled hotly. "It ain't like that. It just—it just, had to be that way is all." He set his cup aside. "I didn't just come into these woods out of the blue one-day lookin' for a run in with some kinda oversized wolf like you and your brothers just did, now did I?" He raised his hand to him, hurling his accusation toward Hank. "But truth be told, I had seen her, scented her, before. Much the way you had, am I right?"

Hank looked up, remembering the powerful odor coming from the woods that all but knocked him out of his boots.

"She found me, son. Granted, I'd been snooping around these woods ever since Ciaran and I first stepped foot in 'em back in the early days. There was always something special here and you, boyo, you've felt it too. I think you said it was like… 'it was like comin' home again'." He smiled warmly at Hank, who flushed red at remembering himself thinking that sorta soft sentiment, but never saying it. "And it is home for me, son. And the gift she's given me is this." Billy Senior stood up and turned around in a circle, his arms held out from his body. "And this, this sure as shootin' is life," he said longingly. "I only wish I could ah brought Ciaran with me, but he was already too long gone under."

Hank looked up suddenly, startled by the thought that there could be others like his grandpa roamin' around this place. "Wait, I thought it was just you? There's more of, of you?" he asked quietly, not certain how to phrase his question.

Billy Senior looked down to the fire for a moment, letting the silence in the moment build. "She's a special creature, son. A god really. And she's older then all these timbers around us, and the ground they sprung from, if the facts be told." Billy Senior's voice took on an odd quality Hank had not really heard before in his grandpa, which was profoundly unsettling. His crotchety, shoot first and ask questions never, grandfather appeared to be, well, happy. And not just a little pep in his step kind of happy, he was downright giddy when he spoke of her. "She's an ancient and beautiful being that lived well before any o' us ever did. Mankind, that is. And she's all that's left of 'em. The last of her kind. The foremother, as we've all taken to callin' her. Those that have been favored by her—her children."

Hank cut him off abruptly, putting his palm in the air. "So, there are more of you. Uhm, more of her children. How many?" he asked tersely.

"Does it really matter, son?" he answered slowly, his voice tinged with joy. "The truth of it is that we're a real family now. And I'm here, well, we're here, together like, so I can ask you just one thing. One very, very important thing. And mind you, boyo, I ain't out there askin' a bunch o' folks this one thing, neither. No sir, just you."

Hank stared at his grandfather, who walked over to him. Placing a surprisingly warm hand on his shoulder, pushing the Savage rifle into Hank's chest.

"The gun belongs to you and you alone, son. Just like I believe, you belong to these here woods. Your real home. Like it is mine," he said thoughtfully. "You see, you is more like me than any other o' my kin. And I sought you out, boyo. To ask you to join us, Hank. Join our family." He smiled, squeezing down on Hank's sagging shoulder. "That day at the edge of the wood, son? You felt it, didn't you?" Hank looked up into his grandpa's face, searching for an answer. "Yes, you did. And it was powerful as well as, well, pungent." He paused. "She'd been watchin' you, boyo. You're a natural. In almost every way to her—to us. She sensed it in you too son, just like she had with me all them years back."

Hank shrugged out from his grandfather's grip. "Wait. What? What is it you're you askin' me exactly?" he finally managed to spit out. "Just 'cause I, I uh, smelt the damn thing taking a dump doesn't mean I'm some kinda wonder boy. Or got some spiritual relation to you or it in any way. Hell's bell's grandpa if you is askin' me to come be a part o' your clan a dead folk that somehow take to still roamin' around these cursed timbers day and night, followin' behind some bitch of a dog or wolf, well shit, I can tell yah plain right here and now, that ain't never gonna happen," he shouted, his tone stretching out, exasperation painted across his every word.

"You need to watch yer tone with yers truly here, boyo. And she ain't no damn bitch of a dog. She's a god and a mother to us, and you best be rememberin' that," his grandfather countered, his tone sharpened and strained to a breaking point. "Damn it boyo, I am askin' you here and now to join together with us. But you've got the facts all twisted about in that head o' yours. We ain't some oddball bunch o' undead monsters creepin' aroun' in the dark shadows," he expounded, his voice calming. "Quite the opposite really, son. We're very much alive, but have just one true mission in this new life o' ours, and it's to protect the very ground yer standin' down on, and that's the plain truth of it. Before the whole lot o' yah up and destroy it once and for all," he said slowly, pronouncing each word emphatically. Reaching out as he spoke, taking another step closer as Hank retreated by two. "And we're goin' to be alive for however long it takes to right this world again son. And we need strong lads just like yourself. Ones ain't afraid to do what it takes to help us get there," Billy Senior finished quietly.

"You *died*! For Christ's sake. grandpa, you're dead, I know you is. We put your cold blue carcass in the got-damn' ground!" Hank exclaimed overwhelmingly, any understanding that he might have had, even thought he had was gone—drained out from him. "And now you, my granddaddy, is askin' me to die too? To join you in death so I can be part o' yer new dead people family?" He felt winded, worn thin. This was beyond too much, his ability to reason any of this closed off in an instance. And he realized that he didn't want the answers no more. The truth he'd sought and come all this way to find, no longer mattered. No sir, in fact, he didn't want any part of any of this at all. Hank, just wanted to get to gone. Gone from this place and the great man that once was his grandfather. To forget any of this ever happened and to never come back this way again.

"Son, slow yourself down some. An' just hear me out now, will yah not?" his grandfather pleaded. "Yah got to see it the ways I do, the ways I always done. 'Cause you and me, we could be a right an' proper team once more, now couldn't we just? And the two of us together, we could make a difference here—for her—for her family.

Can't yah see boyo, she needs us, can't yah get the gunk outta yer silly wee brain to understand that?"

Hank turned his back to his grandfather, bending to begin to pack up his bedroll.

"Don't you never turn your back to me, boy. Don't you never do that—I'll skin yer hide just as fast as you can take to whistlin'…"

Before Billy Senior could get another word out, Hank had spun around, cocking the hammer of his firearm and pointing the barrel just between his grandfather's steel blue eyes. "Don't cha take another step, old man. I don't care how dead or not dead you claim to be. A rifle blast to the forehead up close and personal like, well, its gonna drop you to the ground no matter who you are or what you think you is," he snapped through clenched jaw, breathing out, pushing the rifle barrel flat against his grandfather's long forehead. Seeing his grandfather fully for the first time since he'd arrived some hours back, he noticed that there was something different, something off about him. He looked younger somehow, and he wasn't wearing the old-time mountain man get up he'd been all dressed up in when they last met. He was groomed all funny too. His hair neatly combed and freshly cut, his normally unruly face whiskers all trimmed up in the fashion of the day. Wearing a new red flannel shirt and a fancy waist length sheepskin coat. Hank let his eyes move over the large, once familiar man before him, keeping his Savage rifle pressed firmly to his head. Dark blue denim pants and a pair of fur topped, calf length leather boots that tied off just below the knee, completed his outfit. He was taken back, questioning what it was he was seeing when his grandfather's voice startled him from his thoughts.

"Ah, that's right, son now ain't it? Take a good hard look at me standin' here before yah like I am now." he stated, lifting his hands up toward the trees and turning around in a loose circle. "This is what I've been tryin' to tell you, is all boyo. We is alive son. Oh, very much so. And living just as you is, we're alike you and me. But we're livin' with a purpose now, son. A real and proper plan to change—"

"We ain't nothin' alike Grandpa. Not no more." Hank stated matter-of-fact, feeling the hot tears welling in his tired eyes. "We was once… you and me… I wanted to be just like you, Grandpa. And now, I don't want nothin' to do with you, or any a what yer offerin'. I don't want no part of it." His voice creaking roughly over his words. "So, it'd be best to just let me get my things and head back the way I come. Back to my real family—to your real family, Grandpa. Who I don't got no idea how I'm to explain any o' this to…"

Billy Senior stepped closer to Hank, the rifle barrel pressing deeper into his forehead. "I'm sorry to hear it put the way you put it son, I truly am. But you ain't gonna say nothin' to nobody, boyo about me or anythin' else. You was just huntin' and come up empty, is all. You ain't gonna run yer mouth none 'cause you and I know they ain't gonna believe yah no-how. And you know that to be the truth."

Hank stepped back again, continuing the little dance they'd unintentionally begun. "I'll ask you for those pelts you done stole off us though, Grandpa. And then, well, you got my word. I won't breathe a hint o' any of this to no one no how." Hank paused to look around. "None a what all yah just took to sharin' with me." He squared his shoulders and looked his grandfather in the face. A face he'd always admired and had been trying to emulate since he was just out of short pants. "You got my word."

The quiet rose up between them again, but neither ever looked away from the other. "Okay, boyo, you got yerself a deal. This meetin' of ours never happened. And I know you'll keep your end of the bargain 'cause I, well, trust yah. Always have and always will." He pushed the barrel away from his head gruffly, and held out a large, callused hand. "Shake on it, Henry, and make it so," he said.

Hank, still unsure of what to do next, only hesitated for a second before taking his grandfather's hand in his.

"I'll give you them coyote pelts back, but you got to promise me never to show no one or take them out o' the inners of that house a yers. 'Cause she'd be none too pleased to see her kind's hide skinned and mounted for show, you get me?"

Hank really didn't get his granddad, but nodded yes, just the same. Wanting nothing more than this time with his dead yet now somehow very alive grandfather, to finally end.

"Now, here's the toughest part of it all for both of us, I reckon," he said, holding tight to Hank's hand. "Might be harder for me than you really, 'cause o' the way I feel an' all about cha, boyo. So here it is, you and me, we ain't gonna be seeing one another no more. At least not for a long while anyways. And you, son, you can never come back into these here woods." Billy Senior paused, looking into Hank's face. "And you sure as shit can't hunt no more of her kin. Ever. You tell yer pa these were the animals that got to yer livestock and I be tellin' mine own that yer livestock is now off limits." He breathed in deeply. "It ain't no longer safe for you or any a yours, to come passin' this way again, son." He looked into his Grandson's eyes. Seeing his own within. "These are her woods, now and forever like." Billy Senior spread his arms out then up toward the dense canopy of trees that surrounded them. "The Spotted Green is her family's place now. And no good will ever come to those who enter her uninvited."

Chapter Twenty-Two

Enter at your own peril

The old man didn't even hesitate when he pulled his truck up the Moyers' dirt pack driveway. Cruising right across the lawn and up to the sagging wood gate designed to keep the cows from wandering out onto the highway and getting slaughtered before it was their time to be slaughtered. "One o' you pecker-wood's get yer ass out and open that there gate now. And move like you got a purpose, would yah?"

Being closest to the door (and the furthest away from the old man's cuffing hand), Sean jostled the old truck door open and sprinted over to the gated fence. He couldn't help but notice those same cows, still standing in the same place they'd been standing when he and his friends took to the woods just the day before. *So much has happened*, he thought, his head full of adult words and all the confusing shit that the badass uncle had spewed. But here they stood. Still chewing their whatever it was they chewed and looking at him through those heavily hooded, brown eyes. Not a care in the world. Or maybe they held a secret so great, that only they, the cows of the world, knew the answer to it. Either way, they certainly didn't give a shit about him and their comings or goings.

He unstrapped the frayed rope that held the gate to shut, lifting it as he pushed it open enough so the old man's truck could pass through. Ben's grandpa threw the truck into gear, spitting fresh lawn grass and clods of dark earth up into the blue sky behind them. Sean closed the gate back and hopped into the truck's cab, Ben grabbing him by the shoulder as the old man hit the gas before he was even halfway in the truck itself. The path to their campsite they'd rode over the night before on their bikes had taken them just under three hours to get to. A special place, one they all finally agreed to, deemed the only spot worthy of such an epic campout. Ben pointed the old man in the general direction, as they launched up and over the sloping landscape, the old truck creaking and bouncing along without so much as a slip of the tires. The truck was old but tough, just like its owner.

They'd all been kinda quiet sitting shoulder to shoulder in the trucks cramped quarters. The old man chain smoking his Pall Mall's in one hand and his other, a gnarled fist wrapped tightly around the steering wheel. Now and again, if you were really looking for it, one could just make out the blur of tire tracks their bicycles had left behind the day before. Ominously showing four sets of tracks by the light of day. And when they passed the place where Franky had run one way and Ben and he the other, Sean looked over to Franky. Who had taken to just staring ahead, pretending not to notice. But Sean knew he'd seen it. And recognized the spot where things had fallen apart between them. But he wasn't going to let on to it. He turned to look over at his best friend Ben, who was sitting uncomfortably close to his grandfather, keeping himself occupied by pointing out certain areas of interest along the trail, unnecessary stuff, passing the time was all. Ben couldn't help but notice Sean's persistent glances, doing his best to just ignore him. He knew exactly what Sean was wanting—to tell the old man and Franky the rest of their story. Ben tried his best to brush him off, but to Sean, it was simply too late for secrets, and their friends very life might just depend on him, well, spilling the beans.

"Mr O'Connor?" Sean croaked hoarsely, clearing his throat after the words had already left his mouth. Ben's face turning a brilliant shade of crimson red, shaking his head, urging him to just shut the hell up already. But Sean was pretty well done with holding back, he really couldn't see a downside in telling the whole truth and nothing but. "Uh, uhm, there's something I or, uh, we need to tell you before we get all the way to our campsite Mr O'Connor. Uhm, and it's pretty important, I guess…"

The old man never took his eyes off the rolling grass lands before him, nodding once in acknowledgement. "Well, I suppose if you 'guess' it's 'important', well then shit, by all means do tell it son," was all he said in way of a response. Sean saw that as a pretty good sign, an opportunity to tell the last of it, the most fucked up bit of their already seriously fucked up story. Which truth be told, they'd pretty much left out entirely when they all but confessed to losing their pal Eddie under less than ideal circumstances the night before. And for good reason too, mostly 'cause none of it was all that easy to believe. No matter how many times Sean went over it in his head, it just sounded, for lack of a better way to say it, freakin' bat-shit crazy.

"Okay then, thank you Mr O'Connor. So, we, I mean Ben and I, sir, well, we saw it. Oh, and well, uh, we smelt it, and kinda heard it too. Not just growlin' an' stuff, but singin'. We heard uh, music and singin' and stuff."

The old man's truck rumbled to a metal-on-metal screeching stop, as he slammed his boot down hard on the brake pedal. Throwing the column shifter up into park, he killed the engine, all the while still staring straight ahead. They sat there like that in silence until the old man suddenly reached for his smokes, shaking out a fresh, well if you could call it fresh, cigarette, into his hand and firing it up with the beat-to-shit, once silver, Zippo lighter he'd had on his person for time unknown. Inhaling deeply, he turned to look over at each of the boys, who took turns looking anywhere but in the old man's general direction.

"Ain't nothin' to be ashamed a Sean, er, boys. I been in them parts o' the trees myself more times than you all idiots can count. And the truth of it is this—bad shit happens out there." He paused, then pointed his smoking cigarette in the direction they'd been heading for. "Ain't nothin' to do with what's known to be natural out there in the Spotted Green. Why do you think I been tellin' the lot a you shit-for-brains not to fuck with 'em? Now, you gonna tell me what yah think y'all saw, smelt and heard, or you gonna make me start to guessin'?"

Sean took a moment to let the old man wind down a touch. He, like his pals, was taken by surprise by the old man's surprisingly accommodating point of view. So, Sean broke the silence and took to telling the part of the story he'd been trying his hardest to forget. "Well, I, or we, smelled somethin' really freakin' awful, and then we saw a, ah, wolf—an enormous white wolf. I mean, nothin' like I'd ever seen before, even in books. It must've been some sort of mutant wolf, 'cause it was giant, man. Oh, and then we heard music, and the wolf or creature, well, it heard it too, sir. It sounded like it was actually coming from the forest, kinda like a bunch of musicians were playing right there in the woods for us, or maybe for it, uh, not really sure either way. But then the wolf, well, it sort of was smiling at me, its head bobbing up and down to the tune…"

The next half hour or so was spent sitting in the cab of that old truck, sweating. The heat was unbearable, yet the old man sat perfectly still staring straight ahead, smoking one cigarette after the next while Sean told their story. And when he felt he'd said all he could, he closed by simply saying, "And in the end, the three of us went back to Ben's house, said hello to his parents, and proceeded to demolish a wide variety of nutritious breakfast cereals."

A few more minutes passed in sweaty silence as they stared mindlessly through the windshield glass, the looming blue-gray forest just coming into view across the meandering hills. It was hard to keep from choking on the old man's secondhand smoke, the little in-dash ashtray was already overflowing with crushed and broken butts, smoldering under a thick blue haze of stale smoke. They were wiping their eyes and trying desperately not to cough from the hazy gobs of smoke that filled their lungs. With the passenger side window rolled all the way down, the three boys took turns leaning over one another to stick their heads out into the midday's hot, but smoke free, air.

Without ever saying a word, the old man crushed out his last smoke and turned the truck over. Slamming it into gear, he revved its eager engine and tore off, skidding along back in the general direction Ben had been guiding him in. But he didn't need his grandson's directions. He knew exactly where he was heading. It had been more than sixty years since he'd last passed that way, but it felt like just yesterday when he and Wind had run along this very path. Besides, *it was like comin' home again*, he thought. His granddaddy's face floating before his eyes. He couldn't help but grin at the thought of him. "Been a long while ain't it now. But I's comin' to see you just the same," he muttered quietly, each of the boys turning to look at one another, the same question poised upon their muted lips. "What?"

They bounced up over the final hill in total silence. The old man telling his grandson, who was only trying to guide him to the camp, to just stop talking already. "Shut it, boy. I don't need no directions from y'all. Shit-fire, I know this place longer than the lot o' you's been livin'."

So, they'd driven on quietly, listening to the sound of the wind and the roar of the old motor as they headed ever closer to the place where Eddie had gone missing. The trees somehow looked taller in the light of day, Sean thought. Watching them come into full view, looming gray skyscrapers that all but blotted out the blue in the sky.

"R-ri-right th-the-there," Ben called out, pointing to the peak of the hill rising before them. "R-ri-right, th-thee-there is wah-w-where we set up our c-ca-camp, Gra-gr-grandpa." But the old man only looked out his window for a quick second, nodding his head once before he gunned the accelerator, leaving the boys' campsite in a swirl of tire dust behind them. He was heading straight on, toward the great wooded expanse that now unfolded tenebrously before them. Not a word was spoken, his gaze fixed, locked on the timberline that sprawled ever closer ahead, totally consuming their view through the elderly truck's dirt-streaked windshield.

The old man finally slowed the truck, crawling along then turning to drive in parallel with the edge of the forest's bramble thick border. The boys sat stone still, feeling the clutching unease they'd long associated with the wooded lands in these parts. The old man suddenly stopping, throwing the trucks transmission into park then killing the motor for the second time. They'd come to an abrupt stop just beneath the vast timbers shadowed grove, its gloom-struck veil filtering out most of the light from the midday sun. All the air seemed to just whoosh out from the old man, deflating him to a rare slouching position. He folded his big, roughened hands loosely about the steering wheel, his eyes a hooded mask, stared off across the endless line of foreboding flora, lost in a memory not meant to be shared. "Not with the likes o' you's… well, not yet anyway," he mumbled, turning his questioning gaze onto Ben. "This about the spot you seen it, boy?" he asked his grandson tersely. Who shrugged then looked over to Sean for support.

Oddly enough, Sean had noticed that this wasn't 'about' the right spot, but the exact spot where he and Ben encountered the, well, the oversized, white canine. And had heard the strange music too. He could still make out where the tall grasses that lead up to the forest had been bent and broken, as if something very large had trampled them flat. Yes, very large indeed, Sean thought.

"I thought it might be," the old man responded quietly, never confirming his assumption with either of the boys. "Well, I guess we'd best get ourselves a better look. Let's get to it." He breathed in deep, before jolting the driver side door open. "You all stay close on my tail here and don't… and I mean this shit…" his voice grew gravelly in tone. "Don't, don't you never breech that fuckin' wood-line, Yep, that's right, this very one right here in front a y'all faces." He stabbed his middle finger at the rows of green-black trees that rose up before them. "Until I damn well say so. You get me?" he asked and demanded simultaneously, but again didn't wait for a response. "We move in as one unit, together like. And there ain't no exceptions. Not o' one. Y'all got it?" he insisted, grabbing his rifle from the metal gun rack just behind their heads.

The old man was up and out of the truck before they had a chance to even begin to process any of what they'd just been told. He jammed the hammer back on his old rifle, sighted it toward the trees, then slung it over his shoulder. Ducking quickly out from their view, heading toward the back of the truck.

It was Franky who broke the simmering silence between them. "So? Are one of you goin' to say somethin'?" he rasped, looking intently from Ben to Sean. "Is this it? Is this the place or isn't it?" His voice cracked as it went an octave or so higher. "Whatever this is or isn't, I'm not followin' his ancient ass anywhere. Especially not…" He'd just started to point a trembling finger toward the wall of trees rising threateningly beside them when Ben suddenly jumped out after the old man through the driver's side door he'd left open. A blur of commotion ensuing as he turned to run after his grandfather, disappearing without saying a single word.

Sean looked over to Franky, who appeared to be still on the verge of finishing his point when he answered his own question half-heartedly. "Well, I guess this has got to be it—the freakin' spot." Sean just nodded then put his shoulder to the inside of the passenger side door and pushed hard. The door screeched in protest, finally opening with a series of rust laden, disgruntled squeals. "I'd say we do our best to get with Ben and shit, then follow the old bastard closely. I know he's trying out his best Dirty Harry, tougher-than-nails, tough guy bullshit, but he's obviously got something of plan, which is more than we got at this point," he said, looking back upon Franky's pale, sweat streaked face.

Sean, hopped out from the truck, more than relieved to be rid of the stale cigarette and old man smells that now permeated every inch of the truck's cab. Before his feet could even touch down on the dirt, Franky was literally jammed up right behind him.

"Wait! Dude, just wait up a second, kay?" Which Sean of course obliged, stepping out onto the ground and offering Franky his hand all formal like, "My lady," he teased, to which Franky promptly slapped away his hand and the offer. Even after all the crazy, unexplainable shit they'd been through in the last twenty-four hours or so, Sean had still gotten Franky to giggle a little, which honestly, just felt good.

"What happened over there?" Franky asked, his face suddenly expressionless. "I ain't blind dude, some serious shit went down right there." He pointed directly to the area where the grass was all torn and trampled, with rolled clods of dirt and jagged rocks strewn about. Which lay in stark contrast to the rest of the overly lush, untouched greenery that surrounded the forest.

Following his gaze, the night's most bazaar events took center stage before him, jarring him back there, the thing smiling, staring at him… Franky was watching, Sean could feel his eyes, but the terrifyingly fucked up scene just continued to unfold before him anyway. The strange tune taking flight in his head, the wolf's eyes, turning upon him, measuring him, tasting him… "They were blue. Its eyes were blue," he whispered well under his breath before answering his friend.

"Yeah, you're right Franky, that's uhm, where it all went down. Right on, man, some serious freakin' shit." The images faded from Sean's memory, which was a relief, as he just didn't know if he could keep his shit together if they hadn't. "If you look at it closely, you'll see that's right where Eddie's tracks just stop—like he up and disappeared an' shit, but…" Sean hesitated, trying desperately to conjure words that simply wouldn't come.

"Tracks? Eddie's footprints?" Franky blurted angrily. "Wait, you guys never said nothin' to me about any, uh, tracks or whatever… and Eddie made them? Jesus, why didn't you guys freakin' tell me?" his voice well off-key, climbing upward to a shrilling crescendo. "So, you guys saw him? You saw Eddie there?" Franky accused, throwing his arms up in blunt exasperation. "Right fuckin' there too…" Franky sprung loose, sprinting out from around the truck.

"Woah, Franky, wait!" Sean grabbed him by the collar of his faded tee-shirt just in time to slow him down.

Franky swung around, stepping well within his friend's personal space. Knotted bunches of red-hot anger peppered his cheeks as he leaned into Sean. "You guys didn't even fuckin' tell me?"

Sean slowly backed up a step, palms up. "Look, man, I can only tell you what I know now, okay?" Franky glared at him, temperature crackling, looking more hurt than pissed really, but it was a tough call. His shoulders fell, slouching downward, eyes averted, he skulked past Sean, heading back toward the truck with his head hung low. "We need to stick together on this shit Franky," Sean called over shoulder. "Hey… stop for a second and listen, man. Let's just wait for the old man to come back, then we can all put our heads together and hatch a solid plan to find Eddie, cool?"

Franky slowed, finally stopping in mid-step, his back turned, his voice quiet—softened. "I don't get it. We're friends an' all. We tell each other every damn thing no matter what. But you guys kept this from me. Why? Why didn't you just fuckin' tell me?"

Sean looked down at the grass, delaying, not wanting to answer his question, knowing damn well why they hadn't, he threw out a stumbling response. "We were goin' to, man, I promise yah. But it got all weird an' shit, I don't know Franky, it's just complicated an…"

Franky waved him off curtly, turning back to face his old friend. "Whatever," he whispered, kicking at the dirt. They stood that way for a few uncomfortable seconds before Franky started up the conversation once more. "So, you said that you guys followed Eddie's footprints, or, uh, tracks or somethin', right?"

Sean, looked up, quickly nodding in affirmation, thankful that they'd been able to move on. On from the untold truth of the matter, which was that Ben and he had decided it best not to tell their friend what they thought had really happened to Eddie. They didn't think he would handle it well…

"So, I'm guessin' that means you guys had seen Eddie over there? Is that what you're sayin' without sayin' it?"

Sean looked his friend squarely in the eyes, then shook his head back and forth to affirm the truth, that they hadn't seen Eddie. Not at all

"What the fuck Sean? If you didn't actually see his ass, then how the hell do you know for certain it was him that made the fuckin' tracks? Or if he was even over here at all for Christ's sake?" Franky jabbed a bent finger toward the trampled area in frustration. "For fuck's sake, you guys never seen him at all?" His voice rising, pitching wildly again. "And you expect me, or better yet, any-fuckin'-body to believe that?" Franky's face glistened, an unhealthy glow brewing over his overheated features. "Those tracks could be anybody's, man. And you guys leapt to the conclusion that they were Eddie's?" He smacked his foot to the bare ground, tiny puffs of indignant dust floating up around his person. "What if you guys are fuckin' wrong? And Eddie isn't even out there?" He was shouting now, kicking savagely at the dirt and rocks.

"Franky, it was Eddie who came down here, nobody else," Sean answered calmly, surrender somber on his voice. "Ben and me, well, we followed his, Eddie's boot tracks from the campsite, to right over there." He adjusted his stance then pointed up the hill to where they'd all set up camp the night before, slowly drawing a line from it to the spot where it, whatever it was, purportedly had happened. "We never saw him, Franky. But we saw his boot prints and cigarette butts, dude. And they were his, there's no question." Sean looked to Franky, imploring him to believe it. "Do you remember what Eddie carved into the bottom of his boots? That day we all took to the trail behind his house, in the pouring rain…"

Just as Sean finished regaling Eddie's "F.U." boot tread story, which had led them to the irrefutable proof, the true reasoning behind identifying Eddie's whereabouts and potential struggle in the night, the old man was on them. "Hey, knock that shit off, right now!" he barked, making his way around the truck to where the two of them stood loosely clustered together. "Whatever you two is taken to arguin' 'bout just stow it. It means diddly-squat right here and right now, got me?" He was squinting, glaring down hard at the boys. "So, stop them gums from flappin' and go help your buddy over there carry the rest of the gear." Neither moved a muscle. "I said, find another gear—now git! Move it—pronto!"

Both Franky and Sean jerked mechanically into a fumbling motion, stiffly heading in the opposite direction of the angered old man with the rather large rifle over his shoulder. Who, in all fairness, to Sean anyway, actually did bear a striking resemblance to Clint Eastwood in the Dirty Harry picture. All squinty an' shit, ready to take to firin' in their general direction at any moment. They'd made it past the old geezer without a single bullet hole in their collective hides when they finally sighted Ben, who was trying to shoulder an enormously large, overstuffed, khaki colored duffle bag of some sort. He looked up as they approached, his face slick with a luxurious coating of shiny sweat, well reddened from exertion and of course, the sweltering heat of the day.

"Grandpa bring his pet rock collection?" Franky quipped brightly, his mood swinging upward for the better. Each of them falling into fits of nervy giggling at Franky's well-timed jibe. It felt good, the shit that had been boiling between them since this all began loosening, washing the tension away, at least for the moment. Between bouts of backslapping laughter, Ben dropped the heavy burden to the ground where it landed with a thick and grubby thud.

"Ya-y-you're n-not ga-g-gonna ba-b-believe wha-wa-what he's g-ga-got in heh-h-here."

Sean noted instantly that the faded, olive-green duffle bag was military, just by the color alone. But it also had the name 'Henry William O'Connor' stenciled in black on a hand stitched patch along its zippered opening. And just under the name it read 'Sergeant Major • U.S. Marine Corp'.

"Shit man, I didn't know that the old man was in the army?" he asked, a bit awestruck, staring at the dust covered duffle.

"Ya-y-yeah, he wah-wa-was. A ta-t-total he-he-hero in the wah-wa-war an' sh-sh-shit too," Ben answered proudly, then knelt to unzip the bag, stepping back for his pals to feast their eyes on the treasure within. In turn, each stood perfectly frozen to mute, gob-struck by Ben's big reveal. No one spoke, they just ogled on in a collective silence until Franky finally managed to push out a low and breathy whistle. Ben reached his hand in first, pulling out a long, red stick-like item. Holding it up to the sun's hot white light. Each of them stared up at what appeared to be the largest firecracker they'd ever laid eyes on. Granted, these were way beyond any average run-of-the-mill firecracker, but still... Ben's hand trembling as he held it up. "Shit, there's got to be a hundred of them, no wonder it's so fuckin' heavy," Franky squealed with delight.

Sean looked over to his buddies, his smile fading. "What the hell, man? Why is the old man carryin' around enough dynamite to annihilate an entire city in the back of his truck?" His question was a good one, and they stared at one another in a strange quiet, until both Franky and Ben burst out laughing again.

Ben placed the stick of dynamite gently back into the bag and stood up briskly. He, like the rest, didn't have an answer to why his grandpa had any of this, so he just shrugged and dusted off his hands. But the question remained with them well after their jumpy laughter had finally retreated. They took turns reaching into the open satchel, gripping hold of the precious sticks layered within. An opportunity that just didn't come along every day, and Ben sure as shit wasn't going to deny any of them of it. But his mind wandered, lost in a soupy fog, filled with the previous night's terrors; he caught himself gazing at the grassy area where things had certainly taken a turn. Its torn and matted tufts of grass turning and blowing on the liltingly hot summer breeze. He could still see it, the thing, the monster that had been sitting right there, its blue eyes gazing hungrily back at him. The dry heat of the air picking up, tossing his hair, leaving a wide trail of coldly prickling tingles rising across his sweat sodden spine.

Hank stood back. In his mind, he'd gotten the boys to finally doing something, so he took his time with it. Looking the old tree up and down, trying to place himself back in time all those years past. Not so keen on embracing some of the memories that the past carried, but still, he was amazed it was even still there. "After all this damn time…" he marveled, stepping up to run his fingers along the base of the immense, grizzled old tree. His carvings turned to a fuzzy gray, were thinner, less significant than he'd remembered them to be, but there they were. "H.O.," he whispered longingly, dragging his fingers over the carved letters. Still here, some sixty or so years later, he thought. "Damn. Has it been that long?" he asked of himself, feeling the loss of time fragile against his aging bones. Feeling the sick swell of his own limiting mortality rising to greet him. To slap him in the privates, and shout spit drenched words into his ashen face. *You're older than the dirt son! And your ass belongs to me, old man! Soon… very soon, boyo.* The voice taunting. *Unless o' course…* A haunting thought, one that had provoked him across his life, but never more than now. And as time passed, the louder the voice became. *Tick tock!* It slithered in and out darkly. *It ain't too late, boyo. It's never too late, now is it? My invite is still just as good as the day it were offered to yah…"*

He'd tried to stomp out the words, but they pulled and plucked at him, their memories hovering, closing in around him. "It was the last time I was to see or hear yah, and there ain't gonna be another time. So, you can just shut yer yammerin' trap," Hank growled at the voice and the unwanted memories that unfolded before him. Memories of when he'd last stepped beyond that tree line, into those blackened timbers towering before him. His granddaddy's face, menacingly hollow, his cold, slate blue eyes brooding in shadow. The last words they'd spoken between them, his words coming back... *"Now, here's the hardest part for both of us... might be harder for me... 'cause o' the way I feel an' all about you, boyo..."*

"You ain't real. You ain't so. It's just my imagin—"

"Gra-gr-grandpa?" Ben called out in question. His granddaddy standing there all alone, so still, his hand pressed against one of the many trees that bordered the forest. Something was wrong, something felt wrong, he thought, scrambling quickly to his grandpa's side. "He-hey, Gra-gr-grand-pa-pah?" he asked, softer this time, his pals moving in behind him, stopping at his heels. The old man still hadn't moved a muscle.

"Is he dead?" Franky asked, in a half joking half serious voice. No scurrilous giggles came forth as might have once been expected. Ben's face seemed to be filled with concern. The old man stood frozen under the timbers vast and blue shadowed canopy, head hung to low.

Ben reached out, placing a hand softly on the old man's shoulder. "Heh-h-hey..." was the only word Ben got out before the old man whirled around in a blur, grabbed his grandson by the throat with one hand, then with the other pushed him straight up off the ground to smack into the giant tree he'd just been leaning against.

Without hesitation, Sean leapt forward to help his friend. "Let him go! Mr O'Connor, get the fuck off him—your gonna—"

But before he too could finish, the old man was already releasing the boy, pulling him away from the old tree, dusting off his back with several gruff swats of the hand. "Boy, don't you never sneak up on a man like you just done. Specially one that's taken to his own thoughts and not expectin' some peckerwood to come creepin' up on 'em. Don't you know no better?" He stopped fussing over Ben, who just stood there red faced. "Don't any y'all idiots, know better?" he shouted, looking back over at the boys. "In my day, you might get yourself killed doin' just that. Or at the very least a knife cut to the belly for shitssake, boy," he belted out, the worry hanging on his face in direct conflict with his words.

Ben stared blankly at his grandfather; vibrant red blotches danced angrily about his neck where the old man's iron-like fingers had just sought to choke him out.

"What's the matter with you?" Sean shouted in frustration, standing between the two of them. "You coulda killed him! What the hell?"

Hank turned a cold gaze to Sean, the intensity of the moment growing, ripening. Then, just as suddenly, the old man's eyes softened, crinkling around the edges as he turned back to his grandson. "You got a good friend there, boy," he said, nodding in Sean's general direction. "Brave one too." A hard grin creased his weathered face. "But what he should know," he said, turning back to Ben, "is that you're a helluva lot tougher than he been givin' you credit for." With that, the old man nodded to them both, turned and walked back in the direction of where the truck was still sitting. The air seemed to cool all around them when the old man left.

"What the fuck was that?" Sean questioned Ben, who just shrugged, rubbing at the back of his neck gingerly.

"N-n-no idea," was all he said before turning to follow in his granddaddy's wide footsteps.

The three of them sat on the back of the open tailgate, hot, tired and frustrated by the old man's lack of interest in telling them much of anything now. Even after they'd spent the last hour detailing again and again, their entire night's whopper of a story for him. As he'd insisted that they do, and not to leave anything at all out—no matter how stupid-crazy it might sound.

But after all that, the old man's interest seemed to be elsewhere as he methodically arranged the sticks of dynamite inside his old gunny sack. Carefully stacking each of them gently in place to make room for a compact, time worn and well rusted can of gasoline, several tins of wooden matches, and six boxes of .30 caliber rifle ammunition. When he'd finished his arrangements, he zipped the now tidy duffle closed, then heaved it up into the back of the truck's open cab. Never saying a single word to any of them, even after they'd all stopped talking and took to staring into the day's punch-drunk, sun-bleached heat.

And when they'd tried to ask him anything like; *what was he planning on doing with all that firepower*, he just grinned his grin and stayed as cool as a cucumber. Leaving each of them to come to their own random conclusions, which according to Franky, went something like: "The old man's goin' to blow up the entire woods, set everything a blaze, and then shoot dead whatever tries to make its way outta there."

But what they hadn't seen, hadn't paid attention to, was that the old man had certainly taken a very keen interest in their story, that was a fact. No matter how fucked up it all sounded, and even with the numerous eye-rolls and snickering coming from Franky, the old man kept an alert ear. And finally, when Ben turned to his grandfather asking, "Wh-wha-what about E-ed-eddie, Gra-Grand-pa-pah? W-we-we've beh-b-been at this all mah-mah-mornin' and not even sta-st-started to look for h-h-him," he finally stopped whatever it was he'd been doing and turned to the boys.

His eyes hardened, as if cut from some kinda sparkling stones or somethin'. "We're goin' in them woods to find him. And that's the way of it," he barked, thrusting a gnarled finger at the thickened ridge of trees. "And when you goes in them tall timbers, well, you best be prepared." He nodded, slapping his big hand down hard on his old yet now full, gunny sack. "Now, let's go through it one more time... only this time, you's all be walkin' it with me. Get me?" The boys looked to one another before nodding in agreement with the old man's request. Their collective nerve showing early signs of unraveling, beyond exhausted, just wanting to get to finding their friend already.

They made their way up the hill to the now somewhat infamous campsite. Sean had shared everything and anything he could still remember of the night passed, for what honestly felt like the tenth time. Starting from the day's bright beginnings, selecting their campsite for its primo location, and well, all the other inexplicable shit that happened that night. The dusty embers from their little cook fire still smoldered as Sean, with the help of both Franky and Ben, rounded out the story—their story. Its detail growing more and more fuzzy, distant with the passing of time. Ben pointed out Eddie's spent cigarette butts and his bleared boot-prints still laying claim within the modeling of the hard-packed dirt. And alas, when he faced his granddaddy in the direction the tracks fell to, straight down the hill to the edge of the blue forest, where there appeared to have been a large disturbance in the grass, right where the old man had somehow known to park the truck, everyone just seemed to stop talking altogether. A biting wind blew in, wafting upward the scent of grass and dirt to bluster in tiny circles around them, as if they too were contemplating what to do next.

After a time, they all made their way back down the hill. Both Ben and Sean took turns pointing out rogue boot-prints that were scattered on and around the trail. Eddie's little 'F.U.' trick carving, shown obviously in the tracks of the boot, proving without a doubt that they were his. Stopping together at the "spot." Where they'd seen it, the terrifyingly large, music aficionado, wolf. "That kept starin' at me, grinnin' like some kinda hound from hell…" Sean added tentatively.

The old man bent to knee, examining the larger, more pronounced disturbances at close range. His questioning came so sudden, pressing each of them in rapid fire on their story, challenging their answers, digging deeply into every point made. In the end, he stitched all the different pieces of their story together, corroborating the strange tale, as unbelievable as it seemed, particularly now in the light of day. Sean was able to bring great dimension to the creature's physical appearance, detailing with specificity its odd demeanor, the ghostly white fur, and of course, it's immense size and body mass. But mostly, he spoke to its eyes. "The way they just drew down on me… they were frightening yeah, for sure, dangerous, hungry, but there was something more there too… they were so, so blue…" his voice hushed to whisper. "It was like it, it recognized me or some shit…"

The old man worked the area with painstaking care, flagging both the human and animal tracks. Then, looking directly at the boys, he marked several patches of a blackened substance that appeared to be liberally strewn about the muddled grasses. He used small green branches from the bole of a tree, cutting them away with his knife, then staking each stick deep into the soil to mark its location. He'd warned the boys to mind the "damn markers" 'cause they'd want to get a camera out here later to legitimize the scene and all. "Ain't no one gonna believe any one of us about no animal out here that could make tracks the size o' them. And if them spatterin's is, uh, blood…" he said, staring earnestly at each of the boys shocked faces. "Not sayin' they is or ain't, we just gonna need them to do some testin' right quick is all," he finished, pointing down first at the disproportionally large paw marks that sunk deep into the earth, then over to the suspicious looking dark patches. "So, don't go steppin' nears them markers neither," he'd shouted over his shoulder, jamming the next branch into the ground. "Besides, we need to be sure we're leavin' somthin' for the Johnny Law's to do besides pick at their round asses here, boys. 'Cause they sure as shit is just gonna fuck this all up anyhow if left to their own—that much you can bank on."

When the old man finally spoke again, the boys were passing around a canteen of hot water they'd pulled out from behind the front seat of the truck. Hot and stale as the water was, it still tasted like heaven to each of them, as the afternoon sun set the ground to shimmering in dusty, hot waves.

"Well boys, I believe we's all set to make our move," he said, picking up the duffel bag and all but tossing it over to Ben, who fumbled a little to catch it, but finally got hold of the thing. "You boys take turns toting that "package" on into them woods—yah hear me?" They looked to one another without moving, confused by the old man's request. He came around with absolute purpose, slamming and latching the truck's rear gate. Turning to look at them, which was enough to get the boys moving, but they still didn't really understand where or what it was they were supposed to do.

"Gra-gra-grand-p-pa, w-wa-where's it w-we-we're g-ga-goin' e-ex-exactly?" Ben asked meekly, dropping the heavy duffle to the dirt.

The old man stopped suddenly, turning to look square into Ben's questioning face. "Boy, you got to get them marbles out from yer mouth when you take to speakin'." His voice chiding, but not angry or mean like. The boys took turns looking to the ground, or anywhere else but in the direction of the old man. It wasn't a secret or anything like that really, they all knew how Ben struggled with stammering. The school nurse had once said it had something to do with his nerves, but it wasn't a big deal really, or so they'd thought anyway.

"I'm not lookin' to insult you, boy. But you just got to get that fixed—hear?"

Ben nodded tersely, then looked up, back into the old man's face. Bruised hurt still simmering behind his gaze. Then they all saw the old man do something they'd honestly never seen him do before. Ever. He simply stepped toward his grandson, put both arms around a somewhat shocked Ben, and hugged him tightly against himself.

"You's a good one, son. Don't let no one tell you to different," he said in a matter-of-fact tone. "You're more like me than my shit-for-brains son is, that's for damn sure." And when Ben took to grinning, they all did the same, his grandpa patting him on the back, as he began to unleash his long-awaited plan to a captive, yet happy, little entourage.

They listened intently as the old man began by admonishing them once again. But even that beat the alternative of not knowing what they were doing. "Now, boys, listen up and clean the shit out o' yer ears, 'cause we got to get a move on." The boys gathered around the old man, nodding in all the right places, eager to get to searching for Eddie. "Y'all been mumblin' and scratchin' yourselves about this here firepower I got at the ready." He grinned as he leaned over to take the satchel off his grandson's sagging shoulder. "I'll handle it for now, son, but you boys will be carrying it in, not me." They all felt a bit of swollen pride in the moment when the old man led them to sit under an enormous elm tree that rimmed the forest-line.

They sat in a circle just a few feet from where the wolf, or apparition of one, had shown itself the night before. The old man leaned in close, as if to tell them some sort of intimate secret. "You see that carvin' just above your heads there, boys?" The old man threw his hand up to point out some scratch marks cut into the old elm tree.

"What's an H.O.?" Franky asked, innocently enough.

The old man turned, grinning all lopsided, like some drunken fool might. "H.O.? What you think it stand for, boy?" he asked, letting the question hang out there, savoring the moment. "Well?" he probed, still beaming manically. No one answered. "Well shit, you's all a bunch a dullard's now ain't cha? It stands for Hank O'Connor. H.! O.! For Christ's sake, what'd you think it stood for?" he asked of them a little too cheerfully. To which no one answered, still not following what any of this had to do with anything. "Cut these here initials into that timber myself—Christ must ah been at least sixty some years ago now."

They took turns looking from him, then back to the carving on the tree, still without saying anything. Waiting for the old man to explain what it was they were looking at and why. Which he didn't, not right away that is.

"So? I mean, uhm, well, so what?" Franky mumbled, clearing the way for some well needed explanation.

"So, what? So, what!?" the old man snapped back at them. "That's all the lot o' you's is gettin' from this here carvin'?" He was still pointing at the time-faded initials he'd scratched onto the venerable elm tree many, many years ago. "Ah, for the love of Pete, you still don't get it, do yah?" his voice rising, leveling his question right at Franky. Who just stared back at him in wonder. "Well shit then, let me just explain it like you was simple an' such. Which I'm startin' to believe y'all is. I carved them initials o' mine more than sixty years back, right here. In this very spot. And I brung us right here, to this very place. You all see some relevance in any o' that?" He let his words, his question, sink in—still nothing. "This be the exact same spot where you all, or most y'all, had damn well seen it, comprende?" He exhaled hard and loud. "And this is, or was, well, the exact spot I seen it too."

The old man's breath hitched for just a second, his eyes wandering, glancing back and forth, then back to the tree again.

"Well, that ain't quite right, really now is it?" he spoke quietly. "'Cause I ain't never truly seen it but I did hear and even smell that son of a bitch, that much is for damn certain," he said, letting out a low whistling breath. "These woods, they is cursed and that's the truth of it, and I knew it back then just as I knows it now standin' right here beside her. And that's why I believed you when yah done told me your story." He turned back to them, his eyes ablaze. "This here woods is called The Spotted Green, what it's mostly always been called I reckon. Ever since my own granddaddy and his brother laid claim to her that is. They'd named it such on account o', well, all the strange shit they'd seen in them trees. Things they spotted between the green leaves, or so the story goes. Well, at least that's the way I'd been told it to be," he spoke slowly, watching the boys, their faces blank—quickly filling up with questions yet to be answered.

He held up his hand just the same, signaling for them to 'hold their water' and let him continue without no damn interruptions, which they'd each been prone to do. "You see, my brothers and me been deep in the back o' them woods more than just a handful o' times. I guess we'd come to learn the hard way that them damn trees held their own sort of secrets. And even after my pa and his pa too told us not to get to wanderin' around in 'em, well, we still didn't take to listenin'. Nah, we was o' pigheaded lot, but it didn't take all that long before we actually got our fill o' her. Hard to describe really, we'd all seen and experienced shit we couldn't never explain none out there, but the night I took it upon myself to get me some answers, well sir, to this day, I still wish I'd never gone and done it."

The boys sat still, all eyes on the old man as he took to telling his story.

"You see me and Wind, my stallion back then, helluv an animal, we saddled up one moon bright night and rode ourselves right into the heart o' them damn trees, real deep in, if you take my meaning. All in hopes o' solvin' a riddle I'd been given over to by my granddaddy. Actually lookin' for a sit down with ole William O'Connor Senior himself, who I had suspicion to believe had come to livin' back there in them woods."

Ben looked around, "Wah-wa-wait, your gr-gra-grand-da-dad l-li-lived in the wah-wo-woods?" he asked, not following the old man at all.

"Yes, sir, he did at that after a time. Right out there," he said, throwing a glance over to the dark forest wall. "Your great, great grandpa William, or Billy Senior as he was better known as in these parts, and what we was told to call him when we was growin' up, had, er, taken to livin' in the wild, so to speak."

Ben nodded uncomfortably, remembering the stories of his infamous shoot first and never ask questions, old-timey relative. The splotchy black and white photo that bore the resemblance of a great bear of a man, with an unruly, bristling white beard, and a gaze as hard as iron that stared unflinchingly into the camera lens, still hung in a place of prominence in his family's living room.

"Well, the kicker to my story is a bit of a humdinger now…" he paused, clearing his throat. "Uh, yah see, odd thing of it was, my granddaddy had already been dead for the better part of two years when I seen him again. Just about a mile or so back in these here woods. Yes sir, he was walkin', talkin', an' breathin', just like we all is right here and now.

Franky couldn't help but giggle, it was just his nature when his nerves got the better of him. But the old man's fierce blue eyes struck out to land upon him, pushing any urge of laughing right back down his gullet with a loud gulping sound.

"There's always more to the story than just the one side that be tellin' it," the old man grumbled. "None o' this shit sounds to be true, I know," he stated flatly, staring back at Ben and then Sean. "But it is true lads, hand to God it is. And well, that's why your story, from the night just past, it just fits in with it real fine an' all." His words hung thick between them for a time, the boys each taking to looking down at their sneakers. "There's some powerful magic in these parts, always has been. Old magic some say—" he stopped suddenly, turning his gaze back to the woods. "And that wolf y'all think yah just might o' seen?" He turned back to the three of them again. "Well, that great white bitch is real and it's pure evil. Plain and simple. And she's at the center o' all this shit, includin' your friend gone to missin'.

"My own granddaddy was, as he told me in his own words, 'turned' by the bitch herself. Turned into some kinda undead creature o' sorts," he intoned, letting his words settle heavily on the air. "And the one thing I know for certain, is that she's more than just an overgrown wolf or some kinda dumb animal taken to roamin' these parts. No, she's much more than that, and she turned my granddaddy into one o' her own and that's a fact. Seen it fer myself with my own two eyes. He'd called it 'the favor', that's what she give you when she turns yah into somethin' that can keep to livin' even after they dead an' all. Ah shit, I can't rightly recall much more than that, guessin' I just don't care to no more. Thought I'd left all this shit behind when I left them trees for good all those years ago," he told them, his voice tapering to a whisper.

"Well, until all this new shit here happened with your friend and all." He cast his eyes down before continuing. "The beast, he'd taken to callin' the 'foremother', she, from what I could understand, was more than likely the mother to all this evil doin'. And when she took to favorin' some poor sad sack, she turns 'em into somethin' unlike what's natural in this here world of ours. And in exchange, they be given unlimited time on god's green Earth to do her biddin' and none other. To serve her and the family she's took to creatin'. A family of un-christian like creatures that is."

"Wait, wait… what? Are we talking about an army of undead? Like vampires or zombies, or some shit? Your grandfather was, or is, an undead, er, monster?" Sean asked so suddenly, he flinched at his own voice and the possibility, of course, of being swatted by the old man.

But thankfully, no swatting came his way. In fact, the old man took a minute to pause, leaning back against the tree he'd initialed way back when, a low winded sigh escaping him. "I don't claim to know what they is, or they ain't. They just ain't dead no more," he spoke quietly, as if exhausted by his own thoughts. "See, I buried my grandfather in the spring, two years prior to me sittin' there jawin' with him right back there in them cursed timbers. I'd put his cold, blue corpse in the ground and shoveled the six-foot deep hole closed myself," he said, his voice rising a little more than any of them were comfortable with. Then he waved his hand to the three of them.

"You're all missin' my point. You see, whatever it is you want to call him or them, they simply ain't human no more. But my granddaddy, well, he was more like a recruiter o' sorts." He stopped briefly to contemplate his next words. "Yeah, he was dead an' all, but he looked just the same as I remembered him to look. Maybe even a little better? Like he'd been well fed or somethin'." He flashed a tepid grin around to them. "But he was, well, recruitin' folks for her—the wolf and her, er, family. Tryin' to increase their rank and file if you will." He paused, chewing on his troubled thoughts. "That's what our meetin' in them woods was all about, really. My grandpa, already dead an' all like I explained, was wantin' me to join him and the rest of them un-naturals, and that's, well, just the hard-fact of the matter." He looked across at the boys sitting before him, eyes wide, mouths hung to open.

"But you said no, right? Right, Mr O'Connor?" Franky asked tentatively, sounding more spooked then perhaps he'd intended.

"Well, I'm sittin' right here, ain't I? And I sure as shit ain't lookin' or feelin' no better than my true years. I'm eighty-six years old if I ain't a day. And I feel every shitty inch o' them years, trust me on that one."

The strangeness of the conversation caused the group to grow quiet, ruminating uncomfortably. Each trying to unwind their versions of the events past, and how, if at all, any of this had anything to do with Eddie, who'd been missing for more than eighteen hours now. His unsettling disappearance bringing the unlikely quartet together, here in this place.

"My belief," the old man whispered, breaking open the silent air between them. "Is that they got to your friend there, Eddie. And they've taken him against his will back into the wood, keepin' him hidden deep in there somewhere." The old man grabbed up a fallen branch and started scratching at the dirt between them. "They is just waitin' for now. Waitin' for the dust to clear up and people to go back about their business so they can, uh, change him. That is, give him the favor and what not."

The quiet that settled over them was deafening, no one really believing, but… "Mr O'Connor? So, you think that the wolf mother, the one we seen and well, kinda experienced last night, took Eddie, but didn't hurt him?" Sean asked, deliberately over pronouncing his words, wanting to rationalize what he could. Trying to lay the puzzle pieces into place, to get Eddie back if the old man was indeed right about the way of things out there. Before he could answer, Sean was asking another question that had oddly, not been on anyone else's mind. "No offense, sir…" his words shaky at first. "But don't you think we should get the authorities out here? Tell them what we know and show them all those prints and, well, other stuff?" he asked, his voice cracking. "Maybe we shouldn't be doin' any of this ourselves? I mean, we barely made it out of here last night and Eddie's still missing and that might be his freakin' blood—"

The old man spoke over Sean abruptly. "You boys is out here for one reason and the facts don't lie to yah if you just listen to 'em. Ain't no lawmen, or parent, or any other folks, gonna believe a word o' what you been tellin' me all mornin'." He dropped the stick, clapping the powdery dirt from his hands. "But know this, I do believe you, boys. 'Cause I know what you seen out here is real. And I know what the Spotted Green is from my own experiences with her. And we—just us—got to do the job of real men today." He nodded curtly toward them, his features grim, pulled tight.

"But what if Eddie's really hurt out there? Or the wolf has killed him, or turned him into, uh, the whatever you called it? What can we do?" Sean probed, his growing fears bubbling to the surface all too quickly.

"Damn, boy," the old man practically shouted. "That's what I've been sayin' all along, ain't you listenin'? It's just us now. And we're the only ones that can do a damn thin' about it. And just maybe, put an end to it once an' for all." He slapped his hand down on gunny sack that sat in the center of their little circle. "Let me ask you this, you boys know about uh, nature and all, don't cha? You've been grown in these parts, right?" Each of them took a moment to think, then nodded to the truth of it. "Okay, you seen a kill-spot anywhere?" He paused. "You know what I'm askin' yah don't cha? Don't play coy with me. You seen anything beyond a couple o' tiny wet patches that says your friend might o' met with a more natural-like ending? And to the point, yah don't see no body, nor body parts neither do yah? That's right, and we scoured the entire area all mornin' and afternoon, now didn't we? Shit. What you think, I was just doin' all this for fun?" he stated, his voice strained over, a foreboding unease falling between them.

"And that's exactly why we got to go in alone and if your friend Eddie be in there, hurt or not, I'll track 'em and I'll find 'em. That much I can assure yah of. But if they already turned him, we got ourselves bigger troubles, don't we?" He paused to catch his dust-choked breath. "So, in the end, we got us a chance to finish this. Shit, I shoulda finished it a long time back, just blow up the nest of 'em once an for all. And now, if your friend be one of 'em, you don't want him back no how. And if he ain't, we'll get his ass and bring him back with us." With that, the old man stood, straightening to glare at them one after the next. "The plan, is to go in right here…" He kicked at the lines he'd scratched in the dirt, a crude sort of map taking shape. "We track it from where them paw prints edge the forest rim, all the way to where they end. And I know just as sure as shootin' where that be." He drew a steady finger along the entirety of the main path he'd sketched in the dirt. "We take this here game trail straight in, 'bout a mile or so, then we'll come upon a steep incline, an area with plenty of stacked rocks and old cavern's and such—perfect for settin' in our explosives. I'm pretty sure if they is holed up anywhere, they'd be holed up in them caves. And if we're goin' to find Eddie, that's where they'd be keepin' him, which happens to be the same spot where I'd met my two years in the grave, yet still walkin' and talkin' Granddaddy, all them years back…"

He pointed to the X he'd made at the far end of the dirt scratched map, his voice never wavering in the slightest as he finished the plan he'd outlined, until that is, another spoke out from somewhere, somewhere beyond their little circle.

"No, son. You ain't doin' none ah that and you know it to be true. 'Cause you give me yer word…" The voice, baritone deep, poured out from the forest's stretching shadow. Each of the boys jumping, scrambling backward in crablike unison. "What the fuck?" Franky squealed, pushing himself even further away from the trees. But the old man, he never moved at all, not an inch. He stood still, tossing the stick he'd been using to draw with to the ground, slowly and deliberately clapping the dirt from his hands. The boys, finally able to get to their feet, backpedaled quickly away from the mysterious voice that seemed to have just sprung forth from the trees.

"I thought you might come back here, boyo." The strange voice from the woods spoke rather plainly. "And I bet yah come for the young one that took to missin' ain't cha?" The air was completely still when the old man began to turn, his movements slow, methodical, as he turned toward it. "Well, I can't say that I blame yah none on that score, but yah might be getting' in deeper than yah like if you take my meanin' and such." The old man remained silent as he faced the forest wall. "Ah, but I'll be damned if it doesn't do my old heart good to see you again, boyo…"

The old man moved suddenly to shoulder his rifle, pointing it over the stagger of green brush that surrounded them in a heartbeat. Just as a piercing sound broke through the air, so sudden, so utterly foreign to the wild land they stood upon. This time they all jumped, including the old man. Another blast set the boys flat to the ground on their stomachs, as the now familiar screeching of a siren horn blared to trample out any other sound. And as if on cue, two hulking Ford Broncos in matching black and white came roaring upon them. Tires screeched as each dug all four wheels to grip at the loose grounds, throwing enough debris into the air to dim the sun from their eyes. Finally coming to a skidding stop right alongside the old man's pickup truck. A third vehicle appeared, cresting the hill way too fast, crunching and tearing its way through the tall grasses, slamming to a halt right atop where they'd all just been sitting.

Vehicle doors popping to open from all sides, letting loose a steady stream of Ontario County Police from their official looking vehicles. Amplified through what turned out to be a battery-operated bullhorn, an officer declared their arrival with mechanical authority. His clipped authoritative voice just loud enough to be heard over the wail from the sirens that they'd found somehow necessary to keep rolling. "Put the rifle down and place your hands on top of your head and turn to me," the officer commanded, his voice echoing back and forth across the thick band of trees that lay before them. The boys stayed on the ground, trying to make out what was happening while covering their ears against the deafening blast of the sirens. "Sir. I will not ask you again. Put down your weapon and turn to me. Hands above your head." Several law officers were now closing in around the one speaking, making a show in drawing their weapons while the others positioned themselves behind the many open doors of their glistening, well out of place, police vehicles.

"Dad?" A woman's voice rose above the commotion just as the sirens were finally cut off. "Dad!" Her lovely voice rang out again. "What? Uh, what are you doing out here? Ben, is that you honey?" Ben's mother's voice chimed in, dripping with a serious dose of motherly concern. Mrs O'Connor, Ben's grandmother, appeared by her side. She was wringing nervous hands against what looked to be the same bright blue baking apron she was wearing earlier that very morning. Both women stepping out from behind the authorities' rather over the top cover of the situation.

Ben stood up first, hands in the air, relief washing over his face as he looked back at them. He worshipped his grandpa, and would have, for all intent, followed him to the end of the Earth and back, but this, this scene, the firearms, the wolves and walking dead, was all just too much. More than he could take any more as he began to trot then run to where the two women stood calling to him.

But something was pulling at him, causing him to slow down, stumbling to a standstill. The feeling was so powerful that he instinctively turned around right as Franky sprinted by him, beelining for the officer's car closest to them. "Se-se-sean… wha-wa-w-where is…"

He suddenly noticed that his grandpa was still standing in the same spot along the deep forests edge. He hadn't done anything bad really, yet the cops were acting like he was some kinda terrorist or somethin', he thought. The old man had positioned his rifle against his side, both hands wrapped loosely around it, index finger rigid just above the trigger. He was grinning… all Clint Eastwood style and shit.

Ben's brain jumped back to the "feeling" that had held him, his friend... he turned to look for Sean, noticing instantly that he was no longer lying flat on the ground where he'd just left him. The policeman with the bullhorn was all motion, moving in on his grandfather quickly, followed by two heavily armed look-a-like officers. He heard his grandmother shout to them.

"Ah shit-fire. Don't you hurt that man, he's just tryin' to help is all! Oh, for Pete's sake, come on now, even you all can see that, can't-cha?"

The sweetness in her voice, causing the police men to pause with their firearms still trained on the now grinning old man.

Ben felt an odd sense of panic as he scoured the tree line for Sean, like he'd just up and literally vanished. "How c-ca-could that fuh-fha-fuckin' b-b-be-be?" he whispered breathlessly, subtle movement to his right catching at the corner of his eye. The trees shadows elongated, stretching to take their rightful place under the afternoon's waning sun. A blur of movement in the lower thicket again catching Ben's eye. Turning his attention toward it, watching as several branched limbs quivered then took to shaking. Something was stirring at the base of the tree line. He moved with purpose, ignoring his mother's questioning glances, to where he believed his friend might just be. "A-and he might j-ju-just b-be in tra-tra-trouble..." he told himself, picking up the pace, running toward the forests edge where something or someone was causing those trees to tremble.

Lost in his own troubling thoughts, Ben couldn't help but grin when Sean suddenly appeared before him. "Sh-sh-sean! W-wa-what the..." he shouted, his mind racing, senses on high-alert, he could almost feel the impending danger his friend was about to step into. Sean appeared to be standing alone, there wasn't a soul around him, yet he was—he was talking? Ben thought, he's even gesticulating with his hands as if trying to get his point across to what looked to be a, well, a tree?

Then something moved out from the brush, catching Ben by surprise. He stumbled, realizing that someone, or more accurately, 'the someone', was clearly the person Sean was speaking to. A large adult male stepped forward, out from the scrub trees and their bushy obscurity, placing a firm hand down upon Sean's shoulder. "Wha-wa-what the h-he-hell—Sean!" Ben shouted, rushing up to the two of them, well out of breath as the strange man lifted his large head, a set of piercing blue eyes locking onto his own. Recognition lighting across the elderly man's bearded face. Ben froze, his mind confused, he couldn't speak, or look away from the massive, blue-eyed stranger. Then, just as natural as can be, he smiled warmly back at Ben. But something else suddenly caught the man's eye, his features darkening, the pleasing smile he'd just shown disappearing as he stepped back, vanishing quickly into the dense wood. For the briefest of seconds, Ben had somehow connected with the man, he was so oddly familiar, yet, more than that. Much more than that really,

Ben thought, knowing somehow, almost instinctively that the stranger in the woods was his kin.

Ben's legs just gave way at the thought of it, dropping him down right there on the dirt. Those blue eyes dancing brightly before him, boldly gleaming with undiscovered mischievous… They held a secret. "H-he kn-kn-knew me…" he mumbled. "Ah man, it's tr-tr-true. It's all fuh-fu-fuckin' tr-tr-true," he whispered. Sean made his way over to his friend, placing a shaking hand on his back, then plopped down beside him. "Ii-ii-it wah-wa-was him, wah-wa-wasn't it?" Sean looked over at Ben, and then looked to the ground and nodded silently. "H-h-he was tah-ta-talkin' to m-my gra-gran-fah-father just now—it wah-was h-h-him." The resemblance to the larger-than-life image captured and held still in the old tin-type photo that hung above the mantel in their living room, was simply uncanny. Ben knew every detail of that old photo, remembering every line on the old mountain of a man's face. "Sh-Sh-Sean, wah-wa-what d-d-did he sa-say to y-y-you?" he asked, Sean choosing not to answer, just shook his head slowly while staring at the dirt beneath his feet.

Ben suddenly felt jittery, his stomach lurching uncomfortably as he laid himself out on the ground. He watched as Sean got up and wandered back toward the forest, gazing upward now and again into the blackened rows of murky, grey trees. He appeared to be lost in deep thought, as if contemplating something of great magnitude. Long green leaves hung above him, wavering gently on a breeze that didn't seem to exist. Nothing else moved. Then, as if from a distant world, he heard his grandmother, calling out over the silence that had now taken back its rightful place out here in the wilderness. Calling to his grandfather.

"Please, Henry, do as they're askin' you to do, would you? Just put that gosh-darn Savage rifle o' yours to the ground and come on home with me now."

The brutish tension that had driven the men to the brink of violence seemed to melt away in an instant upon her words. "I won't be askin' you again, husband, now put it down before one o' these yahoo soldier boys take you seriously and starts shootin' at-cha."

The old man, rarely, if ever, listened to anyone, but when it came to his wife, the one true love of his rather cantankerous existence, well, that was a different story entirely. He looked at her and her only, doing what she'd asked of him, dropping his old rifle down to the sun-soaked dirt, grinning all the while.

***

Richie watched the scene with keen interest, slouching further down in the back of the cop's car. A place he'd not wanted to be by any stretch of the imagination, but to witness this shit unfolding, well, everyone has a price, even ole Richie, he thought wildly. He was tense, coiled up like a cobra, ready to spring to life, a hair-trigger fuse just waiting to pop. He still couldn't really believe that his daddy had left him behind and all. And worse yet, taken the side of them three idiot kids. "Not a one pubic hair between the lot o' them fuck-heads neither…" he groused, feeling the simmering fury, sipping on its fire—the temptation burning at him, pushing him on.

When his mom and sister jumped from the car, he'd purposely stayed behind claiming it was better if he didn't get involved in all the nonsense them boys had cooked up. Dragging their grandpa into it all was just bad enough now, wasn't it? He'd told his mother so, and she'd looked at him and nodded in understanding. Truth being, he just preferred to watch them all wet-shit the ole bed from the anonymity and comfort of the cushioned backseat of the cop car. "That way when their sorry asses get hauled in, well, I'll be right here in the cat-bird seat, now won't I?"

He snickered at the thought of it all, until his thoughts shifted, growing dark as they often did. "But I ain't never gonna forgive that old fuck for this one—no sir, never." He seethed, his hot breath clouding the deeply marred plexiglass divider that separated the front and back seats of the police vehicle. "More like separating the good guys from them bad ones as they rode together, justice just waitin' to be served. But not for me though…" Richie mused, a cackle of a laugh breaking his sudden moodiness.

"I ain't headin' back to no institution for nothin' or nobody no time soon—I done my fuckin' time," he advised, straightening up just enough to peer over the front seat, watching as the old man turned, his mom's shrill voice touching down in his ear. He knew that look of his dad's, the one that he held special for just about anyone but him. The only look he ever gave to him was more like something you might equate with a bad case of the runny shits, or feeling the powerfully sickening effects of too much cheap whisky the morning after. "A grimace," he whispered thoughtfully. "Old fucker never wanted to see me comin', only time he'd be close to glad was when I was goin." He grinned at the thought, sucking back the hurt as he had for most all his troubled years.

Something moved along the tree line. A subtle fluttering of branches deep in the brush made the trees' leaves come to shiver. Just enough to catch one's eye. "Well, an eye that knows what to look for, that is," he whispered to himself knowingly. "An eye that's more tuned into the things that move along the undercurrent, slithering here and there, lurking—just waitin' to strike," he stated emphatically. He could almost see the predator that hid behind those trees, almost. But he had always been able to 'see' what others couldn't, it was like some sort of sixth sense or some shit, he thought absently. And his old man, well, he'd noticed it too. Noticed that ole Richie was sorta special in that way o' seeing things in nature, down deep in them dark trees. But did he ever throw him a bone? An encouraging word about his, well, his gift of second sight? "Not once," he answered, indignation settling into a nice hot boil.

Had he ever shown some interest, even just a little, he might have pursued his rather unique talent in a more legitimate way. And things might have been different too… "But he didn't," he stated as a matter of fact, as he'd learned to do often enough over the years. But the old man did know it. He knew that he was better in the bush than anyone else in these parts, including himself. "Damn straight. In them woods, or any wild place you get to, I am the top dog-gone predator. End o' fuckin' story." He was shouting now. Hammering both fists down on the car seat, a single thick runner of white spittle rolling down his chin. He pounded relentlessly on the car's springy seat until the tears that had wanted to come, needed to come, finally did.

Richie's old man was a true woodsman in every sense of the word. As was his pappy and his before that. "It was in the blood," he mumbled, a cold calm coming back over him as he watched the trees. "Not like them weekend fairies that get all dressed up in their expensive gear to go campin' in a fuckin' kiddie park type, no sir—a real outdoorsman if there ever was one," he reflected, whispering quietly. "And he respected the land that God saw to give us and everything on, in, or under it, too—just as his daddy before him did and so on and so forth." Richie sighed. It was a good feeling in knowing he had a place in the family, that he shared the O'Conner outdoorsmen gene. And he had the accolades and gold-colored trophies to prove it. As a kid, he'd won just about every contest he'd entered, from the National Junior Outdoorsman to the American Legion Marksman awards—when it came to huntin', fishin', trappin' and shootin', Richie just flat-out outshone his peers and even some of the adults too. And when he was grown, he'd become known for his skills in these parts and even became one of the most well-respected hunting and fishing guides across the entire New York State tri-county area. Well, that was if you could stand to be around him for any extended period, that is.

You see, Richie was not exactly what one might call, well, humble, or even the slightest bit subtle. No, his demeanor, as some said, was much like a weapon all on its own, landing him in all kinds of tight spots with just about everyone and anyone who chose to hit the woods with him, including the law.

So as the years went by, Richie had learned to keep to himself more and more. You might say he'd grown to like it that way. "Getting close to any o' them shit-heels caused more trouble than worth, no how," he grumbled, almost tasting the bitter memories that came suddenly to roost in his head. "All them dumb-fucks and their shitstorms I put up with," he spat, suddenly feeling hot, his temper rising. The interior of the official vehicle becoming too claustrophobic, his throat suddenly powder-dry, the flamed urge to just bust out and start running, almost overwhelming. He breathed in deeply, wiping at the sweat that rolled loosely into his eyes. Having spent most of his formative years in the Monroe County Correctional Facility, he learned quite readily how to eliminate those moments of feeling boxed in, learning to adjust to a cage and to free his mind if nothing else. And he, more than likely, would have gone on to spend the rest of his days at the Attica Correctional Facility, or worse yet, the infamous Sing Sing Prison, had it not been for the old man, that is.

"The only reason you're still walkin' and talkin'," he muttered, shaking his head, releasing all those old haunts loose across the summer's sky. He didn't want any of them thoughts around, he never did, but he knew what he wanted mattered very, very little in the scheme of things. Because those memories, they never really went away, and in fact, came dancing right on back to him almost every night in all their gloriously brutal detail—as soon as he closed his eyes, that is.

The layering of underbrush, just to the right of where his old man still stood gun on hip, jostled ever so slightly—just enough really. Just enough for someone the likes of Richie to notice. But more importantly, to know that there was something in that very brush, pushing its way forward, waiting to break free from its own treed cage. "Whatever she is, it ain't small-like, and it sure as shit ain't the wind blowin' them branches around neither…" *No*, he thought, *it is something else entirely. Something that knows how to move in the wild, how to move like o' predator stalking its prey.*

The rustling within the forest's lower scrub and bush grew, sending a cool shiver down his backside. Richie knew that whatever it was that caused it was bigger than most animals out there, by the way the upper leaves were jerking around just like the scrub beneath. It was large and on the scent of its prey, pressing hard toward the light of day that lay just outside the timber line.

He turned his head slightly, spotting one of them three nancy-boys that was responsible for putting his old man out here in this world of police shit in the first place, just standin' there, staring off at the trees. His grin came upon him quickly, unexpectedly lifting his sullen mood. "Ah, you little fuck-tard, you done it now." He snickered. "You best get to watchin' your backside cause somethin' is fixin' to bust free from them woods and you might be just the piece o' flesh its fixated on." The thought suddenly connecting, jumping from his head, his muscles tensing, a sudden burst of kinetic energy springing forth as he pushed the car door free to open. "Oh boy, get the fuck back! That thing in the shadow could be the same thing that grabbed your little pal too…"

Stepping outside of the car's open door, he was trembling, knowing what was about to come, had to come, sent Richie's senses into overdrive. Frantically scouring the cop's car for a firearm. "If I had a rifle I could make the shot from here, need be…" he whispered—no one hearing—his head bobbing in and out of the automobile's interior.

The chaos the cops had begun raged on. Now shouting through a bullhorn at his old man. "Drop your weapon or…" Hurling threats and shit at him, their words a distant distraction now. His entire being sharpening down, honed to a fine point the way it always came to be when he sought to make it so. His attention upon the edge of those timbers, right where the boy stood. "Completely, fuckin' clueless too boot," he cursed, his body in full motion now.

Richie had seen some pretty large and dangerous animals out there, and knew that a coyote, if in a pack, might just be bold enough to snatch up a small human, no question in his mind. "If it were hungry enough…" His breathing strangled as he realized there was not a single firearm in the car. "Fucking cops… took it for sure," he said, as his simpleton nephew came suddenly into his sights. He was running right toward the other one, who stood stock still right in front of where the animal had taken to creepin' up to. "Fuckin' idiots. Just beggin' to get to bein' lunch for this thing," Richie squealed, now starting to run toward the boys. "Come on, fucker, come out in the light, let's get a look at-cha… Shit, it's your lucky fuckin' day, a two-fer one smorgasbord of faggoty-ass boy chow."

Richie was sprinting now, not entirely sure what he was doing or going to do, but at the very least he wanted to get a better look at the thing that was movin' around in them woods. "This could be one for the record book, boys—and I'm gonna kill it, skin it, and hang it over my own fuckin' mantle place." He was talking on wildly, feeling the excitement. "I'll be the town's fuckin' hero and shit—if I just had a weapon…" he whispered suddenly, slowing down, the realization hitting him between the eyes. He stopped midstride, watching as his nephew drew closer to the other boy, his troubled thoughts bouncing around in his head. "Half-starved dog is come to sniffin' and there ain't shit I can do," he said, turning back to his old man, sighting the old Savage rifle at his side.

The tree line erupted, spraying leaves loosely outward as the monster within sprung forth. Richie turned back toward the trees, his jaw popped to open as he witnessed the scene now unfolding before his blurred eyes. A large man stepped out from the blue shadowed trees, pushing his way forcefully to stand before the two unexpecting boys. Richie froze entirely, staring at the monster he'd thought to be of the coyote family, but wasn't—at all. It, or he was enormous in size, with shoulder length white colored hair and a mass of coarse looking facial hair that stood thick against his face.

But it was the eyes that caught Richie more than anything else; even from where he stood, they were impossible to miss. There was an intensity there, a ferocity about them that flickered as he glared outward. Their frozen blue color struck to glisten and sparkle wetly upon the afternoon sun's touch. There was something about him—something so hauntingly familiar... Richie was riveted, silently watching on as the strange man again stepped forward, addressing the boy closest to him in a way that almost looked amicable, familiar. And the more he studied the elderly giant of a man the more it seemed he belonged in or to those woods rather than outside of them in the light of day. "An outdoorsman... a true woodsman," he mumbled, motionless before him.

"Aw, come on..." Richie whispered. "Nah, that can't be right... What the fuck?" he pleaded, as the man suddenly looked up from the boy he'd been engaged with—chatting with really—looking up now from his dimwitted nephew, who'd just come to stumble on the little scene, to look directly at him, those eyes a piercing blue, causing Richie to instinctively step backward, recognition of the stranger kicking in. But he never lowered his eyes, as the two men stood locked together in familiarity across the grassy distance. The woodsman's wild-eyed ferocity ever-present as he stared back at Richie, acknowledging him before stepping back to slip silently away beneath the vast wooded canopy. To disappear so quickly, it was if he were never there at all. "And no one here…" Richie said, looking around at the officers who continued pressing their bombastic commands upon his old man, "…is the wiser neither." He turned back toward the boys and the once again stilled forest. "Well, no one but them two peckerwoods that is." Who had remained in place, staring at the spot the old woodsman had appeared out from before sitting down to the ground.

"Well, boys, looks like the three of us got ourselves a little secret, now don't we?" He grinned all shark-like, turning back, his strides long, renewed in purpose as he made his way back to the cop's shiny vehicle. "No one but us little church mice knows the truth of it all, boys—and whatever that mossy old fuck said to yah's, I want to know that too…" he said to himself, pushing his way back inside the car, slouching down deep into the seat's cooled, vinyl cushions. His thoughts jumbled, still not fully believing what he'd just seen, but the image of the elderly man he'd taken to calling the woodsman was simply unmistakable. "There ain't another that looks like him… and maybe all that bullshit the old man has been spoutin' for years about things livin' in them woods is true after all?" he probed, thinking about the old photo still hanging there at his sister's house. His great granddaddy glaring out from the dusty old photograph, all wild and ferocious like.

"Ain't no mistakin' that man," he repeated. *And if he's taken to risin' from the dirt nap he took a century or so back, well, this secret just got a whole lot more interestin'*, he thought incredulously, unable to shake the eerie likeness between the man in the old photo and the guy he'd just seen. "Well, lot's o' strange shit happens out there…" he whispered, trying to think about the possibility of the walking dead logically, but just couldn't get there. "We got us a dead, well, long fuckin' dead, relation that's taken to wanderin' round them damn trees, don't we now, my little nephew? And maybe, just maybe, that shits got somethin' to do with the little disappearin' act your friend took last night too?" he seethed, questioning everything he'd just said, everything he'd just witnessed. "And you, me and your fuckin' little pal there are the only swingin' dicks that knows any of this, right?" His crooked smile curved upward into a cruelly pointed line. "Yeah, that's right. But not for long, boys—not for long. I ain't no good at sharin' nothin' let alone fuckin' secrets," he thundered under breath, his eyes pinned to the two fuck-stick, peckerwood's, who entirely unawares, had gotten to their feet and started to make their way back to the others gathering about his now outlaw status daddy.

SHE

Book Two

A glimpse at part two of the WHITE trilogy.

Prologue

Pieskaret

The young man sat on the hill above his people's village. Watching. He could see their cook fires' smoke rising up to drift on the breath of the father. They made their way, walking in the light of the day under the yellow bird's warmth and protection. He saw them all for what they were and what they'd one day soon become—dead. They would all perish before long, never to be seen on this land or any land again. Their voices to become nothing more than a whisper, forgotten across the many moons of time.

But he, Pieskaret, named for his ancestral line, those who'd come before him, would live on beyond the race of his people. Beyond the day when he'd become chief to the Huron people and conquered so many of the warring tribes that once took both their food and women at will. He'd been told he was given a great gift, the third eye of light which, when possessed, instilled one with a vast and powerful vision and a life beyond the mortal body's normal path. He would walk among those that had passed into the great beyond and in the same way, those that were yet to come. Carrying with him a vision far beyond the current days of light and the many nights of shadow that followed.

He sat very still, absorbing the warmth of the great bird of the sun's gentle touch, feeling its temperate breath tumble all around him. The bitter cold was now behind them and he watched as his people rejoiced, planting new substantive life into the rich black soil the earth provided to them. Pieskaret's mind in great conflict, wanting only to stay in this time, this very moment of great peace and harmony between his people and the land. But he knew as he'd been told; this time and place was no longer meant for him. His journey was to take him far away, beyond this physical space and time, and to prepare himself he must embrace the spirit guide awarded to him. His path would be one of great difficulty, surrounded by blood, death and the many fires of human destruction. But his life's story had been written and so must be done. His tribal elders and council had been very clear in his dream state from the previous night's passing. They sat high upon the great and sacred cliffs of the Huron people, his people. The night air dry, their pyramid of fire cracked and snapped, shooting great bundles of star-like dots across the raven's obsidian skies. The elderly chief of the Huron-Wendat people of old shimmered amongst the fire's glow. His council of eight ghostly figures, the elders of white, all dressed in great furred hides, were truly a vision to behold. Their longhouses of the expansive village, alive and teeming with life of a distant past. Yet here Pieskaret sat amongst them, interacting with the elders of great legend, all in what one might consider, real time.

In this place, the Huronia people and Huron nation were still centuries away from their ultimate demise at the hands of the five nations of the Iroquois Indians. All to one day become Iroquois in mind, body and spirit. But not for those that shared this night's fire. They were the great white elder's; a race long passed that would never suffer the fate of their own people. This weighed heavily on Pieskaret as he sat watching them, then watching their children, knowing all of them would soon come to a blood-soaked ending.

But this was just the beginning. His path was to find her, to find the foremother of white and bring her back from the land of the dead. To revive her spirit was to revive the spirit of the great Huron people as they would live on within her, their ways carried forward years beyond one could count. To a modern world that even Pieskaret, who had visited this strange place of the future, hadn't the words known to describe the vast changes that grew to live there. But she would not only live to see this place of wonder, but would exist within it, changing its destructive path, instilling the ways of their people once again. And he himself would live on as well. In his human form many years beyond his own mortality, all to save her, the last of her kind. She would one day consume his own flesh and blood to bind them together across eternity. And she, Achak of White, would carry on their ancestral vision, finding the one—her chosen mate. A human child who lived and breathed of the time within the Earth's future, but whose soul was one of a far, far older being. And their children would become gods beyond the race of humans. Gods that lived in both human and animal form, able to shift between them at will. Gods that would bring life back to the earth, water and sky, and put an end to man's thirst for the destruction of all they'd held to sacred. The elders had described it this way, decreeing the union between the foremother and the chosen human, a male child of the ways of old, must come to pass.

Yet, he could not help but feel the sadness that now surrounded him, that tore at his very soul. His own wife, their children, soon to be put to the blade. He knew this fate, the fate of all he'd ever loved, must come to pass and that it was simply no longer his place to change its course. No longer his duty to protect and guide his family, his people. Nor was he to remain here, in this time to watch those he'd loved perish, and those that were lucky enough to survive, subjugated to the cruelty of slavery, and the blood adorned sacrifice to come. He pondered upon his troubled thoughts, feeling the warm waters fill within his eyes. Hot to the touch as the drops fell over his painted cheeks.

He moaned low as he saw his wife, Ghigau, and their youngest son of just four winters emerge from their family teepee, where they'd ushered in his new life upon a horn-rimmed moon. A great tangle of thick black hair sat high upon his large and regal head. Already big for his age, he was both larger and stronger than boys of their village twice his age. His name was Esadowa. They'd named him after the wolf, seeing the cunning and ferocity of the animal rooted deep within the child. Perhaps Esadowa was destined for more, the child was thought to be one of great promise, but he knew it was not meant to be in this life. "Your destiny will be taken by human violence," he whispered, the tears falling liberally now.

He removed the war chief headdress that his own tribal leaders had adorned him with, and set it gently upon the sprigs of newly emerging grass. He looked down, not wanting to see any more, not wanting to watch Esodowa, just one of his seven children, run undeterred amongst the many canine animals that served to guard their village from would-be intruders. He rose from the spot just as his youngest son turned, his deep brown eyes locking upon his own, frozen to still in the moment. A flash of bright white emanated from his brown skinned face as a smile grew wide there. His small hand rising, a voice Pieskaret could no longer hear shouting, "Adang! Adang!" Father! Father! he shouted, the twinkling excitement in the boy's beautiful eyes all but stopped Pieskaret's heart from beating on. The joy he felt looking upon his son could not be contained, as he himself smiled back, raising a timid hand upward in response. Just then one of the many native children jumped upon his broad back, releasing peals of childish laughter to float high into the air. Esodowa spun the boy around until they both fell to the ground in a fit of unguarded laughter, rolling atop of each other as the many dogs took their turn barking and playfully nipping at them both. Then they were up and running once more, heading toward the towering tree line the village bordered.

But before disappearing into its leafy canopy, the boy turned back toward Pieskaret, stopping to wave to his father once more. Pieskaret left his hand up in the air as the boy spun around to soon vanish into the shadow of the great timbers. "Into the shadow of the Spotted Green…" he said aloud, remembering the voices of those yet to come who would one day lay claim to these very woods and would indeed name it such.

Pieskaret took one last look at his people from afar, again seeing them all for who they were and were to become. And turned away to begin a new path, across the many miles and many moons unseen. "I will return, my love." He spoke softly to his wife, his cherished one. "I will never forget you, my Ghigau. Love our children while there's still time…" And with that, he began to walk toward what lie ahead, into the vision that the great elders of white had gifted him with.